What the critics said about Jul

"Imagery runs rampant, with delightful
orgy, bombarding all our senses at once, o
delightful and original su
James Waites on Season To Taste, Sydney Morning Herald

"There are profoundly relevant and for some, contentious
considerations here. Flashes of a long and intriguing history:
a rich context".
Frank Gauntlet on Lotus War, Sunday Telegraph

"Julie Janson's dialogue combines the right proportion of sacred and
profane, the hallmark of good erotica: it hits the theatrical G spot".
Colin Rose on Season to Taste, Sydney Morning Herald

"Tough and emotional… at the stirring end, the ghosts of the killed
move in and symbolically reclaim the land".
John McCallum on Black Mary, The Australian

"This is true Australian work. What is Australian art? What is it
about? No matter how much we might dismiss it, Aboriginal people
and convicts, English settlers who are invaders, whatever you want
to call them – forged links. And we never get away from that".
Rhoda Roberts on Black Mary

"Like much of Janson's work, *The Eyes of Marege* – which was
shortlisted for the Patrick White Award and will premiere in
Adelaide before transferring to Sydney – ventures across cultures.
Her previous works have included *Lotus War* and *Tears of the Poppy*,
about Asian politics, while *Gunjies* and her best-known play
Black Mary have dealt with indigenous issues".
Joyce Morgan, Sydney Morning Herald

Julie Janson was born in Boronia Park, Sydney.
She is of Aboriginal descent from the Darug nation.
A graduate of the University of NSW, Sydney College
of the Arts and the University of Sydney.
She is an established playwright with several nominations
for awards including an AWGIE, the Griffin Award
and the Patrick White Award.
Julie was the recipient of the 2013 Australia Council
B R Whiting Studio Residency, Rome.

Julie Janson

THE
Crocodile
HOTEL

cyclops press

www.cyclopspress.com.au

A Cyclops Press Book
Published by Cyclops Press, Australia Pty Ltd
www.cyclopspress.com.au

This edition published in 2015
Copyright © Julie Janson 2015

National Library of Australia Cataloguing-in-Publication entry

Creator:	Janson, Julie, author
Title:	The Crocodile Hotel / Julie Janson
ISBN:	9780980561951 (paperback)
Dewey Number:	A823.3

The author acknowledges the use of the following texts:
Quotes: *Trumby* song written by Slim Dusty (David Gordon Kirkpatrick) and Joe Daly, lyrics @EMI Publishing; *Click Go The Shears* folk song written by C. C. Eynesbury; *Drinkers in the Northern Territory* song written and recorded by Ted Egan; *Rock Around the Clock* song written by Max C. Freedman and James E. Myers.

Design & typesetting by tonygordonprintcouncil.com
Front cover design by Michelle Ball
Front cover photo by Louise Whelan

Printed in Australia by McPherson's Printing Group

For the Darug people

PART ONE

NORTH WIND SEASON, FISHING, HUNTING, PIED GOOSE EGGS READY – 1976

This rainy season is lush and green,
Jane arrives in Lanniwah country in the midst of plenty.
Yams are ready for digging up and roasting.
Crocodiles are nesting. The north wind blows, rain is heavy
and the lightning spirits are everywhere.

CHAPTER 1

Arrival at Harrison Station

Jane Reynolds stared out of the Land Rover's window. The drive from Katherine was a nightmare, it struck deep into her heart, but she was somehow elated, the craving for change always won. Mercifully, her son Aaron stayed sleeping, perspiration on his forehead. This was pitiless heat, searing forty-degree heat suffocating the flat plains and lime green grass spiked with spindly grey-white trees and red boulders thrown like giant's toys on a moonscape that went on and on. The Department driver, resolutely silent for hours, managed a half turn of his head then a nod to outside. It was the Churinga Roadhouse.

He climbed out and leant against the car door, 'How old are you anyway?'

'Twenty seven'

'Old enough, I guess. You can get a feed here if you want.'

'Thanks.' She nudged Aaron and smoothed his hair.

Together they pushed the restaurant door into sudden noise and movement. At any moment, Jane expected an absurdist actor to set their hair on fire. Someone farted. Ghoulish rodeo clowns in red hats laughed. Dusty men in blue singlets. They chewed. Some toothless hippies picked at tinned peas and pineapple. Bushmen, jackaroos, roustabouts and stockmen hunched over plates of chips and gravy.

A bald fat man stood over the bain-marie, sprinkling chicken salt on the yellow food: shrivelled dim sims, chips, pies – all shrinking in the heat. A commercial dishwasher started rumbling. At university she'd worked as a kitchen hand, leered at by the rich boys of Basser College. No blowflies trapped behind glass foodshields back there. Her graduation had been followed by unemployment, a year of staring in cake shop windows, a year of hunger and pregnancy.

Aaron's eyes begged, he held up cans of Coca Cola. She paid the fat man and they got a seat by the jukebox. Kenny Rodgers. *The Northern Territory Times*, grubby from earlier diners, faced her. 'Pol Pot and Khmer Rouge sack head of state'; she spotted another headline: 'Child taken by Croc'. Aaron would not shift from her sight. Vigilance the first word out here, in all things.

She watched the dusty Aboriginal families framed in the greasy windows. Two children blinked with pus-filled eyes in the sunlight. They clutched bright orange Twisties. Their mother stroked their backs in the shade. Single mothers worried about food. She and Aaron had slept next to each other on a small mattress in the share house. No money, no support. Definitely, she must keep hold of this new job.

The fat man pushed an old Aboriginal man in a shredded flannel shirt and no shoes towards the door.

'No humbug here – you know the rules, Sandy,' the fat man said. The old Aboriginal man shuffled towards the road. Jane stood up with a sinking feeling, a slight shaking in her voice. Gough Whitlam's Land Rights speech had barely carried to the Blue Mountains. She urged herself to her feet. She had to speak up.

'Why are you throwing him out?' she said.

'He's dirty.'

'So are those stockmen.'

'He doesn't want to be inside.'

Jane bent towards the old man. 'Would you like to sit down in the air-conditioning?' she said.

The fat man held court.

'Look lady, you're from down south, aren't ya? My place, my rules,' said the fat man.

'It's racist. Let him stay.'

There was a boom of laughter.

'Why don't you piss off? Go on, away you go.'

Jane felt everyone watching; she took Aaron by the hand and walked to the door. The fat man waddled past her and put down a bag of bottles of Coke, placing it outside the door. The old man, breathing heavily, rested on the step. He pulled the bag to him and looked at Jane, his eyes seemed blurred and sightless. She tried to hold his look. She felt useless. It wasn't her business, she had to learn to keep quiet and stop trying to interfere. The roadhouse owner, the fat man, had rights. The customers, the paying ones, were always right, weren't they? She looked back at the faces. Some smirked. Aaron touched the old man's shoulder.

'Want me to carry your bag?' He smiled and saluted at the little blonde boy. Jane assisted the old man to stand, aligning her forearm under his like a tiller to guide him back to his family beneath the tree. The family women averted their eyes. They saw a whitey do-gooder. Aaron put the drinks bag down gently.

'Yeeai, good boy.' The old man touched Aaron's hand and held it for a long moment.

'You okay now?' said Aaron. Jane smiled at the quiet scene the two were making.

In the midst of the doom. Her son, the knower. The children under the tree ripped into the Cokes and swigged. Their eyes were blooms of infection. Did she have some ointment that could help? Who was she to think she could help anybody? She was barely able to help herself. Was this somehow her fault too? The guilt and misery etched on people's faces seemed to go on and on. No one escaped the sense of powerlessness.

Neither blacks nor whites could shake free of how to be around each other. The Department driver was wiping off the windscreen.

To Jane, every broken man on the ground was an incarnation of her mentally ill brother. He would pick up cigarette butts from the streets around Balmain and roll them into smokes with newspaper. He never begged, but suffered the indignity of being thrown from pubs for not having enough money for a beer. His blue eyes and heavy forehead spoke of his Aboriginal grannies. Each tramp was her brother in need. *There but for the grace of God go I.*

Jane bought a box of oranges from the fat man, carried them to the car. They had a long way to go, hundreds of kilometres. The driver put out his cigarette and called to Jane to get back in. The air was a furnace, no air conditioning. It smelt like a decaying cow. She stared out the window: the blue horizon cut the world in two, and it was vast and uplifting. She felt so alive. This was her new life, transmigrated to Mars. Ghost gums, small reptiles flattened on the road and bloated bodies of dead kangaroos. Aaron began to count the dead while a bustard walked slowly along the road oblivious to an approaching eight-carriage road train.

The car turned off the bitumen onto a bulldust track with holes so big that you could lose a car in them. Rainer River, south of Arnhem Land, was scorched country. They drove through hundreds of kilometres of cattle stations with no fences. Stark grey-green beauty.

On Harrison Station, there were soaring wedge-tailed eagles, egrets, blue cranes and galahs. A mirage shimmered, broken-down bulldozers rusted on yellow dirt, water tanks teetered on wooden towers. A meat house, fowl house, dog house and humpies for three hundred people. The Lanniwah houses were made of paper-bark and tin; some were canvas, with pots and billycans hanging in the trees. Mangy dogs lay in heaps on bare earth and the soil glinted with camp pie tins and broken bottles. Pandanus dillybags hung like fruit on bare wooden poles and precious suitcases jutted from beneath iron bedframes. Lanniwah children played on the hills while their parents sat by small fires.

One bent-over old woman with a stick walked by surrounded by blue-and-red dogs. Jane watched her stop and stare at the government Land Rover; she had a magnetic presence. A sense of incredible excitement grew. Jane could see that the demountable school was about four hundred metres from the teacher's place, and the camp was further off near a hill of stone. The big house for the Boss and his family was very close to Jane's new home. It was possible to look into their bedrooms, as they had no curtains; it was uncomfortably close. Still it might be better than television. The pretty lily-covered billabong rippled a short walk from where Jane stood.

Jane lifted her son from the back seat as he woke up. They crawled out of the car; the heat hit them like a shovel. A forty-three-degree haze floated towards her; bleached bones bordered the road. Jane staggered and wondered how anyone could live out here.

Aaron seemed oblivious, and she watched him as he ran around the yard skipping and hooting, exploring their new home at Harrison Station: a large demountable home, a caravan parked on flat orange earth, white painted stones and dozens of shrunken geraniums. Jane took it all in. There was hardly a tree, and the wire mesh fences were falling down – they wouldn't keep out Brahman bulls or dingoes.

'See you later, enjoy yourself. I'll be back after the Wet, maybe five months, with some school supplies,' said the driver.

'Hold on, please – don't leave.'

'Look lady, it's a flaming long way back to civilisation and I'm tonguin' for a cold beer.'

'Wait, what if I need something?' she yelled.

'Like what?'

'Something.'

'You won't be able to call – no phone out here in hell. You had the interview with Mr White at head office. You wanted it. You got it. Good luck, sweetheart.'

He threw their suitcase onto the ground, grunted, spat and headed back to Katherine, a five-hour drive through deep bulldust. Jane watched him go. The hot air choked her and she couldn't catch her breath. She smiled at Aaron. Yep, everything was just great. Her caravan gleamed with round ugly edges. There was nowhere to hide; she was naked.

The landscape was gutted by the annual floods that washed away the topsoil leaving billabongs with stranded twenty-foot long crocodiles. Jane stood battered by dry wind. Blue-grey clouds pulsed with blinding bursts of sunlight. It was an alien landscape with the silver caravans placed like tin cans covered in dust, waiting to be towed away if the numbers at the school dropped. The Department said the people might move on at any moment, looking for seasonal food and ceremony.

God almighty – what had she done? She found it hard to breathe; the isolation was going to kill her. Jane calmed herself by bending down and breathing slowly and repeating, 'I can do this. I can do this'. She squatted on the ground. She doubled over, hands on her knees, time stopped; something was caught in her throat, an eternity of fear. She looked at her hands, the trembling fingers. She saw a round white pebble and stooped to take it in her palm. The stone felt solid: it was a message, and she was feeling space and time in a bright light. She put the stone in her pocket; it would protect her.

Aunty Emily, her Darug aunt, had advised her to take this job: take a chance at a new life, get away from poverty and sadness. To get away from the memories of her father Samuel dying. Jane picked up her suitcase. This would be a great new beginning; she would be a wonderful teacher and her son would thrive on the outdoor adventures. It was going to be all right. She could do this amazing thing.

Jane thought about her place, her Aboriginal blood. It circled in her mind, all the way to the Northern Territory. She knew she was of Aboriginal descent; she had grown up with her father being called 'Abo'. She heard his voice from a distant 1959, when he sat in the backyard of his brick Housing Commission home. "It isn't smart to call yourself an Aboriginal. Your kids might get taken. You won't get a government job," she heard him laugh. He didn't want that kind of job, but his kids might. Many families had lost children with interference from the Aborigines Welfare Board. Samuel's brothers and sisters were quiet on the subject: they learnt table manners and kept the secret. She watched him carve her a yam digging stick entwined with a snake design, as his skin went black in the sun. Her aunts said her father's dark skin was the result of jaundice as a child, but Jane thought that unlikely.

Jane had been called 'a little white blackfeller' when she ran fast in school sports. She had long legs and dark eyes, and a thatch of blonde hair, while her brothers and sister had 'lubra lips'. Jane had known this family secret but it had seemed a distant thing.

She took a wedding ring out of her bag and slid it onto her finger. She unfolded the Education Department appointment letter, 'You have been appointed for one year to Harrison Station School. This position is conditional upon you being a married woman as the accommodation is suitable only for a couple.' She scanned the horizon. No, there did not seem to be any prospect of a husband. The gossips might think that perhaps Jane's husband had run off or never existed.

CHAPTER 2

The Boss

In the distance, six Lanniwah children appeared like drawings in an old picture book: dreamlike and skinny against burning white sunlight. Through squinting eyes, she watched a man on horseback gallop towards them. He whirled a stock whip and cracked it on the ground in front of the children who scattered and hid behind trees. Jane tried to make sense of this scene, to apply her perception of reality to the cowering black children. It was a frightening rush into her deep affinity with her Koori ancestors. Is this what they had experienced? No, he must be playing. He was their friend, surely.

One child had a baby clinging to her back as she crouched with the others behind a thorn bush. The rider flicked the dirt in front of them with the whip. The human shapes were dwarfed against the wide horizontality of barren landscape. He saw her and wheeled the horse around, galloped towards her, jumped the fence to the caravan and dismounted. He was a barrel-chested Chips Rafferty in the *The Overlanders*. He rolled with a cattleman's gait and was joined by his rake-thin wife, Edie. They walked towards Jane.

'Gidday, Mrs Reynolds, welcome to Harrison, I'm Hubert and this is Edie.' His voice was laconic but direct. Jane felt out of place, out of her mind. Her heart was beating as cockatoos screeched all around in a close burst of noise, jarring in the clicking stillness and heat – the terrible inescapable heat.

Jane stretched out her damp hand. 'Good to meet you, Hubert, Edie.'

Edie peered from under her wide-brim hat, her red permed curls swinging to her shoulders.

'Your husband not with you?'

Jane felt the first lie rise up like vomit. 'He's working; he might come later.'

'Later, eh? Oh yeah, when?'

Edie shot an alarmed look at her husband, who licked his dry mouth and stuck a cigarette paper to his lower lip.

'Not sure', said Jane.

'So, you reckon you can handle it by yerself? That'll be worth watching.' said Hubert.

'I'll be fine. I'm a graduate.'

'Where was it? Oxford University or something?' said Edie.

'University of Sydney.'

'You'd better watch out for wild buffalo. If you see one, climb the nearest tree.' Hubert grinned.

Jane laughed but the sound stuck in her throat. They were serious. She beckoned Aaron to her side.

'And don't stand in the doorway. A mob of blacks could come past and you'd be a sitting duck. They'd shoot ya. They're not all bad, but give them a whiff of the booze, they go mad. We prepare for attack.'

Jane kept nodding like a toy carnival dog, looking blankly around for evidence of *dangerous blacks* but all she could see was kilometres of scrappy mulga trees, grey dust and vast nothingness. Hubert looked her over as if she was on sale, coughed, spat a gob of phlegm at a passing red cattle-dog, and then leant back against the fence smoking, tracing the dirt with his boot. There was a long uneasy quiet; no one seemed to know what to say. She sensed some foreboding of a thing that might happen, a fear of the future in that place. It slunk around in grey dirt, a kind of evil.

'Stick to the rules and she'll be right', said Hubert.

'Yeah sure, perhaps you could write them down.'

'No alcohol, it's dry out here. You haven't got bottles of whisky in that bag, have ya?'

'I wouldn't.' She hoped her bottle of Johnnie Walker hadn't broken.

'I would have to confiscate them and drink 'em myself.' He laughed. Edie gazed at Jane's Tibetan dress and dangly earrings, and sniffed.

'Come over later for a cuppa. You can use the old Toyota; you'll need it.'

'Great', said Jane. She eyed the old Toyota's rough appearance but would later be delighted when the engine started. This car would save her life. She realised that despite first impressions, maybe the Barkley family were solid country people who would take care of her and Aaron.

'You know, I can't stand women who talk with a plum in their mouth', said Edie. Jane was compliant. 'Nyeah, I know what ya mean.' She mentally noted that she would have to speak through her nose for the rest of the year. Hubert ruffled Aaron's hair. 'Ya can come up and see me gun. Ya'd like that, I bet. Hey, another thing. I don't want you goin' up to the blacks' camp – it's their place. Ya got that?'

'You're the Boss', Jane said.

'I've staked out the whole one square kilometre for the Aboriginal camp, on the directions of the owners from Singapore', he said.

Oh, the luxury, thought Jane.

'The blacks don't want you. They're like children. We take care of them. Look, they do it tough in the Wet, so I give the old blokes my best lures. I got time for 'em. We help 'em out, but if they step out of line, I'll take the bullwhip to any of 'em. Whip 'em good!'

Jane saw his bravado, but he seemed a frightened man: it was all show. He turned to her and winked. No, he was obviously a racist shit and she would have to deal with him. She was mildly terrified but she pictured confrontations.

Edie was a midwife who with two Aboriginal health workers ran a no-nonsense clinic in an old house on the station. The Lanniwah women gave birth there and she had delivered some hundred babies. In her racism, there was also compassion.

'We know where we stand in the Northern Territory hierarchy. Hugh's a cattle manager but we're not owners', said Edie.

'The government doesn't give us much help when it comes to transport costs, even when we're in drought. The bloody helicopter costs drive cattle prices sky high. It's tough. You know, actually we're like social workers out here, eh Edie – help the dark people get their welfare cheques,' said Hubert.

Jane smiled and kept looking at her dusty shoes.

Edie had married Hubert and adapted quickly to distaste for blacks. She spoke to Jane about her last pregnancy, the adored only boy who was born in Katherine Hospital.

'After one day, I saw my baby was in a plastic crib surrounded by picks.'

'What are picks?' asked Jane.

'Pickaninies, Aboriginal babies', said Edie.

'I took my precious new baby out of that hospital quick smart. Hightailed it back to Harrison.'

Her 'black girl', Gertie, washed and scrubbed for little pay, just tucker.

Jane watched Gertie; she looked like her grandmother. She smelt of rose talcum powder. Her grandma had been born to serve, trained by nuns in an orphanage to polish floors on her knees. She had been fed smears of pink watery jam on sledges of bread. Granny had an education in reading, writing, bed making, pot scrubbing, floor polishing and dishwashing. Like the Children of Canaan in the Bible, to be born black was to be condemned to life as a servant. Such children were half-castes – the brood of black concubines and descendants of ex-convicts. A double stain – double shame.

Jane's great grandmother had her children removed by the Benevolent Society. Benevolent to whom? The English masters and mistresses who received the unpaid indentured servants? Jane had inherited a fear of authority, the police: it had been passed down the generations. There was uncertainty about her place, her right to belong. Jane knew that her family had grown afraid to acknowledge their Aboriginal blood. When her father worked for white people, he had drunk his tea in a tin cup outside their houses on the step, to keep his dark germs away. As a dark child amongst six fairer siblings, he had waited outside the lolly shop, while his whiter brother bought sweets. The sign read, 'No Blackfellas Allowed In Here'.

It was time to come out and own her heritage, to stop apologising for the distant Aboriginal ancestor. To say loudly that the Hawkesbury was her country, that her grandmother was born there, and her great grandmother, and her great great grandmother. She was a descendant of the Buruburongal clan of Freemans Reach Blacks' Camp near Windsor, a member of the Kangaroo Skin People. Jane had been tired of being told it was not her land, no such tribe – she didn't exist – by a mob blown in from the North Coast.

'Are you okay? You dreaming or something? You're miles away.' Edie said.

'Just thinking about something.'

'Gertie's a house-trained domestic so she's valuable, and she knows her place. Gertie can do your washing if you like.' Jane shook her head and kept her eyes down.

'We run the power with a generator and we got a two-way radio, but you can't use that. You come to us for maintenance of the water supply, mail, fuel and food. Any questions?'

'No, all good.' Jane began to move away but Edie whistled her back.

'People in Sydney don't understand what we go through. We lie awake at night wondering if we'll be murdered in our beds. You don't understand how we're stopped from getting rid of the fear. They're a real problem; one day they will all die out. It can't come too soon.' Jane nodded, speechless: if she spoke out now, she would have no choice but to leave, to go back to the mattress in the share house. To poverty. She felt gagged, full of polite meaningless phrases. She would have to wear it.

Jane sat with Aaron on a small hill overlooking the billabong at Harrison and a jabiru, all black and white, lifted off from bright pink water. A kind of ecstasy descended. Hubert drove by in his cattle truck with a perplexed look on his face: *What the hell are they doing out there?*

The next day, Jane shooed the curious Brahman cows from her door and led Aaron over to the Boss's house. Edie licked her cigarette with her pink tongue, and welcomed them.

'Get Missus Reynolds a chair.' Gertie stopped washing a pile of dishes and dragged a plastic chair to the table. Edie was attractive in tight white moleskin pants, like Annie Oakley. She had two girls and a small boy – pretty, pale children. They were curious and looked longingly at Aaron. They soon had him under their collective wings, and giggled and played on the floor amongst clattering Lego pieces.

'Elisha, get a coffee for the teacher.' Edie puffed another cigarette. The eldest girl held a mug with Pablo instant coffee under the hot water tap at the sink, mixed in a spoon of sugar and powdered milk and gave it to Jane.

Jane sipped. 'Lovely.' She looked at the house: corrugated iron and fibro on steel stilts, broken flapping fly-screens. There was poverty in the dirty white walls and plastic chairs. A Laminex table and bench with the School of the Air radio and piles of battered books sat against another wall, and a Hammond organ with sheet music, and flypaper that dangled near her face.

'It's a relief to have a woman to talk to. Gertie doesn't count, she's black and thick as two short planks', Edie said. Gertie gave a vicious slam to the wet clothes. Jane looked out the window and saw Hubert over by his tractor with a young Aboriginal girl sitting on his lap and he was tickling her.

'So, how long you been teachin?'

'One year.'

'Experienced then.' Edie nodded and smirked.

A pink galah flew through a window, perched beside Edie and bent his head for a scratch. Jane felt helpless, like a child, possessed by the older woman. She shook her golden hair. 'You'll have to tie that hair up, the kids are crawling with nits.' If Edie had suddenly thrown the coffee mug out the window and screeched like an orang-utan, it wouldn't have surprised Jane.

Jane knew nothing about the Territory; her experience as a student teacher had been at Leichhardt Boys High School, dealing with boys from the Mediterranean – hairy, dark, with gold chains. 'Hey Miss, you got nice boobs', When they saw their new student teacher, the boys in tight grey shorts had almost taken out their dicks and beaten them on the desk. She learnt to throw boys from the classroom. To pinch ears and throw chalk.

'Will your children enrol with the Lanniwah tomorrow?'

'No, my kids do School of the Air', said Edie. Jane nodded in blank relief. She called Aaron but he wouldn't come. Edie watched as Jane tried to pull Aaron away from his new friends. It was a struggle of wills, but the child won, so Jane went back to her caravan and suddenly felt very alone.

Hubert opened the corrugated iron store twice a week. It was a large building with a small flap that opened for a shop window. Hubert towered over the women, his ledger ready to record each debt. The women queued for hours in the heat for Western cowboy clothes, plastic toys, jeans, cassette players. Hubert had no competition, and robbing Aboriginal people was a sport in the Northern Territory.

'These people, they can't get their unemployment money without us filling out the forms – they can't read.' In reality, Hubert took it all and ran it through his expensive store. He stood at the window and wrote down every item, the powdered milk, packets of tea and flour, a tee shirt, and Donald Cook's baby carrots.

As Gertie hung out washing, Jane handed her some pegs. 'What do they pay you Gertie?' asked Jane.

'For one week, might get ten dollar. Enough for bingo. None left for save', said Gertie.

'You win much?'

'Yeeai, lotta prize'. Jane mentally calculated the small fortune flowing from two hundred unemployment cheques and child endowment. Someone was being ripped off.

Lanniwah women walked past her caravan and waved to Jane. They went the long way around the Boss's house to avoid the snarling cattle dogs. The Boss had trained these dogs to only attack dark skin. Away from the dogs, the Lanniwah children ran and cartwheeled with joy. Jane could imagine running amongst them with Aaron, everyone laughing, just in the fun of being alive.

CHAPTER 3
Identity

On her first night in the caravan Jane was restless. What if no one turned up for school? Would the older women take to her? Make her feel welcome? Jane could hear strange rasping howls. She got up and checked the door. Small trees reached out and ran their branch fingers along the aluminium ... Semi-transparent geckos' eyes twitched. Urgh. She pulled the sheet over her head, wanting to sleep, to be ready for school but the night air suffocated as sweat pooled in her belly button. Forty degrees with just one small fan, and no air conditioner, no television, no communication, not even a radio.

She hated being alone, like herself as a lonely fourteen-year-old girl with her father dead, mother absent, brother mentally ill, sister far away. She stewed and tossed under the plastic ceiling. Maybe someone would report her for being unfit to teach. She thought about her Aboriginal blood. She wondered if the Lanniwah would accept her.

She woke up at dawn; the cattle station was awake. She heard men rounding up animals. Jane looked through the window of the school caravan.

Jane and Aaron swam in the fresh billabong; it was exquisite. It was like the place where her Darug great granny had been born. Great Granny had called her land *nullaburra* country, the wood duck place at Freeman's Reach ... Running fresh water was in the family blood, but it was the salt water that had called her father. He went fishing with the long fishgig he had made of bamboo. A Ned Kelly rig. It was a fantasy that they were a functioning family. It was all dysfunction really. Kooris who fought with each other and other mobs. Jealousies, old burning resentments, feuds with other mobs. Girls raped by cousins, some uncles stinking drunk. Children who looked suspiciously like another man's child. Not nice people. However, generous – they'd give you anything you wanted. Grandma Reynolds cooked roast lamb dinners for thirty, all welcome. She would yell out for them to come, booda, eat! The girls would wait on the men of course. Playing jokes on each other, grown men flicked rubber-band pellet guns and shot each other with potato slug guns, *kerpang*, right on his ear, gotta laugh! Playing harmonica, or for heaven's sake a gumleaf, her Dad's lips would be pursed against the green. It sounded just like a violin.

The Aboriginal Teaching Assistant opened the school, she watched him as she walked up the hill to school. She wanted the first day to be full of promise; she would show them all that she was competent and capable of being head teacher – there were no other teachers. This was a new life and she would forget about the past

Jane stopped at the tin door to the school and the Aboriginal Teaching Assistant was waiting for her. Jane gulped. His thick rich eyelashes – like those of all the Lanniwah people – fluttered downwards as he twisted his fingers nervously. He was handsome, looked fresh and relaxed in his blue checked shirt; he smelt of Old Spice. He had beautiful hands with pale palms. Around his neck, he wore a shark tooth on leather and on his wrists were coloured strings and beads. She could see his shirt lay open to reveal some small raised scars, cicatrices, marks of manhood. David watched her; she felt his eyes on her, and she blushed. She couldn't imagine how he would place her in his microcosm. He smiled at her hippy image, her long neck and slim body, her brown eyes and cascading golden hair, her silk batik kaftan.

He introduced himself: 'I'm David Yaniwuy. I'm the Teaching Assistant'.

'I'm not like the Missus Boss. I am not here to order people about. I am a teacher, I will be learning as much as the children will learn. I am pretty ignorant about Lanniwah culture. You will have to teach me … I hope your people will accept me as a friend', said Jane. David smiled and he searched the floor for some answer to her strange speech. She felt his unease at her closeness as he manoeuvred to place a desk between them. There was a long silence; Jane straightened the pencils. He coughed and finally spoke:

'I only had this job for one year, that how long Harrison Station school been here. Last teacher got bit by a King Brown snake. Nearly finished him up.' David said.

'Maybe you can show me how not to get bitten by a snake or run down by a buffalo'.

Jane watched him walk over the hill to the camp and call the kids. He had the gait of a man brought up horse riding, with bowlegs and a subtle swagger. If his eyes ever met hers, there was a fleeting something, that flickering recognition of a mutual frisson. This was dangerous. *Oh, look out.* Jane pushed it aside, she would have to work with him and she didn't want to jeopardise his position with the Department of Education, or her own. Yes, she would be an upright moral woman, very, very professional – that sounded right.

Jane's main worry was that she had no training in teaching basic literacy. She saw bright-eyed children peeking in at her from outside. Several had snotty noses and running ears; all had scabs all over their legs. Jane piled boxes of tissues on her desk.

Aaron yelled, 'Look, the kids are here!'

She went to the door. 'Come on in and say hello.' The Lanniwah children crowded in. Jane smiled and asked their names. Shirley was fifteen with dark, thick lashes. She stood out from the others with her gold skin, curly blond hair, and a confidence that glowed. Her shyness seemed to be copied from the other girls. The boldness in her stance was magnetic and she obviously had a white father. She held a heavy old book with a gold embossed cover. Jane read the title: *Arabian Nights*. The girls pored over the plastic covers with their intricate silver decorations of Aladdin. Shirley turned the pages of another book – *Sand and Sea* by Norman Lewis, the pages worn with looking.

'Did you bring these lovely books to show me?' asked Jane.

'Yeeai, my daddy book from Borroloola library.' Shirley said.

'We can read them later.'

'We go school one year; dey not readem yet, I can read.' She was a bright teenager, desperate to learn.

'You teachem me read more words, Missus. I love it. My daddy teachem me.'

Lizzy with her huge brown eyes and crown of spun gold, was another young beauty, tall and curvaceous, always smiling. These children gave out a magnetic energy and love.. She cooed: 'We love dis school.'

'Do we have a school cook or cleaner?' asked Jane. David moved to the window and called out in Lanniwah language. A middle-aged woman walked into the schoolroom.

'This one, she works at school too. She Margie. Her daughter Mayda, she oldest girl in school, she eighteen, marry soon.'

Jane smiled and shook Margie's hand; she might like to have a Lanniwah woman friend. Margie held her head low. She was tall and thin, her face round like a brown moon; her eyes stared at the ground. Jane was too talkative. 'Lovely to have such great staff. We will make it a wonderful school', she babbled as silence and uncomfortable shyness sat in the humid air.

David helped Jane unpack boxes of textbooks and sharpen pencils, and they put up alphabet charts and multiplication sheets. Children clustered around a *Women's Weekly* magazine; they touched the picture of roast lamb with a dessert of apple crumble garnished with whipped cream and strawberries. They mimed eating it. They licked their lips and put the picture on the wall. It was a beautiful classroom. She looked with pride at 'her' school. This Aboriginal school.

'Later, you might be come up the camp and meet the headman. He Old Pelican.' David's eyes never met Jane's as he stood awkwardly by a plastic chair and creased his hat.

'I'd like that.'

'I go to Batchelor College near Darwin; getting my certificate soon.'

'Wonderful', said Jane.

'None of these kids can read or write, not even eighteen-year-old ones.'

Jane was not expecting this kind of revelation; her training had been for high school English.

'We can make big books of stories. They can read if we practice enough.' He smiled and kept unpacking resources. David's shyness kept him quietly working in the background at school. She watched how the children adored and respected him. He was a fine Aboriginal Teaching Assistant: his own reading and writing skills were outstanding.

Jane cut oranges into quarters, while David arranged the orange segments on plastic plates. Children appeared in a great mob, giggling and pushing around the school table. David pulled eighteen-year-old Ricky forward and put him in charge of organising the children. The boy was a leader; his dark skin was dusty and he had shining white teeth.

'Ok, line up. When you bin get your fruit, tell Missus Reynolds your name so she can write 'em down', said Ricky.

David gently pushed the smaller children, barefoot and in ragged but clean tee-shirts, into a long line. Four-year-olds squirmed and pushed, queuing with hungry eyes for their little piece of orange, their eyes big as they stared at the fruit.

'They don't get fruit, except wild plum. They love you for dis fruit', said David.

Shirley, with her little cousin clinging to her side, edged slowly up the line. She had never tasted an orange and she watched the boys who already had theirs mince the skin. Fifty pairs of eyes watched every piece. *What if it was all gone?* Jane knew what that felt like, to feel hungry. She took her piece and saw that there was almost none left. Shirley looked behind her at the two remaining children.

'Here, Veronica, eatem up.' She gave her piece away and Aaron took his piece from his mouth and handed it to the last child.

'I'm sorry kids. I haven't any more.' Ricky nodded.

'No worry bout that; we eatem stew for lunch maybe?'

'Yes, plenty of stew.'

The women appeared around lunch time with their hungry toddlers, pushing them gently towards the line of children with their plastic bowls. Hungry eyes. The salted beef hung green from a meat hook at the school camp kitchen. It looked grey and greasy, but Margie made a good dinner with damper for the children's lunch. She added packets of dried vegetables, curry powder and lots of salt. It was beef called 'killer'.

'Back at camp, not much tucker', said David.

Lizzy put her arms around Jane's shoulders. She whispered, 'David, he likem you Missus – you not lonely nomore; and Robert like Shirley.' Shirley punched Lizzy.

'Don't you talk about it – you bad, Lizzy! Shame'.

Jane laughed and kept on working but she was strangely elated. Later, David stood at the school door, but he waited for her to pass and go out first before he lifted down a box of sport equipment. He had manners and as she passed by, she felt the heat from his body, an intake of breath, a sweet exchange of essence. A pulse of attraction so light, barely there but irresistible in her imagination. She let out an inaudible sigh.

Margie was assertive and magnificent and had a smiling face but muttered angrily when Jane attempted to show her how to clean the school equipment and floors. The toilet was overflowing and appalling. Jane guessed that the whole clan used the school toilets. She had made a cartoon poster with all the jobs drawn in hilarious detail. Margie crumpled the drawing in disgust.

'You whitefella alla time bossy.'

Jane sighed, she would clean after the cleaner went home. She asked herself when would colonialism recede? It was embedded in her fairer skin. Incarnate. Her skin would have to be flayed from her flesh, and then she would be the same as them underneath.

At home, a beige turd sat in the caravan toilet, unflushable. Margie had left another calling card. The children nibbled gypsum all day to ease hunger pains, but it bound up their stomachs and made white hard shit.

School days were full. Jane established a routine of alphabet singing, numbers, counting and pre-reading and writing, and David sat patiently with the older boys as they learnt to hold pencils and trace their names. There was something strange about Lanniwah children – they were quiet, they listened in class and it was unbelievable.

The children told Jane stories about their lives, how they hunted goanna or wallaby and stories about their grandparents' time. She had an idea to teach reading and writing by making big books with the children's pictures. She would ask them to tell their story then she would write it down for them and help them learn to read it by rote.

After several days of practice, the children could stand in front of the class and 'read' their story. They showed enormous pride. Soon they could form the letters and copy out their stories. They were writing and publishing their own histories. The big books were the most cared for of all the books and children clustered around the books pointing out their own story.

One day, Shirley walked into the school with Raymond and his friend, Burnie. This old man was well dressed in cowboy shirt and jeans, his face was full of kindness; he touched all the books reverently, then he smiled at Jane, his eyes on hers. The children nudged each other, this man was important. The girls were whispering.

'He your new daddy, Miss Jane.'

Raymond was a white man who had 'gone native', 'living combo'; his home was a shed in clear view from Jane's caravan. He was old and softly spoken, his arm was tattooed with one winding blue mermaid. He had a pile of old books in his home that were oddly marked 'From the Carnegie collection in the USA'. Jane sat with him and Burnie on his old metal bed-frame outside his shed.

'I come from Queensland but got done for cattle duffing. It was a mistake, just a few cleanskins from Brunswick Downs. Black Angus … nice beasts', he said.

Jane saw that Burnie was measuring her character; she was shy with him staring, he seemed to know her already in an unfathomable way. It was like a new world opening for her, this acceptance, it was exhilarating. He kept nodding at her and laughing quietly, then he drew a picture while the others talked. Jane watched an amazing bright flat landscape emerge from the coloured pencils: it was laden with figures of men on horseback and they had guns. He was an extraordinary artist. She leant down to admire it and he tried to push the paper away, he seemed embarrassed. Burnie's head slumped forward. Then he pointed to a hill in the scene; he watched her, then drew a group of black people running away. White men with whips drawn against yellow earth. He pushed the picture towards her. He watched her take it in. She didn't know what to think, to feel.

'You keepem dis picture yerself yeeai? Dat special place, one day, you seeum.'

The mysterious picture was placed carefully in a drawer, she closed it and turned back to Raymond. Later, Jane would look at it, try to make sense of it.

'I was in the lock-up so much at Borroloola that I read through their library. I like a book with meat in it, like Plutarch, Herodotus, Emerson, and Karl Marx.'

'Are you married to Gertie?' she said.

'Yeeai, it was the convention that whitefellas could have intercourse with native women but not marry them. Well bugger that, sorry. We got married in a church. You know about this country? That East Africa Cold Storage Company killed thousands of Aborigines to set up for cattle. Those overlanders, front line troops in an undeclared war. But I never hurt anyone. Did I, Burnie?'

'Good whitefella, Ray, not hurtem any fella.'

'Burnie, he's an important old man, he will take care of you, any problem you can ask him.'

'I'll give Shirley some ice cream for you', she said. Ray nodded a toothless grin.

'Boss gives her plenty of extra tucker, she's his pet.'

'Okay.'

'I like metho better, White Lady. We ran out of Bollinger, eh Burnie. No, you're all right.'

'No good Ray, you gibbit up', said Burnie.

'Jokin'. You know, if anything happened to that little girl I'd neck meself.'

In the late afternoon, the sun was setting and red sparkles bled onto the billabong, Jabirus flew off into the sky. Jane needed companionship: she would be brave. She walked the hundred metres to the camp. Leroy came up to Aaron: he was his best mate; he was eight and wild and cheeky.

'You play wid me, come play near my house', said Leroy. Aaron rushed off.

The heat was unbearable; Jane walked boldly to the edge of the Lanniwah camp and stood still. Some people were afraid of the Boss; she should go away, but she saw David watching her. He seemed amused at her confusion; he beckoned and guided her around the camp. It was spare. Tin shacks and humpies made of corrugated iron and canvas, cardboard, paper-bark, flattened kerosene tins – anything to shelter from the rain and sun. Dilly bags hung from tree poles and mangy camp dogs slept everywhere. Sunshine powdered milk tins were the billycans. Jane saw small fires burning and women squatted before them cooking dampers.

'Children hungry; sometime they get tucker like beef, or might be camp pie.' David sighed.

They walked past Raymond's corrugated iron shed. Shirley and Mayda sidled up to Jane and leant against her shoulder. Mayda had flowers tucked behind her ears; her skin shone like cocoa butter; she had a full woman's figure. She whispered to Jane:

'You likem Lanniwah place?'

'Yes, it's your home, your wonderful country', said Jane.

'You missem that Sydney? You miss your mummy?'

'No, we live here now.'

'Lotta handsome fella in Sydney? Dey like Lanniwah womans?' Mayda said.

David motioned to her to be quiet, pursed his lips to indicate that she should move away.

'Maybe, but you just study school now, okay?' said Jane.

'You leave teacher look around.' David walked ahead.

'We got promise husband; all Lanniwah got dat. We not free, I not need readem.'

'How old are you?'

'I eighteen. I married soon. I run away before dat.'

'Just come to school; you can help me,' said Jane.

'Burnie adopt you for him daughter now. You Lanniwah. Find your skin and family. Burnie mob now, eh?'

'Okay, for Aaron too?'

'Yeeai', Mayda said.

'You got mothers, fathers, daughters, you aunty for me.'

Shirley squeezed her arm and ran off. Jane caught up with David and they strolled past a group of women her age who were making bread, but the Lanniwah women looked suspicious of the new teacher. She was too young. Their eyes never met hers. They turned away and laughed when she and David walked past. Whispering followed their walk.

Someone yelled out:

'Teacher got new blackfella boyfriend!'

David picked up a rock and threw it in the direction of the voice. The women laughed and scattered, but Jane had seen enough and she headed back to her caravan. Her face was hot and red with humiliation, her anxiety rose and she shut the door, she would read a book: there was nothing else to do, she would face her hated solitude.

Jane and Aaron now had a special place in the Lanniwah society but had to learn how to fit into Lanniwah life: being part of a family and clan would have consequences and obligations.

One afternoon after school lunch, Shirley, Mayda and Ricky walked with Jane near the Boss's house. Hubert sat on his veranda smoking and idly set the red heeler dogs on the children: they ran, leaving Jane to fight off the dogs with a stick. She kicked one until it whimpered. It felt good.

'Thanks for calling the dogs off, Boss!'

'No worries, Mrs Reynolds ... My spies tell me that you've been up at the camp!'

'I need to meet parents.'

'They can go to the school. I make the law around here!'

'Sorry, I have to do my job too. Why don't you chain up those dogs? Have you trained them to bite only Lanniwah kids?'

Hubert laughed.

'And tell that girl Shirley to cover up. She walks around with her little titties stickin out.'

Jane was horrified that this boofhead of a man would be spying on the girls; it was sinister. She leaned over the fence to talk to Edie.

Edie was digging in her beloved geranium garden, all red, pink and orange. She looked up and wiped her face as she pushed the trowel into the earth.

'Look at my reds this year; they're good enough to win a prize at the Katherine show. I've even got lemon scented. They were first prize-winners last year. I can bring you some.'

'Lovely geraniums', said Jane.

The children clambered over a broken tractor to look at its new graffiti. Lizzy called out: 'Robert. You bin writin with Texta on the old tractor, "Shirley you sixy gril". It not spelt right. David say you can't spell, Robert! You tryin' to git love from a promise-girl! She promise to an old man. You git a flogging.'

Jane saw Lanniwah women walk past with lowered eyes. She squirmed. She played with the children and ran after little ones as they squealed with joy but longed for female intimacy. So she wrote a long letter to her Sydney friends. She was getting depressed.

One day, Jane noticed an old lady from the camp smiling at her. Jane walked to her fire and sat in silence and added the wood that she had collected with

Aaron. Old Lucy was wizened, her grey hair hung down her back in a dirty pink ribbon. She took Jane's hand and rubbed it against her cheek. Sublime. She gave Jane a gift of a crocodile egg; it was pale greenish white and pulsated, an embryonic reptile inside. Old Lucy's home was a cardboard box house with five mangy dogs and she beckoned with tiny black claws, glaucoma eyes smiling, her dilly bag hung up out of the dogs' reach, a fish head on a tin plate. Jane followed and Lucy took Aaron onto her lap. He squirmed with uncertainty as she crooned in Lanniwah language and tickled him. He looked a bit scared but Jane stroked him and soon he was at home in the old woman's arms.

Jane sat quietly; she watched the changing light and children playing. She knew that too much talk was not right, remembering that white people never stopped talking and asking questions, wanting something. Jane wanted to learn to slow down and watch birds fly past, or ants crawl; she too could settle into the culture and be happy.

CHAPTER 4

Old Ladies and Uncles

Old Lucy and Beatrice shared a camp and Jane watched tobacco from a tin rubbed in old dark hands. This was like Jane's dad, who would roll Champion Fine Cut tobacco in his calloused hands with a cigarette paper stuck to his lip. She had watched him cup his hands around the smoke; she learnt about life at his knee as he squatted with the men, Jane's Koori uncles, on wooden fruit boxes, drinking KB beer from big brown bottles.

When they visited Taree, Uncle Bill would take the kids to the Red Rose Café in town for lime spiders, soda drinks with ice cream, and they sat up with their best manners.

'Nice table manners, kids. Act white. Act white', he'd say. They sucked down the drinks with pleasure.

'I'm going to go to university', said Jane.

'Oh yeah! I got a government scholarship to a Boys' Home, worked all day, no flaming shoes, bringin in the cows, freezing, whipped with a stock whip, but you kids can go to school and learn', said Uncle Bill.

Jane noticed that the café manager wiped down the plastic seats with Pine-O-Clean disinfectant as they left.

Uncle Bill's canvas tent by the railway line leaked; it was grey with mildew. The fettler camp was alive with the smell of burnt rubber and glue used to remake the soles of their boots. Her uncles sat with their harmonicas by a fire. There was a white cockatoo in a cage. The past floated alongside of you – it never left.

Now, Jane searched for a new family amongst the old Lanniwah women. She sat on their blankets in the bough shade by the store, their glaucoma eyes blinking as they chatted mostly in Lanniwah language.

'Some bird dey signs – dat crow up der mean it rain real heavy soon', said Old Lucy. She nodded at Shirley and sure enough, it started to sprinkle from a cloudless sky. A willy wagtail was a messenger that you didn't want frolicking in front of you. Death was coming to someone. Old Lucy sat on a new red blanket and finger knitted dilly bags from hand-rolled string ... She held Jane's hand and stroked it. Jane felt like the old woman could read her spirit. The hippy teachings of the 1969 'Summer of Love' helped: 'Be here now'. It had a resonance, but of course the hippies had been stoned on marijuana and there was none of that at Harrison. Jane sat for hours with the old women as they stroked her wavy golden brown hair and marvelled at the holes in her ears filled with silver and turquoise. She waved vaguely at Hubert who scowled from his veranda. He sure wasn't enjoying a summer of love.

Old Lucy's eyes widened, as she looked sightless in the direction of the big house. Jane didn't know what she was seeing in her memory but Lucy's expression altered as her hands traced the direction of her ancestors. Jane could see that Lucy was living the story; it was as real as the listening children were.

'He moving down river, he camp then move blue lily lagoon. Then another mob lizard come, they got cheeky and bitem painted goanna. See that rock, it got ring inside: sit down place for big snake too.'

Old Lucy tossed back her head and began to sing, her tremulous voice in a minor key; the song tinkled in the quiet air and then rested on one high note. She clapped the rhythm on her wizened thighs and Jane picked up Old Lucy's hand and held it for the song's duration. Jane stood up and thanked Old Lucy, said she would bring her up some tucker.

'I bring you ice cream from freezer; you like that?'

'You granddaughter for me, dat right', said Lucy.

Next day, Jane again waited patiently outside the camp. She wanted to be noticed, to be invited in, the Lanniwah way. Burnie stood up from his corrugated camp and walked in cowboy boots and hat to welcome Jane. He smoothed a place by his fire.

'Sittem here; you my daughter', he said.

For all time now, she was classified as Lelli, a sister to all Lelli moiety women. Likewise, for Jane, men would be her classified sons, brothers or potential husbands. She was disturbed to find out that David was classified as Bulli, a husband. Jane would have to careful not to be seen alone with him. People would talk and laugh at her. She was beginning to find it stressful. Why couldn't they just be normal and follow modern Australian law and not have lots of wives. It was looking like some Arabic custom, where the old men got the girls at all ages and everyone had to respect them and obey no matter how ridiculous and unfair it obviously was.

Jane realised that in the moiety system, everyone was some kind of relative. However, she would often be in the dark – the system was complex. Although, once she had accepted her position, everyone would know what role she had in relation to them: she had sisters, children, fathers, brothers, mothers, and her belonging was forever.

Beatrice was loud, tall and skinny, she was married to an old fellow who had four wives, she was number one and had a commanding presence; she took Jane's Tibetan necklace into her hand and murmured with admiration.

'Where dat from?'

'Tibet.'

'Where dat? Near Borroloola?'

Jane sighed at the prospect of describing the geography of the world outside Lanniwah country. Where to begin? Perhaps with the nearest town, Katherine, then up the Stuart highway to Darwin.

Beatrice had heard about those places. Lot of cars, lot of white people, lot of trouble with grog. Then across the sea. But Beatrice said: 'Across dere, dat home of the dead.'

Hmm … Jane nodded and tried to explain that it was also a place where other kinds of people lived, dark skinned like her.

'More tribe?'

'Err, yes, but many different ones.' Jane tried to draw a map of the world but it seemed downright ridiculous to Aunty Beatrice.

'Who dis Sex Pistols?'

"Punk rock, music, sort of.'

'Anyway, where dat Jesus from?'

The missionaries had been through, leaving behind a mysterious story about a bearded white man who was going to come back some day and save them.

'Yes, maybe it's true – hard to say.'

Old Lucy took Jane for a walk to the metal ring in the tree, Old Lucy stroked the rusted metal but said nothing; she just looked into the distance. They walked back to Lucy's fire and she talked slowly so Jane could follow. The Aboriginal-English 'Kriol' was becoming familiar; it was like Papuan Pidgin English.

The sun set, darkness came and still Jane sat by the fire. Aaron fell asleep in her arms. She touched Lucy's scarred arms and upper chest. The old woman smiled.

'Dis special mark for me.' She took Jane's fingers and rubbed them against her scarred dark flesh. 'Like boomerang mark might be woman stick, dis mark for touch, make it ancestor step on ground', Lucy said. Jane stroked the marks, saw the pain of the incisions made with a sharpened stone. Each cicatrice formed in this way told a story. For Old Lucy, each scar was mourning for a family member long dead.

Jane learnt about female marrnkeetj, clever women who could get out stones put in a body by bilka, clever men. 'Do dat without breaking the skin. Dey keep special stones in cold water. My people dey bin long time dis place. Alla time walk about dis place. Know all the special place, yeeai? Dat one near dat hill, real special, you can't go dere? Men place', she said.

Jane sat quietly and pointed as Lucy looked up into the night. 'That's the Southern Cross', said Jane.

'Look dere. Two sisters dey travel across sky, dey run from old kangaroo. Then dere? dingo star, you callem Sirius. He cheeky fella, he chasem woman .' Old Lucy rolled with laughter, and made a penis of a stick and jerked it up and down. Jane nodded.

Jane nibbled at a wild plum – she spat quietly, it tasted terrible – then sweet bush banana and sugarbag wild honey. The black honey clung to her fingers. The wild food held stories and meaning that described the country. The women each held their Dreaming stories about the country and Jane's mind filled with the landscape's geography, every small tree, every rock, all of it, in a mythic song cycle. Every gift of bush fruit from a child or old person, every warning not go near a certain escarpment or tree was a kind of lesson in cosmology.

Now it was Beatrice's turn to teach. She took Jane by the hand and sat her by her fire, raked the coals with her stick and made tea. Dogs with no hair curled up beside her. Beatrice's long hair down her back was tied with a pristine blue ribbon. Her back was bent in half and she walked with a stick. She had a reputation as a clever woman and wasn't old, maybe forty, but already a magician.

Jane produced sweet biscuits from her bag and opened them for her.

'You like Monte Carlo?' Jane sat quietly and showed Beatrice her photographs of her family in Sydney and Taree.

The next night, Jane opened the school for adult art classes. The adults came to the electric light, the chance to sit at desks and touch books and paints and pencils. Their paintings were full of lore. Old Lucy painted pictures of large red stones over and over again and her paintings always showed men in black hats ... Sometimes, tears ran down Lucy's face. These stones were like the eggs of giant emus: they rose out of the grey earth in isolated plains. Jane respected the old woman's stories, her interweaving of Dreamings and history – they were one and the same.

One afternoon, Jane walked towards these stones; they seemed to rumble. The earth was alive, something was rippling underneath. These stones travelled underground across the land, they tumbled in the old people's dreams. Jane touched the red ochre colour and leant against the rough surface; the rock loomed over her, and she felt as if she was watched. These rocks loomed up against the sky. Her father had pointed out the grey stone cliffs along the Hawkesbury River; they were inaccessible by ordinary people; there were burial places there, he said. Old skeletons of Aborigines thousands of years old. Her dad Samuel knew things about the old people: he had once been the witness to uncovering a Darug woman's bones who had a gypsum cap of clay and her crossed arms hid a small child skeleton, two thousand years old, as old as Christ. It had been reburied in a paperback shroud but had haunted him for years.

In class, the artists saw the earth from above, the bird's eye image of existence, red bursts of song and shape and spirit and sometimes sinister.

Some of the older people painted the men's bullroarers and women's dancing sticks as seen flat against the earth. Space was expanding ever upwards and it brought deep emotional outpourings to talk about the phenomena. Many pictures were stark depictions of loss, of land stolen and lives taken.

'One time, daughter here born, Susan, white man skin. I takem her from Protector Man, alla time runaway, he drive up my place might be stealem her right off my titties. Husband good Wunungah like Ray. He catchem dingo scalp for money. We walk walk. But dat man findem us and takem her. He policeman, he tie her up wid yellafella kid.' Old Beatrice said, and tears dropped on Jane's hand.

'I hear you, mother. Sad time', said Jane.

'Takem long way, nomore seeum. You tellum alla people bout dis. Learnem Lanniwah way.'

Beatrice went into her paper-bark house and came back with an exquisite hand woven dilly bag entwined with soft white feathers. She placed it in Jane's hands.

'Thank you Aunty; it's beautiful.'

'You pay me twenty dollar. I go bingo', said Beatrice.

Jane laughed. 'Okay. Aaron will bring it tomorrow.'

Aaron cuddled up to Jane by the fire.

'Tell me a true story about Grandpa Samuel, like when he was a big boy like me and he ate the galah stew and it was too bony', said Aaron.

'Okay, but then we go home and you go to sleep – we have a big day at school tomorrow'.

CHAPTER 5

Billabong

Leroy and Ricky drove along red paths with their tin trucks made of tin lids and fencing wire. Aaron led the bunch until Robert knocked him over and stole his truck. Ricky yelled at him. Aaron didn't care: this life was unheard of freedom, no strict child-minding centre in Balmain, no hand washing or compulsory sleep time. He was learning to swim – all of the children could swim because they learnt as toddlers and could swim in the billabong before they could walk.

The Lanniwah country was beautiful. Near to her caravan the billabong pool was pink in the sunrise, water dappled like a Monet painting. Piles of small bones and white feathers lay around the shore, pandanus palms fringed the pool and a waterfall cascaded from black rock outcrops.

Every afternoon when the heat in school was terrible, the billabong was lifesaving. Jane and David led the children to swim for hours. Jane and Aaron paddled by the shore, Mayda and Shirley dived into the blue lotus lily pads. Aaron clung to Mayda's neck, dived and laughed; it was complete joy. As Jane swam underneath the cool water, a long necked tortoise's eyes glinted. Small fresh water crocodiles poked their snouts up from the blue water; when they saw Jane, Aaron and Leroy, they submerged.

'Look, Mum, crocodiles. Will they eat me?'

'No, they're freshies. They eat birds and fish, not you – you're too big', said Jane.

But, um, she rather wondered if this was correct: perhaps a really big one, say one and a half metres, might attack a human. Oh great, Aaron eaten before her eyes, how would she explain that? The middle of a pool was a worry: her dad had said to not swim across the middle, a bunyip might live there.

She lay on her back and watched David dive to the bottom, his dark skin glistening beneath the water. He swam under the lily pads, and a green python slid into the clear water. Lizzy and Mayda paddled back with lily stems in their teeth and they showed Jane how to peel and eat them like celery. David emerged dripping, and spoke quietly:

'You happy for this place?' He had streams of water rippling down his body.

'This country is amazing! It puts its arms around me', said Jane.

White cranes, spoonbills and azure kingfishers flew out from the pools nearby as the sky turned pink and the water gleamed pale orange. Melaleuca trees with their peeling bark and grevillea blossoms, fragrant and sticky.

'Dat great ancestral woman's push digging sticks in earth and out come water and all life and they havem babies, hundred tribe and you know dat blood, after birth bringem Dreamtime serpents. Dey smell dat fresh blood', said Lizzy. It was a great mystery and as commonplace as the rain, earth or sun. A woman was sacred because only she could give birth. The girls laughed.

'Mens real jealous of us because we can have baby', said Shirley.

'Is that why women can't go near the men ceremony?' asked Jane.

'True, dey keep sacred things for themselves. Dey frightened dat womens want to take them', said Lizzy.

'You no go to dat men's sacred place. Dey spearem you, sure thing: dat Old Pelican he magic man – watch out', said Shirley.

On the way back from a walk, the bigger girls pointed out caves.

'You no go dere, Missus Jane, for mens, not for womens. Dey killem you', said Mayda.

Jane looked at the secret place; she had heard that there were ancient paintings on the walls, ochres from thousands of years ago. The caves also contained painted bones. The women had said that old people travelled over the country from Rainer Mission to paint the bones and keep them safe from dingoes.

'Dat rainbow snake was angry, not like her babies killed', said Lizzy. Jane had seen photographs of men dressed in tall kapok ceremonial head-dresses.

'Old dingo men', whispered Mayda.

'Like long time olden time?'

'No, last month. Ancestor people but, you know, dog, like great grandfathers, dey real people, live now', said Mayda.

'Bamatji, you callem ironwood, magic power! You sleep under em you not wakem up.' Shirley smiled.

CHAPTER 6

Massacre Story

The children had gone home and Jane watched David as he packed up the schoolbooks. She saw Old Pelican walk past the school on his way up to the store. She put down her files and sat on the teacher's desk looking at David, casual and friendly. Her heart fluttered.

'You reckon I could have a talk with the head man today?' said Jane. Old Pelican was like a chameleon. He would wear a cowboy hat and boots, looking like a stockman, and then sometimes she had seen him looking very old with a white beard, he seemed frail and gentle. He seemed to be changing all the time. 'A shape changer', David whispered.

'He kill lotta people. He's a clever fella. A *werrnggitj* can be man or woman; they good magic, can make someone well. They heal blood. Heal sick people with stones and have spirit with them, get inside people. He can stop that big rain if he wants; he sings backwards. Sings the rain to stop. Powerful old man.'

Old Pelican's camp was apart from the others. He lived in a large paper-bark covered bough shade, a dead wallaby hung with milk cans from a pole. A suitcase was full of neatly piled blankets. The old man sat on an old bedframe while Jane stood back. Old Pelican called out.

'Yeeai. What you wantem?'

'Thank you for meeting me. I'm the new head teacher and I want to know what you would like me to teach the children', said Jane.

'You teacher, you teach 'em. What you ask me for?' Jane couldn't argue with his logic. Old Pelican looked mystified.

He stood up with difficulty and motioned for Jane and David to walk to a nearby flowering tree near the store. He pointed to a heavy metal ring rusted into the bark.

'Dat for chain.'

Jane nodded.

'We takem bones away.'

'What bones?'

The old man tilted his worn hat back from his face. The silence was long and pointed. A white cockatoo flew over them and settled into the tree. Jane felt hot and out of place.

'Yeeai, I there. You see em red dirt near store?'

'Yes, it's bauxite, isn't it?' she said.

'Dat red for reason. I bin little fella. Dem white stock men, maybe twenty of em ride in here. People scared, not seen many Wunungah before.'

'Whitefellas and black police, Queensland boys', said David. He held his head low, staring at the ground. The atmosphere was intense. Jane squirmed.

'Dey think dey gunna get tucker. Dis Wunungah got baccy might be. One fella, he say "We gotta cut wood, why dey do that?" Alla time chainem up, no good. Big shackle chain on dis ring. I little fella, I seeum bag on yarraman, horse, think maybe got damper, bullabingie; we hungry', said Old Pelican.

Jane nodded, not sure where the story was going.

'They want tobacco from Wunungah', said David.

'White settlers did give out flour and sugar', she said.

'Dey roundin Lanniwah up in 1928, dey askem all come and chop up wood with an axe. Dey chop and chop big lotta wood, want em make big fire maybe. Then something funny happen, *Wunungah* holdem gun like dis.' Old Pelican mimed the gun against his shoulder.

'Okay.'

'Mummy say we gunna die for sure.' Old Pelican rubbed his hands over the metal ring. 'Chained 'em up. Just here. Nothin grow now.'

'Why?'

'Dis place, red dirt, see? Here. Blood. You lookem.' Old Pelican looked up at her and directed her eyes to the earth. She was confused: his language was hard to follow.

'I'm sorry', she said. She wondered if that was it. Should she go now?

Time drifted on this plain.

Old Pelican rolled a smoke with gnarled black hands and breathed it in.

'Dey finish up.'

'What? You mean right here? Near where we're standing?' she said.

'The womens scared, start runnin. Mummy runnin wid me, little fella, I run wid her, cryin, she carry coolamon wid baby.'

'Oh God! No.'

White cockatoos flew squawking in a great arc overhead. David kept drawing in the dust with his boot.

'Dey shot all dem Lanniwah men, shot 'em like dey nothing. Like dogs! Daddy he bin shot in head, bang, like that. Den dey run down the womens and hittem wid a stick, not want to wastem bullet, hit 'em all babies wid sticks killem. Smashem head likem watermelon. Throwem on rock. Hittem on head, kick 'em, run horse yarraman over dem. Mummy run real fast to dem hills, pick me up, savem me. Lotta womens run dere, dey stay up dere long time; just get tucker at night-time. Wunungah burn 'em up Lanniwah bodies ... all up wid dat wood dey chop. Yeeai, all burnem. Dey just clearin' for cattle. All Arnhem Land like dat.' Old Pelican's head sank to his chest while tears dribbled across his skin. Jane's tears flowed as well; she felt droplets wet her knees. It was a shock – was it possible? She gulped down the terrible sadness.

'You see the red sand?' David pointed to the store.

'Where everyone lines up for stores?' said Jane.

'Dat one, red from blood, yeeai. Me little fella, I run away, hide in dem cliffs. We real frightened', Old Pelican said as he gazed at the ground.

Jane stared and sobbed quietly. David nodded and touched the old man's shoulder, but the old elder had become calm; he was casual.

'Ok, I go now, grandson. Bringem up big barra tomorrow?'

David nodded at Jane; it was over. The old man walked back to his bed-frame and lay down.

Jane watched him go. It was time remembered, as it was then and now. Old Lucy walked up to them.

'Me, Old Pelican sister.'

She leant on a stick, and Jane realised in that moment that this was a powerful woman – these were remarkable human beings. She had been waiting to meet them her whole life. Several small grandchildren followed, holding onto the edge of the old woman's dress. Edie had told Jane that Lucy was not actually old, maybe only fifty, but she had a degenerative disease that was slowly killing her, shrivelling her skin and muscle; it was like leprosy.

Old Lucy sat on a rug on the ground. Her dogs lay down near her. She pulled Jane to sit beside her and smiled. She was reading her mind, nodded, and spoke in a soft hesitant voice: 'You come to me, granddaughter now, yeeai. Dis place, my great grand mummy country; dis sit down place made long time.'

Two black cockatoos flew overhead. They cried out. Old Lucy listened.

'We hear dat bird for warning. We got rations dem old days. Walkem to old police station near river. Wunungah come with camels, horses – yarraman. Police mans take prisoners and walkem to Katherine town. Neck chain, like dis.'

She put her gnarled hands around her neck in a choking motion. Jane felt like she was drowning, but she had to listen, be a witness. The old woman smoothed a piece of mulga wood; she shifted on the ground; there was a Cycad palm close by with splitting red seeds covered in slow ants. Old Lucy lifted a handful of sand and it trickled through her dark fingers to make a cone. She leant her head against her thin arm, a deep sigh. Jane edged closer and put her hand on Lucy's shoulder, the bones were fragile. The old woman shuddered, tears collected in her eyes. Jane leant towards her face, sniffed the grey hair; it smelt of daisies. Jane thought she would never understand this burden of grief, that her life in comparison had been a breeze and full of joy. Old Lucy looked up and her eyes met Jane's in a deep stare of recognition: it was like she could see all of Jane's inner thoughts, her past lives. There was a burst of white cockatoos overhead, a hundred flashed by squawking loudly. Time disappeared.

'Why did they do that?' said Jane.

'Daddy killem bullock, spear 'im – we hungry.' Lucy pulled her head back and pointed with her lips.

'Which way?' said Jane.

They stared into the distance, looking for a willy willy containing spirits. Old Lucy's hand pinched Jane's in a tight compression.

'Afghan sometime pickem up, takem to Alice Springs, walk with big mob camel.'

Surviving was a miracle. The Harrison history was becoming clearer to Jane as Old Lucy pointed to the hill and smoked her pipe.

'You see that one big hill, dat one big one, lotta cave?' she said.

Jane looked to where the old lady pointed with her lips.

'I seeum', said Jane. The language was getting easier.

'Dey first smellem smoke, big long snake of smoke over dat hill, but smellem man meat cookin. Oh, big trouble comin for sure. Mummy take brother, little Pelican, up dere after mens shootem Daddy. Cuttem up women's heads, lookem like smashed skull, he tellem me, brother tellem story. Aunty head all bin broken, cuttem open like red meat, little teeth white lyin alla bout in dat flesh, likem fruit you know? Me little baby, cry cry alla time. Left in coolamon in bush, alla time cry cry, but mens not see dat coolamon, not till later. Throw em coolamon in dirt like nothin, like we nothin', Lucy said.

Jane held her hand and looked at the crumpled skin and bluish veins that trembled.

'One whitefella takem me to camp. Mummy find em, but later, when she not scared nomore', said Old Lucy.

A silence, while Jane thought of what to say. How did Lucy survive? A baby! What could Jane possibly say in that moment? What could sound as if she comprehended the massacre? Old Lucy drew with a story stick in the dust; it was a kind of map, a memory, a dream. Jane felt sweat running down her back, she lifted the shirt away from her melting skin. Old Lucy took Jane's face in her hands and brought it close enough to breath the same breath. It was slow time, an eternity of breath. The old woman drew a shape of a rifle in the dirt and rubbed it out. Jane stared and then reached out to embrace her, she squeezed the old shuddering body next to her heart. They both laughed in relief. The old woman pointed with her chin towards the hills, where the red rocks stood. That place, where she had been nearly killed by men on horseback, where the men rode the women down and hit them with stirrups, then dismounted and beat them to death with sticks and rocks. And murdered the children the same way with utter disregard as though they were hunting dingo or kangaroo. As though the Lanniwah were rubbish.

'Killem kid with stick. Not wantem wastem bullet'.

'I'm glad you lived; you not get shot', said Jane as she wiped her face of tears.

'Womens run away fast. Stay in cave but cruel hungry, wantem water, fightem over insect, want eatem.'

'They wanted to feed their kids?' said Jane.

"Yeah, gotta eat. Lotta day like dat, hidem then little bit come down, lookem for water. Wunungah leavem now.'

'Did the women learn to work for the cattlemen?'

'Yeeai. Mummy come back down and learnem to work for Wunungah, washem clothes, she keep baby alive, me and Pelican. All live now.'

She held Jane's hand and touched the skin with a stroking motion; she turned the hand upwards and looked at the dark skin lines in Jane's palm. She turned the hand back and ran her nail against the brown moons of Jane's fingers. David's head was low but he looked up at the exposed hand; he saw the colour. Old Lucy nodded at David. She spoke to him in language, then back to Jane.

'You not Wunungah? True, eh? You little bit yellafella?'

Jane nodded. 'Little bit yellafella, that's right, thankyou. My great granny like you.'

'Yeeai. You tellem everyone, remember long time olden time', said Lucy.

Jane nodded and felt a trembling awareness of being in the presence of a survivor, an ancient woman who had seen the white men 'clearing for cattle'. The problem was, how to deal with this terrible information – how could anyone go on after an attempt at genocide? Jane thought that the people had suffered terrible cruelty. It was the remains of that time, that history: a failure to 'manure the ground with them'. It had been a sinister tainted ground, with creeks alive with arsenic, pools of dead parrots and human bones. Did the white settlers' hatred come from a feeling of disgust that Aboriginal people hadn't given up, hadn't conveniently died out? Where was the retribution? The guilt by white people? There was none, and no God to care, just deep ugly anger against a people who had been almost destroyed. *What the hell do you do?* Jane felt the weight of responsibility of this knowledge that no outsider seemed to want. It was a huge honour to be told about these events, an honour, even, to hold the old woman's withered hand.

Jane wanted to know how those Lanniwah warriors had been tricked. Why hadn't they suspected the white men in ghost skins? Did they think they were long lost souls of grandfathers who had come back? Hadn't the chains given them some hint of what was coming? Chains and shackles – yes, she had seen them proudly displayed in the Katherine Museum, not easy to mistake for jewellery. And what about Old Pelican's assertion that their fathers thought they would get tobacco? Was the craving for the white man's drug so strong that the men had thrown away their fear? They had chopped their own funeral pyre – a mountain of wood, enough to burn a tribe. How many? Too many. What, sixty? A hundred? Who knew? Who cared? The Lanniwah, of course. There was mourning for every massacred person. The crying came from a handful of terrified women and children crouching in a cave of ancient paintings – Makassan ships, drawings of the Bainji. Chinese hats and pointy-toed shoes in yellow ochre, x-ray animals, their organs enlarged. And what of the white men? What had they thought about clearing the land, as they had done all over Australia? Men who had travelled from England, that *green and pleasant land*.

She now understood the truth about this place, the terrible, painful truth. In this actual place, maybe a hundred people had been shot down and burnt. The metal ring in the tree told the whole story. David couldn't look at her and she stood alone in the face of this white and black history. The year 1928 when it happened was the year Jane's mother was born: it was only yesterday, less than fifty years ago. Why hadn't anyone told her? Why didn't the world know about this? Were these people supposed to keep this event a secret? They were living on the actual spot where terrible murders had taken place; the soil was full of human fragments, skin and hair.

It was a miasma oozing from the grey earth. You couldn't see it or breathe it but it would never go away – a pool, like blood coming from below, the pitiful dead risen from the ground, burnt skeletons dancing on graves, like a devil-devil dance, criss-crossing red footprints across the escarpment, searching for their loved ones, the spirits searching for home, all the time crying. No wonder the winds howled! How could anyone stand it? How could they go on living?

At last, it was twilight, and cool. Jane sat by the billabong with some children; she made a fire, while David swam with the boys. She watched them dive-bomb each other in the water; she wanted to know what they knew. Did they realise that their parents had been subjugated and beaten, hounded into camps, forced to work, children taken away and locked in repressive orphanages or Christian school dormitories? It was just like her great granny, indentured out to white people as a servant. The other stations around Harrison had few Aboriginal people on them. The cattlemen had forced them to move away ...

David climbed out of the water in his wet jeans. Jane called him over.

'Why do the other stations near here have hardly any Lanniwah?' she asked.

'They run off by *Wunungah* in sixties. I live with father; he did stock work, but told to leave and not come back. So we askem where we goin to go? No tucker, nothing, just his spear and his matches, we walk alla round for weeks until we come here, walk maybe three hundred mile.'

They boiled the billy and David told the story with long quiet gaps.

'Old Pelican, must be maybe fifty now, he run away with his mother after that killing time. Little brother he bin run down by horse, Wunungah hit im with butt of gun. Pelican's mother she run, savem other two children, baby in a coolamon and Pelican run beside her. But she fallem and drop that coolamon, she run to a big cave, special place. She watch that coolamon in grass, real scared. Hearem gunshots, boom, boom, and screaming from Lanniwah women. Dey, you know, rapem them women, then shoot 'em. Next morning, that coolamon and baby all gone.'

David spoke in a steady stream, not looking at the listener, tracing a stick in the dust to draw a map of the scene. Then he was silent for a long time. Jane leant towards David, her shoulder leaning on his. She felt his cool hunched body.

'Lotta womens live in cave for long time too scared to come down. Eat just wild banana, sugarbag.'

Jane had read that 'dispersal' was when the black police came from Queensland wearing cast-off uniforms and paid half white men's pay. Dispersal meant killing blackfellas, or driving them off their land so the pastoralists could bring in their cattle. There would have been billabongs full of blood.

It was time to cook dinner. David and Jane wandered past children as they played a string game with elastic stretched between trees. They jumped and flipped leaving late afternoon shadows. She smelt the warm sweat from his armpits. A man like this was surely unknowable, from ancient lineage: he would give no simple message, no easy communication, each non-verbal sign a mystery. She watched him moving away without a word, stared at the back of his head; his hand rubbed his hair, he could feel her watching. He stopped and stood with his head down, seemed to be waiting for her to call him back, waiting for her to smile and beckon him back to her. She thought of counter-culture freedom, hippy eroticism – *Let the Sunshine In*.

It was cooler and jabirus flew overhead. David walked up towards his shack leaving Jane marooned on a paddock of bones. She called out to him, 'So who are all these Lanniwah?' David looked over his shoulder.

'Dey come from survivors. Lot of old people, they hate Wunungah, white man.'

'Yeah. I see'.

Jane felt sick: she walked upon a blood-soaked country. It had a profound effect – no wonder the women found it hard to accept her. Why would they? As far as they were concerned, she was a Wunungah and part of the generation descended from white murderers. All white Australians would carry that responsibility. Jane struggled to find where she stood. *Was she guilty too?* One of her great grandfathers had been an English ex-convict landowner. Was he guilty, or at least complicit?

The Lanniwah left to go back to camp. Aaron sat in Jane's lap as the sun set ... She could see a sea eagle pecking at the heart of a half-submerged grey dove in the billabong. Its soft down drifted on the top of the water. The poor bird tried to flutter away but the eagle had it gripped it with talons and with a hooked beak was eating its prey alive. Jane couldn't watch.

CHAPTER 7

Plane Trip

In the Wet, it rained and rained at Harrison Station: the road was a roaring river, no longer dirt, just rushing water ... Aaron clung to Jane's back as she waded to school in waist-deep water. She remembered learning to swim in the muddy Hawkesbury River: oyster cuts and rubber tyres and fear of the deep. She had walked the two miles home in bare feet on hot tar; she had sucked black liquorice Choo Choo bars until her tongue turned black. Her father's skin went black as he trowelled concrete in rich people's gardens.

A letter, two weeks old, arrived for Jane. The Education Department inspector wanted to meet her in town. She was in a panic. What did it mean? Was this the end? Had they heard about her being a single mother and she'd be sacked for immorality? Edie had been spying on Jane for weeks. At Harrison Station, Jane watched Hubert drop the big canvas mailbag on her step.

'There's also a letter from the Department of Aboriginal Affairs, wonder what they want?' said Hubert.

'That'd be my business' said Jane.

Edie opened all Jane's letters and they looked pawed over. Hubert stopped on the step and chewed his false teeth.

'You had better watch who you stir up in town – the National First Australia Party blokes have had enough of people from down south mixing it up with the blacks.' Jane nodded; she could see herself run off the property or a man arriving to scare her off.

'Look, Hubert, I respect your opinion, and you mean well, but you are not the police so why don't you and the moral majority mind your own business?'

He looked surprised at her ability to talk back. He sneered and said in a low whisper,

'In town, you know what they call ya?'

'No Hubert, I don't.'

'Slut. Nigger lover.'

She stopped and considered. 'Well, they would, wouldn't they? But you, Hubert, are a gentleman.'

'Righto. Look, I don't think that. I respect you women out here', he said.

'Your husband not comin'?' said Edie.

'No, not coming. Maybe he's dead. Is that okay with you?'

The next day, Jane looked for Hubert, but was told he was off somewhere near the shed, fixing his tractor. She walked down to a rise where the flood had filled a gully with cool water; there were sounds of girls frolicking. She saw Lizzy, Shirley and Mayda swimming in the pool with a blue plastic float. They were climbing on top of it. Their dresses were stuck wetly to their bodies. Jane approached unseen and then she heard a male voice. Hubert burst out of the water from under the girls; he laughed and pushed over the float. He grabbed Shirley around her waist and he flung her into the air, her dress flew up, she squealed.

'No, don't throwem me, Boss!'

He duck-dived and his bare backside shone white in the swirling grey water. Jane stood still, unsure of what she was watching. She felt confused. He was a kindly man after all – or what was it? Mayda saw her standing there in the tree shadows, their eyes met for an instant. Mayda put her hand over her mouth and dived into the water.

'Hey Hubert, Boss, I need to talk to you, where are you?'

Jane heard the girls whispering and him telling them to hush.

'Coming, teacher', he called back. She saw him quickly pull on his jeans over his naked body and hop over the thorn bushes towards her.

'Hi, I have to go to town. I'm sorry to disturb you.'

'No worries, I was just coolin off; come on.' He put on his hat and he looked into her eyes as he slid up his fly zipper very slowly. He did up his turquoise belt; his torso was paunchy but strong. His eyes on hers. She felt very strange. He couldn't stop smiling. He ran his fingers through his thin blond hair; he was handsome but repellent. She watched him hook and tighten the belt; he looked up, his tongue licking his cracked lips.

'What?'

'Nothing'.

She heard Mayda giggling and the other girls whispering. Hubert bowed to the girls and actually flexed his chest.

'You want a tickle too?' he chuckled. The girls flew off into the bush.

'What?'

'Just a joke – can't you take a joke, teacher? Lighten up a bit.'

'I have to meet the Department inspector in town. Can you fly me in?'

'Your funeral. I've only had my licence a few months; I can show off my new plane, well second-hand. It's a Cessna 150 with Omni Vision rear window. Real flash.'

Later, they climbed into the plane. Hawks circled. A jabiru took flight with a flicker of black and white plumage as the Lanniwah stockmen shooed cattle off the runway. Jane gripped the seat as the Boss started the engine and taxied down the red mud and took off.

She watched the purple and red escarpment, cliffs where Jedda had jumped. Wild, white waterfalls and flooding plains were dotted with pelicans, brolgas and boab trees bulbous with water. A herd of water buffalo chewed on pink water lilies. Wild brumbies leapt through water as the plane flew over.

Jane was nervous in Hubert's presence. He picked his scabby knuckles and shifted his stomach behind the flying gear. He smelt of tobacco and Brut aftershave.

'So how's it goin' for yous?'

'Okay. The school is pretty demanding, fifty-two children from four to eighteen. None of them can read or write.'

'Must be hard without your hubby.' He looked back at her, his hairy eyebrows twitching.

'No, not really.'

He gripped the controls and motioned with blubbery lips to the horizon. 'There's the Arnhem highway; we'll be right, just foller her up.'

'Are you an owner of Harrison?'

'Narr, just the hired manager, second in command. I'm a 'yes' man'.

Hubert was deep in thought. He said he wanted a cigarette and a beer and some company of men who knew his world.

'Yeah, the back bar of the Crocodile Hotel, where only men in blue shirts drink.'

'Will you buy a place?'

'We've got four kids, there's not enough money to make a go of it – never will be. It's the federal government's fault, or somebody's, and the cost of trucking two hundred beasts to an abattoir is bloody ridiculous – how can a man make a living? The station makes no money – it's like a terrible mistake. We go through the motions of mustering, what for? Just to count the beasts. The Brahman calves suck their mothers dry, until they're skin and bone. We're like that, exhausted and sucked dry from looking after that tribe. Edie struggling to give medical care in isolation. Watching in despair when a young 'un is dying because she ran out of antibiotics. How do you think that flaming feels? Digging a little grave, but we do it, me and the cattle boys. And for shrunken old people too – shallow graves for people who lived their life under cardboard. No, I don't like this life, but where else do we go? To what? It's the love of these dark people that keeps us here. What is there to keep you? You don't know these people. You'll move on, like all the fly-by-night teachers – you won't look back, will ya?'

'I don't know yet.'

'We keep the flame of English civilisation alive.'

'Do you ever suspect that this country doesn't belong to you? That white people are trespassing?'

'Bugger that.'

He looked down at Jane's legs, nice long brown legs.

'Gee, you'd taste alright.'

'Pardon?' she said.

'Look, I used to be embarrassed about all this stuff, but I like to suck a pussy, sweet and salty, more than anything', he said.

'Too much information, Hubert', said Jane.

'I'm sorry if I offend you, but I have imagined it, you know. Just a quick suck. Look I tried a bit in Singapore, but narrr, not yellow ones. Just you and I up here at two thousand feet in a tin box. I could show you the joy stick.'

'Well, at least you're honest. Can we change the topic?'

'A joke. I wouldn't touch anyone but Edie. A man has to have control in this country, or he could go troppo.' His hand brushed her thigh as he leant forward to adjust the landing gear.

'Don't please', she said. Jumping out of the plane was an option. She was suffocating.

'Sorry, gotta get ready to land.'

He looked very hot and shaky. He had only had a few flights without the instructor; it was a bugger of a thing to land. Jane sensed his fear and felt scared as well. The plane shook and moved from side to side. In the distance the town loomed, Jane held on tight to the vinyl. The air sock bloomed out and beckoned them in, then a man in a battered bush hat waved them down. Thank heavens. They bumped and crunched along the gravel runway, an eagle rose in front of them. Holy hell. Hubert gripped the throttle.

They were about to land and the man at the Katherine airfield waved them down.

'Easy does it, there she goes, nice and smooth.' There were huge bumps; they touched down at the airfield. Hubert's hands shook violently and he reached into his pocket to light a Marlborough, hand cupped against the wind, bushie-style. He looked at her and smiled. Jane watched him; that cupping of the hands always reminded her of her dad. She loved to watch men roll a cigarette and light up: it lit up memories.

Later, Jane left the Education Department office with a pile of books on teaching literacy, and coloured sets of Cuisenaire wood blocks for maths ('four arithmetical operations in one box'). Jane was received as a heroine, a respected and successful teacher. She was smiling. She would be made permanent, a job for life, no fear of unemployment, no grovelling for money. It felt fantastic.

Jane stepped out onto Katherine's main street. Lanniwah men sat in the shade, their heads hung low, waiting for something or someone, a feed or a drink or tobacco or land rights or a woman or the Gunjible police.

A trip to the supermarket, oh joy – air-conditioning! Jane sighed with the relief from the stifling 40 degrees heat. She sat on a seat and watched the white families filling their trolleys with ice cream and nappies while Lanniwah women shopped with one small bag, their babies clinging to their legs. Dark faces looked with hidden envy at the supermarket plenty; young Aboriginal girls roamed the aisles and longingly handled lipsticks and cheap jewellery while the store managers stared at them, willing them to leave. Jane bought a toy red MG car for Aaron, a bottle of Jamieson's whisky and a bag of oranges. She longed for more fresh food, but Hubert had given strict orders about the weight.

The last time she had seen salad was at an education seminar at a nearby cattle station school. Aaron had gone up to some teachers and asked for an apple. He had brought it back to Jane's table and she had cried. It was too much. Still, Hubert had made it clear that the plane could not carry much, and grog was a problem in a dry community. She pushed the bottle deep in her bag. For many years, the elders had forbidden grog: she felt like a criminal.

Hubert took her parcels and books and helped her across the road. He averted his head as her cotton dress billowed upwards.

'Yer meeting go alright?'

'Yes, they gave me reading books. They aren't sending any expert out to help with reading. I wish they would.'

'That's the trouble with you young teachers, not up to the job; you might as well give up.'

'I'm not doing that.'

'You'll get used to the isolation; we been doin' it for twenty years.' She nodded as he heard the clinking of bottles. 'Urgent supplies is it?'

Hubert took her to the Rose Café for lunch, and she was surprised at his gracious behaviour. He ordered a 'surf and turf' and she ate some barramundi. He began an endless dribble of clichés about outback living. Hubert was on a high; he said he liked being seen in town with an attractive young woman: it would make the other cattlemen jealous. They winked at him as they passed. He reached for his cup of tea and nodded back – let them imagine an affair if they liked. Jane smiled again; her lips were stuck to her teeth. He name-dropped, he reminisced, he didn't draw breath.

'My family were old Queensland pioneers, they opened the country up. We fought the Kalkadoons, wiped the buggers out.' He grinned. Jane watched the hairs in his nose flicker; he was panting. Why did he think it was right for his forefathers to have ridden into this land of high red cliffs and shot every

Aborigine? Who gave them the right? They had stolen it all, murdered every person who stood in the way. She could hear a voice in her head shouting. Jane thought that perhaps it was time to tell him that she was of Aboriginal heritage. No, perhaps not.

'Great tall men, all painted up with bones in their noses, big broad shields. My grandpa had one, hung on the lounge room wall at his Riverside property. You know, he had an Aboriginal wife before my grandma. Lots of coloured kids, he treated them well. Winba, his first son: my God he could ride, had such big feet he had to cut a hole in his boots, big black toes stickin out. In fact, he bloody inherited the property, ha! Not my father. Riverside goin to a blackfella!' Jane was listening now.

'What happened to the Kalkadoons?'

He chewed his meat and laughed. 'They were thrown off cliffs, hounded into rivers, some escaped to cause a bloody lot of trouble – should've killed the lot of them.' He bit into a hunk of white bread. As he chewed, she realised that he had false teeth. She was not sure what to say; she ventured, 'That's a terrible story – nothing to brag about. Why do you whitefellas think it's funny?'

Hubert put down his fork.

'Hold on, don't get all righteous on me! It wasn't me. Trouble is, too many look for handouts, won't work. Still, I know a few good blokes – Old Pelican, he'd give you the shirt off his back if he had one.' He roared with laughter. Jane sipped her orange juice.

Jane couldn't eat. She wondered if only Aboriginal people were in possession of memories. Most white people would question the fact that the country had been settled by massacres. If you repeated it again and again – that lie about peaceful settlement – well, it must be true. History books were full of colourful drawings of Leichhardt and his camels. It was a painful falsified history. There was no memory, just half-truths and obedient teachers repeating lies in class. "It doesn't hurt to read pioneer stories to children." Blank faces held passionate views denying the 'black arm-band' view of history. They said, "We have nothing to be sorry for".

'You hear about in 1882 a man, jabbering in German, was seen carried by two Aboriginal women near the Gulf, but the cattle men overlanders shot him and his Aboriginal wives anyway. People thought he might have been

Leichhardt himself after forty years living in the bush.'

The Northern Territory newspaper was in front of Hubert's face. There were fabulous statistics about Territory growth. Compared to last year, the Territory was leaping forward – more beef, better beef exports, live beef – *'Eat more beef!'* There were stories about mineral exploration. Even Hubert was caught up in the fervour. 'Harrison has been earmarked for iron ore. I've alerted the Singapore mob and they're excited. I'm the man; I first saw the lightning flashing along the ironstone out there. It's wasted on cattle and blackfellas.' Jane didn't have an opinion, so he continued: 'What's underneath the ground is the real money, a real winner, a gusher!'

'For whom?'

'The owners, of course. I'm just a manager.'

She hummed; he continued: 'We can open the place up, turn this town into a city, and attract workers. They'll have to improve the freight, maybe another railway. We can fill the roads with trucks full of iron ore, maybe even gold and silver.' His eyes gleamed with imagined wealth. 'And uranium, that's got to be out here somewhere; that's the future – nuclear.'

Jane's mouth gaped open; she couldn't understand his passionate enthusiasm for foreign companies' wealth or for a nuclear industry.

'If it's all mining, where would you go with your cattleman skills?'

He smiled. 'I'll have work – people eat beef but no more mustering with stockmen. It's all helicopters and motorbikes now – we don't need Aboriginal workers.'

Jane imagined Orwell's words *'Our new, happy life'* as she picked at her chips. She sucked her fingers then noticed Hubert's eyes grow large as he looked at her breasts. He sucked in his belly and smoothed his thin hair. She sensed his arousal and closed up her dress. Hubert paid the bill and held open the door to the street.

'Are you finished with town business? Can we go to the airport?' she asked.

'Narr, I got a few more hours at the Stock and Station Agents. You'll find something to do. Go get a facial or something. You women like that. But I can walk down town with ya.'

She imagined the future for the town: more white men crowding the front bar of the Crocodile Hotel, the back bar teeming with out-of-work Aboriginal men and women loading cases of beer into shopping trolleys while their thin children ate chips and drank Coke from baby's bottles. Jane thought about Hubert's rave and could see the potential for the town going the way of so many mining towns: Aboriginal people, denied their land and locked out of employment, turned to prostitution and alcoholism.

Or would it be a new beginning, with land rights, respect, and training for Aboriginal people so that they could take part and become a new middle class, royalties distributed fairly and education paying off with high paying positions in mining and agriculture? She saw them more likely sidelined in humpies on the outskirts of town, like they had always been.

They walked down the street in blazing heat. A paddy wagon drove by and two police officers got out and strolled over to the park. Several Lanniwah youths ran off into the trees and bounded over a fence. Some elders watched with bored expressions as the police approached. One old man was peeling the gold tissue from a Benson and Hedges pack with a razor blade. Jane wanted to get close to the scene. Hubert held back and leant against a wall to light a cigarette. She walked up to a metal seat in the shade and sat down to watch the theatre of cruelty.

The police were young; they leant down to speak to an old man and his wife. Jane strained to hear. The old man gestured towards the running boys with his lips and shook his head; he seemed to be saying that he knew nothing. One of the police pushed a flagon bottle with his foot, the old man covered it with a blanket. The police drove off. Jane walked over and knelt down.

'You okay, Aunty? You got trouble with police?'

The old woman looked up at Jane through cloudy eyes. She smiled with no teeth and said, 'Yeeai, bulliman all humbug.'

Jane nodded and gave the woman ten dollars. 'You get tucker.'

The woman smiled.

'Yeeai, I get bread and baloney.' She tucked the money into her bra and Jane heard Hubert laugh.

'You can't save the whole world, Jane.'

Jane thought about what it was like, this living in a police state. She had seen plenty of police action in her life. One day in Taree, she had watched her Koori cousins put in a paddy wagon; she had frozen to the spot. The boys gave cheek, dared to speak back: they were defiant young hotheads. Jane had run up the road to defend them, grabbed the arm of the arresting female officer and tried to pull the boys out of the wagon. She had been arrested as well, shoved against the vehicle and handcuffed. She yelled: 'You can't arrest us, we've done nothing wrong! You're picking on little boys, why don't you pick on someone your own size?' Hanging out on the street were unemployed white youths who guffawed at the scene as the police drove her away.

Jane had seethed at her impotence and later hammered on the cell door. A big copper had stared at her. 'What do you want? Oh, it's a phone call, is it? You want to call your solicitor, do you?' She nodded. 'Give me a break', he said.

'You and your cousins have been charged with resisting arrest; assaulting an officer and using obscene language', he smirked.

'I want to make a statement', said Jane.

'Well, when you are bailed. Got two hundred dollars on you? No? I thought not. You better call Armidale and get free help from the Aboriginal Legal Service. Good luck!' He had slammed the door.

Jane had heard a constant refrain from her father: 'Stick up for the underdog. If you are the only person in the room who believes something, then stand your ground.' No one had stood up for them, they had spent the night in gaol, and in the morning, her Uncle Bill had arrived with bail money.

Jane sat down next to the old woman, but Hubert had finished his smoke.

'For Christ's sake, Jane, move on. You're a teacher, not bloody Christ. Let's go get a drink, you'd like that, I bet.' Hubert took her arm and pulled Jane to her feet. They moved off towards the shops.

'I just wanted to help.'

'Flamin' Mother Teresa you are. Oops, lady present.'

CHAPTER 8

Making Friends

Hubert went off to do some business and Jane bought a city newspaper, she read, 'Viking Two space vehicle orbits Mars' and 'South Vietnam and North Vietnam united in Socialist Republic of Vietnam', so all her uni Moratorium protests and guerrilla street theatre were not in vain. It seemed so far away from her current universe.

Katherine was made for white people; it had neat flowerbeds and shops with shiny clean windows. It had an Anzac memorial for dead soldiers, but none for the massacred Aborigines.

There was an address by the local historical society in the old airfield museum. The speaker said it was necessary to forget the past and to reconstruct it as a peaceful settlement. The local non-Aboriginal Katherine community liked historical re-enactments about pioneers with children dressed in lace bonnets dancing English folk dances. The memories to be preserved were of brave white men and lonely women battling savage blacks who were treacherous cannibals, who stole everything, and could not be trusted. Yes, that was a comforting story. Still, some of her ancestors were pioneers; she remembered that she was also one of them. It could be confusing.

There was a murmur of approval around the room as the speaker suggested they all stand to sing their national Australian anthem. They sang, 'Advance Australia Fair'.

She saw that it was a history scraped clean and rewritten to fit current thought, one of gold prospectors, overland telegraph, and Afghan camel drivers. 'It looked like it had been strained through an Afghan camel-drivers underpants', was one of her dad's sayings. It was a story of sturdy cattlemen, loyal Aboriginal trackers. Why, it was what made this country what it was, a man's country. It was a story of mixed-blood children removed from the corrupting influence of tribal blacks; they were often homeless and destitute, somehow lost in their own land. Accused of thieving or begging. There was a photograph on the wall. It showed pretty Aboriginal girls who wore pink bows and party dresses, *like Topsy,* their new white parents smiling benignly. They meant well. Jane nodded automatically while her heart beat loudly. She didn't trust herself to be quiet. She might tear loose, swear or get really angry. She would be calm and respectful and listen. If not, they might have her taken away for disturbing the peace – *mad as a cut snake.*

The museum had photographs of planes, mining equipment, and cattlemen. There were Aboriginal shadows in the background, but some pictures were of men on horseback with belts of ammunition, as if they were going off to a foreign war. They wore digger hats with cockades of emu feathers; they smiled at the photographer with what seemed like insolence. Beside them was a patrol of black police officers in uniforms, leather boots and swords, their eyes stared into Jane's. The photo Jane remembered, of her father in army uniform in the war, would not have been out of place. They all smiled for the camera and the caption simply read, 'Early police took care of pioneer safety'.

She gazed at the curling photos of women in long white lace dresses picnicking on the river with children in straw hats, and standing to the side, an Aboriginal servant holding a white baby. The pioneers sat on cane chairs and tables in the shade of gum trees. Rifles stood against the tree. These were *We of the Never Never* images ... Jane remembered her granny's house, withered potted palms, mattresses on the floor, concrete laundry tubs filled with cracked dishes, a black wood fuel oven and scones lifted out in a mist of steam. A cream lace tablecloth.

A neck chain and huge iron manacles in a glass case drew Jane's attention. These chains dragged Aboriginal prisoners back to Darwin. Laid on a white crochet doily were fragments of Victorian crockery, baby buttons and a pair of lady's silk gloves. In another case was a wooden cradle with the caption 'Made by Mr Gunn for his first born'. In the last case were some old boomerangs and spears. No caption.

Jane moved from the exhibit to another dusty room and other visitors followed. A man in shorts, pink tie and white socks stood near her.

'Gee, the early settlers did it tough. Nice collection isn't it?' he said. Jane breathed deeply. Now was not the best time to reveal herself, but she couldn't stop.

'It is a reconstructed past. It's devoid of Aboriginal history. They either don't exist or weren't important enough, just flora and fauna.'

She realised that her thoughts and beliefs were *very threatening to white people,* but she couldn't keep quiet – she would be complicit. At Harrison, the men had been ordered to cut up the wood for their own funeral pyre. To heap the logs into a mountain. Chains had been looped through manacles, like the ones in the glass case. They had been shot even though the Lanniwah held axes – how had it happened? They might have thrown them like stone tomahawks straight through the white men's heads. Listlessness covered her, she lacked the will to fight this consensus view that white was right.

~~~

Jane looked at the window of the Australian Womens' Association; she might even get a lamington cake. The shop had a sign that said 'Women welcome. Make *new friends* in Katherine'. Yes, that sounded great, that's what she needed, new friends. Women of the world, unite. The window had decorations from Christmas and a plate of fresh scones, crocheted baby booties and lace doilies. A bell tinkled as she sat down at the table and smiled at the sunburnt women who welcomed her. It was great start. Who cared if what was she wearing looked a bit strange? Was that an embroidered see-through ethnic blouse? Well, she looked almost like a hippy with that long gold hair.

Some women were obviously from the landed gentry. They spoke about horses, gymkhanas, polo, and the Bachelor and Spinster ball. Everyone had a nickname like Poopsy, Tricksie and Floss. They wore pastel linen dresses or riding pants bought from a catalogue, had smooth blond bobs and black velvet headbands, discreet gold earrings and old money taste. Jane imagined their all-white gardenia gardens and perfectly matched silver cutlery. Still, it was her lucky day, they said. There was to be an address by the regional president of the AWA and there was a semi-circle of plastic chairs lined up in the shop.

Jane nodded at the women as they moved aside to let her in.

An overhead fan turned in the heat. It started with a demonstration of a recipe for lamingtons, 'Dip the sponge into runny chocolate icing'. Then magically the atmosphere intensified as the president began talking about the subject of schools. They smiled at her but were sniffing out unorthodoxy. Perhaps they had heard about Jane – she shuddered to think about what they might have heard, so chose an expression of optimistic niceness. She could recognise some of them as members of the evangelical mission, or 'the anti-sex league'. They would see through her and her Indian cotton skirt. The president warmed up her theme of cleanliness: one could keep a class free of contagious diseases if one acted appropriately. Apparently, in NSW it was easy to have Aboriginal children, or as she called them 'our dark brethren', removed from your local school. Simply make a complaint to the school principal or directly to the Northern Territory Department of Education.

Jane sucked in breath and sweat dribbled down her back. Now, she could speak up now.

'The children can be expelled for health reasons', said the president. Jane was stuck to her seat, scone crumbs stared back at her from the floral porcelain. Her head was beating.

Some of the women lapped up the information, and they made notes on paper napkins. A few looked mortified. Jane was in the presence of a horrible ecstasy of caring. She could see herself losing control, her mind full of the history of this place. Who was it that profited from the slavery of Aboriginal people and smashed holes in babies' skulls, wiped their white grandfathers' sabres and guns after a nigger hunt, a bushwhack? 'Out, out, damned spot'. It was like a current of electricity that filled the room. Some muttered kindly that it was a shame 'but they would all die out'. They felt sad about it, but it was nature, the survival of the fittest.

Jane stood up slowly. The president spoke directly to her: 'So nice to have a new member in our midst'. Jane took a pink iced cake from the plate and stuffed it in her purse, then wrapped three lamingtons in a napkin. She reached for the sandwiches. The women stared. 'Don't mind me,' Jane moved towards the exit but at the last moment found her voice.

'Have you heard of Martin Luther King? Or Charlie Perkins? Perhaps

Pearl Gibbs? Kath Walker? You've heard of her surely? The rules about denying Aboriginal children schooling are terrible and cruel! I teach in an outback school and the children love to learn. They are bright intelligent people and respectful.'

'Someone whispered, 'Don't get upset, dearie.'

Jane smiled. 'The cakes are a bit dry, try using real butter and not Tulip margarine.' She was learning to hide her feelings.

Jane slammed the screen door ... As she walked away, one of the women followed her and touched her on the shoulder.

'Hey, don't go. It's not always like that. Many of us raise funds for the Aboriginal children in the hospital; we pay for a layette for new babies. We're not all racists.'

The fair woman brushed her hair from her face and smiled. Jane stood in front of her and couldn't speak. She nodded and thanked the woman; they shook hands and parted. Jane knew that there was kindness in the outback; she just had to look for it. She hurried off to meet Hubert.

Cattlemen lounged outside the hardware store and nudged each other as Jane passed. One smirked and yelled: 'Hey, nice sort. You wanna get lucky?' Jane observed the women looking at her, but she held her head up and strode forward. Her feminism often cut out when it came to using her beauty for her advantage. To survive in a male dominated world she had to be smart enough to know the allies from the spies. She had to identify who could accept her.

She wondered again if she should tell Hubert about her Aboriginal heritage. Somehow, spending her life denying her Aboriginality was becoming untenable. Maybe she was a fraud – she wasn't Aboriginal like the Lanniwah, they certainly didn't see her as one of them, not black enough. No, she might as well keep quiet, and enjoy the lovely wages. Jane stood in between, acceptable to neither side, suspecting she might be a traitor to the Aboriginal cause – if she couldn't take the racism then she didn't deserve to be accepted. She wondered if she was ashamed or just being pragmatic while working for a greater good. What if she came out to Hubert and he complained about having an Aboriginal teacher? What if he told the department about her non-appearing husband? Worst of all, she might lose her job; go back to poverty in Sydney, share houses and handouts from a pension or charity. It made her want to vomit. She spiralled into fears of unemployment and homelessness, the picture of herself hitchhiking with her baby on her hip with nowhere to sleep that night. The status as an unmarried fair Aboriginal mother: it was a position that came pretty low in the secret Australian caste system.

Jane and Hubert walked along the quiet riverbank. It was a clear, blue-sky day, champagne pink gum trees stretched along the levee bank. Jane flicked flies from her face.

Suddenly, a heavy stocking, full of wet sand, like stone, flew past Jane's head. It fell with a thud at her side. Hubert yelled, 'Jesus Christ, somebody hates you!'

He jumped down the levee bank and ran over to a hill. He was a hero. He searched but they had disappeared like the white rabbit.

'The idiot has gone!' he shouted. Jane was alarmed. No one had ever tried to hurt her before. Hubert picked up the heavy stocking.

'Someone has taken the time to fill this up with wet sand, it's like a cudgel, and it could have fractured your skull or killed you. Or me.' She touched the weapon, ran her finger over it.

'Nice quality panty hose', she said.

He dusted his Akubra. 'Maybe it's time for you to get out of the Territory.'

'Nope', she said.

An eagle cruised overhead, swooped, landed on a wallaby carcass and began to pick out its eyes. Jane asked herself if her country had always been this way, seething in anger, a treacherous place where nothing was, as it seemed. They walked back to the main road where the familiar sign said 'Welcome to the Northern Territory, God's own country'.

Hubert and Jane arrived at the airport. Some skinny dogs ran across the tarmac, then a black rock wallaby bounced by. He told Jane that he had young women begging him for a dance at the Katherine Picnic Race Ball; he could rumba with the best of them and his Hammond organ playing fantastic, sexy, every woman's dream.

Jane sweated on the plastic seat as Hubert took off in the Cessna. He pulled on the throttle; the plane shook, then was steady. He stared out the window, leaning and squinting through at the vast grey and green land. He smelt of beer.

'You know, I'm not really a hard man.'

Jane shifted nervously – not again! Please, could they just fly? Her dress crawled up her backside and the vinyl seat became glued to her skin. She could smell his strong scent of masculinity, his hands stained yellow with tobacco.

The sound of the plane roared in Jane's ears. They flew for twenty minutes without speaking. It was a beautiful flight; she watched the ochre coloured landscape, like a Utopia earth painting. Exquisite and serene, she was so happy. Suddenly the top of Hubert's head began to sink towards Jane's knees. Was he falling asleep or having heart attack?

A rising panic, not again. 'Are you okay?' she whispered.

He let out a wild moan and began to cry. This was alarming: she could see herself trying to fly the Cessna and nose-diving into a waterfall or the flooded desert.

Hubert wiped his nose with his sleeve; he peered upward and sniffled. 'It's Edie, she doesn't understand me.'

'Oh, okay, I'm sure she tries, Hubert. It's hard on a woman, the isolation.'

He clenched his fist and slammed it against the dashboard. A gauge flickered red. The tears rolled down his face. He whispered; 'She's a real bitch at times. Gives me flamin' hell. Sorry, shouldn't swear.'

Jane breathed out.

He wept openly now while still flying the plane. She tentatively patted his big back as it hunched over the controls, and felt a rising panic.

'There, there, it'll be alright.'

He looked up with piggy red eyes, and his lips distorted. He yelled; 'You've got to believe me, I don't touch little girls; it's not like that, it was ...'

'I haven't heard a thing. Please, don't worry ...'

The sound of the engine buzzed in Jane's head. She begged it to drown out Hubert's conversation.

'She sang me, you know, the girls have magic love songs. They're like Greek sirens. You try to block out the singing, but it gets in yer mind and torments you. Girls take up their cat's cradle strings, their breasts move, they twist their girdles, it's all in the song, drives a man mad. They flutter their lashes and purse their lips to show pink inside, and weave the song like string. Oh, you think I'm crazy.' Hubert coughed and laid his hand on her knee. She was trapped like an insect under a bull.

'Hadn't you better watch where we're going?'

He stirred and looked at the looming landscape.

'Yeah, it's fine. I just wanted one person to believe me. You believe me don't you? Because my own bleedin' wife doesn't. She thinks I'm a low down liar and gin jockey.'

Jane grimaced and slid her knee away from his sweaty hand.

'All women get stressed out here; it'll be alright', she said.

'You believe me?'

'Yes, yes, no worries. I'm sure you're not a liar', she said.

Her mouth was as dusty as Gravox powder. She dribbled inconsequential babble. She had a vision of him naked with his dick in his hand, covered in blood, still crying. Hubert took out a handkerchief and blew his nose.

'Sorry, Jane, sorry for using the whip on the kids. You know a man goes a bit troppo out here. You believe me.' The roar of the engine filled the air. His eyes looked fiercely into hers. She spoke in a monotone, would tell him anything he wanted, would do anything. She wanted to live.

'Sure, stuff happens, not your fault.'

She did not believe him; she loathed him. He was a pathetic weak lustful man, probably a child abuser, and children would never recover from him. Jane wished that he would fling himself out of the cockpit and smash onto the purple and yellow sandstone below. A Hubert of strawberry jam. They were flying over that cliff again, where Jedda had jumped to escape her tribal husband. Hubert stopped sobbing. He flew the plane on a steady course and they didn't speak again. Embarrassment stuck to the windshield.

Below them, a hundred pale grey donkeys ran through white water, spooked by the plane. Jane wondered if any native animal could survive in the onslaught of European ferals, and she reflected on the desecration of the land in such a short two hundred years.

He landed the plane, another hair-raising set of bumps. Jane laughed outright in relief.

'Great flying Hubert, we must do it again sometime.' It was a weird inner world where her brain was ripping with images of violence, but on the outside, she could be the polite and modest young teacher, grateful and oozing respect.

He mumbled and lumbered back to his house.

Jane went to her caravan and opened the bottle of whiskey.

Old Lucy sat outside cooking beef ribs on a fire.

'You okay, my daught?' She said.

'I have a dress for you. See. I care.' She pulled the floral shift from a bag with a flourish. Old Lucy touched its newness.

'Me gibbit young womans, me no needem. Good one, eh?'

'You cookem dinner for me and Aaron?'

'Yeeai, cookem. Good tucker, for blackfella. You see how we cookem.'

The old woman bustled about the small kitchen; the flour for damper flew into the air. It was like having granny back: it was peaceful, listening to the soft muttering language.

CHAPTER 9
Ceremony

Each day at Harrison was a revelation. Jane expected that a disaster would wake her up. She could make some horrible mistake. She waited for the visit from the school inspector, who would come unannounced and find her swimming with the children or asleep and snoring under her desk after lunch. The Department would realise that Jane was incompetent, that her lesson plans were rubbish and that she couldn't survive this remote posting. And that she was a bald-faced liar. They might ask her to leave and she would be swallowed by an unemployment queue. She would be homeless again and desperate.

'Mrs Reynolds, you reckon we're made of money and it's all right to let the older people use the school after dark?'

'Some are learning to read', said Jane.

'It uses too much electricity, we won't be responsible for the bills', said Edie.

'They want to paint, maybe they can sell the works. Burnie's acrylics are beautiful, and he paints the Dreaming of the escarpment.'

'Dreaming, my arse! Just turn off the lights.'

The children pointed out bright pink flowers on a tree. Leroy grinned and yelled, he dressed in feathers and had fish dangling from a line, and he hung around Aaron's neck and whispered to him.

'Now pelicans lay egg on beach', said Leroy.

'Leroy drew a big picture with eggs as big as people, he drew Aaron digging in the sand, he drew his whole family, trees and the billabong – all were equal in the cosmology.

'North east wind blowing, then yam leaf change colour, pelican egg, goose eatem now', said Ricky.

Jane had to learn about survival in the new environment, that it was crucial. The children at school taught her; she had as much to learn as they did. Ancestral beings inhabited the landscape; they were not just stories to the Lanniwah but actual living beings. 'You gotta watch out, you might be upset someone, clever one, makem curse on you. You listen and not makem mistake. Some white fella makem mistake, big one, then he bin finish up, real true', said Shirley.

'Ask the old people if I can see a corroboree', said Jane. A real one, a ceremony, that's what she longed for.

A few days later, Jane sat with Aaron in her arms, patting him to keep still. The ceremony was beginning ... She had felt frustrated with waiting, hadn't they said it would be after lunch? That was hours ago. Maybe there would be nothing, something would happen to prevent it. Some fight between families, someone flogged with a waddy.

The sound of didgeridoos came over the hill. The sound grew louder, clapping sticks and boomerangs; they were singing a welcome song, thousands of years old, and a hundred men and woman danced into view. The audience was only Jane and a few women and schoolchildren. The immaculate dancers moved across the earth as if it was a skin, thudding their feet to wake up spirits. The women told Jane that the earth was marked like scarred bodies, the cicatrices on old men and women. Jane felt an extraordinary rush of emotion – nothing like this had ever happened to her. The totemic ancestors came alive in front of them: wallaby, dingo, bush turkey, snakes, goanna, all transformed by the performance. No camera, it would seem rude, just experience; something to tell her grandchildren about one day.

The men wore white strings of feathers and kapok on their heads. Their bodies gleamed with white ochre paint, and the women wore cotton dresses but had ochre daubed on their faces and arms. They came in a long advancing line, a hundred dancers to welcome her, they surged over the hill, the sound of ten didgeridoos, white feathers moved to the music.

Then suddenly the welcome dance was over. Old men and women called out to dancers to announce the next piece, devil-devil dance, with the children screaming in delight at the skeletons dancing with jagged limbs. The young men sucked in their cheeks, hollowed like skulls, their arms like disjointed limbs of rattling ghosts. The didgeridoos roared, and clap sticks kept up the urgent rhythmic beat.

The old men sat and sang and small boys danced alongside their fathers. The old women beat time on their laps in a separate group. Dappled light from the setting sun shone on their bodies. The men wore sarongs of red cotton cloth around their waists. Jane was electrified; they were in front of her, the stamping sent dust flying. They pounded the ground with their feet. Gum leaves rustled in huge bunches tied to knees and elbows. Aaron jumped up and joined the little boys. Jane noticed David playing the didgeridoo amongst the painted men with the red ochred drone pipe balanced on his right foot, the sound a rhythmic dittamoo, dittamoo, brrrrrrrh, dit, dit dit, and the sharp clicking sticks, click, click. Jane was mesmerised. He mesmerised her.

Some women held bunches of leaves in their hands, they rustled in time with the rhythm. These were display ceremonies, not sacred but for public celebration. They welcomed this new teacher over a three-hour corroboree. Each dance took about ten minutes, then the dancers would move to the side, some sitting by small fires (blackfella fires), chatting. One of the younger women came up to Jane, and with lots of laughter brought her up to dance a Brolga dance. She held her arms high and on the beat raised them up and down like the bird while Aaron hid his face in her dress.

Amongst the joyful performance there was a murmur, all eyes turned to the intruder. Edie walked over and gave Jane a message.

'I heard on the radio telephone. That school inspector will be out soon to see you; he has to come before the flood gets worse.'

'Thanks.'

Edie walked away then thinking better of it came back. Jane froze, not another reprimand. She walked away from the dancers and stood under a tree with Edie.

'You better be up to date with the paper work; they look at that. And I'll have to tell him about your extra-curricular activities', said Edie.

'Like what?'

'Burning up power, that's what.'

'You don't have to tell me how to do my job.'

'Keep your shirt on. You're doing all right ... Look, why don't you come over for dinner and meet the new Minister. He's a philosophical man. You might learn something.'

'Sure.'

'And where exactly is your husband?'

Jane had no reply, she felt anxious, and a sickness in her head, it was not easy keeping peace with Edie. It was a constant learning curve to follow Lanniwah law – and then the unwritten rules of the cattle station were worse.

Jane sat up in the night and wrote endless lesson plans. It was best to be prepared; she hated examinations. It terrified her. Facing authority was the worst thing. Maybe she would fail.

CHAPTER 10

Edie Cooks Dinner

Edie welcomed Jane and Aaron into her dining room; it shone with neon light. Jane was excited: it was a night out. Aaron had put on his best shirt and Jane was dressed as conservatively as possible, trying to fit in. The newly arrived missionary, Reverend Thomas Wiltshire, sat upright at the table, his eyes beaming at Jane. He was forty with an intelligent gaze, curly hair, a pencil moustache and lips that needed constant licking; he wore long white socks and sandals.

Hubert gave a begrudging rave about how generous the Singapore owners were in allowing the Reverend, and the Lanniwah for that matter, to stay on the consortium's land.

'This place had a station manager with a reputation for liking horses and dogs. I was walking up the stairs in front of him, and the Boss says: 'Hey, you've got a nice arse. If you were a kelpie, I'd root you.' The men laughed and Jane watched Edie hang her head.

'The neighbouring stations had run the buggers off ... they would take a shotgun to any blackfella who crossed the leasehold boundary.'

'They seem to need to travel across the land for their beliefs, the ceremonies protect the cosmology and earth', Jane said.

'Bull crap. The station has the legal right to lock them out; the blacks are darn lucky that I'm a kind man.'

'Very kind', murmured Jane.

It was a special night, Jane's new second-hand blue Toyota had arrived. She had paid for it with a cheque that Hubert had accepted. The long wheel based four-wheel drive meant freedom for Jane and she celebrated its arrival.

It was her first vehicle.

'Here's a toast to Mrs Reynolds' new Toyota!' said Hubert. They raised their glasses of cordial.

Hubert chewed while cutting up his children's meat.

'They're witch doctors. Clever, you call 'em, clever? Putting filthy stones into people's stomachs. Real clever. Some of the cures can kill someone, or drive 'em mad, poisoned with ant bed and thorny devils. Nice medicine. Edie has had men hobble over to the clinic with spears hanging out, dragging along the ground, sticking out of their thighs. "Missus helpem me." That's their law for you. They want our medicine for the agony. Hey Jane, don't look like that. You gotta watch out for those young blades, eh Jane; they're too bloody cheeky. They think they can have any woman, black or white. Real casual about it, then they piss off. I'm not judging the dark people, it's their culture. Pass the tomato sauce, Edie', he said.

'I know how to look after myself', Jane said.

'I bet you do.'

Edie looked hard at Jane. 'Did you hear about that Jimmie Governor? He hacked open women and children with an axe.'

Reverend Wiltshire was playing with his food, his hand had a tremor, Edie watched him place his fork down. 'Now, let's be kind; we use Christianity for compassion with Aboriginal suffering, it is a well-embedded praxis in contemporary belief. Mrs Jane, you can call on me if you need spiritual help, I am also a trained service provider for scripture classes in schools. I know I seem formal, I make mistakes, but I do have a heart.'

'Service provider', said Jane.

'I try to have a spiritual insight into rural Aboriginal people, I have asked myself why I pursue a Ministry in this area and it's because I strive for insight into their minds. Compassion is from the Latin: to suffer with, have mercy. I see suffering out here amongst Aboriginal people. I was blind but now I see. God is immanent, pervasive, the only religion where we die but don't die. '

'Pass the salt, Edie. Nice weather we got.' Hubert coughed.

'That is true of Lanniwah beliefs as well, the ancestors are alive and part of the landscape, never ending and do not die.' Jane looked intensely at the Reverend.

'Jane, we will have some excellent spiritual discussions.'

Edie laughed, then focused on Jane.

'I know the Katherine school inspector has a terrible habit of transferring teachers who don't cut the mustard', said Edie.

'More white sauce, Reverend? We're usually asked to make a report about each teacher. We ran the last fella off', said Hubert. Edie tittered.

'What for?'

'Breakin' the rules', Edie laughed with a raucous grunting sound.

'And he nearly died of snake bite, stupid bastard', said Hubert.

'Poor man.'

'Came hopping up the steps holding his leg', said Edie.

'Oh no.'

'He'd cut the bite marks, blood pouring down. I said, Edie, get a band aid! Better make it a big one!'

Edie, Hubert were weeping with laughter.

Jane thought, "Are they stoned?" She pictured the man writhing in pain. Alone, frightened. It must have been horrific; those King Brown snakes were deadly. Maybe he didn't tie the wound up with a tight bandage. What would she do? Maybe she should leave tomorrow, no, tonight, just zoom away, and get as far as possible away from these savage loonies and poisonous snakes. No, she would be fine: she was brave, she knew about snakes and racists.

'This steak Diane is tough', said Hubert. Edie grimaced as Hubert shifted in his chair and smiled at Jane. He looked into her eyes and slipped his tongue out.

'I cooked it long enough', said Edie.

Jane lifted the dark strings of meat from the pinkish gravy. She nibbled.

'She can't cook, she just burns everything', Hubert said.

'I try, but you haven't bought me a new stove', Edie whined.

'She was a real shocker when I married her, couldn't boil an egg.'

'You like it, don't you, Reverend?'

'It is a lovely dinner, Edie. We are grateful', Jane said.

'You kids remember her chicken with lemon essence? Nearly poisoned us', said Hubert. The children had alarmed faces.

'I like it. Mum's a good cook', said Elisha.

'She couldn't boil water.' Hubert laughed and held his sides. There was silence.

He removed a piece of gristle from his mouth as Edie carefully placed her knife and fork by her dish and stared into her lap. The children were frozen over their plates, balls of meat stuck in their cheeks.

'Except the time that I tipped a wee boiling kettle on your dick because you were fecking a girl from the camp. Running around with your little willy hanging out.'

The children's eyes became saucers. They ducked. The Reverend choked. Jane cut up her meat and pushed the mash onto her fork.

'She's kidding. Aren't you, darling?' said Hubert. He lifted his knife and ran his finger down it. He licked the gravy.

'Sure, you wouldn't do a thing like that, would you?'

'Lovely potatoes.'

'Thankyou, Jane, they are instant.' Edie smiled. Her face a clown mask.

'Anyway, it's better than blackfella tucker', said Hubert.

'Actually, the food up at camp is fantastic: try grilled fish on coals and fresh damper, yum', said Jane. The table went quiet.

'Sure it is' said Hubert. He guffawed and choked.

The Wet season continued with more teeming rain. As water flooded all around the station, Jane watched it slowly move from the billabong to an inland sea right outside her door. She walked to school with her books on her head. The silver caravan stood isolated but dry. She wondered if the water would flood her home; maybe she would have to move, but where? The thought of having to stay with Hubert and Edie made her feel physically sick.

It was a grey-sky day, even coolish, and Jane had swum in the flooded billabong with Aaron. She worried that a big salty croc might have swum from Harrison River into their billabong during the flood. David said they would be fine. Jane clung to David's words; she dreamt about him. He was an impossibility as a lover, too complicated for her to consider.

Hubert started up his aluminium boat and puttered around the road, now a river, with Old Pelican beside him. They shared a packet of smokes. They went to visit outlying herds of cattle and on motor bikes pushed them further away onto dry land. Little herds of Brahman cattle stood around scraggly trees chewing on bark, their hunger terrible.

Jane watched with sadness at the cattle trying to find something to eat, their big Indian eyes pleading. She fed one some bread. Hubert and Old Pelican stood next to her.

'If they bloody starve, they bloody starve', said Hubert.

'Can't you hand-feed them?'

'Oh sure, come on over, Betsy the cow, sit down in the lounge room and have a plate of bloody salad.'

'I only meant, you'd save the cattle so you could then butcher them. It's all about the money; everything is really, isn't it?'

'Narr, the prices are so low, it's barely worth mustering and driving them to slaughter. A man can only do his best in this God forsaken country.' Hubert spoke with a boisterous joviality. Old Pelican nodded.

'We get killer later?' he said.

'Yep. At least the dark people get a feed. Nobody starves on this station, and there are three hundred of them. Prime fresh beef every week, plenty of store tucker, paid for by our taxes. They love the work. Out there on 'out stations', livin' on their so-called country, they're starving on lily root, aren't they, Pelican? Lily root for God's sake! How would you like to live on that tasteless shit? And tortoises, poor harmless tortoises, baked alive. Pelican doesn't want to go back to traditional times. You'd starve to death, just like you used to.' Hubert handed the old man some food wrapped in a tea towel.

'Wunungah before want us starve to death then we no more problem.' Old Pelican spat.

'Well, you can give that lunch back then', said Hubert.

'The cattle have eaten up the land, there's hardly any bush tucker left', she said.

'They bloody love me.'

'I'm sure they do. They depend on you like we do.'

'He good Boss', said Old Pelican. Jane looked at him; he was such a sycophant and good at pretending to agree with Hubert, but there was a deep something else inside that old man: he was secretive and she feared him. When she saw him walking alone a shiver went up her back.

Jane looked over at Old Pelican and he smiled back.

'That inspector might have to fly in. I hope you're ready. He's a mean shit of a bloke ... He'll eat her up and spit her out, eh Pelican?'

'Yeeai, he real cruel.'

Old Pelican laughed and slapped his womerah? against his leg. She watched the old man sharing a scone with Hubert; he munched and wiped his beard with his gnarled hand. He ate slowly and kept staring into the distance.

CHAPTER 11
Toyota Breakdown

The flood subsided and Jane decided to risk the bogs to go on a school visit to Rainer River; it was a hundred kilometres but she had a winch for when the car was stuck in mud. She ignored the feeling of dread, the sense of oncoming disaster. Jane drove, with Mayda holding Aaron, and Shirley pressed next to her in the front of the Toyota truck. They were in an isolated place: sometimes no cars would pass for days. You could die in a place like this. It smelt of rotting animal corpses. Twelve school kids sat on the back, three in the front.

Suddenly there was a big noise, a growling roar and smoke rolled from the engine – the worst possible thing to happen out there, broken something, cracked gasket, what was it called? The head or something. Whatever it was, it was bad, very bad. Black oil dripped out the bottom of the truck onto the muddy dirt. Jane took a cloth and undid the radiator. Steam rushed out; there was white oily stuff in the water. She crawled under the car to stare at something greasy. Yep, it looked like an engine. No, it was stuffed. She would be alright, someone would come in an hour or so; she could have a sleep.

The truck was a bomb. A wind sprang up from nowhere, willy-willies, malevolent spirits teased them. She had no hope, no idea where she was in this nameless place. A bustard strode along the road and past the truck. She asked him the way home.

The children were relying on her and her pathetic skills and judgement. There was one plastic jerry can of water ... The boys put a canvas over the back to make a shade while Jane dozed in the heat. She dreamt that she was travelling amongst haunted things, blood cracked a ghost's face, and she saw herself torn by wedge tail eagles, and she dreamt that she had gone out with a tortoise once. She saw her father's body floating in the green sea, but she couldn't reach him. She dreamt of her brother running naked across a road wearing a tea cosy as a hat. She had sore, chafed lips, cracked and stuck. She woke up with a start and the children stared at her.

They sat in the dirt on the side of the road near a prickle tree for two hours fanning away the flies as Aaron sang songs.

'Click go the shears boys, click, click, click ...'

'Enough Aaron. Okay, you kids sit in that shade, don't drink all the water', said Jane. Lizzy looked at a mirage of water glistening across the plain.

'We can walk home Miss Jane. Robert and Shirley know de way cross our country, take two, maybe three days', said Mayda.

Robert shook his head.

'I not sure. Don't know 'im.' He pursed his lips towards Shirley; she had the power of seeing pathways through stone escarpments and ravines. She stared in the direction of their homeland. It was a gleaming pathway, like a shining snail trail, moving as a lightning snake over mulga, scrub and rivers. For Shirley, the way home shone like silver.

'We can go dis way, Miss Jane. You can foller me. I can do it', said Shirley.

Jane stroked the young girl's hair. 'No, Shirley, we must stay put and wait for help.'

'There's no help out here, just bad mens. I know the way, dis way.' Shirley looked down the empty road and pointed with her lips to the south.

'No far, maybe two day walk.'

What about water?'

'We find plenty. Native well there, lot of well. My mummy show me, special place little water snake place', said Shirley.

'She can do it, she know dat track' said Mayda. The older girls nodded. Jane shuddered with the responsibility of fifteen Lanniwah children; she could see the newspaper headline: 'Negligent teacher leads Aboriginal children to their death in desert'.

'No, we stay here. It's a lovely spot, nice shade', she said.

'Yeeai.'

Hours passed.

'Get some wood for a fire. It's getting cold.' Fear hovered as the sun set. Fear was like an old man ghost. Only silence. Later, stars came out in a shower of bright sparks. Shirley crept under Jane's her arm and whispered, 'Dis debil debil place, bad mens, Miss Jane.' The children huddled under blankets. Hours went by and Jane fell asleep. Shirley flew across the ochre landscape with her hair in flames, shooting through the hills a few metres above ground, a swift rush of wind over the floodplain, over the heads of water buffalo and wild yellow camels. She was an angel, with Lanniwah children flying behind in her wake.

The darkness overwhelmed them. Things were scarier in the dark. Bad mens. Jane thought about her mistake of trusting the old Toyota. Cheap as chips. Mayda gazed into the growing darkness, where Jane could see nothing.

'Look out, here come 'nother truck.' The other children gathered around and nodded wildly. Jane couldn't hear anything, then there was a little hum in the far distance.

'What is it, Mummy?' said Aaron.

'Oh no', Mayda sighed.

'What?'

'Dat one Harry, drunk stockman from Rainer River. He bin after barra. He Bossman's boy, dat Hubert, dat his boy. He bin drinkin grog. He bin fight, he bin swear. He bin chasim womens. His daddy not want 'im.'

Jane stood on the road and watched the dust barrelling towards them. She ran into the middle of the road and waved frantically as the light hit her.

'Please help!' Jane waved at the vehicle and it stopped.

The driver pointed a torch at her; she shaded her eyes from the glare.

'Hi Harry! I'm the new teacher at Harrison. Hey mate, take us home.'

It was a battered brown cattle truck, with a dead something on the back. Harry climbed out of the cabin; he staggered as Jane looked at the dead crocodile. The green brown fins stood up and glassy eyes rolled back under yellow lids as big as saucers. Blackish liquid bubbled out of the great jaws, and the teeth shone in the night, yellow fence pickets, sharp as needles. She remembered that it was now illegal to shoot them, but here it was, stinking on the back of a rusty truck. Crocodile legs stood up with toes and claws reaching into the black night, a serpent's tail leaning over the side. It was a Brueghel painting, a Flemish night on Purgatory Mountain. Aaron stepped forward and touched the tail.

Harry was twenty but looked thirty in tight dirty jeans and a big silver belt buckle. His new black Akubra hat was pushed low over his eyes, his sun beaten face a mass of crinkles. He was skinny and dangerous.

'Ya look done in', he drawled, and sucked on a cigarette. A flicker of sex passed his eyes. Flicking his eyes at Mayda, he pursed his lips, and then grinned. Jane was aware that, yes, he seemed to be slurring his words, he was drunk, he was most probably a pig, but she willed him to be a civilised, helpful, non-racist gentleman.

'I'm so glad to see you. We've been here for hours. My hero.'

'Ya got a tinny or two for a thirsty bloke?' He looked idly at the supplies on her vehicle. Jane ignored the pleading eyes of the Lanniwah girls.

'There's beer in the back, sorry it's a bit warm. You like Fourex?' She handed the beer to him and he cracked and swigged it in a second, then wiped his hand across his crooked mouth and stared openly at her breasts.

'You should carry a rifle – ya never know. Could run into a tractor load of drunk blackfellas.' Jane nodded blankly. He kept on: 'I wouldn't leave ya. You know I'm Hubert's son? The shithead! Bush hospitality. Yeah … we're known all over the world. You got a tomato in that esky? I haven't seen a tomato for a year. Or an apple?' She nodded and went to the box of Woolworths groceries, chose a tomato and handed it to Harry. He ate it in one bite.

'We live on beef and tins at the Rainer. Real kind of ya.'

Mayda pulled nervously on Jane's arm. She whispered, 'He bad, Missus.'

Harry kicked at the Toyota tyres. 'Stuffed eh? I can take ya. She's a flat-bed truck. I'll put the croc off into the bush and come back later; he's not goin' anywhere, eh? You can tie the kids on with a rope. You got another few beers?' He took a rope and tied the children onto the back of his truck. They looked very frightened.

'You big girls can tieem little ones on. Well, how about that, fresh produce and a nice piece. I'm doin' alright for a bushie.'

Harry heaved the body of the crocodile onto the side of the road and covered it with a tarpaulin.

'He bin drinkin, Missus. He no good Wunungah'.

Jane didn't listen. 'We've been here for hours already. We have to go with him ... He's Hubert's son so we'll be fine.' Jane spoke in a hushed tone as the children looked miserably at the greyish blood staining the truck floor. Their little hands gripped the rope that was tightened around them. Jane climbed into the cabin with Shirley and Aaron and the raving loony drunk. Harry started up the truck and it lurched away. He began singing:

'They've got some jolly good drinkers in the Northern Territory. From Katherine down to Alice, it's still the same old story.' Jane thought he was very kind really; he was going out of his way. He was generous and quite nice under the tough appearance ... but Harry gunned it. He tore down the road at eighty kilometres per hour.

'Slow down! You're going too fast. You'll kill the children', Jane yelled.

His face transformed into a grimace of nastiness. Little mean eyes darted over her.

'Shut up, I'm drivin my way. You do-gooders from down south, you know nothin'!' He drove along the Arnhem Highway, a dirt road with Brahman cattle in the moonlight. He hunched over the wheel, insane, foot pressed to the floor.

'For God's sake stop, slow down you'll kill the kids. Please. Oh God in heaven, look after these kids', she shouted.

'I like you.' He turned his face, puffing Marlboros, eyes mad.

'We'll hit a bullock, you idiot, slow down!' The children screamed on the back as they held on to the one thin rope that stopped them being thrown off the racing truck. Suddenly, with a majestic grace, a Brahman bull strolled onto the road. Jane watched in horror, a slow motion collision and a slam of brakes into the thumping animal, a crash. They were thrown forward, necks wrenched. The bull rolled in front of them, tinkling glass, truck lights smashed. The bull staggered up and hobbled off into the bush.

'Stupid cunt. Get the pickaninnies off.'

Jane had already leapt out of the cabin and was helping the children off the flat top. White eyes in the black.

'Where's my bloody smokes?'

Harry scrambled in the truck for his cigarettes as Jane huddled on the side of the road with the terrified children.

'We'll light a fire and wait', Jane said. They gathered some wood and lit it. Harry put a tin of water on the fire.

'Look at that, didn't spill a drop. That's what I call impressive driving.' He smoked and gazed into the fire. The older girls moved away with the small children, they rocked them in their laps. Jane edged away from the fire and clutched onto Shirley. She watched him sideways and twitched when he made a slight movement. Harry's snake eyes flickered around Jane.

He moved closer to her, brushed prickles from the ground between them. Jane edged away.

'You've got nice legs. How about it?'

Silence and alarm filled the air.

'Go away. The Boss will come soon.'

'Not likely. Tell the pickaninnies to piss off so we can have a bit of privacy. You're lovely.'

'I'm married. Just stay away!' Harry thrust his chin upwards in sign language to the children. 'Get!' Their fear of the stockman pulsed.

He pulled her towards him.

'No. I said no!'

She shoved him away. He pushed against her chest shoving her down on the ground as he reached to undo his belt. One hand held Jane fast, a clenched fist at her throat. She could feel his erection. She shouted and pushed, her eyes wild. Terror choked her voice, she was strangling and coughing, her pulse raced. Then Mayda and Robert burst out of the darkness with a heavy branch of a tree, they slammed it into Harry's back, dropped the branch and ran away.

'You little pick bastards!' He pushed Jane away and stood up, swinging around looking for his attackers. Jane scrambled into the bushes, her panting mixed with the sound of Aaron's cries. The children huddled near her, she could hear the terror in their breathing, they hid behind mulga bushes. No one spoke. They watched Harry as he lumbered to the truck cabin. He reached in and drew out a shot gun. Harry stared into the black night. Whimpering from the Lanniwah children.

'Where are you? Damn bitch!'

He aimed into the sky and bang, a shot rang out with a burst of light and red sparks. Aaron began to scream; Harry turned and walked towards them. Jane felt as though she would faint with fear, she pulled Aaron into her arms and ran to some rocks with all the children behind her. A black wallaby jumped. She stopped and whispered for them to be quiet and placed Aaron into Shirley's lap. She grabbed Jane's arm and looked into her eyes. Shirley's head shook from side to side 'Don't go!' Jane used sign language for them to stay and be quiet; she walked out into the clearing. She stood in front of Harry, her legs shook.

'Look Harry, don't be silly, we are just a dumb bunch of women and kids, you wouldn't want to hurt us.'

He turned to the side, spat and laughed.

'Yep, that's right.'

'And if you touch those kids, I'll tear your flaming head off.'

He stood very still and began to walk towards her. His cigarette dangled from his bottom lip. The gun was tucked under his arm like a Sunday newspaper. His hand fumbled for his fly zipper.

Then the deus ex machina arrived – the distant sound of an approaching car. Shirley cried out: 'Missus, look! Car with Lanniwah men and old lady comin.' An absurd image, a Mini Moke car loaded with Lanniwah men and one ancient lady, arrived out of the blackness. Jane ran out in front of the headlights.

'Please, help us. Can you give us a ride to Harrison Station?' she begged. Her urgent pleading face was white. Harry walked up and placed his gun on his truck and strolled over to the car. He edged Jane out of the way, leant like a Boss on the bonnet of the car and lit his last cigarette, he tossed the packet away. So slow, so easy.

'You mob go that way back along Harrison, and tell dat Boss Barkley that Miss Teacher she okay. I look after dis mob.'

'No, we want a lift. Don't listen to him. Please! I really need to get these children home', Jane yelled with wild eyes. She was envisioning herself raped, bashed, the children terrified and running away in the bush, lost, dead. The old Lanniwah woman, a little white scarf around her head with daisies on it, sucked on her pipe. She looked deeply at Jane and then at Harry and measured the moment.

'Dis white woman scared of dis white man. You boys take dem. I wait here smoke me pipe.' The children cheered and helped the old lady climb out onto the ground as her boys gathered around her and the children took their place in the car, all crowded on top of each other giggling ... Jane placed Aaron amongst them and the elder held out her hand to Jane; it was tiny and fragile, high veins criss crossed the black skin, the hand trembled a little like a small bird. Jane took it in hers and stroked the back of the hand with her thumb. Their eyes met, and there was a sigh of simultaneous breath ... Through the old woman's eyes came her heart. Jane was amazed that she could show such kindness, someone who had certainly witnessed her people's massacre, starvation and dispersal and been treated like dirt by white people. Who had suffered countless humiliations? The old hand withdrew and she took a packet of tobacco from her bra inside her dress and offered it to Harry. He mumbled and took a pinch, he inclined his chin upwards, and the old lady gave him a cigarette paper to roll a smoke, a wordless peace offering. He couldn't look at Jane. The old woman actually felt sorry for him too, she had seen his panic and Jane's, and she had not judged this desperate drunk man. How could this eighty year old be so full of compassion? Where did her sublime goodness come from? Why was there no hatred and desire for revenge? Jane wanted to say: "You sensed my fear and you helped us, you smile and sit gracefully down beside a man who is drunk and possibly evil ... But you have his measure, you can read his pathetic life, you have pity. You offered him a smoke. I want to be like you, full of heart and forgiveness."

Jane laughed.

'My guardian angel.'

The old woman nodded and puffed on the pipe, smoke whirled around her head, a halo. They drove into the tall, grey elephant grass beside the road, everyone smiling as the Mini Moke climbed the bank. From the top of the rise Jane looked back to see the old lady sitting companionably with Harry ... She held Aaron close and watched the disappearing fire light out the back of the Mini Moke.

They arrived at the sister cattle station to Harrison and were dropped off down by the manager's house. Jane ventured up to the front door where a white cow's skull glinted in the light from the lamp by the door. She rapped and waited. A soft tread behind the door, a weathered country woman opened the door a fraction, pink chipped finger nails clutched the door frame, a large diamond shone on a ring.

'Hi, I am the teacher from Harrison, we broke down and I have fifteen children with me, we have hardly any food or water, we ...' She was cut off as the fly screen door slammed.

'You can drink from the tank by the cattle pen, use the tin cup.' The woman looked through the fly screen window and hissed. So this was the famous outback hospitality! Jane wandered back to the children and squatted on the ground amongst the cow dung and helped them drink water from one tin mug. Once again Jane thought about people's capacity to forget simple compassion and kindness. To consider, how would I like to be treated in this situation? Without this feeling for others, all horrors, even Aboriginal massacres, were possible.

Sometime later, a silent stockman drove them home in his truck ... Jane stared at the dark landscape, hard dark trees. Aaron was curled up in her lap. She felt an overwhelming need to protect him, she stroked his back. She wanted to take him away, back to the city where he would be safe. The Territory was too tough, too unknown; it had a hard unforgiving brutality. She looked at the bent white gums, they bowed down to some avenging god. Jane hated the place. A male domain, dominated by cruelty and harsh landscape. The ground grew little food, it was like the moon, no one should be forced to endure it. She wanted a peaceful life, with soft green trees and a beautiful home. She would save every bit of money and escape as soon as possible. She ran her fingers through her hair, it needed a wash. She was getting dandruff. The Lanniwah children were subdued; every one slept.

At Harrison, the parents were relieved to see their little ones. Jane felt ashamed of her lack of preparedness for disaster, her failure to check the oil, but they hugged her; they were happy.

As she put Aaron into his bed, she felt enormous relief ... Jane would never allow this to happen to her again, she would be alert. There was a surge of strength in her head, she felt like the Hulk, powerful, invincible. She had taken Harry on, she had faced him, and she hadn't run away, she had stared him down. It was possible she would have torn him apart with her hands if she had to. No one threatened her kids and got away with it. She would rather die than give in.

CHAPTER 12

School Inspector And Land Rights

The country was in Jane's bones but she cried for home (wherever that was) and it rained and rained in torrential streams with sheets of white lightning in the iron-stone country. She knew the school inspector was on his way. The little caravan shook with thunder like bombs. *Gurrling*, it was hot. Magpie geese gathered in huge flocks. Away by the coast, sea turtles laid eggs. The lightning spirits struck the land with tongues of flame, fertilising the earth and bringing new growth. Barramundi slept on floating lime-green lily pads. The floodplains were dotted with ti-tree swamps and exquisite billabongs fringed with pandanus. It would flood and devil-devil were rumoured to be on the march. Jane had listened to old ladies telling stories about the poisonous death adder hidden in leaves. A storm rolled across the black sky and a dingo appeared with electric blue fur, Jane nudged Aaron to look and they stared in amazement as it leapt down the rocks.

'Holy Christ, what is that?' She reached for her camera, but the dingo had evaporated and the storm passed with no rain.

Jane prepared for the long awaited inspection but the Department man had not arrived; the waiting drove her crazy. What if he arrived by plane and found her lost in the bush or half-naked sunbaking by the billabong, as she often did? Or up a tree escaping green ants? What if he wrote a negative report? What if Edie and Hubert didn't think her up to the job? What if he heard that she had lied about being married? Yes, she would tell the inspector that her husband had died, suddenly, of a rare disease. Or he was killed on the last plane out of Vietnam. He was an army hero. A dead one. She worried all week. No, she was going to be fine, she had an honours degree in Drama, she was an excellent teacher, and she had distinctions in the psychology of education. She was very, very competent and many a smart private school would love to employ her – why she could most probably get a position at Frensham with nice white girls to teach.

The inspector didn't come; Jane gave up posting a child look out at the school window. She stopped writing lesson plans; she did a lot of drama and art in class. They had fun. She forgot about him – he wouldn't come in this terrible weather.

'You carry that torch at night and look out.' One old lady bent close to Jane and whispered. Shirley translated. 'She say, devil-devil proper bad one, can sing someone, take away their spirit.'

The bigger girls whispered about the Nella Mugga-Mugga.

'The little hairy people who angry and hungry; they live in stone country', said Lizzy.

'They takem you away for sure, they stealem young girls', said Mayda.

'There might be giant dogs who attack people and rip them to bits', Aaron squealed in terror.

'When you in bush, real dark, der red eyes, dat him, he might eat you', said Lizzy.

Jane thought about the Lanniwah families in their rough shelters. They would be soaked through. David had told her, 'It's nothing; it's the Wet. Flooding every year'. Jane walked chest-deep in grey swirling water across from her caravan to the school. She carried books and clothes on her head and hoped the crocs didn't come. 'Dey fresh water missus. Not eatem you', Shirley had said.

Wet children shivered outside the school.

'Why are you kids standing outside in the rain, it's only seven o'clock? You're soaked, poor beggars'.

'We not beggar. We Lanniwah.'

Jane hustled them inside. 'Come in, get changed. Shirley, get the dry clothes from the cupboard.'

'Missus, we wet. We hungry. Why we got no tin of pie like you.'

Jane rubbed them down with towels. 'You're shivering. We got hot stew for dinner and damper!'

'We bin sleeping under a bit of tin', said Lizzy.

Shirley nudged her.

'Don't tell her dat. We okay. You make us shamed.'

Jane realised that some of the children only had chaff bags for blankets. She felt so awful she wanted to give them hers. She made a note to buy blankets in town. She gave out school towels. She felt angry that some blankets ended up on the rubbish piles – couldn't they look after anything?

Hubert pulled up outside the school; he had new cotton blankets.

'Thought youse might like some of these; they're new.'

'Thanks, we appreciate it.'

'I heard you had a bit of trouble with poor Harry. We don't see him much … You're not piss-weak like some of those teachers, you're goin' okay. I found it hard to be accepted out here when we first came, but the mob got used to me', said Hubert.

'I don't want to be accepted by people like Harry. Sorry, I never will. He's an idiot!'

'You never will, sweetheart.'

The truck thundered away spraying Jane with mud.

Every day Jane worried about the arrival of the inspector, but the road and airfield were empty except for cows.

Shirley became devoted to Jane; she was the first one at the door in the morning. She had bathed in the billabong and carried her baby cousin on her hip. Raymond had taught Shirley to read and she loved reading magazines thrown out by Missus Boss. Her mother was Gertie the domestic servant, so Shirley had a special place. Edie gave her clothes. Shirley dreamed of going to Katherine and seeing a rodeo or movies. Like most of the children, she had never been there – it was the magic Land of Oz. She studied hard and was the last child to leave the school to eat dinner at lunchtime. She wanted to be a teacher and help her people. She sometimes drove Jane crazy.

Jane turned the school into a drama room for a maths and speaking exercise that lasted for hours; they made the chairs into seats on Connair, or Qantas.

'We're going on an imaginary trip to Sydney to see the Opera House. You, Robert and Ricky, can dress up as pilots or air stewards. Lizzy, you collect the tickets and tell everyone to fasten their seat belts. Okay. Look out the windows and see the city down below'. They practiced their English, their manners, and the fun they would have on the journey ... The children arrived in Sydney and bought things at the play shops. They practiced asking for drinks and jeans. They counted out their money and asked for the correct change; it was exciting to learn in this way. Outside a bustard picked at a green melon in the mud, Jane watched it. It was ridiculous, really – how would any of them ever get down south?

'At my place, I got a concrete floor, real flash. You come up to camp and meet my family', said David.

Jane wasn't sure if this meant he had a wife. He smiled, she was excited and happy. 'I'm not married yet; just meet mother, father, brother, sister, big mobs', he said.

He could read her mind.

After school, Jane took Aaron and walked with Shirley to find David at his brother's camp. Sammy was making tea and David leapt up and beckoned them to his fire. They ate damper and golden syrup; no one said much, the young men reached for the syrup can and poured it thickly on the damper. It was awkward and Jane felt uncomfortable being the only adult woman: she noticed Lanniwah eyes watching her every move. Jane waved goodbye and went with the usual group of followers up the hill behind the camp. David and Sammy followed at a distance.

'Don't go dat way Miss: not woman place, lizard man place. You follow me', said Shirley.

Jane nodded. She puzzled about this way of viewing the world, where people of the past were both human and animal but also ancestors. A clever woman carried her spirit familiars in a dilly bag. A *kaggatta clever woman* gained power from a grave or blood of a dead man. The causes of death were said to be contagion, swallowing a bone, eating too much clay. Jane heard that you could die from handling cycad nut, snakebite, sea wasp sting, even a death adder on the road. *Wemmi ti,* this was sickness with no cause. If anyone died, it could be *wangginawaggi* or *bilka*.

They looked down from the escarpment to the camp. Children flicked stones down the cliff.

'Everyone lives in tin shacks. What does the Department do with all that money?'

'They don't spend it on houses, dat for sure', said David.

Shirley pointed to the distance and tugged Jane's arm.

'Some fella comin; look plane dere', said Leroy.

'Might be government man,' said David.

'I've got to get back', said Jane. She felt rising panic, it might be the inspector. Leroy helped her down the rocks, she rushed towards the school. What if he was already in the classroom? It was a wreck from drama games. He wouldn't understand.

The next morning, it got hotter and hotter and the rain went on and on. Jane felt like she would explode. She heard laughter from inside Hubert's house and then a man with a folder, dressed in beige shorts and tie, walked outside with Hubert, they sat down to drink tea. Jane thought he was a stock agent. His plane was fancy enough. She relaxed. She was mistaken.

John Pageworthy had been a Department of Education inspector for years. He was zealous and careful. He looked constantly at his clipboard. He arrived at the school just on the morning that Jane had sent all the children to the billabong with Margie. There was a community meeting in the school about land rights. Mr Pageworthy looked surprised, fingered the school lesson plans and registers. Jane invited him to sit down at a small desk, where he sat awkwardly and opened a new page on his clipboard. He rapped his pencil and coughed. Jane thought he smelt funny, like bad fish. He had spit collecting in the corner of his mouth. David had a look of horror on his face. Jane waved at him.

'I have come a long way Mrs Reynolds and I am due back in town by eight o'clock.'

'I'm sorry, but I had no warning that you were arriving today. The Lanniwah are having a meeting', she said.

'Do you consider that this community meeting is part of your school responsibilities?' he said.

'Well, it is part of being in a community. They have no other buildings. Just tin humpies.'

Old Pelican and Burnie were at the front of the room; behind them was a large collage of alphabet and Lanniwah words. David stood nearby; he was answering questions.

'Not crown land – dat mean we can't make it claim', said David.

'Excuse me. I have to explain something', said Jane.

'You have to give me your day books', said the inspector.

She ignored him and stood next to David.

'I have written a letter to the big fellas at the Department of Aboriginal Affairs again about Lanniwah land rights. I have been talking about this process to David', she said to the elders.

Old Pelican began to yell in Lanniwah language. He was pointing at Mr Pageworthy. Old Pelican was getting agitated; he kept slapping his woomerah against his leg.

'Might be we shootem all gubberment men', he said. Mr Pageworthy's face turned whiter than usual.

'Okay. Let's wrap up the meeting until tomorrow', said Jane. She tried to shoo everyone out of the school. No one moved. She was impotent. The Lanniwah ignored Mr Pageworthy; they were agitated and wanted action.

'You writem letter, we sign 'im', Old Pelican said.

'You tell him talk about this wid dat Chief Minister fella, he got big nose, big job, he can gibbit land back', said Old Lucy. She walked over to Mr Pageworthy and pushed her bony finger in his narrow chest, he looked alarmed.

'They want Aboriginal land rights to the Harrison Station', Jane explained.

'I am a school inspector, not the Prime Minister.'

'There's no grass for stock anyway. In the Dry, it's just dust', she said to no one.

The inspector was getting angry. He clicked his pen frequently, he sat apart at Jane's desk and read the lesson plans and marked them with red ink. His neck grew red.

'I can go over the records of attendance when the elders have gone', she said.

'Where exactly are your students?'

'Sport, swimming practice, you know freestyle, butterfly, in the billabong, there's a school sports carnival coming up', she said hopefully.

'Of course, they are practicing at eleven am. The whole fifty two of them.'

'Miss Jane, you writem up letter now, we not wait no more!' Old Pelican was full of energy; he was about to claim his people's land, and no white fella in beige shorts was going to stand in his way. Margie arrived back with all the children. Dripping wet, noisy, unruly, they crowded into the school. David quickly saw the disintegrating situation and spoke to Old Pelican.

'Grandfather, teacher got big fella Boss from Katherine to talk to, we come back later, eh?' said David. Jane opened the door and invited the Lanniwah to leave.

'I come over later, we writem 'nother good letter', she said.

Old Lucy watched her and touched Jane on the arm.

'Okay, we come back 'nother time eh? Dat fella come for testem you, granddaughter?'

Mr Pageworthy tapped his pen again, and Old Pelican walked towards him. Jane saw a flash of anger on the old man's face. This was not a good sign.

'You go back Katherine. Dis teacher best one, you write dat. Den you get plane and go back now, you not bugger up dis school', Old Pelican said. The Lanniwah parents left the school, the children sat in neat rows, all very quiet. David sat beside the children.

Jane smiled at them and pulled up a child's chair next to the inspector.

'Bush schools, eh? You never know what to expect.'

'Quite the contrary, Mrs Reynolds, I expect standards, high ones, and children sitting at desks learning to read and write. But perhaps you don't. Perhaps you have some Sydney ideas about creativity; I can see all the papier mache and paintings on the walls. Nice if you are in a city Performing Arts High school – but not so useful out here in the outback. We care for our students. We have a responsibility to these poor native underprivileged persons. Perhaps you should reconsider your future. But now, time's up and I will be having a formal meeting with the station manager and his wife – they have been sharing certain facts with me, very interesting. So excuse me.' He walked out of the room. Jane put her head down and sighed, fearing the worst. It was all too hard. Tears dribbled on her day book.

The children had been listening, they looked at her, and she blew her nose and forced a smile.

'All okay. We're all good; he said you are wonderful.'

David took out a picture book and began to read aloud.

Some weeks later, while Jane expected a letter from the Department to arrive any day, instead the letter about land rights came back. It had been opened. Hubert had had a good look and scowled over his veranda at this do-good southerner with her political ideas.

'Any trouble up at the camp because of you, and I'll take the bullwhip to you, whip you good!' However, the letter said that despite the obvious long-term association of the Lanniwah people with Harrison Station, they had no legal rights to the land. The Singapore consortium was within their legal rights as leaseholders to run the Lanniwah off at any time. It said that the Lanniwah didn't meet the criteria. This was leasehold, not crown land. The land was owned by a Singapore consortium. *Jesus wept.* The Lanniwah also didn't have rights to move around to sacred sites for essential renewal of spirit ceremony: it might disturb the cattle. She still had a thought that eventually truth would win. After the dark there would be light.

Jane was astounded at the casual injustice; she again asked the children. 'Who owns this country?' They yelled as one, 'We do!'

Jane had been involved in land rights marches in Sydney and it felt like the 1970s had been alive with Black Power and Aboriginal activism. The Redfern mob had accomplished so much down south.

She sat with Old Burnie as he painted a vivid landscape from birds-eye perspective, bold orange swirls, mauve and green, the teeming waterfalls in the wet. David handed him the acrylic paint from the school cupboard.

'The Koories in Sydney set up an Aboriginal Medical Service in Redfern and that movement is spreading all over New South Wales', she said.

'We only got bit a clinic, no doctor', said Old Burnie.

'What's that Black Power?' said David.

'It's not like that. They got the Aboriginal Legal Service, and it was pushed forward by these young Aboriginal law students and their white supporters.'

'No Black Power?'

'Well, kind of. People visited the United States; they came back, and they wanted a bit of Black Power and guns', she said.

Burnie stopped painting and scratched his head.

'No good', he said.

'There were some very violent protest marches; you know, cheeky fellas.'

'No good: gun no good, gaol no good', said Burnie.

'Now, some blackfellas become big fella politicians.'

'I heard that.'

Jane didn't tell them that she had also attended marches and had been caught up in feminist protests as well; she had ripped her bra off in Hyde Park with some Koori women. *Arr, sisterhood!*

However, it was like land rights in the Northern Territory hadn't quite arrived despite the Northern Territory Land Rights Act. Hubert laughed about how he had run off some Koori people from down south who wanted to talk to 'his' blacks.

'They drove up to my house, the hide o' them, wearin' land rights bloody tee-shirts! They were goin' on about Aborigines living in this country for forty thousand years. What bunk. I ran 'em out with a shotgun blast.'

Jane smiled weakly. 'They are getting land rights in other places.' She felt exhausted: maybe she should just shut up, and play it safe, be a nice calm sweet mother and teacher, find a boyfriend and settle down in the Sydney suburbs. Somewhere nice and middle class like Mosman. Study Cordon Bleu cooking. She could get a perm and have a facial. She would be a new person, she might marry a doctor: her mother would like that.

'Aboriginal rights will be extinguished or it will be like a flaming Berlin wall running down the whole country. You talk like that and I will run you off too, you watch me!' Hubert sneered, and then farted loudly like the crack of doom.

He stomped off, puffing Marlboro. Jane thought it was crazy that an Australian cattleman would fight for the right for Singapore businesspersons to buy more Mercedes, destroy Hubert's own country, and at the same time treat Aboriginal people like so much vermin. Mind you, Hubert made a lot of money from the Lanniwah by skimming off their welfare cheques. *In a two horse race, always back self-interest.*

In the privacy of the caravan, Jane developed endless strategies, but mostly she just wrote letters to members of parliament. She couldn't just do nothing. Jane wondered if this limp action was the result of having become a government employee, relying on them for her wages. (That money was adding up). Jane poured over the booklet that arrived by post. She read the details of the 1975 Act that outlawed racial discrimination in Australian society. Really? No one seemed to take notice of that in the Territory.

'It clear we own dis place, alla time walk about dis place, grandfather time all over, sit down place Dreaming place, little frill neck goanna place, dey still here today. Not Singapore Dreaming place. Not queen place, not crown place.' Old Pelican said.

'Lanniwah always live on this land. That government want make us Aboriginal people slaves on our own country', David said.

'Old men talk about dat Gurindji mob; dey standem up, walk off Wave Hill Station.' Old Pelican raised his voice; he was emphatic.

'You tellem bout dat.'

'They weren't going to work for old man Vestey for nothing, but what dey get? Dey hungry.'

'Well, they had their homeland handed back by Gough Whitlam. That red sand trickling in Vincent Lingiari's hand. We saw it on the TV.'

Jane feeling like a messenger of doom, a mouthpiece for the bloody government. She made dinner. Aaron chattered; she was dying of loneliness; she wanted romantic love. She wanted some hot sex. She ached for it.

A letter arrived from Mr Pageworthy. He needed more information and asked her to send in her year's program, in duplicate on a carbon copy. There was no carbon paper. She wished he would drop dead and be found with his beige shorts around his knees in some cheap motel with a bong by the bed.

Jane saw how the Boss could be cruel and treat the Lanniwah like dirt, except he did respect the old men, like Old Pelican. He would sit on the fence at the back of Hubert's veranda and smoke with him; they were good friends. She watched them from her caravan, they were on the fence talking for hours about something, smoking and laughing. What were they talking about? Maybe fishing lures and cattle station business. It was amazing.

Hubert and Old Pelican had a grudging mutual respect. The Lanniwah elder had walked hundreds of kilometres across his mother country, he could sing the song lines, knew the real ceremony; he was a maker of men from boys. He made her shiver. Jane saw Hubert pass him the Drum tobacco.

'Take what you need. We got plenty.'

The sun was setting and the old man lifted himself heavily from the fence.

Jane guessed that there would be no mention of land rights in those conversations. Old Pelican was shrewd and knew how to keep the peace. He was an actor.

Jane heard nothing from the Education Department, and hoped it meant she had passed inspection, somehow.

CHAPTER 13

A Storm

Sheets of white lightning summoned the Lightning people spirits. Jane peeped out the window and could almost see the old women spirits breaking stones and throwing them from the cliff top. She guessed that spirit familiars of her old lady friends walked the earth, murmuring. Jane hoped they could protect her ... Inside the caravan, Jane's body boiled.. Her blanket was damp with humidity, and warm, too warm. She clutched little Aaron, terrified and crying. She rocked him back and forth and sang broken lullabies.

Rain pounded down in sheets and the thunder and lightning crashed around the ironstone. Purple light shattered the darkness, great flashes of electricity ripped along the ridges. Jane and Aaron huddled in one bed in terror, it felt like the end of the world. The whole plain lit up in jagged lightning bolts. Each one like a bomb in intensity, they coursed through the land and Jane's body shook. The rain was in sheets of teeming water, it thundered on the roof and the caravan felt like a tiny box about to blow apart.

Afterwards the earth smelt of sweet ozone, of life and rebirth. For the Lanniwah, the rising flood had ceremonies and stories, it explained the world. The water rose slowly, with flocks of white birds, pelicans and white herons descending where there had been gullies of dust.

Jane could see Aaron was happy, he ran about all day with Lanniwah kindergarten children and he was a prince, a leader at school. He had new friends in the big house who thought he was cute. Every day after school, he ran over as the Boss's children finished their School of the Air lessons. He seemed blissfully at ease.

Shirley loved sitting with Jane on the caravan steps...

'This country where we belong, we lucky because dis country teachem us. And Boss, he teachem me 'bout music; I play organ, he good boss', said Shirley

'Everyone know dere place. Mummy teachem, Granny teachem.' Jane saw that it was the past, present and future.

'We can't leave it dis place – we die, spirit finish up.'

Jane, who had grown up in Darug country, thought the giant eel sign she saw everywhere was the symbol for the Parramatta rugby league club, 'Go the mighty Eels'. It was much later that she learnt that Garangatch the Eel was a Darug and Gandungurra creation ancestor. Now that was a revelation. Had the Englishmen who took the country hunted her great great grand mother for sport? Did they laugh and make bets about who could shoot her down?

In Lanniwah country, it was important for Jane to be placed in a classification system – a 'skin' or moiety. Old Pelican had determined Jane's moiety.

'You granddaughter for me now, yeeai. You learnem 'bout dat. Burnie your daddy now. You not talkem alla 'bout son in law. Taboo for you. You learnem dat fella could be husband yeeai? Who im, who dat Bulli right husband for you'. Old Pelican laughed at her squirming. Jane was about to enter a parallel universe where *nothing was as it seemed*. A tree was not just a tree but also often a repository for an old person's spirit. 'Don't touch dat tree, Miss Jane. That old woman place; she live dere', said Lizzy.

The old people mostly spoke in Lanniwah language and creole, and used English in a broken pattern that followed the Lanniwah grammar. The children spoke several languages from their mother's or father's side. They spoke a musical sounding Aboriginal English, and they worked hard in school learning Standard English. Jane picked up the intonations of Aboriginal English quickly and Aaron was fluent in a few weeks.

As the rain kept coming, brown water crept along the road. This was the only road out of the station and now it was a river. Jane was marooned and there was no possibility of escape except by Hubert's plane, and that seemed impossible – he barely spoke to her

One day after school, Jane watched David and Aaron talking, and Aaron's endless questions. He was very popular and everyone knew his name. The

Lanniwah called out to him when he went past and he played all over the cattle station. He collected stick insects and a spiny desert lizard he kept in a shoebox. He amazed Jane with his curiosity and love of nature. Jane was proud of him and imagined he would be a naturalist saving species. David walked with him and explained the Aboriginal universe.

'You see that rock, not just rock but little fella like you, he go foot walking then he steal food then he turned to stone', said David.

'When? That's just a story.'

'No, true! That boy stealem his mother's food: he was punished.'

'I won't steal, ever. Witches eat children if they steal', said Aaron.

David held the child's hand and smiled.

'You see billabong, that place for little lizard, golden one, special place here.' David spoke softly.

Jane listened to how the seasons gave different things, and ceremony had to happen to make sure the flowers bloomed or the rain came.

'We learn a little bit at a time; as people grow up, learn more. When they old they like big library', David said.

Suddenly a bomb of black mud hit Jane on the shoulder. She swerved to see Aaron and Leroy making mud pies and laughing at her.

Jane listened to the boys.

'My daddy is dead; he died when I was in Mummy's tummy.' The other boy nodded. Jane went up to Aaron and took his hand, she needed to talk. 'Come here, darling, I want to tell you something. Your daddy is not dead; he had to go away', she said.

'We can find him, then', Aaron said.

'No. He wouldn't want that.' Jane smiled a limp smile.

'But he will. He must be just lost a bit. He will want us.'

'Maybe one day, but not now, Aaron. You can look when you are a big boy.'

'I'm a big boy now. I want my daddy.'

Aaron ran to their caravan and took a blue Japanese cloth from the wall. It had a white bird flying across it, a crane. Aaron made a Superman cape and the little boys tore it from his back. Later, Jane found it a rag in the dirt. She was furious, insane with frustration and old grief. She yelled at him.

'You naughty boy! That was my special thing from daddy. You stole it. You wrecked it. I can't stand you being so naughty. I will send you away to the children's home, and you will never see me again!' Aaron's face was a mask of white. He let out a piercing scream, ran to his bed, and wept. Of course, Jane was sorry; she touched his back, and he shuddered.

Next day, Edie was at Jane's side, walking to the store. It was cheque day and she had to open up. Jane carried a pile of children's workbooks; her body bent over, her face haggard, she was exhausted. Edie watched her sideways.

'You want to burn out? You do too much for them. You'll be carried off in an ambulance babbling like a lunatic'.

'I'm okay – it's just so many to teach to read', she said.

Edie thrust a letter into Jane's hand. 'It's just come from the Department. You want to open it. It's a few weeks old'.

The letter announced the assignment of another teacher to Harrison Station, who would be flown out from Katherine the next month. Jane dropped her books and hugged Edie.

'Hey, watch it.' Edie pushed her away and picked up her hat from the dust.

It was a miracle! Another teacher was coming to Harrison on secondment. Jane prayed that they would be human. She put the book pile on her head and waded to school, Aaron swimming behind her as trees and occasional dead cows floated by. Gertie hung out washing from the big house veranda, and the dogs howled on their chains as the flood licked at their kennels.

~~~

Jane had organised a theatre night for the school and the children had been rehearsing for weeks. The girls arrived at school breathless and giggling. They were nervous, had never performed for their families before. Jane put lipstick on their mouths and blue eye shadow on eyelids. They looked gorgeous.

The senior students had written their own play about Dracula and the Indians, a mix of American movies and horror. Ricky played Dracula, with white make-up and dripping red lipstick blood. 'I want ? suckem your neck.'

Back stage, inside the school, David smiled at Jane; he was a reliable stage manager.

'You are really something', she said.

'What thing?'

'Wonderful', she said.

He froze, and then his eyes met hers – at last, a burst of connection.

'This night, mean a lot, like nothing they done before, you know, really good, makem kids feel real strong. Train em up. You not like all Wunungah', he said.

'I have a grandma who is Aboriginal', she said.

'You carrying dat blood. You beautiful, pink lips; you make me … you know.'

'I don't know. What?' she said.

'Wantem you.'

It was out, the thought, the spoken desire. She blushed, taken totally by surprise at his boldness. He looked down, his feet shuffled, a nervous moment.

'Oh that, okay … well, thank you, we work together … it's …'

His eyes and lips motioned towards the billabong.

'You wantem come?' His head inclined. 'With me, tonight?'

'No, I can't', she said. He looked down; he seemed devastated. His eyelashes fluttered. She watched the top of his head, the Brylcreemed curls bouncing. His lips trembled. Children piled into the classroom to change their paper costumes, screaming with joy. David walked outside. Jane breathed out; she could barely believe what had just happened. It changed everything.

Jane wasn't proud of herself, she hid in the storeroom, she clutched her thighs together, she was burning up with longing. No, it was ridiculous! Not now, not here; she couldn't be in love with her teaching assistant even if he was the right subsection. It was utterly unthinkable. She would not give in. She would be strong, she would live on raging hot fantasy, but she felt extreme desire for this lovely man. She pounded the wall next to her head and sank on her knees in tears, and then the storeroom door opened. David looked at her, he took in her body, he looked at her brown legs pressed together, her hand pinching her thigh, her eyes burning with want. He nodded and his head dropped to his chest. He sighed. She pushed her hand across her mouth willing the feelings to evaporate. He turned slowly and shut the door. She leant against it and sobbed.

However, David didn't speak alone to her again; he hid behind his professional work, and Jane tiptoed around him. She pushed away any romantic thoughts about him. It was impossible; it was not the way to progress with her position or the trust of the community. She would find someone else. There were single men in Katherine; she would look out for a likely person. Maybe a pilot or an engineer, someone with a degree, a man who was tall and kind, non-racist, someone she could trust.

Storms rocked the country and every night thunder men threw their spears into the ground.

PART TWO

NORTH EAST WIND BLOWING, END OF WET SEASON, PELICANS NESTING – 1976

This is the beginning of the dry season. It is the time for fruiting trees and a cold strong wind. Jane settles into life with the Lanniwah. She learns how to collect fruit and hunt tortoises. Crocodile hatchlings are carried in their mothers' mouths.

CHAPTER 1

Meeting Orlando

Jane escaped the waterlogged station to attend the Katherine Education Conference. She looked at the delegates as they signed in and a young man caught her attention, he looked exotic as she watched him walk out the door.

That night in Katherine, there was a dinner dance at the school gymnasium. Ten minutes before she walked in, she had a crisis of confidence. What could she wear? She tried on different combinations of transparent cotton – no, they were all wrong. A black sleeveless velvet dress, long – silly really, but it would do. Jane felt high anxiety, she tried some red lipstick, she looked like a harlot, and she rubbed it off. Perhaps this would be a chance to meet someone, find a lover. Her yearning consumed her. Behind her were the years of dressing in black, clutching a book of poems and haunting libraries and coffee shops, the search for an artist to love. Waiting for her destiny. Outside the entrance, she sat on a bench, caught her breath to summon up courage. There was no point going into the hall. People might stare, but it was only a gathering of lonely teachers – no one would care. Get a grip! Her heart pounded.

It was a relief to hear rock and roll music. It was a Jerry Lee Lewis song, 'Great Balls of Fire' – oh yes, bring it on! Gum leaves and tropical flowers decorated the green corrugated-iron walls. Jane's eyes scanned the hall; balloons drifted amongst party pies. She looked around wishing she could talk to someone, anyone. She would settle for an entertaining old woman, there would be no eligible men. She felt like an awkward wallflower at a scout hall stomp in 1965. She began to dance self-consciously, alone.

Jane saw a dark haired young man across the floor. She asked someone who he was. His name was Orlando. Jane saw his jiving, rhythmic dance moves, and his seductive smiles. She walked across the floor towards him and time slowed down, he watched her approach, he stood with his hands on his hips, she felt full of light. What was happening to her? His eyes were fire and his lips beckoned.

'Would you like to dance with me?' He breathed into her ear.

'Please take me away.'

He put out his hand and took hers; he pressed it to his heart. They began to slow waltz; they slid into an embrace. Hot electricity passed between them.

Jane surrendered to his touch, knew that she would follow him anywhere and that he would eventually run off, and leave her because that is what always happened. But, oh, God, she was weak at the knees at his dark curls and blue eyes. A 1950s style band was on the stage murdering a snare drum. Orlando groaned and knocked back neat vodka from a bottle. He ate a pickled cucumber from a dish. She expected him to smash his glass in a fireplace. He poured her vodka; she threw it back, wiped her mouth with her hand, and felt utterly wild and uninhibited.

'*Na Zdorovie*', he said. They got drunk. Orlando grabbed Jane's hand and led her away, into the darkness of the school hall. She was aware that her dress was limp with heat and perspiration, and it stuck to her breast and her nipples. She pulled the fabric away and fanned herself. His hand rested on her waist, pulsating with fire.

'I have been waiting for a transfer to a permanent teaching position. I'm tired of Katherine town. I'm envious of the travelling musicians doing concerts and tours. I've met some who are Afghan and Aboriginal. You should hear the drums, zithers, and Arabic sounds. Sorry I talk too much, eh?' he said.

'What on earth are you doing in the Territory?' she said as she swallowed another vodka.

'The outback called me as if I was a boy wanting to join a carnival circuit ... I'm drawn to Aboriginal communities in a way that ... well; I just had to get up here.'

Jane nodded and touched his hand. 'You are very attractive. I'm glad you're here. Are you married? Do you have a girl friend?'

'Straight to the point eh?' He whispered. 'No.'

'Good.'

They searched each other's eyes.

'Come outside, you're beautiful.' They glanced at the room of drunk teachers, exhausted sunburnt people with worn out eyes, Christian people who would be horrified to know that Jane and Orlando were about to share a joint in the bush outside the tuck-shop. He leant towards her and kissed her. That first kiss.

The night throbbed with heat. He stroked her hair and breathed it in, lifting her curls into his face, absorbing her femininity and sweet Indian perfume. She sank into his arms, already in love; she began to breathe hard as he ran his fingers inside her dress. He lifted the hem and suddenly his fingers found her knickers and stroked softly.

'Don't stop', she said.

She panted and leant against him in a trembling orgasm. Jane looked into his smiling eyes. She drew breath and she could feel his muscled chest and pushed her hands up under his shirt. She was about to make a huge mistake, she would fall for him, it was madness, it would end in misery. She would throw away her feminist creed and high principles with her overalls and books by Simone de Beauvoir, she would shape change overnight into a licking, panting, sex-starved animal. An unmarried mother, available, fuckable, wet and luscious on all fours, wanting his body. To him, she would be just another slice off a cut loaf of bread, an easy lay, a town spinster, a town bike. But she sank into his warmth, his easy laugh and searching eyes, and he pushed urgently against her. She put her hand down his jeans and softly stroked him. He sighed and his breathing began to race. It was too late to walk away and be sensible. She peered back at the teaching crowd where tongues would already be wagging and her reputation shot to pieces. She might as well give a plenary session, 'Naked sex show from Kings Cross and the non-Feminist position', on the Outback Education Conference table.

'Damn, someone's coming over', he said.

'I don't care.'

Jane's mind raced ahead. She could see the lustful bed, the Desdemona begging for his gripping hands round her throat. There was a possibility that she could turn into a limp soft thing, and he would grin at how easy it had been to seduce her. No, she would say no, not this again, not another man to muck up her life. Together they would walk in the grevillea-studded land, perfumed and hot, a sweet hell with temptation and devils, but Jane didn't care anymore, she wanted him badly.

It was all over, her cover as a wife waiting for her returning husband was blown. People were glancing over at them, at this very public seduction. She had no discretion, she would most probably be sacked, certainly lose her position as head teacher, lose her precious job with a traditional Aboriginal mob. She would lose the community respect given to a married woman and become an object of scorn and lust. She would have to put up with drunken white men banging on her motel door begging for 'Just one root, darlin'. Jane had stepped into oblivion. Orlando smoothed down her dress and took her hand.

'Come on, back to the party, I'll get you a nice lemonade.' He looked with a smile, his eyes linked with hers. She was his, and in half an hour, he would be inside her.

The next morning outside the motel, she leant against her lover. He helped carry her bag to the street to find her truck. He kissed her openly and waved good-bye. She was devastated and stared out the rear window at his figure against the pink gum trees. The conference had gone by in a daze and Harrison beckoned.

She drove with a fixed gaze past grey trees, an unconscious view of the straight monotonous road. Feeling elated, on fire, a glowing realisation that love was happening. She sang aloud to the blue sky, she would find a way to have this man in her life. Her mind was full of the memory of his body, lithe and strong. The endless night of lovemaking, no sleep, the crying out in ecstasy. He was wonderful; she was alive again. The miracle of finding a true lover like this, the excitement, and the purity of joy

At last, a second teacher would arrive. Fifty-two children were too many for one person so Jane had written and complained. He was handsome, he was single, he was twenty-eight, he was a songwriter, and he was a gift. He was the substitute teacher, Mr Orlando Kerekov, and she already loved him. He arrived one afternoon from a light plane dressed in RM Williams clothes, tight white moleskin pants, elastic-sided boots, a white lapelled shirt – Territory costume, but with long black hair. His head was straight out of a Russian fairy tale. She watched him throw his swag outside her teacher's caravan, and then he reached into the back of his bag and brought out a guitar and a didgeridoo. Jane melted.

'Hello, head teacher Mrs Reynolds. You surprised to see me again?' He grinned.

'How on earth did you arrange this posting?' she said.

'I was owed a few favours by my boss in the Katherine office. So where do I sleep?' He winked at her.

'The letter said the Department would transport a new caravan home out here in a month', she said.

'Right, that means six months. I'll make a camp with my swag, no worries.'

'Maybe you should stay with the Boss? '

'You don't mean that?'

'Stay where you like.'

Jane felt rising panic, this could be a terrible mistake. He would take over her school, he was a male, and he wouldn't be able to help himself. However, he was beautiful.

He rolled out his sleeping gear and set out a fold-down chair next to it. He was home. She made him some tea and sat outside with him. They ate beef stew for dinner, Orlando eating with a ravenous appetite. He licked the plate like a Russian peasant. He put on a cassette of classical music – a Shostakovich quartet. Then he played Frank Zappa and the Mothers of Invention on the cassette player, the discordant sounds set the dogs off. He took Jane by the hand and danced; she felt his warm body and the tension of electric frisson.

Aaron placed himself on the stranger's lap, put on his hat and asked a hundred questions.

'Why is your name funny?'

'My Mama and Papa were born in St Petersburg in Russia; they came to Australia after the war. Stalin wanted to send them to Siberia', said Orlando.

'Where's Russia?'

'As far away as you can imagine, it's really cold and there are great onion shaped domes on churches, covered in icing sugar', said Orlando.

'Like Hansel and Gretel?'

'Mmm, the witches are called Baba Yaga. They eat children', said Orlando.

He snatched at Aaron's leg, he squealed. Jane studied him and watched Aaron bond instantly. She had longed for something better for her child.

'How come your first name is not Russian?' she asked.

'Mama arrived as a refugee. She wanted me to have an Italian name so I would fit in out west. She chose a girly name and the boys at Narragingy High beat the shit out of me for it.' He laughed. Jane smiled and he stared into her eyes.

'You look so Territory now', she said.

'Been here five years. I'm even learning to play didgeridoo.'

'So you think you're an Aborigine.'

'No, just learning to play. You right with that?'

'I grew up near where you did, in Richmond, just down the line.'

'You're not from a refugee family though? Are you? You're kind of exotic and dark. You'd be what?' Jane looked at him and said nothing for a while.

'Aboriginal family from way back, Darug mob. You won't have heard of us. Everyone says we died out'. She didn't want him to know everything yet, about the poverty, the ragged clothes and poor food. He smiled and put out his hand to shake hers.

'It's an honour to meet a First Australian', he said.

Jane wondered if he was being sarcastic. Would he at any moment tell her she couldn't be Aboriginal? He leant forward; it was a slow inclination of his head. The black curls framed his face, red lips. He tilted her chin and lightly kissed her mouth. He tasted her tongue. Warmth came over Jane, she was accepted for who she was, and she didn't have to explain that they hadn't died out, or be told that she didn't look very dark. So many people in her life had told her that she couldn't be Aboriginal, that she was too white, that all the Hawkesbury mob were dead, no survivors. She loved him already for his acceptance: he was no racist and he had the most important trait of all, compassion.

Jane served a dessert of bread and butter pudding, Orlando continued to eat like a famished man, running his fingers around the dish. He licked it and smacked his lips. Aaron never stopped asking questions, but Jane put him to bed with a made-up story. She tucked him in and slipped outside to the fire.

Orlando's voice seduced her. She wanted to distrust him but he made a startling impression. His eyes moved over her hungry body. Soft and alive, she tingled with anticipation; her eyes were unwavering in his, her will draining away.

'I had better go to sleep, I've got to meet the kids on Monday', he said. Jane was disappointed, which was an understatement – her thighs were aching – but to cover her embarrassment she stood up and threw the tea from the billy into the fire, she didn't look at him.

'Okay, good night.' She moved towards her door and stopped.

'Yep, you want to say something?'

'Just that I am so glad you are here; thank you for taking this job.'

'I wouldn't want to be anywhere else on the whole planet. We'll have a great time.' He grinned at her, got into his swag, and turned his back.

She went to her room and crawled into bed, she was restless, frustrated and unable to sleep, and she peeked out the window at him asleep with his arms tucked in like a baby.

Next morning, Orlando swept his new camp of dust and strolled over to Jane's caravan. Aaron was first at his side.

'You want to have swim with me in the billabong?'

They ran to the water and jumped in. Orlando came back to the caravan home. Jane saw how he let his eyes move over her breasts; she couldn't believe her luck.

'I have to tell you that I probably won't be here long, just until the Department finds a permanent teacher to work with you.'

'We can make the most of it', she said.

She saw him naked in the river, naked in her arms and she clutched her dress between her knees.

That night, after Aaron was asleep, Orlando made a fire and boiled a billy; he called her over to the fire.

'Come and have a cuppa?' he said.

Jane saw him watching her in the fire light. She leant on the door with a moment of doubt; saw her past outrageous love life thick with pulsing memories. Somehow, her parents' fighting was tied up in it all – a sticky spider cocoon of betrayals, a surge of furious emotion.

Her father had never been at home, was always working, his dark back bent to a concrete mixer in the sun or on the railways. There was the spectre of Aaron's feckless father, a painful love. It rushed past as Jane stepped out of the caravan. It seemed like a portentous moment. The future opened up like a chasm. The hair on her neck prickled. Orlando's smile drew her to him; it was inevitable that they would be lovers – she had known it from the first moment. The night stretched out before her; it was delicious. Orlando played his guitar and half sang a song, he sounded slightly ridiculous but he had a wonderful melodic voice. Jane pulled a sarong around her and sat on his swag, the fire warming her legs. Orlando held the mug and smiled into her eyes as she held out her hand for the tea.

'You're so pretty.'

He poured some forbidden vodka into her tea.

'I shouldn't', she murmured.

'Yes, you should.'

She shook her head then grabbed the bottle out of his hands. She threw out the tea and half-filled her mug with vodka. Thank heavens! A drink! Jane sipped delicately.

'Oh, this is so good.'

She was exhilarated by her first taste of alcohol in a few months. The dry community with an alcohol ban – it was best for the Lanniwah but she missed the occasional drink. She kept her eyes on his, gently ran her fingers down his face and dipped them into his mouth. He watched and allowed them to touch his tongue. She shook a little.

'This is a bad idea.'

'Nope.' His hand travelled down her Indian cotton blouse and rested on her nipple. He rubbed it delicately between his fingers. Jane moaned softly. She watched the tanned face, his dark eyebrows, the inside of his lips glistening pink, his teeth so white. When she kissed his face, it was damp and salty. His black curls flowed down the back of his neck. He held her in broad arms. She sighed.

'I can't help myself.'

Orlando opened up the swag and she crawled in under the canvas. It smelt of eucalyptus and maleness. He pressed his body against her, gentle and strong, his mouth electric excitement. He tried to compose his face and smile.

'Don't worry, trust me. I've got condoms.'

He lifted her skirt and pulled her pants down. He buried his face in her thighs. He ran his hands down her legs and gently kissed her breasts, teased the brown nipples. In a second, he was inside her body, thrusting with passion. She moved over on top of him, they stared into each other's eyes; they were in a wild tempestuous lust. Her hunger for him was desperate and uninhibited. Jane arched her back; she shimmered in the fire light. He murmured loving words; he loved her body, her delicious sweet fanny. She guessed it would all end badly, but for the moment, it was exactly what she wanted. She cried out in love, tears trickled from her eyes and they lay back panting and began all over again.

Over in the big house, Hubert and Edie were arguing again. Hubert's loud voice penetrated the darkness, then a crash of bottles.

Aaron woke up and called out for his mother. Jane jumped up from Orlando's bed. She wrapped a sarong around her and ran into the caravan.

'Okay, Aaron, Mummy's coming. It's alright, sweetie.'

She put him back in his bed and sang a song. Outside, Orlando lay back in the swag grinning. She watched through the louvres as he rubbed his hands across his face and breathed in. She guessed they smelt of her fanny. She saw him pour vodka and roll a joint.

'I regard teaching as a necessary evil. I love the children but I couldn't be bothered with the paper work. Life is for living and not boring me to death. I like to write poems.' He lay on his back with no shirt on, strumming.

'Do people in town fall about laughing when you tell them that?'

'Yep, some do. I don't mind. I grew up mostly with my mother. She was mad as a cut snake. I couldn't face her. The war nearly destroyed my parents and after building a fibro house out west, my father ran off with a Ukrainian truck driver with enormous tits. Like balloons. He just sent money and cards to Mama and she sort of clung to me. Arrgh, the Ruskie strangle hold.'

'So you ran away to the Territory.'

'Yes, you could say that, but hey, I give her half my pay. And I love the mysterious Aboriginal world, the heart-breakingly beautiful sunsets. I want to know what all the Dreaming stuff means. I want to find out if I believe it. A double reality.'

'You didn't come for the money?' she said. He smiled and she knew that her whole existence was transforming and that she could be happy with him as the second teacher and together they would be able to teach fifty-two children to read and she would have a lot of great sex.

CHAPTER 2

Meeting The New Teacher

School began with the ringing of the bell. Children had bathed in the billabong and lined up outside the school. They looked at Orlando, who stood grinning and waving. Jane saw the girls giggling. David stood back and watched the children's reactions to a new teacher; he hung his head: he could read Jane's admiration of the new teacher. She felt torn by this experience, confused in her attraction to both these men.

'We are very lucky. We have Mr Orlando to teach the senior class. He has come from Katherine and he has some fruit and lollies for you at recess time', Jane said. The children whooped and laughed.

'I am so happy to be able to teach you for a while. I might not be here for all the rest of the year, but I will try my best to teach you well', said Orlando.

'Where you got well? We got Lanniwah well, not far', said Ricky. Orlando shook his head.

'No well, just ... Hey, let's go inside and make a start on reading. I hear you have made some big books. You can show me. Then we can have a music lesson, some of you can learn to play guitar. We'll start a rock band. If your head teacher agrees.' The older children crowded around him stroking his brown arms. They loved him already.

Over the next few weeks, Jane found her job easier with a second teacher. She could work with David teaching the alphabet to the little ones or take her twenty-six children out to play with water measuring. David put out the coloured buckets to fill. He looked over at Orlando who was under a tree playing his guitar and teaching the children to sing a Rolling Stones song. David avoided talking to Jane except for schoolwork.

She felt his growing distance.

It was sport time after lunch. The red lilies were out and the whole school plunged into the cool billabong. They grabbed Jane by the shoulders and played diving games. One five-year-old child called out to her,

'You swim wid me?'

'I swim wid you!' Jane said, as he jumped into her arms. Such love in these children. They showed no fear of the outsiders; they loved Orlando straight away, so unlike their suspicious parents. The girls swam like fish around Jane and peeled the lily stems. They chomped down on stalks, like celery, and their eyes shone. Mayda and Lizzy swam under the water and emerged next to Orlando, they ate lily stalks with their teeth, and they laughed at him while the peel slid off their pink lips. He swam away. Aaron paddled by with his little mates – everyone wanted to be his best friend.

Orlando swam out a long way to keep a distance from the young girls. He practiced diving for fresh water mussels with Ricky and Robert. He averted his eyes from all the females when they climbed out of the water with their thin dresses clinging to their bodies.

Never had Jane felt so free and happy; it was a most romantic and blissful life. She looked at Orlando and he blew her a kiss. Mayda and Lizzy giggled and shrieked. They knew everything about Jane and Orlando.

As the flood subsided, Orlando settled into the school. He was amusing and brilliant, and required hardly any work or discipline from the children. They learnt to sing dozens of songs. He taught Ricky and the oldest boys to play guitar and they jammed while the other children picked nits from each-other's hair.

Jane was not amused, but the children thought Orlando was hilarious. He acted out funny stories and led them in wild, free-expression dances where they ran around outside the demountable classroom in the dirt. Jane had great ideas for art and drama and they wore crepe paper costumes and performed outlandish Dreamtime dance drama that ended with everyone running into the billabong.

The children learnt to tell the time with a cardboard clock while Jane and Orlando rocked and rolled. 'One o'clock, two o'clock, three o'clock, rock, we're going to rock around the clock tonight ...' Jane ploughed on with alphabet chanting, and pre-writing exercises. She taught the bright ones new vocabulary and carefully repeated pronunciation, and she watched Orlando's unconventional music methods as he tore over the plain with children chasing him. He was a mad thing.

'Could you just stay inside sometimes and work on maths?' said Jane

'Don't be conventional, Miss. We are the new thing in Territory music.'

'Just stay for a few hours: they need to learn to read.'

'They need rhythm and blues and love!'

'For God sake, help me.'

'Nope.'

'Dick!'

'Look, I'm on a spiritual journey. Last year I went on a vision quest near Uluru. A Native American shaman called White Foot led us. I didn't eat or drink anything for three days. I went to a sweat lodge and ate peyote. I meditated on a hill. It was amazing', he said.

'What happened?'

'I was hoping to see my spirit guide: it would open my eyes.'

'And did you?' She was beginning to realise that he would never help with the washing up, ever.

'I saw a frothy caramel milkshake. Little dribbles of cold water ran down its sides.'

Jane realised that a man who had a milkshake as his spirit familiar could not possibly be trusted.

Lanniwah children sat in her lap and played with her hair. They drew figures of men in lap-laps with spears, grannies surrounded by dogs, bright red fires and yellow sunsets, kangaroos and turtles, jabirus and bush turkeys. Some boys drew guitars, penises, and guns. She loved to hear them reading, all her work was paying off. They wrote about grandparents: 'My grandfather walk around Arnhem Land, he bin carry lot of spears, he kill lot of people.' They drew pictures with Texta colour pens of warrior men and women carrying coolamons full of bush tucker. One drew, in bright reds and yellows, Granny Lucy surrounded by blue dogs sitting by a fire, shining blue skies, staring at a pile of red rocks – 'She always draw dem rocks.' They drew sacred waterfalls and all of it with a flat dimension, no perspective, no lessons in art from Giotto in their school. Everything had equivalent value, a fish, a flower, an insect or a man were all drawn the same size because all had equal importance in the Aboriginal Dreaming cosmos.

Ricky drew a Texta colour picture of the store and he also drew the tree with the metal ring, but it was out of proportion, the rusted reddish ring shone as a huge circular form out of the small tree.

"What is this place?' said Jane.

'Killing place', said Ricky. David was on the lookout for boys who drew with their shirts over their heads sniffing the heady Texta fumes.

Orlando worked well with David. They took the older children on walks to talk to Old Pelican who showed them his paintings and therefore their history. Jane was happy. It was a perfect scenario, two teachers and an Aboriginal teaching assistant made a functioning remote school. She pushed thoughts of loving David out of her mind: a whitefella was safe.

CHAPTER 3

Dinner Again At Edie's House

Edie suggested they have dinner for the new teacher. She asked Jane to bring a plate of something from a tin. Edie had picked some of her red geraniums from the garden, and put them in a vase on the table. Jane sat sipping tea.

'These are my favourite, Rouge Cardinale geraniums, and second best are the small pink Lotusland ones,' said Edie.

'Nice, it's incredible that the bullocks don't eat them.'

'I'd shoot them first.'

Edie cooked as the children tore around with Aaron playing chasings. She wore a red Chinese dress; it was peculiar. Jane observed that Hubert liked having other men to talk to – Orlando and the Reverend, they would have to do. He smoked and chatted over a cup of tea in the afternoon light.

Phrases like 'living in sin', and 'defacto couple' floated around. No one mentioned them ... The flagrant breaking of Hubert's rule not to visit the black's camp, hung in the air like a dead crow.

'So your teaching assistant's alright?' said Hubert.

'The kids love him.'

'Oh yeah, everybody loves that smartarse fella.' Hubert smirked at Jane.

'Apparently, I am his brother in their moiety system.' Orlando said.

'But you're not a real relation, just adopted into their dumb clan system.'

'It's not dumb', said Jane.

'No, but say if I wanted to marry a young woman here. I wouldn't worry about what darn subsection she was, I would just have her. I mean if my dear wife was dead or something ...'

'You wouldn't be accepted.'

'So what?'

'Well, I'm not flamin dead but you might be if you keep this up.' Edie said.

'You're right, mate,' said Orlando.

'Boss, call me Boss, everyone does,' said Hubert.

'Okay, Boss. I really appreciate the welcome you have given me.'

'No worries.'

'What's the story with Gertie's daughter?' said Orlando.

'Shirley's half white. Only race on earth where the colour gene is recessive on the female side,' said Hubert. 'But she could pass; her kids will be quarter caste.'

Jane flinched at the description but the two teachers lounged on Hubert's veranda. Gertie was sweeping the floor behind them and the cattle dogs slouched under the fence. Hubert shook his head at Orlando.

'It's easy to be tempted, you'd know that', said Hubert. Silence. Orlando looked embarrassed. Jane nudged him.

'Those eye-lashes, their black pussies waving in your face, whoa, tempting all right.' Edie came out to the table, threw down a bowl of red jelly, and tinned fruit. Hubert rolled a cigarette and looked over at Edie. She snarled. Orlando shook his head at the offered tobacco pouch.

'It's a crime Hubert, if they're underage girls', Jane said. Hubert nodded. 'No, I'm not saying ... I couldn't ... Hey, looks like rain.'

The Reverend Wiltshire arrived and took a stool. The tone shifted. Edie became animated and girlish, giggling, and offered him a drink of warmish green cordial. Jane unwrapped her contribution of savouries: Kraft cheese on Jatz with pickled onions. The minister was nervous, and slapped mosquitos as he joined in the discussion.

'How's your tent Reverend? Comfy, I bet', said Hubert.

'It's not comfortable. Too many rocks, but that was the place you told me to camp.'

'Too right. Want to keep an eye on you. Don't want you becoming an Abo.'

'Actually, some of the young Aboriginal men are a profound inspiration to me, like David. He brought the boys to Sunday school. We talked about the love of Jesus, his teachings. Yes, to be a teacher is a calling. It shows a true dedication to human beings. Like Jane here.'

'It's the children. I love them.'

'There are many temptations in the bush and many young white men have been seduced by the Aboriginal way of life.'

'They live combo. It's shocking' said Hubert. He ate a pickled onion while staring at Jane's mouth.

'This place. What an opportunity! Give me an Aborigine for a day and I can teach him about the love of Jesus. My arms reach out to them. I feel a power that is profound and I am open to learning about the comparative aspects of their religion. A shared spiritual insight.'

'Or teach him how to bow down to the white cattle man and be beaten and subjected to inhumane treatment at the hands of missionaries and be grateful? How about we repeat the story all over this country? You'd appreciate that would you, Reverend?' said Orlando.

'You a commo radical or something?' Hubert laughed. Jane hid her face.

'Perhaps you, Orlando, might be happier studying anthropology back at your university or returning to ... what were you? A poet was it ... in Glebe. This calling is not meant for everyone.' the Reverend pondered.

'Make a lot of money do they? Glebe poets?' said Hubert.

Jane offered more canapés of biscuits and bright green gherkins. She tried not to think about the secret that the women had suggested about Edie. Surely, that was evil gossip, but she eyed Edie with new appreciation.

They finished eating. Everyone said how nice it was – the custard and jelly had been lovely.

Orlando declined the offer of a lift back to Katherine and assured the Minister that he would work harder at his spiritual life. Edie hugged Jane and she felt excruciated.

'We all try to get along with the Aboriginal people here. Take that Old Pelican: he has wisdom and magical powers. How about you join him and me for a little prayer in the youth bible classes?' said the Reverend.

'Sounds informative. I'll try to make it', Jane lied.

Edie called her children with a loud whistle.

'Time for bed, say goodnight to Mrs Reynolds and Mr Pepepov.'

'That's Kerekov', said Orlando.

'Good night', they called out. The children went to bed and Hubert rolled another smoke. Later, Jane saw Hubert and Edie walk hand in hand down towards the billabong; they looked happy and in love ... Jane had a twinge of envy like a hit of drugs. She sat outside her caravan with Orlando.

'I bet they're talking about us. I told them I was married. Oops.'

'They'll think you're a slut', said Orlando.

'They wouldn't use that language.'

'A loose woman.'

'Thanks.'

'Maybe, they think I forced myself on you.'

'I bet they think I'm a sex starved nympho from Sydney.'

'Well, that'd be right', he said. She punched his arm.

'I reckon Hubert will think that your reputation will end up smashing you in the face. I can just hear him saying, "If some cattle men get wind of it, they'll be sniffin' around for a go. Linin' up outside her caravan." Don't worry, darling, I will protect you', he said.

Jane wondered what that meant, 'protect you'. Was it a kind of commitment? No, too soon. He would be off as soon as he could. She could never trust him – or could she? There would be a moment when he also told her that he needed something else. She would fail again, or not.

That night, Jane heard a noise outside her window. Orlando was asleep beside her snoring gently. She saw a figure standing at the window right near her head. She was very still. She tried to wake her lover, but he was fast asleep. Jane slowly pulled back the sheet and sat up quickly. The dark shadow of a big shape leapt from sight. She looked out the window and pulled herself up on the sill. It was a naked white man in a blanket, crouched down on the dirt trying to hide, but her eyes met his for a fleeting second and he got up and hurtled back into the night like Dracula. Dogs barked wildly. Jane thought he was a pathetic peeping Tom, whoever he was.

Jane imagined that another dinner for the teachers and the Reverend might not be happening any time soon, even if she did bring a plate.

CHAPTER 4

Daniel

Orlando's friend arrived to stay for a few days. Daniel was a twenty-nine-year-old builder who worked for contractors and had a range of racist and sexist jokes. He had taken Orlando with him to visit the contractors' camp outside of Katherine. In town, the builders liked to hang around the Crocodile Hotel, but as 'fly-in-fly-outs', in an Aboriginal community they were outsiders with no place in the kinship system.

Daniel rode his motorbike straight up to Jane's caravan. He was blond and rugged; he hitched his R M Williams jeans, brushed down his red Bob Dylan tee shirt and gave her a shy smile.

'Gidday Jane, I hear you're a wonderful teacher.'

Daniel cooked them a lamb roast with tomato puree and garlic. He had a secret bottle of red wine. He was funny and outrageous, self-deprecating, fantastically politically incorrect. Jane told herself that she tolerated him for Orlando's sake. He looked around her caravan and saw a valuable bark painting on the wall.

'Hey, that's nice; worth a bit, eh?' he said.

'It's a Dreaming story by an old friend, my adoptive father Old Burnie', said Jane.

'Bet you got it for next to nothing.'

'No, she paid a lot for it', said Orlando. Daniel leaned over to the bark and scratched the ochre with his nail. He nodded.

'Sorry, that was rude. Hey, I might not look it, but I had a good education, I forgot my manners.'

Daniel had blazing blue eyes, and he grinned with white teeth ... He was a mystery: something hidden inside him; he was intelligent and competed madly with Orlando to outdo him. The men had chemistry between them. He seemed to adore Orlando and yet baited him. She felt admired but completely left out, like an ornament.

There was a sound of laughing out in the bush. A high squeal and whispering. Out of the night, Mayda and Lizzy stood giggling in the caravan light. Jane saw them through the window and opened the door. They were wearing their best clothes with pink flowers in their hair, their hands held over their mouths.

'Come in, you want something?' Jane said.

'Nothin, just ...' Mayda dropped her head.

'What? Come and have a cordial, or a biscuit? Is everything okay?'

'We going back. Goodnight ... Daniel!' They hid their faces, then slowly Mayda lifted her head and stared at Daniel; they ran off laughing.

Jane sat back down at the table. 'That was strange', said Jane.

'Just kids, they're always curious', said Orlando.

Daniel was a mate and mates were hard to find. Later after some drinks, Daniel took Jane in his arms and rock and rolled in the caravan kitchen as he smiled at Orlando. Aaron hit Daniel with a plastic Robin Hood sword.

'Don't touch my mother', Aaron said.

'Look out, Oedipus!' Daniel said.

Jane laid out the dinner on the Laminex table; she served the food, and listened to their banter. Daniel laughed and wrestled with Aaron. They made a Lego castle. Then Jane took her son to bed and read him a story while the two men told wild loud lying stories.

'Daniel! Can you can read me. *The Magic Pudding?*' Aaron called out.

Daniel took the book and looked embarrassed.

'Mate. Not now', he said.

'I can make it up. I know it all', said Aaron. He told the story to Daniel who sat on his bed to listen, then returned to the table.

Daniel brought out a hashish joint; yes, that was good. Everything was funny: Dan balanced a glass on his forehead, hilarious, and laugh – she couldn't stop: everything, her whole existence was so damn funny. The lights in the big house went on; that was funny. The food tasted so yummy; Dan had a Cadbury's chocolate, food of the gods.

Orlando cleared the table with Daniel and washed up while Jane listened to the men. Now she felt excluded; it was like being the audience at a movie: the men were very entertaining but she waited in vain for a moment when she could join in. They became riotously stoned. Her jealousy grew; Daniel had all Orlando's attention. She was not important.

'Cyclone Tracy. You remember how we saw the pink cement mixer truck fly over our head?' said Daniel.

'And the howling banshee screams from the wind?

'You pulled your flatmate under a mattress in the bath, wouldn't let her out. That was cool.'

'We were saved by the plumbing fixtures, the whole house blew away', said Orlando. Jane stroked Orlando's hair, he flinched and she dropped her hand. Daniel watched and caught her eye. She looked away at Daniel and raised her eyebrows. Orlando saw her.

'I stayed in a house a few years after Tracy, just slept on a concrete floor with a mozzie net, no walls', she said.

'The smell of the rotting Christmas turkeys inside smashed freezers, what a stink. Wild dogs tore into garbage, no water to drink, it was like in Vietnam', said Daniel.

'You weren't there, honey. We lost everything: all I had left was my shorts, didn't even have a pair of thongs.'

She stood up and moved to her bedroom. 'I'm going to bed', she muttered.

'Goodnight, teacher', said Daniel.

She found him amusing but strange. His masculine private school boy persona had an animal energy. She had met men like him before; she spoke but he ignored her ... a subtle misogyny.

'Why don't you come over to the Crocodile Hotel one day? We'll have a real booze up.' Daniel called out.

The next night, Orlando went to bed early, leaving Jane to entertain Daniel outside next to a fire. They were drunk.

'The enemy is inside your head', said Jane.

'Are you a stupid shrink or something? I had enough of that pycho stuff in the army', said Daniel.

'No, just observant. I can help you to learn to read', she said.

'Piss off! I've had more spastic teachers try to do the remedial thing on me than you could count. You should throw Orly out, he doesn't deserve a woman like you', he said.

'It's not your business; you haven't even got a girlfriend, what would you know? You pretend to love Orlando, and try to stab him in the back.' Jane stood up as he grabbed her hand. She stared at it.

'Have a bit of pity. A man gets so desperate. I was in hell when I was conscripted. I just need someone to talk to.' Daniel said.

'We've drunk too much', she said.

'Sorry, I'm screwed up, it's self-loathing; up here I drink, it's not cool, and I'm used to people punching my head in pubs. I learnt to box in Nam. I like the taste of blood in my mouth', he said. Jane walked into her caravan and turned off the light.

On the Saturday morning, Aaron ran off to play with his friends to make a road from the school to his caravan. It was a very long project; they were digging rivers. Daniel ate breakfast inside with Orlando, laughter seeped out the windows. Eavesdropping seemed inevitable. Jane leant against the aluminium concertina door – it was the only way to find out what was going on with Orlando. She suspected that she was developing a paranoid psychosis, an obsession with him that verged on insanity. It was a delicious falling out of love and she craved the drama of it. The tone of the men's talk was conspiratorial.

'Mate, you didn't. You're making it up!' said Daniel.

'All night long, smooth as silk.'

Jane banged the door open.

'What is?' she said.

'Nothing', said Orlando.

'Or should I say, who is?' she said.

'Just bloke talk, Janey. Janey, forget it', said Daniel.

The weekend filled with a claustrophobic atmosphere, where each person tried to score a witty bite off the other.

'My family are from Bourke in New South Wales. We had a small property but we went broke in a drought, shot all the sheep and buried them in a mass grave. But I actually went to a good school – Shore, believe it or not', said Daniel.

'That's a shame about going broke. Is that why you're so pissed off with the world?' she asked.

'Could be; what's your excuse?

'You don't need to know.'

'Try me.'

'Okay, working class western suburbs, fighting tattooed older brothers and sister. They chain-smoked from fourteen years old, lived on instant coffee and lay on the lounge watching TV all day. I have a memory of one brother grovelling and crawling across the carpet to beg for a smoke. He licked his brother's foot for it. Yep, lazy good-for-nothings on the dole.'

'What happened to you?' he said.

'I dreamt of a better life. I hung on the front gate, looked down the street of Housing Commission red brick houses, and knew I had to get out. I left home at sixteen, and I worked as a cleaner in the mental hospital. I got a break. A teacher's scholarship and I went to university. I learnt to copy how white students acted, found a plum in my mouth and lied about my background. I wanted to fit in but I never fooled their eastern suburbs snob mothers. They picked me in a second. My family are ... they couldn't help me and I certainly couldn't help them.'

'That's shit', he said.

'Maybe, but I did find out that there's a huge world of people a million times worse off than me. People who live under a bit of tin in a dust storm with babies and eyes full of pus. Women who are beaten up because they chase the wrong-side man, old men and women who remember horrific things, and none of it is their fault.'

'Yeah, yeah. Heard it all before. They'll die out, drink themselves to death.'

'That so? Well, don't give me any crap about why am I wasting my life on Aboriginal people. I am one of them', she said. He went very quiet and looked hard at her.

'Narr ... Look, I'm not a racist but ... look at them pissing their welfare cheques against the wall – what hope is there?' His voice trailed off as she walked away and slammed her bedroom door.

She heard him ride away towards the Lanniwah camp on his motorbike.

He stopped. Jane listened, but nothing. She prayed that he wasn't sniffing around the young women; it could be dangerous.

The next morning, Daniel's swag was empty; he hadn't slept in it. She looked around; maybe he was having a wash in the billabong. Jane saw him walking out of the bush. She heard a girlish whispering. Jane darted inside. Daniel walked into the caravan kitchen and asked for a cup of tea. He looked exhausted but elated. He was about to leave.

'Thanks for the dinner and hospitality. I appreciate it. You forgive me for being an idiot, I hope', he said. Jane shook his hand and helped him carry his swag to his bike. He waved and rode out of the station, did a 'wheelie' in the dirt and disappeared into the trees. Orlando swept the ground near the fire.

'You did a line for him. You wanted him', he said.

'No, he's a dickhead. It's not like that. I love you.'

'Not what I saw', he said.

'Don't be jealous.'

'What I don't get is you thinking that it's alright to flirt with any bloke you like, while I'm not allowed to have female friends.'

'I didn't flirt', she said.

'That's good; I'll remember that line for when I need it.'

A few hours later, Jane stood in the caravan kitchen staring at the Olivetti typewriter on the Laminex table. He had written another poem. It beckoned from the roller, floating, flapping. Jane ripped it out and sat, tired, on the plastic chair. Heat hung, so hot, the hum of the fridge, the sound of a dingo strolling by with a 'who gives a shit' attitude. She read with a furtive dirty haste. Her breath quickened. Yes, this was it – a poem about making love to a Lanniwah woman in the river.

He had talent, this twenty-eight-year-old man. The description in the poetry was clear. Her heart beat and thumped as heat rose in her chest, face hot, sweating. He had the girl on the Toyota bonnet and again waist deep in the cool fresh water. Palm fronds tickled. It was near where they had picnicked with Aaron, cooked sausages on the fire. White sand, a pretty place. He described the girl's dark hips when she had gyrated in front of the pub's jukebox. She had slithered and pulsed. Singing him to her with her luscious sexy black eyes darting into his. His urgent longings and having her later in the river. He said that her wet vagina was like a secret cave.

Jane ripped the poetry in two pieces and gently placed this proof of infidelity back on the typewriter. She waited for his return from the school, for him to know that she knew. Her excitement mounted at the prospect of a fight, a real fight with vicious plate throwing – it would be good to hear a crashing plate, see him duck and quiver. And he walked into her trap; she asked him, 'Why?' His answer the exquisite male logic:

'I had to have a girl when you were busy – what other chance would I have?' Jane laughed and was struck dumb by the purity of the lust. She had developed an addiction to the fights. Lusting for them. Horrific angry word throwing. Then the sex, sublime, hot, vicious and terrible.

She realised that she would never know much about this whitefella, a secret men's business suited his character well, and all his business was pretty well secret. Jane hoped that Daniel would not come back. He was big trouble.

CHAPTER 5

Lovers

The nights were long, but there was a feeling of growing love, and Orlando and Jane told each other stories. The lack of radio, television and phone made them reliant on a few library books or each other and they were both great storytellers. They absorbed each other's histories. They outdid each other with snake stories: black snakes, brown snakes, and death adders – all part of western Sydney childhood.

There were dinners with Edie and her family in the caravan. Jane was still wearing Tibetan dresses and she had Buddhas around the caravan. They had removed the kitchen table and Hubert and Edie were required to sit on the floor and eat Indian curry and chapattis with their fingers. Incense burned ominously and Jane saw Hubert being downright uncomfortable in his tight RM Williams jeans, his scrotum pressed against the low makeshift dinner table. Edie seemed horrified.

'He doesn't like curry, only white sauce on his steak', said Edie.

'She's right. I can eat anything. I even ate a black snake once. Real bony'

'Well, I'd better get back home, I'll have time to slit my wrists before bed', Edie laughed.

It hadn't gone well, the mutual suspicion snaked around the room. Still both couples were lonely. Orlando stretched in the chair. A brilliant funny storyteller, it was his turn and his eyes were bright. He acted out bits by stepping into character. He did great impersonations of Hubert and Edie. 'I'll whip you good, boy.' He mimed the whipping and cringing.

'Let's hear about your life in Burma as a monk. I've been longing to hear the next episode.'

Orlando sat astride the table to demonstrate how he had gone to the pit toilet each morning and had to fight off the pigs in Goa who wanted to eat his shit fresh from his bum.

'My turn, do you want to hear about how I danced in a see-through body-suit at the Cell Block Theatre. It was an unrehearsed performance to beat poetry. Or how I was member of a free theatre troupe and I emerged naked from a box of offal while transvestite queens rushed past on roller skates?' He fell asleep before she got to the good part. She carefully laid the pink sheet over him.

Jane began to find out about her new lover. He was musical and vain, loved pictures of himself and asked Jane to draw his portrait. With Orlando sex could be moments away, so she learnt to not bend over in front of him when sweeping, her swaying backside drove him crazy. He had lust-making black hair on the back of his hands just like a monkey. Jane was entranced. She had not had a lover who was so excited about her body. His eyes blazed as they held each other. He licked her thighs and caressed her skin. He lay his head on her mound of Venus and sighed.

Jane sensed that he had old guilt following him around; he was secretive about his emotions while she was naked and loud. He had sudden outbursts of repressed jealousy and anger that surprised her, frightened her.

'Go on, burn the love letters! If you love me you will', he said. She cried.

'You're frozen inside: you have cold hands.'

They were affectionate and cuddled openly in front of Aaron, so he reacted and hugged Jane with fierce possession.

Aaron glared at Orlando. 'She's my mummy – you can't have her.'

'It's okay, mate. I love her in a different way. She loves you best. I want to protect her.'

'He won't hurt me, Aaron. You don't have to save me. I love you: you're my little boy', she said.

She walked down a path alone. There were snake tracks in the sand, thick nasty tracks. Jane flicked a long stick in the tussocks to drive away King Browns. There was stillness in the air, some strange feeling, hair on her neck prickled. The grass moved, a hissing, then a huge brown snake leapt up in front of her, six feet high and flexed to strike, its beady black eyes staring, and tongue flickering, hideous, the devil of all fear. She nearly wet her pants in terror. Its eyes gripped hers and she couldn't move. Jane moved very slowly backwards, her stare still fixed. She looked sideways and the snake still didn't move. She saw a heavy stick on the ground, and while still staring into the snake's eyes she picked it up. The image of the snake's head as it lunged forward, the purplish forked tongue and the bite of poison. Jane imagined it flooding her nervous system and slowly paralysing her heart. Her hand came up slowly holding the stick and she hit out at the ground near the snake with all her strength. The snake swung back its head to hiss and fell to the ground and she watched it slither away. Yes, it was fleeing, more scared of her than she was of it. Of course. No worries. Poor thing. Lovely creature really.

Her steps were full of shivering fear; she tiptoed along the path with her weapon, but again the sound of a hiss. The snake was following her! A rush of terror. 'Help, help, please someone!' A scream, but her voice made the reptile even angrier but then she watched it … the shimmering scales and stillness, it was beautiful. It spoke to her of ancient stories, a creature imbued with magical qualities, a creator of the landscape. Like the great Anangu pythons called Kuniya who were also women who fought the poisonous Liru snake. These animals were a protected and feared species and Jane stayed still as the land spoke to her. The King Brown swept away into the grey grass and was gone.

Jane walked through desert daisies and pink starflowers. She stood on a rock above the grass and breathed deeply. She thought about David and how things might have been different for her. The sun was warm on her back, and she watched red and blue dragon flies dart in the rushes.

Orlando joined her by the billabong, he arrived like a floating ghost, and she jumped in fear. Then reached out for him, for his reassurance and love.

'I'm sorry, I was angry. Let's not be like that, the jealous thing, it's poison', he said.

She held him tight and they hugged and sobbed on the sand bank. There was too much isolation to hurt each other, and too many snakes.

CHAPTER 6

Katherine Town

As the Wet subsided, the road became passable with a winch on the Toyota. The town of Katherine was the holy grail of good times in school holidays for Jane and Orlando. They went off to the Regional Education meeting. They drove in and went to the evening folk club. Peter, Paul and Mary still sang at this club, pale imitators drawling away. Some talented musicians and singers appeared, wine and beer flowed, it was a release and they could get drunk. ' I love Katherine, the best place in the world, so sophisticated, so cultured, so alcohol sodden, yippee!' She turned up the music and sang aloud,' Y.M.C.A.!.'

At the club, one hip-looking young man played the viola de gamba (of all things), sometimes accompanied by Orlando on guitar or didgeridoo. He said he was a historian; his wife was with him; she was also beautiful and magnetic. Jane felt a strong need to know them. Jane looked around the party – it was rocking and people were drinking large amounts of beer. She had a familiar burst of insecurity; it took her by the throat. Yes, that'd be right: Orlando was now stalking the most attractive woman in the room. She was dark-haired with pale skin, and busty. Some of the Katherine teachers looked at Jane with a sort of pity – they knew Orlando well. One female teacher took her by the arm.

'Be careful; he has a reputation. A ladies man.'

Jane clutched her beer stubby holder. The headman from the office of Road Planning and Construction was leering. He wore a short-sleeved shirt over a beer belly, shorts that barely concealed his manliness, and thongs. Arr, yes, the answer to single women's prayers.

'You new in town, eh? My spies tell me yer single.'

'Hmm', she said.

'You teach the dark people long?'

She could feel the heat rising in her throat, not another conversation where she had to explain her work. 'On a cattle station, its challenging work', she said.

'I could come out and visit? Live alone, do you?' The big man leant towards her, his thick and hairy arm pinned her against the concrete wall, and then he twisted his head as a young Chinese girl walked past in a miniskirt.

'Take a squiz of that! I could eat off that black arse.'

He grinned back at Jane. She pushed his arm away and hissed into his ear. 'Why don't you piss off, you chauvinist, racist dickhead!', she walked away.

'Lezzo!' he spat back.

Orlando spent the entire party glued to the dark-haired woman's side. Jane observed that the pretty face and deep cleavage fascinated him. Jane thought he was imagining placing his penis in between those breasts. He preened and told jokes; the girl laughed; they shared cigarettes; he gazed into her eyes. This felt like hell. Jane clenched her teeth. Yes, she would run away. Why did she always choose such faithless men?

Orlando sensed that Jane was watching; he waved her over.

'Jane, this is Marcia. She's going to give a talk about innovative pedagogy.'

Marcia nodded while looking over her shoulder. Orlando smiled as Marcia beckoned him with a curled red fingernail. He was positively panting. Jane had on a coat of invisibility. Yes, that was it; she did not actually exist. Perhaps she wasn't beautiful enough, and that mouth – she spoke up; not good, not quiet, not compliant enough.

The people at the party all asked, 'How's Orlando going? We miss him in town. How are his songs coming along?' Jane mumbled. She was sure that when she got dressed at the motel there had been someone looking back from the mirror. She had applied ruby lipstick and cleaned her teeth. Yes, she seemed to exist. What's more, she had been with a lovely man. They had hot fantastic rude sex. He had breathed in her ear and called her his little whore. Yes, it was fast-pumping wipe-it-off kind of sex before they came to the party. Hadn't they? Maybe she smelt. Did she have bad breath? She hadn't looked desperate; no one had whispered about her, or had they? Was she a joke? God she hated that, people laughing at her. She imagined driving down the road, but she didn't have the car keys. He had them in his pocket, of course. Jane felt like a puppy dog, powerless and pathetic.

The effect of being in a relationship with a charismatic clown dawned upon her: she was *second fiddle*. He used these rare social occasions to shine as a hilarious mimic, while she found herself talking all night to old women in corners. Soon she would dissolve, leaving behind a pool of greasy sweat.

'Orlando, I'm going back to the motel.' He looked alarmed.

'Not yet. I haven't had enough vodka.'

'You'll be fine.'

She walked onto the Katherine Street, a carload of cowboy hoons roared past.

'Hey, darling, want a root? Can we all gang bang you?'

They were all shitheads really, what exactly were men made of? As she walked away, it felt like she was leaving this short relationship forever – it felt incredibly pleasant and liberating.

The next day, the Katherine Regional Education meeting began with a dinner. Jane managed to find herself opposite a balding man who luxuriously picked his teeth, sniffed, and examined the toothpick before the meal. He was sweating and rivulets of perspiration dropped on his plate. His wife had a strange orange fuzz perm. She leant forward conspiratorially as she sipped a glass of Porphyry Pearl.

'The remote Aboriginal schools are challenging aren't they? I am concentrating on teaching cleanliness.'

'I'm teaching reading', said Jane.

By the end of the meal, Orlando was slurring his jokes and he seemed to have his hand up the panties of pretty Marcia. Jane looked and he sat up trying to appear sober. Jane wanted to scream in jealous rage: she wanted to tear Marcia's eyes out, cut her tits off and feed them to the crocodiles.

The next day presentations were endless. She thought: could I go now? God she hated meetings and talks by the dullest people in the universe. The Education Department's expert on 'Methodology, Pedagogy, Objectives:? Evaluation and Strategies for Educational Outcomes' – oh groan! – spoke for two hours. Jane's hangover pulsated. She found her head dropping onto the table, her mouth a dirty cocky cage. She snored. Dribble seemed to have collected on her conference folder. God, had she fallen asleep? Orlando nudged her; his hangover was non-existent. She hated him. He was intelligent, well read, alert, and had his hand up in the air.

'I have a question, are the pedagogical outcomes measurable in a cognitive philosophical paradigm? In addition, are the consequences of using this measuring device comparable to the outcomes measured by other educational mechanisms? Alternatively, all of the above? Oh, and who won last night's raffle? I was dying to get my hands on that meat tray.'

Someone yelled: 'Get your hand off it, Orlly.'

The room laughed. Jane looked at him sideways; she didn't recognise him. Who was this pompous educational theorist?

She had a dreamlike memory of the end of the previous night. Arrgh, it was coming back. That's right, focus. Orlando was dancing on the pool table with a flowerpot on his head. At one stage he might have hung his willy out of his fly with the trouser pockets turned inside out, 'dancing the elephant', he said. No, it wasn't possible; he couldn't have. Then the brunette had disappeared with him into the ladies toilet; she had come out ten minutes later, brushing her skirt. There seemed to be flecks of semen on her blouse. Jane imagined Orlando pumping Marcia's pussy standing up in the cubicle, tight black dress pulled up to her armpits. A rootin' tootin' Territory lad. It couldn't have been like that. It wasn't possible. He loved Jane; no man could be so awful.

Later in the motel, the row began.

'How could you? Everyone at the conference saw you go in there with her! How does that make me look?' Jane said.

'Who cares what people think?'

'I care.'

'Well, that shows how middle-class you are. We are not married; we are friends.'

'We are teachers. We have to be respectable', she said.

'No one tells me how to behave, I do what I want, and I always have. We Russians beat the Germans.'

'Why are you doing this to me? I don't deserve it.'

'It's not all about you. I have my needs. Get over it, it doesn't mean anything. I love you.'

She looked away, the words 'break up' and 'affair over' floated on the flocked purple wallpaper. They got into bed and turned their backs. She felt terrible, she wanted to choke him and spit fire in his face.

'I hope you get the clap', she hissed.

A few days later, the gift was crabs. They itched and crawled in her pants. She searched with disgust and cursed the brunette. Orlando came back from the chemist with DDT lotion.

'This will kill them. Sorry, Jane.' She watched him cover his pubic area with white lotion.

The town of Katherine had all the aspects of a social world: dinners, pubs, and drunkenness, vomiting in gutters, prostitutes, desperate people, self-delusion, cruelty and loads of good wholesome fun. Jane hoped that in the future Orlando could avoid the temptations that were around every corner. She loved being in a couple but he was a man with roving eyes; every attractive woman they met was a rival; it could be exhausting.

The next day Jane made friends with the historians. They were so courageous and eccentric that the Department of Education didn't know how to treat them. In the battered Suzuki, alone, Rosie had travelled one thousand kilometres to record stories from Aboriginal informants. She was young, tall, dark and striking, had babies and loved writing true history. They had applied for a grant to write a social history book for the Northern Territory.

'They wanted a book about brave pioneers battling the Australian outback, maybe a mention of attacks by treacherous natives on valiant men installing the telegraph line from Adelaide to Darwin. Nice photos. It was suggested that some cartoons from the *Bulletin* could show a few Chinese at Halls Creek in coolie hats and pigtails. Gold, Afghans and the outback spirit. Yes, that would be good, with lots of lively folk memories', said Brian.

'And photographs of the first town mayor, with his wife in a pith helmet,' said Rosie.

Jane visited them in town and sat on the plastic lounge in their demountable house – this was the only accommodation available, at the army aerodrome. Jane and Rosie discussed the work of historians.

'Why is it that concerned citizens always refer to the 'Aboriginal problem', and what to do about infant mortality, alcoholism, poverty, unemployment? Those people talk with a mock sorrowful expression. It's an ecstasy of mourning for a 'passing people'; the need to 'smooth the dying pillow'. It's an orgy of 'tut tut' grief', said Jane.

'There was ignorance about the vibrant and growing Aboriginal communities, both urban and rural, so oral history is all that remains.'

'Thank heavens for you two', said Jane.

'There are a few records of the killings, rapes and poisonings. Aboriginal people had learnt to lie to protect themselves from any do-gooder reaction down south – and the backlash up here? It might be a knee-jerk response, kids taken. How could human memory be trusted? White people tend to only believe paper records, and if it wasn't written down then it didn't happen.'

'It's like a series of victories over Aboriginal people's stories, so they could massage history into noble events ... I saw the museum, oh dear, these stories revealed sugar-coated fairy tales where the Wunungah husband went on ..."

'Nigger hunts and bushwhacks to clear the land of Aborigines.'

'Yep and the 'little missus' supervised the starching of cotton lace tablecloths, nice. I like a good table cloth...'

Brian continued:

'Instead, after a year of research, and travel to so many towns and Aboriginal communities, Rosie and I produced a huge document full of damning revelations about the treatment of Aboriginal people at the hands of white Australians. There were massacres; land was stolen, destroyed, water holes poisoned. Children were taken and the Aboriginal families never saw them again. Men set fire to dying Aborigines. Aboriginal woman were raped, half-caste babies killed with sticks by their white fathers or buried alive – you can listen to the recordings'.

Jane listened to the tapes of oral histories Rosie and Brian had gathered while squatting by campfires, listening for days to Aboriginal stories that made your hair curl, their cassette recorder burning with horror. They would sit near to sites that frothed with corpses, where people who had speared a cow were murdered and left in the burning sun for dingos to eat. No burial markers – the earth was made of skin and bones, hearts and lungs.

The couple would joke about how to approach old white cattlemen who had reputations for murder. They described it to Jane: 'Um, hi, nice place you got here. Killed any Aboriginal people lately?'

However, in reality, they had devised lists of non-confronting questions, with gentle probing about their families and long ownership of the land, which might lead to sub-textual replies.

Jane went with them on an interview with an old cattleman.

'Was it leasehold or freehold? Did any Aborigines live here?' asked Rosie.

'No, not now. Maybe once, but they had moved on long ago', the old man said.

'Gone where?' asked Brian as he wrote studious notes.

'Dunno mate, walkabout, you know how they are. Government gives them everything these days and they just drink grog, piss it up against the wall.' Brian nodded sagely and carefully tucked away the tape recorder. The old cattleman called him back.

'They used to say, when it came to darkies, shoot, shovel and shut up.'

Jane heard from Brian about what happened when the *History of the Northern Territory* publication was ready. The Department of Education was horrified. The Director brought Brian and Rosie into his office. Brian imitated the director:

'This is not what we wanted. Why are there so many Aboriginal stories? Why haven't you researchers spoken to any of the local historical societies? Have you read any of the pioneer diaries or brave stories of Leichhardt and his journey to Port Essington or Stuart? These were explorers of real courage. In addition, what are these wild and unsubstantiated claims that a well-known and respected pioneer, one George Renway, had shot hundreds of Aborigines around Rainer River in the early 1900s? It is ridiculous! Renway's grandson is the head of the local Rotary Club and Chairman of the Shire Council, and he will tell you that it was positively insulting. No, it will not do, we cannot publish this document! The Department is sorry, but it has been a waste of funds and we suggest that you, Brian and Rosie, might like to go back to teaching. That would suit you better, don't you think? And would you like a remote school on the Gulf, one hundred kilometres from Borroloola?' They all laughed.

Brian asked Jane if he could get permission to visit Harrison Station, he would send a letter to Old Pelican for Jane to deliver. There was a huge story to record out there. Rosie and Brian would record it. They would publish all the stories themselves, with tapes of the interviews.

As Jane came out of their house, she noticed that there were men watching her from a car. They looked like city fellas, and one man in a suit jumped out and took a photograph of her. She walked over to them. Perhaps they were lost and she could help them. They drove off.

'You're committing a crime by even thinking about land rights. You won't find much support for a land rights march. If someone puts up a land rights flag, they'll burn it and they'll track you down and crucify you ', said Brian.

'My letters arrive opened. Edie says she doesn't know why.'

'They spy on you; they have nothing else to do. Us southerners, we are monsters who want to destroy the real Territory. We are the commos and agent provocateurs; we have been watched and photographed. Its common knowledge', Rosie said.

Jane thought that perhaps they were being paranoid, but her friends shook their heads.

'No, there are National First Australia Party spies, really. They pay private detectives to watch us agitators.'

Jane thought that she would be found out and her modest activities in black rights would be monitored – even the CIA was obvious in small towns. She met an American man dressed in the clothes of a Christian linguist: long white socks, buttoned down white shirt, freshly ironed Bermuda shorts, hair glued in place. She saw him at Aboriginal meetings taking copious notes and even openly recording the speeches on a tape recorder. Jane sauntered up to him and smiled.

'Who are you? Are you CIA?' he was startled.

'Ha, no ma'am, just a Christian on God's work.'

'Are you making files about outspoken Aboriginal people? Why would you do that?' He looked very uncomfortable and adjusted his glasses.

'The Missionary Fellowship Group is translating the New Testament.'

'Do you report to ASIO or CIA headquarters? Are you using surveillance on us pathetic teacher activists?' asked Jane. The man laughed and wiped sweat with a handkerchief. He blew his nose and looked lovingly at his snot;

he neatly folded the hanky back into his shirt pocket.

'No, Ma'am, I'm here for Jesus Christ. The devil is among us. Maybe you are suffering from paranoia?'

'What is it? A worldwide conspiracy? Do you think that the Black Panther Party is on the move in the Northern Territory?'

'He moved away. Jane turned her back and saw him taking photographs of Lanniwah men and of the outspoken elders. It was a mystery. Perhaps the missionary work was all above board; these men were working against social injustice. Doing wonderful things for Aboriginal people. They could save the languages.

Jane felt fearless in the face of these men. She had seen her father leave the Communist party because he was threatened with dismissal from his job on the railways. Karl Marx's ideas flowed in her childhood home. They argued about equality, the evil of inherited wealth, the working class, and how to stand up for your beliefs. There would be no bowing to old money and the squattocracy like their grandparents had to. Still, Jane had feelings of panic when she spotted these men taking her photo. What if she became destitute again? The men in black cars might take *her* child.

'Who are you? What on earth would you take my photo for?' she said.

'It's nothing sweetheart. It's for the girly page in *The Sun*'.

'Are you the National First Australia Party? Looking for reds under the bed, are you?' she shouted at the man in the suit.

'Just ASIO, darling', he laughed.

Jane leant down. The nervous man sat there writing notes. He looked down her blouse.

'What are you doing spying on me?' she said.

The driver started the engine and rolled up the window. She went around the front and kicked at the car's headlights. The man in the suit stared. She slammed her fist into the window (Ouch, that hurt!).

'Stop following me!' she shouted.

In Katherine, she had become an active letter writer to newspapers and government officials. She was riding a wave of political change. She made sure that she could get away from school long enough to attend the historic signing of Northern Territory mining agreements. Jane made super eight films.

It seemed important to document the workings of a police state. She paid the price in the suspicion, or downright hatred, she encountered. In the past, she had feared arrest for having kept a little grass, but in the Territory, she was an obvious target ... It came to nothing: she was free up there; no one cared; she could do what she liked; be who she liked.

A week later, Orlando called out that he had seen the historians driving up the muddy track. Brian's old Suzuki car crawled through mud and his first sight of Jane was in her purple see-through purple harem pants as she bent to tend her Chinese cabbages. She looked up.

'Welcome to Harrison and Lanniwah country.'

'You look like a hippy, so out of place on a Territory cattle station.'

'She's doing a remarkable job', said Orlando.

Jane and Orlando made them welcome and on the first night the visitors brought out a bottle of dry white wine and had even brought salad – they had a party. Jane's need to talk was fierce; she began long monologues with patient Brian smiling – he had learnt to be a good listener and speaker.

'Revolutions are made by people having one voice: this is the genius of the Black Power movement; its one mind set, the spirit of international rising against colonial hegemony. In Sydney, they are protesting, staging sit-ins. The old order will be overthrown, but it will be gradual.'

Rosie sighed. 'Aboriginal people in remote places don't hear about this movement ... except from people like us. We are dangerous.' Jane pushed her chair back:

'Yes, they have heard about it. Whispers. They know about their own violation, the bizarre and brutal history; they live it every day, walk past the site of murder every day, and feel the oppression every day. The men work for nothing and the women boil clothes in ten-gallon drums, they are paid with flour. Subsistence living. It's demeaning. Like my family's life.'

'You can hear their stories, Jane. Human inquiry; find out the mystery and pathos. The killings all over this country were repetitive and gross. Stories hidden in mangroves, black stinking mud like old bodies decaying. Their history is full of rivers and wetlands polluted by death. The rising of the tide, it sometimes brings reptilian giants, they are king. Everything scatters in fear. They are an allegory that shows humanity's cruelty and survival.' Brian spoke calmly while pouring everyone another wine.

Orlando entertained with stories of ceremonies. Isolation in the remote stations drove people mad.

Next day, Old Pelican walked up to meet them. He was crooked with a lame leg, had a carved stick to lean on, clean-shaven and he wore new cowboy clothes with fringed pockets, and elastic-sided black-brown boots. A handsome devil with white slicked down hair, so different to the old person Jane had first met. He beckoned them over near the store, dusted off a place under a tree. He sat for hours with Brian, Rosie and Jane; they brewed tea and ate damper with jam, Old Pelican smoked tobacco that Brian had given him. There were some gifts for him, new blankets and more tobacco; he smoothed the grey wool and rubbed his chin. The old man looked hard at Brian.

'You tellem true, eh? Not bunkum.'

'I will, old man, I promise to tell true.'

'They are good people, trust them', said Jane.

The old man nodded and they started up the tape recorder.

'Old people, they hide little fellas from dat East Africa Cold Storage Company; they come first, might be 1890. Government send em up to clean up Lanniwah, Aboriginal people. Body all pile up dat Rainer River. Dat Constable William, he in charge Native Police, he killem thousands our people.'

'I heard about that, they had an enquiry but the premier of South Australia, he defended that fella. He was found guilty.'

'Nope. Dat not right. He say not guilty! You Wunungah make up all rubbish one story, I not talk 'bout it no more.' Old Pelican was angry. Brian sat quietly.

Hubert rode up on his motorbike; he revved the engine and blew dust over Brian and Rosie.

'Who gave you permission to talk to my blacks?'

'They're not your blacks!' said Rosie.

'We asked Old Pelican and the other elders', said Brian.

'Elders my arse! A group of pathetic bludgers. You come up to my house first and you ask permission from me, not them. They don't run the show, I do. You got that, townies?'

'Sure, we're sorry for not observing station protocols. It won't happen again', said Brian.

'Alright, I accept yer apology. You can come over later and meet the Missus. Show some respect. See you later for smoko, Pelican.'

'They didn't know you ruled with an iron hand, Hubert', said Orlando. Jane nodded to him to be quiet. Hubert roared away on the bike.

Brian offered Pelican a photograph from a library. A mounted constable, William Smith was dressed in white shirt, white moleskin trousers with a broad leather belt and a pistol on the side in a holster. A white felt hat tilted back to reveal his moustachioed face. He wore black leather knee-high boots and leant against a carbine rifle. Next to him, a member of the native police was bare chested with a belt of carbine shells across his chest. He pointed into the distance while the constable looked on. Around them, other members of the force squatted with belts of shells and rifles.

'It was a posed studio shot, well lit and decorated with salt bush branches – that's right, presumably for fond colonial memories. Proud moments for generations to look back on, sitting in pride of place on the mantelpiece', said Brian.

'There is no history, just different versions of the past, different eyes. If we try to prove one version it doesn't clarify the problem; other sets of so-called proofs are equally possible', said Rosie.

'What you say? Talkem plain for me, not big corrugated-iron word – you bunkum', said Old Pelican.

'Yeeai, old man. We listen, not talk.'

Brian tramped through the bush with Old Pelican and Old Lucy; they spoke with him all day. Jane and Orlando kept busy at school but watched the comings and goings of the historians.

Hubert came over to where they sat with Old Pelican.

'You finish with these southerners, old man? Hope they pay you,' said Hubert.

'Yeeai, Boss.'

Hubert turned to Brian.

'You can pay the old fella, okay? And you don't want to leave your departure too late – you might get stuck in a bog, and I'm not gunna come and dig you out. Orlando has pissed off to some corroborree – he won't be able to help you either. He's turnin into a blackfella.'

Brian and Rosie packed up their camp and the old Suzuki car lumbered down the road as Jane watched them leave. She felt lost without them. They were her lifeline, a piece of sanity.

CHAPTER 7

The Wet

There were no vegetables in the Wet and there was a lack of vitamin C. Jane imagined that this was possibly causing the crash of relationships. The flood came up quickly and Aaron told Jane it was great that he could jump from the caravan for a swim. Jane eyed the water for snakes and crocs. Jane's garden of Chinese cabbages drowned. Edie showed Jane how to cook green papaw and some kinds of grass. Jane made ice cream from tinned mix and once she gave some to Margie to take back to camp. After that, Lanniwah people yelled out asking her constantly for ice cream; she tried to keep up with the demand, but gave up.

Edie gave out free advice on how to cook beef.

'You can grill the ribs on gidjee coals. Frying the liver is good, but there's no onions or bacon.'

'Aaron won't eat liver.'

'What about a nice curry? And there's beef and white sauce, followed by jelly with custard, custard with tinned fruit, custard with jam roly-poly. All nice.'

'It's so monotonous,' said Jane. She thought all Edie's cooking tasted like vomit.

'Then go back to Balmain and you can eat frog legs and goose livers at some fancy restaurant ... You know this place is haunted. You can feel it, taste it.' Edie escorted Jane out, and slammed the kitchen door ... Jane stood outside and wondered if Edie was turning on her. It must be the Wet.

However, Jane had food, and the Lanniwah had so little. The people were always hungry: they lived on little fish from the billabong, beef, tea, sugar and damper; sometimes there was bush tucker like bush banana or a tortoise.

In the mid-morning, Jane sat outside her caravan eating damper with the schoolchildren. A group of Lanniwah elders waved to Hubert; he walked to the fence and held a meeting. Old Pelican tried to mediate with the Boss because they wanted to carry out a renewal ceremony at a nearby lagoon; they wanted to harvest lily seedpods.

'We gotta make that ceremony or big trouble, like ants comes to eat alla Lanniwah', said Old Pelican.

'The cattle come first and I don't want anyone moving about and frightening my cattle', said Hubert. Old Pelican twitched and struck his woomera against his leg; he looked angry. Mayda and Shirley stared at the scene – no one liked to see Old Pelican angry.

Later, the music drifted into the school, the children became restless. There was a big men's ceremony beginning up behind the hills near the camp. Orlando slipped out of the classroom. Jane followed him.

'Where are you going?' said Jane

'Can't a man do anything without being questioned?'

'I will have to take your class', she said.

'That's right, sorry.'

Orlando disappeared with a group of painted men and older boys. David went with them. However, David returned before lunch without Orlando, Ricky and Robert. He taught maths to the older children while Jane continued with reading and writing. David watched her pride in each story. After the school day was over, there was still no sign of Orlando and the boys. Aaron pulled David's arm.

'Why did Orly go? I want him to read to me', said Aaron.

'No worry, Aaron. They back tonight maybe. You go home', said David. Aaron ran outside to play.

Jane smiled and put away books; a pile slipped from a shelf and hit her on the head. David rushed to pick her up from the floor, his arm around her back to support her.

'You okay?'

'Yeah, just bumped my head. That shelf's too high', she said.

He took her arm to help her get up. She looked into his eyes. He turned away.

'Thank you.' She laughed.

There was a silence between them. Then Orlando came to the door. He surveyed the scene and Jane moved awkwardly away from David. Orlando wiped his face, the ochre smeared across it.

'Miss me?' said Orlando.

Embarrassment was in the air. David shuffled to get his hat, mumbled goodbye and tore out into the afternoon light, and then he looked back to the caravan school. She stood watching him. An arc of black cockatoos flew by, and then she blushed.

Orlando held Jane, his face ablaze,

'They put stones in me', he said. Aaron climbed into his arms.

'Are you going to be my Dad?' said Aaron.

'Don't know, mate', said Orlando.

Next morning, Jane went to the store and lined up with the women from the camp. Beatrice leant against the corrugated iron shelf. Hubert glared at her.

'Before you can have any sugar you must pay back what you owe.'

'Just little bit tea, little bit flour.' Beatrice whined.

'Fill in your welfare forms and we will get money for you so you can bloody buy food.' Hubert was exasperated and his face grimaced at Jane. She was supposed to sympathise.

'But I not want hand out, just gib job. I workem like all mens. I ride; I muster alla time good work.'

Hubert slapped the counter to stop Beatrice as she reached for a packet of tea.

'You are holdin up the queue. Move away. You are causing trouble. Are you mad? Learn to write your name and we can fill in the papers. Raymond, push her out of the way, will ya?' Raymond looked away.

Beatrice stood her ground and Hubert leapt out of the door and lifted her aside. She raised her fist and he stood in front of her breathing hard. Jane moved next to the old woman, reached onto the counter, and held out a packet of sugar. Hubert grabbed her hand and his face relaxed.

'She has to learn.'

'Beatrice is fifty; she deserves respect and kindness.' Jane stared into the Boss's eyes and he lifted his hand. The sugar was given to Beatrice.

'Put it on my bill.'

'We will.' Edie licked her pencil.

Beatrice accepted the bag and walked away with dignity.

Jane was at the counter and she piled up the tins of fruit and powdered ice cream. Her overflowing string bag of stores made the women around her stare. Orlando, impatient, stood next to her to help carry the supplies.

'When will you ever have enough, Jane?' he whispered.

'Thankyou Edie, could I have another two tins of peaches please?'

'We look so greedy.'

'I never had enough to eat as a child, so now I can afford it I will buy plenty. There will never be an empty cupboard at my place, Okay? And I feed half the starving school children who come to play with Aaron.' She hauled away the huge shopping bag and flung it into the Toyota.

Orlando watched Jane; he looked wary and concerned.

'I love you; don't go all troppo on me. I'm going back to the ceremony'.

'I want more equality in doing housework', she said.

'Not this again. A clean caravan for what? For who?'

He sometimes attempted to cook some exotic concoction using fish and vegetables. It was disgusting but he swallowed it with tea. He demanded that Jane clean his boots. This was too much. Jane felt isolated; the role of wife sat heavily on her. Surely, it was supposed to be better than this. She sensed that it was all a mistake.

'I don't want to be like a 1950s house wife, welcoming my 'husband' home at the end of the day in lipstick and crutchless knickers with a chop on a plate', she said.

'Sounds alright', he said.

'How did the feminist thing happen? I can work a full time job, raise my child, do all the washing, cooking, shopping and still be a brilliant anthropologist conversationalist at night while having raging hot sex'.

'Okay, let's go back to the crutchless knickers part, what colour are they?'

'Just stop. I'm exhausted with feeling this burning rage beneath a pleasant smiling surface. *Keep a happy face,* that's what my mother said'.

'Don't wreck it, Jane. What we have, it's special.'

Orlando strolled up to the men's camp. She watched him walk away and thought he might leave soon. She wouldn't cope. But she was glad that she was near Arnhem Land – it was nicer somehow than her old university life. My God, she needed whisky and the bottle was empty – Orlando had drunk it all. God, she hated him sometimes.

CHAPTER 8

Old Pelican

The hot humid morning lay around them, the heat so languid and unforgiving. The nights were restless and full of dreams. Jane stood at the stove cooking while Old Lucy recounted a dream about Old Pelican that she had the night before.

'For God's sake, don't say his name, he will come. You know he's psychic – whenever I think about him, he appears. He's scary.' She scraped the fat from the pan and laid eggs on a platter. The sound of cockatoos, bullocks and a weird whistling. They looked at each other; Lucy rubbed her head and shook her body in a shudder. There was a faint movement outside the caravan, a soft padding of bare feet. At that moment, Old Pelican stood at the door. His piercing black eyes stared at Old Lucy. A broad grin and his teeth shone, perfect for an old man.

'You tellem me your dream.' Jane looked uncomfortable; he sighed and she laughed. She ushered the old man into the van. His eyes flickered over the breakfast: there was the smell of supermarket bacon and he breathed it in. She served her old grandfather a breakfast of eggs and bacon, and he ate hungrily.

'Year, tellem me now.'

'There's an old man walking, he stares and he swings his woomera in his hand', said Jane.

Old Pelican listened closely as Jane fidgeted. 'Yeeai. Where dat place?'

'Don't know; it was a dream.'

'Might be here eh?'

'Might be; might be Sydney.'

'Dis place. Who comes?'

'Another man has a shovel spear between his toes, pulling it along in the dirt behind him.' Old Pelican leaned forward, eyes searching. Old Lucy put her hand on Jane's arm.

'Who dat one?' Jane shifted nervously.

'Don't know.'

'You tell me dat name, eh?'

She shrugged her shoulders. Jane guessed that he knew exactly who it was but she was afraid to tell. She went on. 'So no one can see that spear. He brings it up and throws it right through the old man.'

'No good. Thank you. I know 'im, might be Wunungah, you know 'im, yeeai', Old Pelican said. He went out the door whistling, he swung his woomera from hand to hand.

Jane looked down to Old Lucy. 'I don't want to be responsible for some bloke being speared just because I saw something in a dream.'

'Not worry.'

'I have to train myself not to even *think* his name, because if I do, every time, he stops me in the middle of the road and commands me to take him somewhere, like the store, and he expects me to pay for anything he wants. It's fair enough but so strange', Jane said.

'Dat one in our head powerful. He killem might be ten men.'

'No.'

Old Lucy, David, and Jane packed up some children onto the back of the Toyota and headed down to the distant river. As they passed the camp, Old Pelican called out to Jane:

'You get big mob fish for me, yeeai?'

'Okay old man, I already gave you some yesterday,' said Jane.

'Later, you bring five fat one now. You better watch out, I singem.'

The elder watched them drive by, David shook his head.

'That old fella, he got magic; gotta watch him, he see everything', said David.

They drove for a few hours across a grey and green landscape. When they arrived at the river, Jane ran into the water and cooled off. She stood waist deep and beckoned to the children. They held back nervously.

'Come in, it's lovely.' The children stood away from the bank silent and staring, reluctant to swim. Robert and Ricky broke big branches from trees and hit the water, splashing and shouting. David spoke to them and they threw rocks and bellowed out in Lanniwah language.

'Must be a ceremony to welcome spirits of the river', said Jane.

It took some minutes before it dawned upon her that there could be big salt-water crocodiles. She realised that the plain stupidity of her decisions as a teacher was overwhelming. They waited and checked the riverbank and surface of the water, then everyone jumped in the river and they all forgot about the crocs – they made too much noise for an attack. The boys caught fish and they cooked them on the fire, they ate damper and drank tea.

David plunged into the water to untangle a lure, his rippling skin breaking through the surface of lily pads. He took her breath away. She pushed away the attraction. It was ridiculous; she must maintain her respect as a head teacher. Any way he was too shy; he seemed to lack courage. She didn't like weak men. Yes men. She liked strength and she had responsibilities that other women couldn't dream of. Many of her uni friends still lived at home with their parents. Still, when David's smiling face emerged from the water with another fish she was relieved that such a kind joyful man shared their remote school and the kids loved him. Aaron jumped in the lagoon on David's shoulders and he wrestled with him amongst lily pads.

As it got dark, they arrived back at Harrison.

'Here old man, we got your fish; we must've been lucky', said Jane. They put a bag of fish to next to Old Pelican's fire.

'Dat country belong us; dat fish belong us, not you', said Old Pelican. He threw the fish on the ashes and turned his back.

CHAPTER 9

David And Missionaries

A month later, Orlando went to town and stayed. He had been asked to go back to his town job. Jane was devastated. She felt the billowing onset of sadness. It had been good and bad but she would miss his laughter and jokes, his warm love.

Jane heard that more missionaries were coming to camp at Harrison; they would stay for a long time in tents and caravans. She hoped for some friends. She searched the road but all she saw was cattle trucks.

There was a crunching sound outside her home, Jane ran out to find a huge bullock casually eating all her garden.

'Get away, damn you! Shoo, shoo!'

Hubert rode up to Jane on his motor bike. She looked at the bare ground where her cabbages had been.

'The cattle are destroying my garden and all the biodiversity – there'll be no native plants left', she said.

Hubert shook his head. 'Now that's a big word for a little lady. And bullshit ... Don't mind my language ... They eat up the rubbish plants, bits of wattle or mulga, no good for anything', he said.

'It's home for wild life', said Jane.

'Who needs that? We'd be better off without King Brown snakes. How would you like a seven-foot king in yer bed, eh? Kill you stone dead. Or maybe you like a long snake eh?' He snickered. Jane ignored him.

'The cattle pollute the water holes', said Jane.

'It's a competitive industry. Australia has to grow. This meat industry is our future. You can't sell Aboriginal culture. Trade is what makes this country great, not spiritual oogie-boogie. I want to feed my kids, give them a good start-up farm back in Queensland, and let them grow rich on fat cattle.' He was so certain. She nodded mechanically, it was no use arguing.

'Why did you let missionaries come?'

'Why did you let Orlando sleep with you?'

'My business.'

'That's right. You could bloody do with a bit of spiritual guidance.'

'So could you.'

'Come up an watch us castrate the yearlings; you'd like that.'

Later, Jane sat on the railing and watched men brand the yearlings. She flinched as Hubert seized the branding iron and plunged it into a flank – the smell of burnt flesh, the howls of a cow's pain. Hubert looked up, saw Jane on the fence, grinned and sniffed the branding iron, then looked annoyed – it was really no place for a woman. David was also watching from the fence, and would think she was out of place. She wondered if he could see her sadness but she couldn't read his face. He was a shy man in front of his mob, his head always tilted down, his hat shading his eyes.

Jane tipped her head towards the billabong; David replied with a slight lift of his head.

'I don't like the stink of the cattle, pushin' them around. I like huntin'. Real clean to get a wild animal, sometimes I get goanna from seeing him near the tractor', he said. It was the most he had spoken to her in months.

'It's good to get fresh meat. You use a spear or gun?' she asked.

'I hunt by myself, I love early time, you know when dark gone. You can track a wallaby or family of kangaroo. I like might be own new Land Cruiser one day or something flash, maybe white or red.' He knew that Jane liked him. She blushed when he looked at her. She was fidgety when they had to work close to each other.

'You smell good, like sweet flower or somethin'. But your nose holes, they too small like white woman', Jane laughed.

'I straight talk and if a woman wantem me, well it be cruel to say no. Woman gotta be right subsection, skin for me. I don't care if people talk about me.'

'I have to care', said Jane.

'You going to that church when they start up. I like Jesus', said David.

'I don't know; depends on how desperate I am'.

There was a Christian revival in the 1970s in the Arnhem Land region. The arrival of Pentecostal missionaries had brought 'the Light'. After their arrival in Lanniwah country, they sang all night, just like a ceremony. 'Yes, Jesus loves you, the Bible tells me so ...' Boys stopped sniffing petrol and there were spiritual visitations, singing, 'Halleluiah' and baptisms. Entire families committed themselves to Christ. Everyone played American cassette tape recordings of testimonies of converts, 'We are saved'.

It was like America, like Southern revival meetings with Lanniwah boys striding around the small settlement all washed for church. 'We gottem new clothes.' Everyone was polished and shining for God. Aaron ran to the meetings with Edie's children, joined in the singing of hymns and ate lots of lollies given out by women with bad haircuts and sensible sandals and socks. Jane was horrified but kept a polite distance. It was painful to refuse some company – her sadness was killing her.

The Reverend welcomed the new missionary families as they got out of their trucks. They had jubilation on their faces; it could have been the Promised Land. They had come to save the heathen world. They set up tents and caravans in a circle, started up a generator with a sound system and loud speakers and aimed it towards the Lanniwah camp. 'Build on the rock and not upon the sand ...' They seemed to be waiting for an Indian attack.

The sound of the church bell rang out from the church tent and the missionaries did the rounds collecting people. They took them in the old truck to church – it was one tent with space on the ground at the back for the Aboriginal brethren.

Evangelism gripped the region. The cow cocky wives, looking forward to a break from station monotony, arrived at the tent mission in droves. Edie and Hubert were there in their best clothes. The tent filled with ecstasy. Reverend Wiltshire was good looking, mesmerizing, sexy. He had a microphone. Jane huddled near the door, ready to escape as the voices rose.

'God is great, long live Jesus.' A hymn sung by Barry Manilow started up from a cassette player. Stamping legs throbbed rhythmically, the tent swayed, the chanting built to frenzy.

166

The minister shouted: 'Are you with me?'

The room replied in a swoon, 'We are with you!'

David watched Jane from down the back.

Jane saw Edie rise from her seat as if hypnotised.

'Take me oh Lord, into your heart. I am ready to be reborn in Christ!'

Wiltshire took her hand and led her to the platform, flapping his hands all around Edie, flapping up and down like he was putting out a fire.

'Out, out devils.' She fell into his arms. Well, who wouldn't?

'When the son of God descends in glory, we shall all gather and he will divide the sheep from the goats.'

Jane wondered where the sheep and goats were. She would have liked a leg of lamb with garlic and lemon. She sensed the metaphor meant the literal and moral exclusion area between black and white, Christian and non-Christian. Some of the women moved forward to hold Edie just as she began to speak in tongues. Jane's eyes met the minister's briefly; he seemed to be saying; 'I know this is ridiculous, but here we are.'

Jane began to sway; she felt a high energy coming. The Reverend smiled, a conspirator, then raised up his muscled arms in a Jesus pose, prayed aloud and the room was hushed as Jane moved in a hypnotic swaying and chanting.

'Jesus is coming. For there shall be great tribulation. Prepare for the end of history.' Jane felt lifted by the pulse and they took her into their grasp. What on earth was she doing? It was confronting; she must be really desperate for friends. Clammy female hands were on her head, some women had BO (all that crimplene), and oh no, they lifted her to heaven, the grey mildewed tent roof.

'Oppose witchcraft! Strike out the rulers of darkness!' shouted Edie.

'Where is he, Mummy? I can't see Jesus', said Aaron. The Reverend's eyes fell on Jane again; the look seemed to convey a message. 'I can read you. I know who you are.'

Edie opened her eyes and looked at Jane; it was look of devotion. Her red curls she tied in a knot on top of her head, a crown of thorns. Any minute stigmata? In a sea of brainwashed homemakers, could she be part of it, or go outside and sit with the sane Lanniwah women under a tree?

It seemed more likely that the devil-worshippers were inside the tent, moaning in group oblivion. Dixie had an intelligent light in her face. She looked at Jane. 'I think you are our enemy.'

'Stop! I can't believe in this shit!' shouted Jane.

Jane felt suddenly naked and cold. She watched the Evangelist women hunch their shoulders, their eyes averted. They fingered their thick wedding rings. David stood up at the back and laughed aloud. It was embarrassing. Jane watched Dixie rise and go to the tea urn, a look of disgust on her face. Jane was not sure if she should leave. It seemed that her evil non-conformist thoughts were being telegraphed out of her head; the tiny congregation could turn on her in disapproval, and they could sense her alien presence. They knew she was an unmarried mother, a fornicator (she wasn't alone there) and an agitator for Aboriginal rights. Maybe they would rip her to pieces, tear her blonde hair out by its black roots, and eat her heart on a Jatz biscuit. They had tea with a cream and jam sponge cake, light as a feather, and David helped the Reverend pack up. Jane went back to her caravan with Aaron, there in her yard were three Brahman bulls, and they had eaten her washing off the rotary clothesline. Aaron got down on his little knees and prayed for them to leave.

Next day, David moved over to stand near to Jane at the school barbecue with the travelling evangelical missionaries. The Reverend was talking about his efforts to raise money towards the ongoing medical supplies for the clinic. Edie leant forward and nodded at him. She was strangely dressed in a cocktail dress of Chinese brocade and high heels, and was speaking with a plum in her mouth.

David whispered, 'You come with me tonight?'

Jane smiled as she handed David a sausage on a plate. The Reverend stared at her sternly, fingering his cross.

'People will talk', said Jane.

'You come.'

David looked down and mumbled. He looked uncomfortable with so many white people looking at him. Over at the teaching assistant's table, the Lanniwah women stared and giggled. Mayda was serving drinks. She passed a glass of cordial to Jane, pursed her lips towards David and smiled.

'One look at you, Miss Jane, and everybody know it all – before it even starts they know you bin lookin' for each other', said Mayda.

'The old ladies sung us, I reckon', said David.

David ate and tried to talk to the Reverend who was grinning over lime cordial. Jane pushed a burnt chop around her plate. She smiled at David.

'What happened to Orlando?' he said.

'He went away months ago. He sometimes works for the university in Darwin, and in Katherine. He commutes, sort of. He's gone, that's all. It's okay, really. He wanted to go.'

David's eyes found Jane's brown eyes. He swam in them. He smiled and moved to touch her leg with his. She felt a surge of nerves and strolled away to get salad of tinned peas, beetroot and pineapple. She wanted to be with David. She no longer cared if white people would condemn her, or the Lanniwah. She no longer worried about her job. She would take on the fight. Who cared? She would get another job, or live in a tin shed. The taboo around a teacher and a traditional man could be broken.

Jane sat at a table. The Reverend followed her and sat opposite. David found a place, laughed, and chatted with the students. 'Any one going to, you know, to evangelical bible reading class tomorrow?'

The Reverend looked up expectantly.

'You goin', Jane?' said David. His eyes betrayed him. Jane thought it was the furthest thing from her mind. She was rolling in the surf, video clip style, wrapped around his body, gasping.

The evening progressed and the missionaries wandered off holding sleepy children. David reached under the table

'Your hand burns', he whispered.

'Stop looking at me.'

His hot eyes followed her, and then he looked down, ashamed..

She whispered, 'Hey, I keep looking behind, trying to see which pretty girl you're lookin' at.' Her fears were all gone – she could do whatever she wanted.

'It's you.'

'I'm ugly. Stop looking. People are watching.'

David held her mouth in his eyes.

'I'm lookin'. You lookin' back. You got brazen eyes; I catch 'em and hook 'em in. Eh, come later and meet me.'

'I've got to go to bed.'

'Can I come?' he whispered.

Then they were on the billabong beach in the dark. He kissed her ear and neck, fingers already in her pants. She breathed hard. 'Jeez, you black men are fast.'

He kissed with a fire that took her breath away. It was an explosion of heat.

'I don't care if anyone sees. Oh shit, it's a missionary lady.'

'She chasing a dog.' David was soft and tender.

'Be quiet', she said.

'You lie under me and pretend you dead. She'll go.'

Jane was trying to get up. 'Oh God, let me up. I'm goin' home. Bad idea', she said.

He smiled and helped her up. He brushed the casuarina needles from her dress.

'Come fishing tomorrow?'

There was a long pause.

'Yeah, I'll come.'

Jane woke in the night. She could hear a Lanniwah song, a love song, calling a man to a woman. Jane wanted to take David's body and lick him and mount him and nibble and eat his flesh, gobbling. Or fill him full of spears like Saint Sebastian. She hated him because he would eventually become unavailable. Culturally different, he might see her with contempt afterwards. Oh, the angst and the lust of it.

The next afternoon after class, Jane leant over a washbasin and wrung out a shirt. She was hot, and tipped fresh water over her breasts to cool down. At that moment, she looked up. David stood by the gate looking. Her tee shirt clung to her nipples. She plucked it free. His eyes burnt, and then he hung his head in the familiar shyness and walked off.

That night, Jane snuck over to David's camp. The fire smouldered. David slept in the open on a mattress. His college satchel hung from a nail in a bough. Billycans were next to bags of flour and suitcases. There was a long shovel nose spear, three-pronged spears and a fine woomera leaning against the branch. The dogs growled at her. It was madness. Her heart pounded as she crept near.

'David, wake up', she whispered.

'What? Jane, you not come here.' He sat up and dragged her over to his bed. David kissed her hungrily, his eyes open and laughing. Jane hugged him and fell into his arms. She was in love with his difference, his gentleness and his sexy smooth skin. He covered them both with a new blanket and held her against his chest. She smelt his pungent masculine scent.

'I have to be quick. Aaron is with Edie's children', she said. His eyes were bright in the darkness and he stroked her legs and laid his curly head against her breast. He tasted her nipples and nuzzled into her. Jane breathed as though her heart would explode, she panted and touched his dark chest, her fingers traced the raised scars. He nodded at her and whispered.

'Now?'

She pulled him urgently to her and he slipped into her wetness; he sighed as he made love to her. Her head arched back in joy, this was a lover who she had longed for and now he was with her.

CHAPTER 10

Sports Carnival

At school the next day Jane gave balls to the girls. They ran outside to play captain ball. The school regional athletics day was coming up, and Jane was on fire with the desire to prove her school was great. They wanted Harrison to win. Ricky was a good runner, faster than any child in the school. Rumours ran through the school: that passionate teacher from Germany was training the Rainer River School. They heard that he was a fierce competitor and had the teams trained to win with mathematical precision. Tunnel ball, captain ball, all were very fast teams. Jane imagined a man in a severe uniform with a whistle and blue staring eyes.

She feared that she would not have the necessary commitment to bring home the Remote School Trophy. All that whistle blowing and repetition – no, she couldn't see it. Then there was the problem of sports uniforms – they had none – and she could see no way to raise the money to buy some. Anyway, where on earth could they be bought? All the children wore grubby worn out-tee shirts and shorts. David was very good at ball sports, and trained the boys every afternoon in forty-degree heat. Jane preferred high jump and sprinting. They marked out an athletics course on prickly earth. The children had no shoes, not one pair between them, even Jane went bare foot.

On the day before the carnival, fifteen chosen children piled onto the back of the Toyota, screaming with happiness. Many had not been to Katherine before and had been practicing their manners for buying ice cream in a real shop. Jane had turned the school into a living drama role-play for the children to practice their 'good English'. They waved goodbye to their mothers and crying sisters and brothers who were left behind.

The trip was dusty and Jane fed the children sandwiches and milk on the five-hour journey. At last, they drove into Katherine sports ground and were ticked off a list by the local school principal.

'I welcome all the remote school teachers and children. We have some dedicated Katherine teachers who are very friendly, they are here to make you all feel at home. There's a barbecue and then mattresses with sheets will be spread out in the hall', he said. Excited children ran around wildly.

The Woolworths supermarket was well packed and air-conditioned. Aboriginal families sat quietly on the cool floor; old men sat cross-legged with empty laps, hoping for a relation to come by and give them lunch. Jane found it unbearable to see old people so thin and unwashed. She watched quietly to see what people were buying. Some white men came out of the grog shop with shopping trolleys laden with cartons of beer, and then she saw two Aboriginal mothers come out with a similar load of beer. Jane looked away; not her business. She wondered where the food was. The skinny children clustered around eating lollies and drinking Coke.

In the school hall, the Lanniwah children had the barbecue provided by smiling town teachers. The children had a shower and went to sleep.

All was calm then in the middle of the night, a noise woke David. He looked outside the hall and woke Jane. 'There drunk men outside, they call for their nephews.'

Jane got dressed and went outside into the blackness with David, standing behind him while he attempted a friendly negotiation.

'You fellas can't come in here – we got little ones sleeping.'

Ricky stepped forward.

'Hello, Uncle, you wantem me?'

The drunken man staggered and reached out for the boy. Jane watched him warily as the uncle embraced the frightened teenager

'You givem me twenty dollar.'

'No gottem money, Uncle. Teacher got 'im.' Ricky was shamefaced.

David began talking softly and asked the uncles to leave.

'You come back tomorrow, see kids runnin. Make you real proud.'

'You come wid me!' The drunkest uncle lurched forward and took Ricky by the arm. David argued, but a punch swung wildly near his head. David ducked and put up his fists, drew in his breath. The air was electric with violence. Jane jumped forward and gently pushed David back.

'Let me talk – he won't dare hit a woman.'

She walked out to meet the two swaying men. They wore dirty tee-shirts, and looked like they always slept rough.

'Sorry, you should go. We teachers here: we look after these kids; not your job, our job! Get!' she said.

The children were huddled behind her, they sucked in terror and the next moment the man's arm shot out, with one huge punch knocked Jane to the ground. She saw stars, hit the ground and felt a thunder of pain shoot through her skull, ears ringing. Children cried and screamed. Mayda held onto a screaming Aaron. The man stood over Jane with his fist clenched, but he looked remorseful and David pushed the man away and shouted at him:

'What you doing? You hit the head teacher! I call the police; you go to gaol!'

The Lanniwah man had no teeth; his face crumpled and he began to cry. His bare chest had many cicatrices raised on the black skin; he must have been a highly initiated man. Jane raised herself up on her elbow and pulled her jaw from side to side. She was dizzy and disoriented.

'My teeth are all loose! Shit, that was hard.' She spat blood onto the ground and held her chin. The children gathered around her and touched her hair, their eyes shining with concern. Her body shook with fear and anger, but her voice was powerful and full of authority. She got up on her feet and wiped the blood from her mouth. She faced the men.

'You shame these kids – they wantem look up to Uncle. You come back tomorrow, makem proud. See them run better than all the white kids', she said. The drunk men swore and turned. They called out for money and walked into the night. Ricky was upset and his head leant on his chest.

'Don't worry, Ricky. You okay with us', David said, as he hugged the youth. Many children were awake, and whispering went on into the night. David held a wet cloth with ice to Jane's face. It was the first time he had touched her in weeks.

The next day was the sports carnival. Mayda marked off the children's names and lined them up. When they entered the grounds, they were shamed that they were the only school without uniforms. The Katherine schools had shiny blue tee-shirts and sparkling white shorts, so the Lanniwah children cringed in embarrassment. David gave them a pep talk.

'It's not the uniform that wins. It's the faster team, and you are all real fast. Go out and show them how you can win.'

They all cheered and entered their races. Ricky lined up with the white Katherine school athletes, who wore new running spikes and knelt for the starter's gun. Ricky just stood in jeans with fists out ready to run. The gun went off and Ricky streaked down the running track, the two hundred metres flew by; he won with ease, the white boys puffing behind him. The Lanniwah children cheered and jumped. After the final, the white boys shook Ricky's hand.

'You are the best runner; you won first place. Good on you.'

The dreaded Rainer School team arrived on a cattle truck and precision-marched out onto the oval in crisp white uniforms, looking like Hitler Youth. The Harrison school team cringed; they looked ragged with sores on their legs. It was a shame job. But Jane had a fighting spirit – she went to every child whispering some magic incantation for power. The tunnel ball competition began. Mayda was captain and she lined up Shirley, Lizzy and the others.

They had fierce concentration and played hard but lost. The final point score reflected the extra points from team games. Amongst the few remote schools, Harrison came second. Jane couldn't believe how important this result was to her. She was elated. She could do this thing, leading a school to victory.

'That team might be cheat: those kids older than dat", said David.

'Leave it alone; the judges know best', said Jane.

'Dey bush champions.'

The children were transported back to Harrison on Hubert's truck. It was school holidays and Jane stayed on in town for work and a few days later she drove the long road back with David at her side.

A silent time at midnight and a long drive back down the highway to the station … Jane drove and David watched the road. The moon was full and cast a pale shine on the ghostly bitumen. She had Aaron tucked up beside her, and David sat with his arm out the window. The closeness was comforting.

Jane whispered. 'Scary at night, you reckon?'

'Yeah, real quiet. Drive slow. Gotta watch out for 'roos and pigs', David said.

'More like bullocks: they just wander on the road.'

Jane drove for hundreds of kilometres, concentrating fiercely to stay awake. They stared for hours. David changed the country music cassettes; they sang along to Slim Dusty. Then a strange powerful mist crept along the bitumen; it had wisps of figures; it was elusive and like a coming fog of mysterious power. They both were silent … a tension filled the vehicle.

In her head, a screen of a long moonlit road. She saw something, but didn't speak. Her hair prickled on her skull, a cold shiver ran down her face and into her torso. She shook her head, there was a vision of something, a terrible thing that was coming, but what? It was in her mind – a picture of a pale weeping man, standing on the road, covered in blood and his face was transformed with terror. He pleaded for them to stop, begged them to stop. He looked like Daniel. *No way.* It was not him. He was at a mining camp. David's leg was close and hot. The man was hurt. In her head, she would get in the back of the truck with him and rip her dress into bandages. She could feel the ripping of cloth between her teeth, the cotton stuck in her teeth. Her hands tensed against the steering wheel, they were white and bony. She would save him. She wondered: *How do you stop arterial bleeding?* Pressure. Yeah. Oh, God. The road went on and on – the eerie tension, the strange light.

Meanwhile David was staring at the road. Later, he said it was funny because there was a bend and there were no bends on that road. In his head, he saw around the bend; it was the only one on the road. He looked at Jane. 'Somethin' there. See 'im?'

Jane's face was pale. 'I know!', she whispered.

'Narr, he gone. Might be somethin' scared, I reckon.'

David laughed in relief. He looked at Jane and his voice trembled. 'Ya know what? I thought dere was …'

'What?'

He could see her fright. 'A man … blood, might be.'

'Bleeding. Oh God! You're sweating. What's wrong? Your face is pale', said Jane.

'You know dat, I wasn't goin' to stop.'

'I would have ...he was bleeding.'

The next morning, at school, Jane told the story to the older girls. They gathered around her desk, big eyes and hushed voices.

'Last night, we saw something on the road.'

'What you see?', said Shirley.

'I saw a bleeding man on the road.'

Lizzy joined in:

'Who dat?'

'I don't know. Maybe Wunungah man', said Jane.

'Shoulda take us. We look after you. You no good widout us', giggled Shirley.

Jane kept up the story to an enthralled audience of kids. 'He was covered in blood, he was hurt very badly. Then he was gone. Disappeared.'

There was quiet. Ricky touched her on the shoulder. 'Dat alright, Missus. You saw a new ghost. We callem *cheeky fellas*. He fresh killed.'

'No worries. See em alla time. But you no go in bush widout us; them wild fellas might steal you.' Shirley smiled and played with Jane's long hair.

Jane piled all Orlando's possessions – notebooks, penknife, prayer flags, hash pipe, Indian dream catchers – into a box and pushed them out the door. Maybe she would set them on fire.

CHAPTER 11

Ceremony

Another day and the sound of the didgeridoo and singing had been going all morning ... Jane lay on her bed and the throbbing sound of ceremony saturated her body. It was mesmerising; the sound called her. It blocked out all other thoughts. It was summoning all the people. It was impossible to work.

With the roar of a motorbike ... there was Daniel again: he couldn't stay away. Daniel stood astride his blue BMW , took off his helmet and ruffled his dusty blond hair. Jane waved to him but she was annoyed.

'You need permission from the Boss if you want to stay a while', said Jane.

'Darlin', I can go where I like, but alright, I'll tell him I'm here.'

'You should ask the head man too,' said Jane.

Daniel walked over to the Boss's house and knocked on their door. Jane watched him laughing with Hubert as they smoked outside on the veranda. She watched their easy masculine conversation; she was aching for friendships. She was tired of being ignored, her advice treated with disregard. As though she knew nothing.

Aaron had created a long road with stones under the washing line and set up toy animals on farms out in the yard. Jane hung out washing on the bent rotary clothesline and saw Daniel playing with Aaron. Eventually Daniel knocked on her caravan door.

'I've been invited to ceremony.'

Daniel picked up Aaron and swung him around then placed him gently on the ground.

'That's a bad idea.'

'Come on, it's started', Daniel swept Aaron up, laughing, onto his shoulders, and carried him towards the Lanniwah camp.

Jane followed behind and waited for someone to ask her to sit down. She saw Old Lucy nodding at her. Jane sat next to Old Lucy, who removed sand and casuarina pods from the blanket and patted it. Jane saw Daniel shake hands with Burnie and Old Pelican. It seemed fine. The young women whispered and snuck looks at Daniel.

It was a special ceremony. Jane hid with Old Lucy for the sacred business and the women cowered under blankets with Aaron and the other small children, but he fidgeted and asked why the older boys had gone with the Lanniwah men.

'It's sacred business, for initiated men only. Circumcised men', said Jane as she looked out for Daniel. Old Lucy pulled off the blanket.

'You got sugar? We makem billy-can tea.'

'Aren't we supposed to hide for hours for this ceremony?'

'We waitem for mens chase us with fire sticks. Good fun dat bit. We got powder milk, Beatrice, you bringem up', Lucy said. Shirley stretched out her legs by the fire and massaged them with Brylcreem.

'Makem shiny', she said. Suddenly, there was a very loud noise. Jane's head reeled from the explosion and Aaron buried his head in her lap.

'What was that? A gunshot? So loud?'

Jane saw a terrifying fire sculpture like a burning Satan twenty feet tall with horns, hideous and frightening. She wondered if she had seen the devil. She looked over at the figure, not Satan after all; it seemed to be a construction from pandanus palm leaves and sticks. Still it was strangely eerie. From the distance came singing, throbbing didgeridoos, clattering of boomerangs, rhythmic pulling towards the sound ... Jane sat transfixed while Old Lucy patted her hand. Jane stood up, searching for signs in the distance.

'You go down dere they killem you – dat man's business.'

'Okay, I will stay here', said Jane.

'You got instant coffee? I likem dat Pablo coffee ... Dat nephew, he lovem you. Wantem.'

'Who?' said Jane?

'You know 'im, David.' She whispered and pointed her lips towards his camp. The old lady pressed Jane's hand and giggled.

'You sit here. I teachem you 'bout dis dance', Lucy said. She painted Jane's face, red ochre with dots for water. A water cleansing ceremony – they would clean the spirits from a dead woman's house.

Jane watched the women and Old Lucy pulled her up to dance with them, she followed the rhythm and swung her hips and lifted her feet in the dust, her elbows pushed out at the sides. The women moved their hands with a piece of stick held between them. They swung from side to side in a pulsating exciting dance that went on and on in a mesmerising rhythm. Jane saw Daniel watching the young women. Those swaying bottoms.

The ceremony went on for hours. The men and boys' steps were more spectacular – devil-devils came alive with bulging eyes. They conjured ghost skeletons that frightened the children.

Aaron jumped up and began dancing with the little boys. Jane saw David in the middle, and watched him dance with Aaron. David had painted himself up with white ochre; he wore a grass headdress and carried a ceremonial stick. They were re-enacting the sea-crossing journey of the Dreaming sister and brother from another place. These were some of the great creation ancestral beings.

Jane realised that something was wrong: Daniel was dancing with high stupid kicks and mocking the dancers with his flamboyant gyrating hips. Jane was mortified. The girls watched him and hid their faces in laughter. He danced up in front of Mayda and wiggled his hips, his eyes on her lithe body. She sat down with the women and hid her face in a blanket. Jane squirmed knowing that Mayda was a promised wife to Old Pelican, and he was watching, staring at this Wunungah interloper.

Old Pelican stopped singing and stood up. 'This Wunungah cheeky fella. He show no respect.' Daniel danced like a wild white man. He was *a funny bloke,* he mocked and cavorted, he moonwalked backwards across the sand. The old men watched and muttered. The Lanniwah children squealed and laughed, hands over mouths. They didn't want anyone seeing them, didn't want to be told off, but they were gripped by the sense of danger in the dance. White ochre streamed with perspiration down Daniel's face, knees lifted too high.

Daniel made a mockery of this solemn occasion, Old Burnie watched with an angry face. He was also *bilka*, a clever man, capable of curing illness or other skills, like flying across the night sky on feathers of fire. His mysterious powers were not to be ignored. You could die so easily. The old man beckoned to Jane, she bent down to listen.

'Daughter, you tell 'im go back to his place, leave Lanniwah place', Burnie said.

Jane didn't know what to do. She nodded but stood still. People were looking.

Old Pelican commanded the music to stop. There was tension in the air as he walked in front of Daniel. Old Lucy walked a few steps behind him, she carried a big waddy stick.

'You go. We not wantem you here!' he said.

'It's a free country', said Daniel.

Everyone stared. Jane cringed in embarrassment. David stepped in front of Daniel. He took his arm.

'Come on, fella. Let's go.'

'Narr, I'm an Australian and this is Australia. I can go where ever I want – no Abo can tell me to get off my own country.'

The air crackled with tension. Jane watched, hoping Daniel would just leave and not come back, but instead he picked up one of Old Pelican's spears. She gasped. This was very bad. He held the spear out in front of the old man. The Lanniwah were quiet. Jane stood up, she had to say something.

'Dan, put it down! Don't be so stupid.'

'You go. Wunungah not wanted here!' said Old Pelican.

'Stop dat fella, daught. You stop 'im!' Old Lucy yelled.

Daniel took the spear and it began to bend in his hands; no, this couldn't be happening, it was a bad movie. He broke it over his knee in front of the old man. The carved wood splintered. Jane was unable to speak; she hid her face. Would the headman kill him right now? Daniel threw it at Old Pelican's feet. Jane clutched her face: was Dan suicidal? Did he understand what *a tribal challenge* was? David shook his head and waited.

The old man laughed and turned to look at his tribal brothers. They were hanging their heads. Old Lucy stood up, she shook her waddy at Daniel. She was dangerous and she pushed Daniel away down the path towards Jane's caravan. People yelled behind them. The old lady belted him with her waddy.

'Get out of it! I get it, I'm going!' said Daniel. He skipped out of Old Lucy's reach and ran down the track.

'You get, we no wantem you here! We not want cheeky whiteman on our country, we proud people. We killem! No more have Wunungah cheeky for us mob!', Old Lucy yelled. Jane followed them.

'You idiot, Dan. Go away! Don't come back!' shouted Jane.

Daniel rode away on his motorbike in a dust cloud. Jane breathed easier and went back to apologise to the elders. She sensed something vast and sad, a thing that hovered.

'Sorry for that man. He won't be back.' Jane was ashamed.

The finale of the ceremony came in the late afternoon when the fifty painted people danced down the path to the billabong, and everyone danced into the water. Coloured water trickled from Jane's face; Dan's presence was her fault.

The rain came in the night. In the early morning, Shirley and Ricky stood at the school caravan door, soaked, with scabies sores, skinny and hungry, all grins and white teeth. Jane felt amazed that she was teaching in this remote place where no one had a waterproof house, yet the children were all affection and laughter, then quiet as can be when the lesson began, with respect for teachers that was wonderful. There was no sign of David or the older boys until midday. School began without them and Jane took over all the classes.

David came back from the ceremony one evening a few days later, his eyes shining and hair tangled. Aaron sat on his lap and Jane felt her self growing in love towards this remarkable man.

CHAPTER 12

Gossip

Gossip was always possible, especially with the new missionary neighbours. It had the capacity to destroy people. Jane was away overnight at a nearby community meeting at Rainer River and Orlando arrived from Katherine to run the school. On her return, he told her about an incident. He had played guitar all day to the children and they made up songs; they all had academic free time. Late that night, the stars were bright. There was knock on the aluminium door of the caravan. Orlando was reading in bed.

'Who's that? Okay, I'm coming' said Orlando.

He opened the caravan door and there was a young woman from the camp. He said he didn't know her name. She stood there wrapped in a blanket, shining black eyes and a wide luscious smile. She looked up at him coyly then dropped the blanket. Her skin was the colour of cream and caramel, her big nipples stood up and invited. Skin soft and smooth. Beckoning. It was a moment from Xavier Herbert and a hungry man's dream. She was Australia's history and love all together. Lubra. *She of the Never Never.*

'I said: what are you doing? Cover yourself up for God's sake! He had turned his head away, and asked her to put the blanket back on.' The girl smiled with long dark eye lashes, her body shimmering. Small upright golden breasts, glossy dark skin, a small mound of Venus with a fluffy bush of black hair. *Yes, I will tell it all, the details, yes.* She let him look, for a long while, and then she giggled, coyly wrapped herself up and strolled back to her camp. 'I swear it's true.' Jane listened with fascination.

'I don't know why you are telling me this.'

Orlando said: 'I lay hot on the bed, I was swimming in lust. I always have a battle with the devil living in my penis. I tossed in sweat, gnawed my fingernails, and I slammed my fist into the pillow. I rooted the bed. I knew at that moment that I could do this, have self-control, as other men did. Then I masturbated and lay panting, I was miserably aware that I am a weak man.'

Jane breathed out: okay.

'Did you know her name?'

'No, never seen her before.' She saw that he was lying.

However, Jane heard later that someone saw him having her in the river, by moonlit pandanus, watched by crocodiles, and again in the Toyota truck, their bodies clinging together in lust under the yellow moon with all the eyes watching from far away. Jane fumed. She felt the jealousy eat her up. She didn't want to believe it. It was evil, dirty, shitty gossip. She shut her ears to Gertie; she was just stirring trouble. She hated the way the Lanniwah enjoyed gossip; the women lived for it. It was like going back to her childhood, nasty horrible things said that broke up families, tore apart lovers – sent her father away. Jane put up her chin and felt ferocious.

'Don't spread that stuff around, Gertie. You know nothing. Mind your own business! How do you know it wasn't your husband Ray? Yeah, how about that?'

Gossip went around like lightning. Orlando hung his head and described the scene of the dropped blanket again to Hubert as he was burning off, flicking his cigarettes into the brown grass. Jane chewed her nails in silence beside him.

'Getting a bit of the velvet are ya, mate? Mix it with the gins, you'll get shot. Yella kids runnin' round town.'

'No, I didn't. I can't help looking, they sing me. She made some sort of magic. Those old men put some stones into me in initiation. I can't help it; it's a powerful magic. The young women can pull you in. It's like a potion you can't resist. You don't believe me', Orlando said. Jane shoved him and looked at Hubert.

'He's weak as piss. Sung you! This blackfella country will drive you insane', Hubert said and laughed.

'Some things; they showed me stuff, like I can't talk about it', said Orlando.

'Forget it. You're going troppo. Gotta be on guard. Gotta watch those young ones', said Hubert.

'Yeah, I know.'

'Now look, I bring Edie presents home from my trips to the East, silks and stuff. Arr, the women like that kind of thing. I bought her a lovely bit with red embroidery of the phoenix, and gold tassels from a little back street in Chinatown. Lovely … Mate, you take care of Jane. She's real good with those kids. Don't let her burn out. Hey mate, many a good man has been destroyed by the temptation up here'. Hubert got on his motorbike and roared away.

At the caravan, Orlando clenched his fist for the first time. Jane thought he was going to hit her; she was shocked by his impulse for violence, could see his teeth gritted, imagined him crushing her nose. He glared, the tension was terrible, she didn't flinch, and she looked back and swallowed hard.

'You are a traitorous liar too', he said.

'Oh is that it? Try harder', she said.

He continued with tears dribbling, 'Can't you see what you've done? Having a quiet fling in Katherine is one thing. I heard you are having an affair with David!'

'You had sex with Aboriginal girls you picked up in the pub. You could have dozens of half caste kids running around the town', she said. She ignored his particular accusation. It seemed safer.

'Everything we do in this community is transparent. You've destroyed all our work here; no-one will respect us now with this gossip. I look like a fool and you look like a slut', he said. She raised her hand. He grabbed it and twisted as Jane cringed and fell against the table. She bruised her arm; it stung. He crashed outside in a fury, slammed the wire door off its hinges. He cried in rage as he picked up a wooden chair and smashed it again and again against the ground. It hung in bits from his grip. Aaron woke up and stood at the door in his pyjamas. He had wet his pants.

The missionary neighbours came out of their caravans, staring open-mouthed. It was better than the movies.

Jane stormed out the door, ran to the wire fence and bellowed. 'What do you think you're looking at? Go on piss off, you mindless missionaries! You wouldn't have the guts to have a fight. You're weak indoctrinated whiteys with no passion, just heads full of inane Bible quotations. Praise the Lord!'

Orlando laughed, and called out to Jane.

'You tell 'em, Jane'. She swerved and then stepped up to the fence. Dixie, the missionary mother, was quivering. She smoothed her apron.

'When you arrived here, I asked you why you had come to this place. All you could come up with was that God had told you to come. Like you had some individual chat line to God, like you were the chosen ones. You didn't come to escape your boring Epping Baptist Church upbringings or your sad sexless empty marriage. You came because God told you to come and save the natives! What bullshit!'

Dixie's face was a mask of horror. She sat down on a plastic chair. Jane slammed her door. An hour later, Dixie knocked. She was holding a dish of food with a potholder.

CHAPTER 13

Disaster

After putting Aaron to sleep, Jane went out to lie under the dark blue sky. The Milky Way was a pathway for a Dreamtime serpent, its black undulating form slithering above. White pulsating stars, tiny sparkling lights going on and on: the vastness was exquisite, so vast and never ending.

The next morning, she walked into the schoolroom where the Lanniwah girls held out their hands to her to press. They nodded to each other. Jane was oblivious to the atmosphere of impending doom that hung around her like a lame dog. David was occasionally absent from school. If he did come, he was quiet and withdrawn.

It was time for the monthly teachers' meeting; Orlando was present to help with school planning, and he made himself at home on a swag near the school. David sat with his head down on a little school chair.

'David, can you take the minutes?' said Jane.

'Yeeai, I got a pen. You tell me what to write.'

'Yep, she's the head teacher. You do what she says: she's the boss', said Orlando.

'We have to keep up with lesson plans, and write up the day book', said Jane.

'Very important, someone might want to read them in hell.'

'I'm just trying to keep the records properly. Can we keep to the agenda?' Jane said.

'Yes, let's do that. Can you spell agenda, David?'

'Do you want to say something, Orlly?'

'Why don't you just tell him what to do? This meeting stuff is just going through the motions. You'll make all the decisions any way', said Orlando. He picked up his guitar and strummed. David leant on his knees; his head couldn't get any lower.

'I don't. Let's discuss student behaviour, item two', said Jane.

'Let's not. I'm going for a swim. David, you want to come for a swim? Oh, I forgot, you usually swim with Miss.' He stood up whistling, put his guitar over his shoulder and walked out. The schoolroom was very quiet.

Orlando was a person for truth. When it suited him. Jane thought he had no rights to say anything about her life. He seemed to want to confront David and it would be an awkward moment between the men. However, it would be liberating, the truth: everyone liked the truth; it would feel fantastic. They all walked down by the billabong, Orlando pulled aside a bush for David to pass. He picked up some gum leaves, rubbed them in his hands and inhaled.

'You're sleeping with my woman', said Orlando.

'Narr', said David.

'I'm not your woman! You left me. Stop this please', said Jane.

'Everyone says you are. Please don't tell a lie.'

'It's none of your business, Orlly!'

'Not sleeping. Just, you know, one time', said David. Orlando stared at the top of David's head.

'Please, look at me.'

Jane chewed her fingers. David lowered his chin to his chest. Orlando grabbed David's arm, Jane pushed Orlando's hand away. 'Don't.'

'Okay, don't look at me, but I feel like hitting you.'

'You can try that', said David as he looked into his rival's eyes. The two men stood staring at each other. David put his head down again.

Orlando spoke with a trembling voice: 'I helped you. I showed you how to teach maths. I thought we were friends. You betrayed me, white-anted me.'

David hung his head again.

'Great choice of words.'

'I'm sorry, you like my brother. I did the wrong thing. She's not happy', David said.

'Happy, what the hell does that mean? Happy – no one's happy. I think about killing myself every day', Orlando said.

'She alone woman, not mine', said David.

'Maybe she likes your skin – it's black, and mine's too pale.'

David was alert; he looked afraid of the direction of the conversation.

'You've wrecked my relationship. What about the kids we teach?'

'Look who's talking. You screw around, you left us!'

David moved away into the bush.

Orlando yelled; 'Yeah, run away! That's easy for you – no responsibility, just run and keep running! Go walkabout!'

Jane felt a rush of anxiety; her head pulsed. She looked at Orlando and he was crying in humiliation. It was an act of stupid jealousy. She once had wanted Orlando at the school: he was a fantastic creative teacher, but that was over; they managed without him. Why had he come back? Just another egotistical whitefella who thought he knew it all. He walked calmly up to her.

'I'm breaking up with you', he said.

'I thought we gave up on each other a while ago.'

'I'm living with a wonderful woman that I met at the conference.'

She picked up a rock and threw it for old times' sake. It spun in the air and smashed against the road. He had her left months ago; it was simply his shell of a body that stood there. She felt an enormous relief.

Orlando walked up towards the camp; he would sit with the men. She knew what it was like to be alone, sad with her child. She could contemplate her future. Jane sat on her front step and saw that the vast bright blue sky was half the world. It was never ending.

PART THREE

HONEY COLLECTING SEASON, FLYING FOXES ARE FAT – 1976

Stringy bark flowers are sweet smelling, and Lanniwah children are eating sugar bag wild honey. Fresh water swamps are drying out and Jane watches the burning off of grasses.

CHAPTER 1

No Shoes

Jane was waiting for a visit from Brian and Rosie. The letter had said they would arrive soon. Weeks passed and Sunday afternoon at the station stretched out in a sweaty gloom. Jane saw Lanniwah children lined up outside the store to get lollies. Edie's children already had theirs. Elisha licked her lollypop luxuriously at the Lanniwah. David strolled up and bought sweets to share amongst the children. He smiled at Jane.

Jane knew this scene, the segregation. When Aboriginal people went to the movies in Taree, they had to sit in the front where a dirty rope separated the sections. She had sat up front with her Koori cousins just to thumb her nose at the other part of her family who thought they were white. Most of her friends were black, didn't wear shoes; she played with them on the river and built rafts, fished for flathead and made little fires to cook on.

Jane tried to remember if the racism was obvious. Well no, not really. The white women would ridicule her teenage purple-dyed hair or long second-hand dresses. Samuel was horrified that his daughter wore recycled clothes; that meant real poverty. Although, he didn't offer Jane or her siblings any money and kept putting all his earnings down on horse races or buying rounds for his mates at the pub.

Childhood was made of colourful tableaus in the back yard while her dad cut off the chickens' heads and the family plucked them, flies covering their feathered blood-speckled hands. Her mother called it 'making money for Christmas'. Jane recalled that they ate endless meals of tripe and onions. Jane would cross the paddock and skirt around the cows to avoid the embarrassment of going to the local shop to ask for a half pound of broken Arnotts biscuits.

The train had roared past; someone chucked a rock at her and yelled:

'Black slut.' She'd picked it up and hurled it back.

Then, the time her father had lost his job, 'laid off', there were gloomy no-meat nights, just a fried egg on bread. Jane's English grandmother said, 'Sam is a wonderful man, but not a good provider'. Her mother had developed malnutrition with sunken dark eyes from going without so the four children could eat. Fear had lurked in the kitchen and arguments poured out of their parents' bedroom.

Jane sometimes wished all of them would vanish from her consciousness – the whole lot of them, her dad, sister and her brothers – just evaporate; her brain cleansed, instead of them hanging around cluttering her present existence. If the memories could just *give her a break.*

In Harrison, it was moving towards the Dry; a northeast wind blew, mud had changed into bogs and cracked earth, people collected sugar bag honey and dust began to billow along the road and still no sign of her historian friends. She searched the road for dust, for their rattling car and companionship, but they didn't materialise.

There was a week of dreams and supernatural events and plain, sad signals that something was brewing. Jane had a dream: a neon sign – 'The Crocodile Hotel'. David walked into the back bar (a man walked into a bar). A young Lanniwah girl, lithe and golden, a yella fella, danced a slow dance in front of a jukebox. Elvis sang, 'Don't step on my blue suede shoes'. David danced near the girl, grinning. He had asked around and found out that she was the right moiety for him, 'right way' potential wife. He motioned his head and she fluttered her eyelashes, flashed her eyes, and was keen. She pinned frangipani flowers over her ears and chattered to her friends. Jane wandered if she herself was in love with the coquette. Anything was possible in a dream. The girl swayed her hips in her faded jeans. David followed her out into the night. Jane woke. It was so erotic.

The next day, Jane felt embarrassed by her dream. It was as though David knew about it, knew her lust. He sensed her prickly mood.

They sat outside after lunch with Margie. David talked, about more dreams and Dreaming, like the 'proper way' for people to care for land; the 'right skin' had to look after the people's land.

'This place for girl frill-neck lizard sitdown place', Margie said.

'Do you ever get sick of those stories? Having to think about everywhere you put your foot?'

'Dis true for dis place. No other thing true like dis.' Margie frowned and David spoke:

'Yeeai. We look after country. One mob light fires for other mob with kerosene fire sticks, but in old story, one old man, *Nagaran*, he burn grasses, little fire spread ceremony all about country. Old Pelican. His mother, she smell smoke dat day. She see smoke coming, and something strange, it smell like meat, man meat, Wunungah bin killem all other mob in Arnhem Land.'

Jane looked to the horizon, a flicker of yellow flame, walking fire. They watched a dry season fire approach, the air smelling of eucalypt smoke. Whistling kites and chicken hawks dived on the hot winds, feasted on lizards. Jane saw it coming – oh great, a fire to burn down her caravan.

David took off his hat and ruffled his black hair. She watched. He looked into her face and then away. He was very uncomfortable. Jane reached out her hand to touch his, he let her stroke his warm skin. It tingled, flames shot through to her vagina. She hated herself. Couldn't she just be there? Wasn't it enough to have this spiritual experience? To feel all calm inside, why couldn't she just meditate and practice desire-controlling yoga like other people? Downward dog or lifting tiger or something. Why did she have to change it all? Jane had let loose some kind of lustful monster; she fantasised and became obsessed. David looked down at her hand on his skin, he leant his curly head against it, and warmth pulsated between them. He knew about her: he sensed everything.

David was on her mind all day, all night. She wrote his name in the sand and made up scenarios involving hot rapid sex up against walls. She stayed back at school and stared at his classroom in the hope he would also stay back. He didn't. She lounged outside the store hoping he would come in to buy food. Jane was in the grip of intense burning love – she couldn't get David out of her head. Someone must have sung her, made her a victim. She left scribbled letters at his house and his Lanniwah brothers smiled, polite as always. 'David, I need to see you, I am going mad. I want you. Meet me.'

Eventually, Jane got up in the middle of the night while Aaron slept. She couldn't sleep. She knew she was being a *bad mother*. She wrapped herself in a sarong and, naked underneath, she walked to David's home. Insane. She stopped half way, such a stupid thing to do; she would turn back. It was crazy. She was imagining the same story that happened to Orlando: she would be the girl in a blanket. Excitement pulsed; she was nervous but inflamed. She wanted to experience this, to feel him against her, the fire of it.

Dogs howled. She scratched at his window and her eyes darted, her chest throbbed, the fly screen was broken, his hand slid out and grabbed her wrist.

'What you doin', bub?'

'I want you. I can't stand it.' David opened the window and lifted her inside. His bed had been moved inside on a concrete floor, no sheets, just a blanket. He pushed a dog from the bed.

'Come here, you okay now. I love you', he said. She whimpered, he stroked her and she knew it would be hard for him to make love to a crying woman.

She walked home into the humid breeze. She took the red path that wove through the Lanniwah camp. Some twenty people lay asleep on blankets by smouldering fires. She tiptoed through the camp, a short cut, but a stick cracked and two men, now awake, called out:

'Wey, ghost. Who dere?'

Jane panicked: how to explain her presence in the camp? Like a spirit running through the pandanus. The men grabbed spears and womerahs; she heard them running after her. They shouted, 'Ghost, stop!'

Her heart was beating fast and her breath sped up. Luckily, she had been a school champion sprinter; she jumped logs and ran to her home. A shovel spear swished past her head. It landed with a sickening thud next to her leg. It would have sliced her open. She stood still, what to do? Move slowly – no run, escape. Jane dropped to the ground, she slithered along the dirt – what on earth was she doing? She made it to her door and shut it carefully after her. She leant against it panting. How could she have been so stupid? She could have been killed. Chest heaving, she gasped for air. Her son stood in the room.

'Where were you, Mummy? I was scared.'

'Sorry, darling. I wasn't far. I'm here now.'

Jane crept into bed beside Aaron, his little form trembled. She lay awake all night, electric with love and fear. She thought about her need for security and fear of abandonment. Maybe this kind warm deep Lanniwah man would be someone to love forever.

The next day, Jane learnt about David's new promised wife. The older girls at school loved Jane, and spoke in hushed tones about David.

'He got new one, Miss Jane. We cry for you. She young pretty one from Gove', said Mayda. Jane patted the girls on their shoulders and smiled.

'It's okay, don't worry. I don't think about that stuff. He's my friend, my teaching assistant, that's all.'

She couldn't tell the truth and when David left the school for the day, she ran on and on, through the back camps, mad with jealousy. She was afraid of the smell of dust, dog shit, cooking meat. Some wild animal, some kind of reptile with speckles, had been beaten with sticks, and now lay on the coals, alive, skin curling, its legs stuck up in the air with crinkled claws. She ran in the heat from her jealous anger. Vicious thoughts burst open the door to David's ragged house. She would discover him with this new girl, like two backed beasts, her red cotton shift bunched up at the waist, his buttocks pushing into her. The girl's squealing pleasure. She could see herself opening a tub of Dulux paint, yes, yellow and viscous, pouring it over them or ripping the girl to pieces.

The sound of distant clap-sticks and cicadas, a child crying. Now, Jane hated David, hated his easy way with women, and hated how easily she had said yes. She wanted to have him to herself. They could run away together; go to Darwin. She could get a good job; he could too. They could live in a nice, new, clean white town house in Casuarina. They'd go to the Parap market on Saturday, drink mango smoothies and buy tropical flowers. There were plenty of mixed couples there – or were there? They could be free of prying eyes and Christian condemnation. How dare people judge her? Orlando was promiscuous; no one accused him of being immoral. It was a double standard, always!

The air was full of smoke, someone was burning off the dry grass, and fires trickled between the houses. Flies stuck to her face and eyes. This land had become a dirty, smelly place full of rubbish. She didn't want to be there anymore. She hated everyone and everything about the place. She was going crazy. She fell on her bed and cried with shivering convulsive sobs.

The fan whirred; she heard a distant didgeridoo playing. An old man had been singing since dawn. It was cooler. Jane felt better: everything was going to be good: she would get over this silly infatuation and she would never go near David again.

The dreams of little lizards, crocodiles, sea turtles and caramel milk shakes tormented Jane. She crawled under the teacher's desk in the classroom and slept.

A spasm of sadness as Jane hung out the washing. Her arms ached from work, and red dust stained the clothes. Grief took her away, left her sobbing, for whom? David? Orlando? Her dad? For lost loves? Her body shook; she knew this feeling, the helplessness in the hands of some thief, the savage shaking. She put down the wash basket: Aaron must not see her like this. The Boss mustn't know – he would say she was losing it.

A wild bullock stood in front of Jane, fiery eyed, nostrils flared, pawing the dust. She moved slowly, backing away; she had taken the wrong turn on the track; fear stuck to her sweaty skin. 'Climb a tree.' She hid until the bullock wandered off. Green ants stunk in her hair, ashamed: everyone knew about the affair. A dark shadow of doom approached. She could see it rolling across the plain, grey and ominous and full of destruction of her job, home, family. She tried to psycho-analyse herself. What was it? It was a blur. Being all alone in this country was dangerous. For Lanniwah, a lone person might be someone who had transgressed, outcast, to be avoided.

She tidied up her room and then unpacked a small worn handcrafted cedar box with metal corners that she had brought with her.

It had belonged to her father, long ago. Aaron asked about the contents. There were old Box Brownie photos of his war time in Borneo; Sam standing next to his mates, slouch hats on, leaning on shovels; Japanese prisoners of war also leaning in the sun with well-fed smiling faces. One picture was of a radiant-eyed young Indonesian girl, in her best sarong, love shining out to Jane's father, written underneath, 'Don't ask'. Old bullets from the war, a fishing sinker and big Japanese teeth. He had dug gold teeth from dead men and they rattled in the bottom of the box.

She held up the large metal fishing sinker – yes, that was the one, from the rock ledge, the night he had drowned. She took it from Aaron's hand.

'Not that, darling. You can't play with this: its Mummy's special treasure. It was my dad's.'

She placed the silver coloured sinker back, heavy with memories. Her dad had sat on her bed with her (to her amazement) and sobbed uncontrollably. Shuddering tears, nose running, gasping tears of sadness, his heart somehow broken. He gave Jane this precious box of treasure – teeth, for heaven's sake, to a fourteen-year-old girl. 'Keep this safe sweetie, my princess. I don't know what is going to happen to me', he said, as if it was the crown jewels. Yes, that had been when the snowy owl had come, sitting every night over the back door, with the broken fly screen flapping in their poverty.

Brian and Rosie arrived to visit Old Pelican and Jane. Oh joy, oh joy! They parked their Suzuki under a tree. Brian cooked dinner for Jane and sat with Aaron in his knee. Rosie took him away and put him to bed. Jane poured cask wine into plastic cups and they sat by the campfire outside the caravan. Jane broke down and told them she had an affair with David. They nodded and toasted her courage or madness and the isolation and the beauty of Lanniwah country. Living in the Territory could drive you wild or drive you troppo, like Xavier Herbert addicts, with between-culture obsessions and loneliness.

'It was born in me. I'm not consciously making these wild decisions; maybe I'm pre-programmed to be a bad seed, and can't help being attracted to men like this. It's positively Freudian. I loved my tall dark dad. David looks a bit like him – well, so did Orlando for that matter. What hope do I have?'

Brain and Rosie listened as they always did to these deprived and isolated folk. Then Brian took some papers from his brief case, he laid them on the table and began to read.

'You wanted to know about this place, its history, we found it: Report of a Special Board created by the Federal Ministry in 1930, to inquire into the killing of Aborigines by police parties and East Africa Cold Storage Company cattlemen.'

'You found it.'

'It's not pleasant, but it helps us find the truth.'

'Old Lucy and Pelican are witnesses.'

'Listen: Mr R M Whiley, police inspector of South Australia, decided that shootings had been justified, necessary in self defence.'

Rosie spoke up: 'Police investigating police. 'This is what they wrote: Police had been been attacked by blacks with boomerangs, spears, nulla nullas and tomahawks. There was not a scintilla of evidence that the shootings had been in the nature of a reprisal or punitive expedition. Why had thirty Aboriginal women at Harrison been permitted to run free if a massacre had been intended?'

'They were run down by men on horses who smashed their heads in with pieces of wood. The report is all lies.' Jane sighed.

'It was not believable that the constable would have dismounted and gone amongst the blacks, if a massacre was intended. The blacks were a willing work party in the chopping of firewood. They expected payment in tobacco. Further, the police on evidence could have shot a hundred blacks with ease had they so wished.'

'Then there would have been no Lanniwah left to to talk.'

'Okay, we are getting to the end here: the Board found that no provocation had been given to the Aborigines which could account for their attacks on whitemen. The tribe had advanced while on a maurauding expedition threatening to wipe out settlers and working boys.'

'Old Pelican said they were hungry and hoped for some flour.'

Rosie paced the floor and took hold of the paper.

'We found this report at the Museum of South Australia. It is damning evidence. We will include it verbatim in our writing.'

'You can show David and Old Pelican. The metal ring in the tree is a memorial.' Jane sighed.

Brian held Jane in an affectionate hug:

'Not all white men are monsters. Rosie and I are working to uncover this history, despite the holdups, we will get it published.' They waved goodbye and drove off.

The following days were so slow. Jane didn't go near David after school hours. She could hear people gossiping about David and teacher; it was like a chattering noise that beat in her brain.

CHAPTER 2

Another Love Affair

Edie stared across the road in a floating bad mood as she brought Jane the mail; there was an old newspaper with headlines "Capture of Gang of Four: Cultural revolution ends", Jane shrugged: it didn't relate to anything in her universe. Edie held out another item, she pushed it towards Jane as though it was a turd. It was opened. The letter from the Northern Territory Education Department said it all: 'Inspector's report of misconduct: Failure to comply with Department regulations; possible recall or Dismissal. Another inspection is proposed.' Someone had told the Department. Jane was obviously a fallen woman – not a vanguard for the sexual revolution and political activism, but immoral, and therefore a bad teacher and terrible mother. Sex had been her downfall, and it was obvious that she was some kind of social deviant. She didn't fit into respectable society; she was 'a bad moral influence'.

She dragged herself to school but the older children like Ricky and Mayda were doing most of the teaching while she wallowed at her desk.

Later in her caravan, Aaron sat on the bed.

'Don't be sad, Mummy.' He patted her head.

'Don't cry; it will make your face red. I will make you happy.' He used his kindest voice. 'Would you like me to make a cup of tea? I can make Vegemite biscuits too.'

'Make some powdered milk first', she said.

He ran to the kitchen to make Mummy better. He was the man of the house again.

Edie walked into the caravan, sat down and, with no polite waiting, sat back on a chair and lit a cigarette.

'You pushed that Orlando away', she said.

Jane was astounded.

'What are you talking about? He left months ago. We had a fight like you and Hubert', said Jane.

Edie chewed her plaits.

'He was nice, he could sing, and play guitar. I miss that, and you couldn't keep him', Edie said.

Jane turned her back and put on the kettle, went through the motions of making tea. 'You have no right to talk about my private life', said Jane.

'Why not, there's not much else to talk about out here. He seemed to be in love with you. What did you do to wreck it?' said Edie.

Jane planted the cups of tea on the table. Edie sipped.

'He had someone else, and Hubert didn't help, as you know. Or have you forgotten? He threatened to kill my teaching assistant,' said Jane.

'Just a bit of fun – you southerners can't take a joke.'

'No, guess not.'

'You're not married are you? Never have been? So Aaron is a bastard?'

'That's right, but you knew that', said Jane. The air was like syrup.

'You were too smart for him or you thought so.'

'Enough, Edie...' Jane replied. Anger rose up in her chest.

'But you have your eyes on a blackfella don't you? Now they're both gone', Edie continued, as Jane snatched the tea from Edie's hand and threw it down the sink.

'Please excuse me, but why don't you rack off?' Jane walked to the screen door and opened it. Edie giggled and stood up.

'I know when I'm not wanted', Edie said.

'Get out! I don't need your patronising advice', said Jane as Edie tossed her hair and walked down the steps.

'People won't like it: moral danger for kids, sex with a darkie, not good', said Edie.

'Why, you tried one?'

Edie's voice was tight and sinister. She was a dog sniffing a scared rabbit.

'Bye, thanks for the tea. Next time make sure the water boils', said Edie.

Jane leant out of the window as Edie stepped over Aaron's toy cars.

'He's a man, not a darkie, he's Lanniwah. And anyway, I'm Aboriginal as well. I'm a Darug woman from Sydney!' Jane shouted.

Edie stopped. Her shape was a silhouette, the ringlets swung back and forth. Jane watched her back in the midday sun. Edie turned and leant on her knees to hiss: 'Well, that would explain a few things. You're a black whore, not a pure white teacher after all', she said.

'Pure, who is pure? You sound like a Nazi! No one is pure, the whole human race is from bloody Africa!', said Jane as Edie strode back to her house.

Jane slammed the tinny door and sat on her lounge. She had finally told the truth, it felt recklessly good. She was in the mood to destroy something. She went outside and grabbed a shovel. What could she kill? The chickens? That bloody red dog? No, it would be nasty and messy – all that fur and feathers, too cruel. Jane saw Edie's precious geranium garden. She jumped over the fence, swung the tool and smashed the plants to bits. She took particular pleasure in crunching up the prize winning lemon-scented variety. She cut deep into their little flower heads. Edie looked over the veranda, her mouth gaping. Jane threw the shovel onto the dirt. She felt great.

'I hate geraniums!' Jane shouted.

After this breakdown in communication, Edie stopped allowing her children to play at Jane's caravan. Aaron was welcome at the big house but he was aware of the frosty atmosphere.

'Why can't Elisha come here to play? She's a good girl', said Aaron. Jane patted his head.

'She just can't.'

'I'm going to be a scientist when I grow up. I need roads to go bush. I can ask Edie if Elisha can help.'

Jane fell into a sweaty lump of tears. She was bold in the daylight, a bright competent teacher but at sunset she embraced a deep gloom. She felt worthless: she deserved the pain, she was not good enough. She longed for connection, to be part of a family that functioned. Sobbing came naturally. She went about the caravan with tears rolling down, splashing in the curry. It was humiliating, the affairs, ignominious moral squalor; she was still waiting for her future and all she had was teaching. The Sundays were gloomy, she watched happy groups of Lanniwah going fishing, they belonged to each other.

She was determined not to fail, not to die like a dog. She clenched her fists and drew wild charcoal sketches of hell.

The mail truck from town arrived and the bag disappeared into the big house. Jane had an idea that she might not receive any mail again, and then she would be really cut off. That would be the moment to shine as an outback Aboriginal woman, or go stark raving mad and take up being an axe murderer. Edie would be first.

David was back at school the next day, as though nothing had happened. Jane saw him strolling about with the children. Jane went walking alone. She needed some space to think about David, but the place seemed full of death. Shattered bones littered the stony ground, thorn bushes reached out, spiky insects and huge jumping ants populated the land. Grey sand, orange sand, speckled black crawling things, prickly melons on vines. There was nowhere to lie down, the earth looked utterly alien.

In the morning light, amongst crackling leaves and the smell of eucalyptus, she found a creek. It felt like a more peaceful place. The sound of water running comforted. She bent to pick up leaves, tried to blow them into a tune. Then she heard human sounds, panting, moaning, and a gurgling laugh. She thought that she should disappear as soon as possible. She was quiet and still, then walked softly and saw a ute parked near a kapok tree. The Reverend Wiltshire was making love to Edie, doggy style. The Reverend groaned and collapsed on the grass and shuddered. They kissed gently and Edie wiped her fanny with a lace hanky, pulled up her knickers and threw the cloth onto a thorn bush. The minister lay on the ground and cried. Suddenly, Edie turned around and gazed at the rock where Jane was hiding. Jane quivered with expectation as Edie walked towards her and seemed to be about to speak. But she turned slowly around and went back towards the ute, Jane's heart beating furiously.

Jane slid down into the grass and stayed hidden until Reverend Wiltshire stood up and broke a branch from a kapok tree. Jane watched as the Reverend knelt down and whipped himself with the fluffy leaves. He could have chosen a thorn bush. He whimpered and muttered a prayer. He then got into the ute emblazoned with 'God Saves' and drove off with Edie. A white dingo sniffed around the tree.

That night, Jane invited David to dinner and made a special fish barbecue.

She saw Aaron watch with curiosity as she flirted, so she stopped smiling and her conversation took on a professional tone. She didn't want to confuse her son.

The next day, David walked down near the billabong. Green ants made nests above his head in a tree.

'Are you following me?'

'No, just walking', she said.

'Hey, I'm goin fishin'.'

' So am I.'

'You a real strong good woman.'

'I want you' said Jane.

She knew there were eyes in the bushes. 'They all lookin when we walk to the creek. People laugh, you know, whisper. Might as well just doori out here on the road', David said. 'There no secrets in dis place.'

She was uneasy. He stopped and held out his hand. She was lost in those brown eyes, so soft. He murmured as he stroked her long hair.

'I don't wanna shame you.'

'Then go away', she said. Nevertheless, he led her to a grassy bank hidden by pandanus palms.

'Come walk with me, take off your, you know, dress. Lie on the grass with me. You want me? Come on, bub.'

She could smell the nectar blossoms; she closed her eyes and breathed in the pandanus. She ached for his love. The sand flies swooped.

'You wanna make babies, Jane? You got real pretty skin. Like you want me for lover? You shiverin'. I'm not gammon, your eyes flashin' and sweat on your lip, your breasts, real fine.'

'This is the last time', Jane whispered. Oh, sure thing, they all say that!

'Sure, bub, last time' he said.

She no longer cared what people thought. Jane wrapped her legs around David. He nuzzled her soft hair. He said she smelt good. He lay down on the sand and pulled her towards him. No talking now, just love. Dark skin on gold, they tumbled over and swam in sweat. He was like a dangerous drug; he sent bursts of light through her head. She sighed and murmured like a sea siren: this was heaven. Sweat on his lips, pink on the inside of his mouth, a fire and blasting passion shooting through her arched body, and sweet release.

Later, he lit a cigarette. 'Good barramundi here. I spear one fella this long last night.'

Sometimes, in a bitter inner world, Jane had a tortured anxiety about her future: she knew she it couldn't be with David. Her mind wandered again, perhaps she could fly to Darwin, take a dream along sex strewn pathways. For David she would even give up drinking. Her lust for her favourite drink – whisky with ice. She could taste it all smooth and silky in her throat. God, she loved whisky. Here there was none, only warmish cordial. She remembered once drinking a whole bottle of Jamieson's whisky by herself at a school camp when teaching in Sydney. She had awoken after sleeping with a long haired musician teacher, and felt wretched, hung over, an appalling taste in her mouth. No, she would have to learn to be a teetotaller for David. And she would make a move, and apply for a new school, a transfer, a new place with him.

Jane wasn't the only crazy woman at Harrison Station. She could hear Hubert yelling at Edie again over at the big house. Edie and Hubert's relationship was getting more dysfunctional, their fights a hushed seething or shouting match. He played the Hammond organ loudly late at night; it sounded like the theme from *Psycho*. He sang drunkenly. One day, Edie threw a mattress and a pile of cowboy clothes over the balcony while her children ran around the house screaming.

'And don't come back, you cowardly snake!' Edie yelled. Hubert ran down the steps and pulled the mattress back up the stairs with his daughters pulling at the top.

'You'll be going back to dirty old Manchester with the cheapest air fare I can find, and you can live on chip butties', he shouted back. The front door slammed and more shouting went on. Jane listened; it was better than television.

His truck roared off down the road to the nearby sister station. Edie was crying; it was that deep shuddering crying. Then the door slammed and she locked herself in her house while her children whispered.

In the morning, a cloud floated over. Old Lucy stood outside the Boss's house looking up and listening intently. Jane felt a strange atmosphere, like a fog from the big house. Old Lucy was breaking the rules but she called to Jane and took her by the hand and walked up the steps. They peered into the kitchen. They heard children's whispers. Elisha said that Edie couldn't get out of bed. Gertie stood stock still in the room. Lucy nodded to her and crept into the master bedroom; the faded pink chenille bed cover was on the floor. Poor Elisha looked frightened.

'Mum won't get up. Gertie gave the little ones cornflakes for little lunch', Elisha said.

The smallest child took Old Lucy's hand.

'Mummy said Daddy's got a secret.'

Lucy saw that Edie had lain all night by a lamp, watching cockroaches on the floor. She twitched in a damp sheet. Jane opened the window and fresh air poured in. Lucy looked out and there was the familiar white dingo walking around the house sniffing for food. Lucy took Elisha by the hand.

'Mummy be alright. She real tired.'

Old Lucy told Jane that she would sit with Gertie to watch over Edie.

However, a few hours later Jane was working on her school program when Old Lucy banged on the door. She had a vision: Edie was eating pills. Jane remembered seeing the white pills in a bottle by the bed, so Jane tore out of the caravan and strode up the shaking aluminium stairs. Old Lucy climbed slowly behind her. All the children were playing table tennis under the veranda. Old Lucy said she saw Edie reach for the bottle of sleeping tablets and count them out in a pile, a pale hand shivering and fingers stuffing each tiny white fragment into her mouth.

'Missus eatem might be a hundred pill. Sure thing dat enough for finish up'. Old Lucy pushed open the bedroom door. Gertie brought water in a saucepan. The bedroom was hushed with a pause between laboured breaths. Old Lucy sat down and began bathing Edie's head. Jane touched the sweat-soaked sleeping form. She bent down to Edie's face and noticed brown froth on her lips. There was no time to panic, Lucy pushed Edie onto her side, Jane began cleaning her mouth of vomit. Lucy went to the open window, leant out and called to Elisha.

'Elly, gettem Boss, in dat truck! You big girl; you drivem'. Jane pulled Edie on to her back and gave her mouth to mouth. Her mouth tasted of sick. The still white face gaped. No breath. Jane thumped at Edie's chest, thump, thump, then again.

'Breathe, Edie, you stupid bitch, breathe! Breathe! Don't you die on me!' Jane yelled. She tried to remember resuscitation, was it three breaths and ten heart thumps or the other way around? The eyes flickered open and then Edie coughed. Lucy smoothed the hair out of Edie's eyes. Jane looked around the room, she had a moment of confusion, where was the bathroom? She ran to the kitchen, took a packet of salt, Lucy brought water and she poured the salt into a saucepan of warm water, and stirred. Edie was moaning which Jane took to be a good sign. If she was semi-conscious, Edie might be able to swallow salt water. Lucy lifted the inert woman into her lap and held her head up; she nursed her and sung in Lanniwah.

'Edie, Edie, wake up, you have to drink this now! Edie!' Jane lifted Edie's head and shouted at the dribbling woman. She held her tight against her chest and kept her head up. Just at that moment, the youngest child burst into the room.

'Mum, Mum! What you doing to my Mum?' she said.

Gertie beckoned the children to her.

'Mummy sick, you be quiet now. Come in kitchen, we waitem.' They crept out and sat outside the door with Gertie's big arms around them all. Inside the bedroom, Jane held Edie's mouth and forced her to drink the warm water and it poured down her face. She sat astride the limp body and Old Lucy held the head up as Jane scooped cup after cup into Edie's mouth. At last, Edie vomited a stream of dissolving pills dripped onto the floor. Lucy laughed and cried.

Hubert came into the room; his eyes met Jane's. He had a look of compassion and terror.

'Is she going to be okay?' Hubert whispered.

'I don't know. You better fly her to the hospital', Jane patted his hand.

Edie murmured and sat up. She stared like a banshee. 'I want Wilt, where's Wilt? There are ghosts here on this station. I see them. Can't you hear them late at night? All the crying?'

Hubert took her hand.

'It's alright, love', he said.

Edie snatched her hand away.

'I hate you. I want Wilt.'

Old Lucy quietly moved into the corner.

'She must want the last rites', said Hubert.

'I guess so', said Jane.

'I'll get him.'

'You no wantem dat fella', said Lucy.

"What you doin' in my house, old woman? No blackfella up here!' Hubert glared at Lucy.

She shook her head.

"Savem Missus, Boss.'

Hubert held her gaze, his head dropped.

'Sorry, Lucy, I don't know what to say. Thankyou.'

She nodded and walked with dignity down the stairs. He called out.

'You wantem tobacco?'

Old Lucy looked up and shook her head.

'No wantem your bacca. No wantem nothin from you fellas.'

Jane watched Hubert approach Edie's bed and lay his head gently against her chest. He took up the end of her red curls, twisted it around his fingers, and breathed in. Edie's hand stroked his head, she murmured and he gave a great sigh. He nuzzled her neck and laid his cheek up against her pale face; he cried and softly hummed against her skin. Tenderly he rocked his head, lay his big frame down next to her, and fully embraced her light body. His knee wrapped around her oblivious to Jane's presence. He pulled Edie to him and buried his face in her body. Jane stood unsure of when to move; she felt that she had always been alone and had never been loved or cared for and all her life she would wait for this kind of love.

He carried Edie down the stairs.

Jane read a scribbled note from Edie: 'Maybe the kids would have been better adopted out from the beginning. I am a failure as a mother, and I can't go on being a wife. Stuff being a good wife'.

Gertie read to the children and Jane went back to her home to bathe Aaron. She sat on the side of the small bath and stroked the water. It was soothing, she liked water. She heard Neil Young singing from the cassette player; he was soothing.

Edie's galah was her friend; and Jane had him sit by her side while she scratched his head. The dingo, now sitting under a bloodwood tree, coughed outside. Old Lucy sat outside Edie's house and sang a long rippling Lanniwah song, the night filled up with tremulous notes.

Jane dreamt of the suicide attempt, but it was somehow Old Lucy who had swallowed the pills with warm milk and Jane floated with her in warm brown water. She sank beneath it in the tiny square bath where she curled into a foetus shape and held Lucy cupped beside her. There was a bubbling in her ears and they kept their heads above water and floated in a boat down an underground river, splashing water on the sides, their hands languid in white foam. The river cave was cool and Lucy drank the water until it began to drown her, delicious and dark and warm. She sank to the bottom. The next day, Lucy called out to Jane:

'You dream 'bout something, me not dead. True, eh?' she chuckled.

A few days later, Edie came back from town with Hubert. At first no one spoke of the incident; it hadn't happened. Jane looked at Edie as she sat hunched over a small mean cigarette. She was not psychotic, she was the camp's midwife, invaluable as a nurse, as a person. Jane even loved her a bit – after all, Lucy had wanted her saved.

'I have seen a thing or two and stitched many legs after a goring by a bullock. One bloke had his intestines hanging out', Edie said. In her chatting, she hid her real despair but reminded Jane that she was a bush nurse who cared for people.

'You might not know it, but I look after everyone, black, white and brindle. You reckon I discriminate, but I don't. I use my best medicines on all of them. I actually love them all. Old Lucy knows that. That old woman knows everything that goes on. I shouldn't have tried to kill myself. I would rather have killed Hubert; that old lady would have some magic to do that', she said.

'She's a real joker', Hubert said. Jane smiled awkwardly at Edie.

'Don't have any more children. They'll just grow up and become a pack of dingos wanting to drink your blood', Edie said.

Elisha let out a wail, she ran from her mother's side. She sniffed and Jane held out her hand and rubbed the child's arm. 'Don't worry, darling, we all get a bit crazy out here', Jane said. She walked towards home but Edie followed for a moment on the steps.

'Don't you tell Hugh what you saw.'

'Or what?'

'You'll have to go.'

Jane moved away and sat next to Old Lucy outside. The elder smoked a wooden pipe and tore up pandanus between her thorny nails. Aaron sat beside her plaiting the string.

'We're all in a kind of hell', said Jane.

'Dat womans real sad, but she not gottem bad heart; we know all 'bout dat.'

'You were strong, Aunty. How did you know she was trying to die?'

'Spirit tellem me'

'How that happen?'

'Just come sittem near me, say come now.'

'What did it look like?'

'Dat Missus spirit lookem like her. Me face alla cold down side, can feelem.'

'You helped save her. Even though she treats you so badly.'

'Help alla fella: no fella should be killem for nothin.' Old Lucy walked slowly up to her camp with her dogs by her side, Jane watched her go.

CHAPTER 3

Dance

It was a quiet cool evening on the station. The waters had long subsided leaving dried mud on grasses and trees, and it was the beginning of the luscious Dry. Jane and David prepared to run the school dance at Harrison. The little cassette player sat on a school desk in the paddock, blaring out Johnny Cash, Charlie Pride, Elvis Presley, Slim Dusty or even the Rolling Stones. The community loved to dance. Sammy was the disc jockey. He beamed at David. 'Now, dis one for all the kiddies out der, 'I wanna hold your hand' by Beatles.' Everyone squealed.

The children loved to rock and roll; jive was fast and exciting to watch. The kids loved to stand around singing, 'One o'clock, two o'clock, three o'clock, rock! Let's rock around the clock tonight …' Grown Lanniwah men in tight jeans and shiny cowboy boots moved seductively as they smoothed their perfect Akubra hats and danced with the kids – frenzied boys dancing with boys, girls dancing with girls, no touching the opposite sex allowed. A wild bunch of small boys with Aaron in the lead tore around with their tin trucks.

Suddenly, Hubert and Edie arrived at the dance, the country and western music was too much to resist. David's eyes met Jane's; he whistled. Hubert grabbed Jane and pulled her close for a slow waltz to Slim Dusty. (She nearly fainted – was he drunk?) The Boss was full of grace: he held Jane tenderly and waltzed around the dirt dance floor, then changed gear with his hand held gently behind his back as he slow waltzed in front of her.

As Jane swooshed past, Old Lucy began to choke with laughter, and cried out, 'Oh, look out!'

Meanwhile Edie danced with the Reverend, who was dressed in a sports jacket. Her head pulled back, she seemed to swoon and her flaming hair flowed behind her, like in a Botticelli painting. The Reverend danced with jerky strange steps, as if he was breaking glass. Sweat lit up his forehead; he wiped his eyes with a handkerchief and looked like a happy man. He twirled Edie and around she spun. 'Oh, Wilt. Stop it', she said, and laughed, swinging her head back.

The music revved up and Hubert jived with Jane (he was definitely high on something – Jane wished she had some). She was amazed at his gyrating hips. She was amazed that the couple were even there. He looked occasionally into Jane's face with a self-conscious smile and twirled her around in a delicate pirouette. He was light on his big feet, a man with rhythm.

Elisha led the other children in rock and roll. They had the time of their lives but did not go near the Lanniwah dancers. After a few dances, Edie gathered up her brood, and took them, whining all the way, home to bed.

The black sky pinpointed with stars, an impossibly beautiful sky reaching down to the Arnhem Land horizon. The older Lanniwah girls arrived at the dance smelling of lavender eau de cologne, their hair in ponytails and glitter bands – a late night entrance. Then 'Greased Lightning' poured out of the cassette player. Hubert tipped his white Akubra hat and skidded to his knees in front of Shirley. He had the John Travolta rhythm and a cigarillo like Clint Eastwood's in his teeth. He jumped up and jived in front of the girls. They giggled and hid their faces.

'The Shimmy Shimmy Shake' blared out. Mayda moved towards David, her eyes on his, she shimmied and her round breasts wiggled in the firelight. She was a disco dancer. The girls wiggled their hips and Jane saw Hubert staring at their slim backsides, his face transfixed. That rock and roll music got into people's bodies and took them away.

Shirley and Lizzy ran up to Jane. Shirley held Jane's hand, her eyes aglow with the magic of a night out. Shirley had just turned fifteen, she showed Jane a ring, a present from someone, she didn't know who. She found the present wrapped in newspaper outside her shed. Jane guessed it was from poor love-struck Robert.

Shirley's father, Raymond, stood a way off, gleaming with pride next to his wife Gertie.

'Missus, you dancem wid us girls?' Shirley held Jane's hands. Jane swung the girls around in rock and roll wildness. David watched as she danced. He was always the showman. He taught the boys some hip gyrating moves, which sent them into hysterics. They mimicked him, the same boys who would disappear one day soon for initiation.

In the firelight, Jane could see that Hubert had left and was lurking in his truck in the darkness. His cigarette burned, he flicked the ash out the window and gazed with fierce lust at the young girls' little backsides in the jeans he had just sold them. David looked over at Jane, a fleeting moment of connection and longing.

Some days after the dance, Jane was worried that Shirley hadn't come to school. She looked out the caravan door towards Raymond's shed, but no, she was not around.

'She bin gone Missus Jane, but now we findem her', Lizzy said.

'Where was she?'

'She bin gettim some clothes. Missus sent for her, but red dog bittem Shirley and he pullim her to Boss truck, slam door.' Jane sat Lizzy down and held her hand.

'Shirley cry now, Boss drive and, you know, he gets her.'

'Take me to her, Lizzy', said Jane. They walked to a bough shade near the womens' sacred site, where Shirley lay on a blanket in the dust. She looked up and then hid her head under the grey blanket.

'Tellem Miss Jane', said Lizzy.

Shirley sat up and wiped her nose. 'He say, he not know why he do it, but say he had a right – me half white anyway. He say, "Stay away from young men".'

'Did he hurt you?'

'He open the truck door and he naked. He say little golden Shirley, little golden Shirley, all grown up now, promise him really by Raymond, but my Daddy not do dat', said Shirley.

'You tell Missus more', said Lizzy.

'Me shame. After dance. He take hair, pull, and tear my dress off. I scared and cry alla time, he do it, I scratch him face.'

'After that, he got off, try kiss her but she cry', said Lizzy.

'I say, "You bad man. I hate you!"'

'It's okay, Shirley. We will help you', said Jane.

'He gottem dressed and give me his belt; it got silver buckle, blue stone. He say Edie buy it at show. Nice one', said Shirley. Jane stroked Shirley's back and the girl hid her body in the blanket.

Lizzy stood up and took Jane's hand. They walked away. 'He lock her in truck, Missus; no water, she near bin finish up.'

Jane saw Hubert walk over to the cattle yards where the men were working. He looked like he didn't have a care in the world.

The voices of the old women whispered as Jane listened to the story of how Old Lucy had sent a spirit message to Shirley telling her to live. The sun had beaten down on the tin roof of the truck and Shirley had given up banging and shouting. When the women had found her collapsed in the cow dung, her heart was racing as the heat climbed to over forty-five degrees. She was perishing, needed water. Water would make it all right. Her lips had been stuck to the flesh, her tongue swollen and tasting of blood. Old Lucy said maybe she would die, no school any more, just a spirit world for her.

The next day Shirley came to school. She was subdued and sat quietly at her desk practicing her cursive writing. Her work was neat and she wrote twice as much as any other student. This day she only copied the shapes of letters; she did not listen to stories or join in chanting the alphabet.

Jane put her arm around her. 'You okay, Shirley?' Jane asked. But Shirley shrugged off Jane's arm and kept writing the curling letters.

The turquoise inlay belt lay on her desk, a coiled blue snake. Jane watched it all day and at lunchtime as the other children left the room, she touched Shirley on the arm.

'What's this?'

'Belt.'

'Yes. You want me to give it back?'

'Boss belt.'

'I see.'

Jane covered the object with her hand and Shirley bolted from the room. Jane rolled it up, this piece of evidence, a coiled sliver of truth. Hubert was a kind man most of the time but he was a rapist and she would somehow make him pay. She felt confused and didn't know if the item could somehow protect the girl from future abuse. The word 'abuse', slippery like the ground after the flood had subsided, all grey and murky, sat in her head. Her fierce protective feelings for these children were as strong as her fury about the terrible bloody past. One more child stuffed up by a selfish pig of a man.

Jane stared out the window, she looked for some kind of sign, but it was just dust now, the Dry in full swing, willy-willies, wild little spirit men with a mischievous intent, tore up the hills. There was no clear path of what to do. Maybe the crow squawking in the tree – was that a sign? Well, she couldn't read it. She was helpless. The burden of the school was crippling her, but somehow this thing, this evidence would help her to discover a new depth of strength. She would confront him. Her hair stood on end at the prospect. Maybe it would all turn sour and she would be forced to quit her job, the only real job she had ever had. It was nerve wracking.

At the end of the day, Jane stood at Hubert's door, her heart beating, throbbing. He motioned to her to come in. He sat at the table with an overflowing ashtray and she put the belt down in front of him. The blue stones glistened and the silver snakehead shone.

'What's that for?' he said.

'You lose it?'

'Might have – what's it to you?'

'Shirley gave it to me.' Hubert pushed away from the table and stood up; his fist banged the table. She jumped.

'Just leave the bleedin' belt!' He picked it up, unfurled it and lashed it across the table. Jane was still, in front of a mad buffalo. She nodded and turned to leave.

'Did you rape her?'

Edie walked into the kitchen, her fierce eyes on Jane.

'What did you say?'

'Leave her to me, Edie. What the hell? You start accusing people and you'll be run off. You know bleeding nothing ... Look, kids tell fibs, you know how they can make up stuff. Have a heart. I love these kids. You know me Jane, big hearted Hubert.'

Jane swallowed. He wouldn't look at her. She moved towards the door, the air thick with fear. He sobbed.

'She just turned fifteen. I could report you.'

Edie leapt at Jane and swung her fist, Jane ducked.

'Who do you think you are? Coming in here accusing my husband? I'll punch your face in.'

'Just try' said Jane.

'She's a little liar – they all are, believe me. You watch it. I can have you out of here in the blink of an eye. Or you might meet with an accident.'

Hubert caught hold of Edie as she fumed. She pushed him away and sat at the table sulking; steam seemed to spurt from her nose; her hand trembled as she lit a cigarette. His hand reached out to touch her; she shoved it away.

'Get out!' said Edie.

'I love that little girl of Gertie's like my own, wouldn't hurt her,' murmured Hubert.

That shithead. Jane shook as she went down the steps. She felt a terrible rage and compassion for the girl. She was torn between going to the police and letting the old people work it out. Maybe they could sing him. She would have to leave Harrison if she spoke out, and she knew that Hubert drank beer with the local police.

Later in the night, Jane lay awake listening to movement outside her van. Was it Hubert? Her fear turned the night into a sweaty ordeal. She was alone; someone might break the pathetic aluminium lock and rape her. Her imagination was alive with terrible pictures of Shirley in the truck. A dog started barking. He barked and barked until the night was quiet.

The next day, the school seemed back to normal. Shirley played chasings with the little children. Then, Mayda looked over and motioned to Jane with her lips and eyes that there was trouble over at the Boss's house. Jane nodded, she didn't know what was going on but she guessed that Edie was having her say. Jane couldn't read the undercurrents and spoke to David about it. Jane knew how Hubert had the girl in his truck, no one seemed to know where, and had left her to 'perish with no water'. She had nearly died, but no police arrived; there were only muttering rumours. It was too terrible to contemplate.

'What's going on?' Jane asked David.

'Not sure. Maybe Missus know about everything. Gertie maybe talk', David said. He looked worried and worked with his head down all afternoon with the younger boys. They were learning their times tables and it was a noisy exercise. Jane would not even ask David what would happen about Shirley: it was up to him to tell her if he had a mind to.

Outside Raymond's shack, half a cow hung bleeding and flies buzzed. Jane was out of her depth, her confidence shrunk to nothing, and she didn't know what to do. Jane and David sat with Raymond, Sammy and Burnie. Robert stood nearby; he was upset and wanted know what everyone would do about Shirley.

'Mr Raymond, you shootem Boss, yeeai?' said Robert.

'That won't help, Robert. You go back down camp. This elder business and me.'

'I lub her', said Robert.

'We all love her', said Jane.

Robert slunk away. They all knew about the rape, and wanted to know what David could do from his position as teacher's assistant.

'Nothing', said David.

Jane nodded with compliance. *Lily livered coward.* She looked at him and hated his weakness.

'Mr Barkley Boss. Who will believe dat girl?' said David. The men sat with their hats twirling in their hands.

'Dis thing never happen all the time Mr Hubert bin boss. I not understand, we think him good man, trustem. Maybe dat girl she sung him, wid magic, he can't fight dat', said Burnie.

'Powerful magic, that love magic', Raymond said.

David shook his head. 'She only fifteen, too young.'

Burnie agreed. Raymond said nothing. A tear ran down his face, he was a man destroyed. David put his arm around the old white man.

'He's a sneak like Iago, tells you one thing but tricks you. I should shoot him', said Raymond.

'Your Wunungah mob no good, eh Ray?' said Burnie.

Raymond nodded his white head. 'No good, I maybe kill him. She's my only little girl'.

'No talk of dat. We see what happens, eh?' said David.

'We might be pray for her', said Sammy.

Jane watched and felt a passionate rage inside.

'I hate you all! Won't anyone stick up for this girl? Because I will. I'll tell the police!'

'Don't do that – make big trouble.'

Raymond held up his hand. Jane nodded to him.

'Long time ago, we had another baby, a little boy called Tom, after my dad. The Protector of Aborigines drove up and took him. Just like that. I argued with the man but he was adamant that the law was the law. No cohabiting with natives, and all half-caste children to be taken. It was raining. He was only two. He put him over his shoulder like a bag of spuds. *Summum ius, summa iniuria* – the greater the law, the greater the injustice. Never seen him since.' Raymond sniffed and wiped his eyes with his shirt. Jane looked away.

'They said it was for the good of the children. They thought they were doing the right thing. It's paternalism – a sickness of white people; their atrocities; well, it kills you. My dad, you see, he was removed too', said Jane. The men sat in quiet contemplation, looked at her and nodded.

'You get Gertie to come down to the school. I can give Shirley some new clothes', said David.

'That's not going to help, is it? What is a girl worth? A new shirt for Ray? A few packets of tobacco, some rum maybe?' said Jane. David's head bent low. Raymond sighed.

'Shame job', said David.

'It's not her shame, or your shame. A girl has been assaulted. I have to report it. It's my duty of care. I can't just leave it up to all of you', said Jane.

'What you tellem? They ask for proof, what you got? Nothin'. David showed his rage, he punched his hand into the ground. He hid it, but she saw his hatred burning.

'I'm gunna take a truck to Rainer cattle station, and then hitch a ride into town. Might be talk to the Katherine police', said David. The men's faces were alight with fear because police were always terrible trouble, never justice.

'Maybe you can see the Department fellas, at that Education office', said Raymond.

Jane thought this would be of no interest to them.

Old Pelican strolled up and sat on a box. The men bent their heads towards him.

'I get pay from Boss, new boots and Akubra, nice one – what you want? You father, I payem you half, eh?'

The next morning, David came to see Jane; he told her about another dream, that he had a bull charge at him, he lost blood.

'Dat animal king of horns, a wild buffalo, he got little mean eyes real low and stare for me, he maybe Wunungah'.

'Maybe you want to get away from this station, be free of the Wunungah?'

'Might be, but not you. I don't want to leave you', he said.

That night Jane sat with David and Old Lucy by their fire.

'Might be Kadaitcha man gettim. Him move like lightning, got feather feet. Dat Boss better watch' im', said Old Lucy.

'He won't know what hit him, never see 'em comin', said David. Jane felt a shiver up her spine; her hair prickled; she felt cold. She stared at the land in the moonlight, and realised that she couldn't see it, couldn't understand it. The people and the land were one and it was not her country.

David didn't go anywhere; he just mumbled and turned the other cheek. Jane made a report and posted it. She wasn't going to be weak.

CHAPTER 4

Hubert And The Whip

Hubert played Hammond organ, even Bach, up at the tent church on Sundays. Jane saw the congregation through the tent door. She stood outside and listened; the music was sublime. Edie and Hubert told her that they were thinking of being 'born again'.

After church, Hubert walked over to talk to Jane; he threw lighted matches on the ground to burn the dry grass as they talked.

'I've got something to show the little fella.'

Jane hoped it wasn't a new bible or his privates.

Aaron followed Hubert and his three children to a dead tree that had collapsed. Underneath, yelping in the dust, were some half-dingo pups. The children picked them up and stroked their golden fur. Jane watched Hubert slung his whip over his shoulder and hold out a puppy.

'You choose one, Aaron. They're ready to leave their mother. They can lap milk.'

Aaron was very happy. He took a little male puppy and squeezed it under his tee shirt. He ran home with the gift.

'He's half dingo; his dad is the white dingo. I'm calling him Flash.' Aaron ran off.

The dog came to lick her hand, he understood. Little Flash followed her around, wanted to be near in case he was called for. He licked the tears from her face. A dog didn't stab you in the back; a dog was faithful and kind.

A group of Lanniwah men came with David to Jane's van. She invited them in. They had a serious problem – not enough food. David spoke for them and explained that the Boss was cranky. The other men, their heads down, eyes lowered, creased their perfect Akubras in their hands. There was an atmosphere of fear and anger, and Jane felt out of her depth again.

'Boss says the cattle boys can't work no more. He got no work. No work, no meat!' said David.

'What can I do?' she said.

David looked through the window at Hubert tying up his horses.

The air between them all was thick. Jane chopped at some steak and piled it into a pot. The men watched the meat.

'We can't keep the whole mob on school food. There isn't enough for the kids', she said. The silence grew.

'David, say something!' Jane pleaded. He shrugged his shoulders.

'I don't know what to do', he said.

'We can write to the Department of Aboriginal Affairs. I can teach the older girls how to make a vegetable pie. And there are fish. We can take the big kids fishing at Limmeer lagoon – lots of barramundi', she said.

'He locked gate to lagoon, he say no one to worry cattle', said David. He shook his head.

'Just cut the chain with a bloody boltcutter', said Jane.

'Maybe we write a good letter, tell 'em what happen, 'bout dat girl', said David.

'You and your pathetic letters! Why don't you be a man? I thought you blackfellas had some courage.'

'I'm not gunna fight him or you', said David.

'Look, I'm angry too, but we can't shoot ourselves in the foot. We rely on Hubert for everything', said Jane.

'So, you're a coward too', said David.

The quiet was chilling. She kept stirring tinned vegetables into the stew. As she bent down to find another tin, the men walked out of the caravan and back to camp. She ran after them.

'I'll bring up some stew when it's cooked, I can leave it at Burnie's.'

David put on his hat and walked past her in the direction of the Boss.

'Don't go near him, David!' she cried out.

David moved across the paddock towards Hubert. He seemed to be yelling at the Boss. A slow motion scene unfolded. Hubert saw him coming and sooled his dogs onto him. Jane was horrified. The red cattle dog nipped at David's heels. He kicked hard and it ran away yelping.

'Oh no, please don't, David. Leave it!' Jane shouted.

She yelled at his back, but he was already silhouetted against bright blue sky, his tall frame and long hair against Hubert's belly and bowlegs. They looked like a Javanese shadow puppet play with absurd characters and big noses. She heard David bellow:

'You hate Aborigine. You push our people round like dirt. We starvin'. You come from that Queensland to run dis station for what? Rich Chinese businessmen. You steal welfare cheques from our mob. You should be locked up. You nothin but a gin-jockey crook!'

Jane saw that he was magnificent. She heard him yell with a pent up aggression that defied being punched in the mouth.

Hubert fumed. 'A crook? I'll teach you a lesson you won't forget, boy!'

He ran to his truck and grabbed the stockwhip, swung it around his head and brought it cracking down on David's back. Hubert was red in the face and sweat poured down his shirt. He rolled the whip up.

'Go on, get off my place! Piss off! I'm Boss here. You're nothing but a lousy assistant teacher. You're nothin!'

'Not your place; dis country my place.'

The bullwhip cracked again, hitting the earth next to David. He cringed and ducked, but didn't seem to be afraid. He looked like he was enjoying the drama of it.

'That's right, Hubert, you coward, use a whip. You're too weak to face up to a man without it!' said Jane

David jumped at the next whip crack and began to look like a rodeo clown. Aaron put down his puppy and ran across towards him crying and shouting.

'Leave him alone! he didn't do anything!' Jane rushed to pull the child out of reach of the whip. Now incensed, she ran and faced Hubert.

'Don't hurt my little boy! You touch him and I will kill you!'

Hubert looked at little Aaron and slowly rolled the whip into his hand. He calmly walked towards his house. Then, as if in reverse motion, he turned and hissed at David.

'I'll give you until tomorrow morning to pack up and piss off Harrison

Station. Don't let me find you here or I won't be responsible for what happens to you. I'm warning you!'

David picked up his Akubra hat and dusted it off. Jane hung like a crow on the horizon, frozen. Hubert stood with his whip curled around his fist.

'Maybe you'd like to as well, Mrs Reynolds.'

'I need this job more than anything!' she said.

'She not leavin and I not goin' off my country. Dis Lanniwah place, not yours! You have to shoot me first!' David said.

Old Lucy and Beatrice appeared magically next to Jane. They had their waddies. They looked over at Hubert.

'You Boss fella not hurtem dat young one, or we killem you!'

'I am in my rights to drive the lot of you off! Go on, go back to yer garbage dump, get outa my sight.' Hubert swaggered over to his truck and got in.

The old ladies gathered up Aaron and brought him to Jane's caravan.

'Will he shoot you with his gun? He shoots dogs. I saw him try to kill a dingo', Aaron said.

'Dat Boss, he can't stop us. It's okay, just a joke. Don't be frighten, Jane look after you. She tough one, your mum', said David.

Aaron hung onto David, and then Jane put out her arms and took hold of her little boy. She soothed him.

'You want some banana custard for sweets?'

Jane watched the big house and saw Edie come out onto the veranda for a smoke. She stared at David with a vicious hatred.

'We need you, David', Jane begged.

I not goin anywhere. Eh, Aunty?'

Jane was in shock and could barely speak. She was at the drowning point of life.

'You could apologise', she whispered.

'Narr, dat not goin to happen, you know dat. Dat whip. Can't take that. He will forget bout dis, no worries. I got a job here. I stay alright.'

Late that night, Aaron heard Jane crying in her bed. She wept uncontrollably, sobbed and gulped for air, ashamed to cry in front of Aaron, her soaked pillow bunched up in her fist. She was a sad pathetic wretch; she hugged her child and they slept in each other's arms.

Jane felt responsible for David standing up, but it was his own choice, his own road. She was proud of him.

Jane thought about it. She was what? 'A bit Aboriginal, a drop of blood'. *What part of you is actually Aboriginal?* Who was she? What on earth was she doing? The men's fight over her was awful. She was an idiot to let it go so far. She was about to throw away everything. Somehow, she felt liberated. David had stood up to Hubert, and so had she. She had a voice and would use it.

~~~

Weeks later, the wind blew up black clouds, howling. Aaron cuddled up beside Jane in the bed, she read him a story. She could hear the rev of the Boss's truck and the Lanniwah men – had they been drinking?

'That Boss can't drive for shit', Sammy yelled in the dark.

Hubert was crashing gears, going too fast on the corrugations.

'Hey, look out!' another voice yelled.

Jane listened to the night, the smell of fear in her armpits. She sat up, alert. Listen! What truck is it? Hubert's. Going too fast. *He must have a skin-full,* thought Jane. He was about half a kilometre away, wrecking the gears. The truckload of men sounded very drunk. *I bet he's got a truckload of blackfellas; must be coming back from the rodeo.*

Jane could hear Hubert singing a country and western song: 'Trumby was a ringer, and a bloody good one at that. His skin was black but his heart was white, and that's what matters most' Jane could picture him driving, scratching his mosquito bites, smoking Marlboro, drunk on booze bought at the Crocodile Hotel.

Jane and Aaron crawled up to look out the window. 'What's happening, Mummy?'

She imagined Hubert squinting in the dark. Hubert's voice, his deep tobacco-ravaged bark, in her mind. 'The buffalo can break yer bull bar. They get real wild when you shoot the buggers. Put a couple of bullets in em.'

The headlights got closer. Jane's heart beat fast. Something awful would happen. Or maybe they were just happy drunks – yes having a great time, lucky things. Jane listened intently as the truck pulled up outside her caravan.

It was so quiet. Hubert didn't get out; he would be brooding, picking scabs.

'Come on, you mob. We better walk', Sammy called out.

Hubert was growling like an animal.

'Stupid Wunungah bastard. You gin-tailer!' a man yelled.

Jane slipped down under the window to hide, Aaron beside her. She heard the truck door open, peeped through the window and saw Hubert get out of the truck cabin, his fists raised.

'Alright, youse fellas, who called me that? I never touched that girl. She lied. Who drank all me Fourex. Was that you? Get off me truck, you can walk! David, you think you're too smart – a teaching assistant! What would you know?'

'You too weak, old man Boss. Let's walk, eh?' David said.

The Lanniwah men climbed off the back of the cattle truck; they were light on their feet.

'I'll have youse one by one. Ungrateful black bastards. I drive yer into town and you bloody abuse me all the way. I bring all your food out, look after your pensions', yelled Hubert.

Jane could see David standing tall. His fists raised. He seemed suddenly wanting to be free of the unending humiliation, the Boss and his aggressive bullying. She guessed that David's manhood demanded that he stand up for once.

'Boss, we don' wanna fight. You too drunk', said David.

Some of the Lanniwah men scattered, they ran through the bush like disappearing rabbits. David was still there beside the truck with Sammy and Old Burnie.

'Walk away from him. Leave him! Don't fight him', Sammy said.

Hubert staggered towards David and slammed a heavy fist in the young man's face. Jane jumped and shivered. Aaron began to cry. There was a sound of punches thumping in the quiet. A crack and groan; someone else was crying; it sounded like Sammy. Jane was transfixed, her heart thumping.

She could see Hubert swaying from side to side, he was punch drunk or just drunk. He threw another heavy punch at David but it missed. Hubert's shirt was open; his chest heaved in the light, he was sweating and it dribbled down his face. His tongue poked out like a Maori warrior. Was he ill? Jane pictured herself getting between them, stopping the fight but she couldn't move. Such stupid men – why were they trying to kill each other?

'Come on, you blackfellas, is that all you got? Fight you black bastard! Too full of gin piss? Come on, fight!' yelled Hubert. David's voice was low and urgent, then there was the sound of brutal punches and cracking bone, grunting, then there was silence. Jane peeked out. She could see shadowy heads down. Shadowy men. The Lanniwah man standing with fists over a slumped body of Hubert.

'I maybe kill 'im, that Boss.'

There was a sudden quiet and Aaron froze next to Jane.

'That's David's voice. I didn't know he had the guts. I reckon he hit Hubert', Jane whispered. There was the sound of a dingo, a night bird, then no sound.

'What's happening, Mummy?' Aaron whimpered.

'He had it coming.' Jane stepped out into the night. 'Oh hell.' She whispered to Aaron, 'Don't worry, sweetie; just silly men fighting. You stay inside.'

'No, I want to come. I'm scared!' Aaron said.

'Okay, you bring the first aid box. It's under the sink!'

Aaron carried the box with the importance of an ambulance man. Hubert was unconscious on the dirt with Old Burnie and Sammy standing over him with terror on their faces. She saw blood on David's shirt. He was rubbing his knuckles. She looked at David and he looked away. Jane bent down to feel for a pulse on Hubert's wrist. His arm was at a strange angle. She looked at again at David, his eyes in a panic.

She touched him on the shoulder. 'It's okay, David, be calm', she said.

'He hit me first. He punched me.' He rubbed his jaw.

Jane examined the limb. It looked broken, crooked. Hubert was knocked out, his face puffed with blood and cuts.

'Doesn't look good. Someone will have to drive him to hospital. Get Edie'.

'I'll get her', David said.

'No, don't. Run. For God's sake, don't just stand there. We'll look after him. He hit his head. Oh God, just pray he's not going to die.'

The Lanniwah men ran into the night as dogs howled and a dark wind whistled through the trees. Jane called after David:

'Don't tell anyone you hit him!'

Jane gently tilted Hubert's body into recovery position and told Aaron to take the torch and run to get Edie. However, the little boy was terrified, so Jane grabbed a towel from her caravan and placed it under Hubert's head. She took Aaron's hand and ran with him.

The lights in the Boss's house were all ablaze. The dogs on chains howled and barked; it was a cacophony of noise. Edie tore down the steps and assumed control of the situation. In no time, she was driving into the night towards the next cattle station with Hubert on the back seat.

At that precise moment, Jane felt relieved that Hubert was on his way to town. She was miserable and realised that it was a terrible thing to have happened – what about poor Hubert? What if David was up for murder. David might face banishment from his country or life in prison; it would kill him. You couldn't beat up a station manager and get away with it. It'd be a miracle if someone didn't try to shoot David. It might even be Edie, she was capable of it – no one touched her man and got away with it. *Stand by your man.* Jane cried large hot tears; Aaron sat with her until he fell asleep. She swallowed some aspirin with milk and begged the night to end. She was frightened for David but somehow she admired him. He wasn't a coward. He stood up for himself; he would be a strong man with his people respecting him, and stories would be repeated about this night.

A few hours later, Jane was asleep. A pebble clattered against her window. David stood outside. She went into the darkness and with intense emotion they embraced.

'I want to say goodbye for you; maybe gone long time', said David.

'You have to get away now, before policemans come.'

'I'm not scared, not like wild fella. I can face 'em up.' He held out his hand to her.

'No, you have to run. Just go now, please! You wouldn't get justice.'

'I want lotta thing in my life, good job. I not just a fella to sit down alla time. You my woman now', he said.

'Yes'.

David clenched his teeth, to keep them from chattering. He had wanted to face the Wunungah for a long time.

'I sick of that Boss business, alla time make us feel bad. I getting education now, all I want. Then for all kids we learn 'em up. I don't wanna run alla time.'

He turned and walked towards the waiting cattle truck. Burnie would take him away and bring back the truck. She watched his back and felt bereft. David stopped and lit a cigarette. She stood waiting, longing for a kiss, watching as he moved into the shadows. She stood for a long time as the vehicle disappeared amongst the shadows of gum trees.

David would stay put at a secret location until things calmed down. The men told Jane that all the Lanniwah were pleased that the Boss had got his due, that one of their men had stood up to him. He most probably deserved the payback after what he had handed out over ten years.

'We sick of it, working for nothin'; sick of being warned off our country', said Burnie.

Jane thought that after things died down, if Hubert was okay, then David would end up in Darwin and go to the Department of Education, or he would front up to the Katherine area office, bold as can be. She imagined him asking for a transfer and going back to college. She wanted him safe.

Was it possible to reverse the action, press a rewind button on the cassette player, and replay what had happened? Where was her intuition? She wasn't sure that she hadn't had a hand in David getting away; he needed to avoid the onslaught of recriminations about their affair. She should never have given in to temptation. No one would respect her. She thought that she might feel better now – abandonment felt somehow normal. She had learned that behaviour. Would it feel better when everything she loved disappeared? Did she want the feeling of betrayal? If every man left then she would be normal. Was desertion a state that felt good, leaving just her and her child? Alone.

She remembered that moment in time when she had lent across the divide and touched David's hand, their eyes meeting, him flustered and unsure, squeezing her fingers, an unmistakable invitation.

In a strange way, she also had compassion for Hubert. He was a flawed man, a terrible man, but some kind of victim too. Jane wished he would just pack up his truck with his wife, kids and guns and drive home to Queensland or wherever he belonged with all the other rednecks, rapists, rodeo riders and raving xenophobic loons.

~~~

The next day, there was a hush in the school. Young girls gathered around Shirley. They whispered and peered out the windows. They wrote notes to each other, giggled, and tore them up. Mayda asked why David hadn't turned up for work.

'Maybe he's had to go off on ceremony business. They won't tell us; maybe he will come back', said Jane. The children knew where he had gone: the rumours about the fight were pulsating through the camp.

'That Boss he gunna die for sure', said Mayda.

Burnie motioned to Jane to talk outside the school. The windows swarmed with children trying to lip-read. Apparently, Edie drove Hubert to the next station late at night, and in the morning, the station manager had flown them to Katherine hospital. Hubert had a fractured skull and broken limbs. It wasn't good; he was really sick. No one talked about who was in the fight. All the fellas were too drunk, no one remembered. Sure, they couldn't remember a thing.

Some days later, Edie drove back down the road; she saw Gertie and the children running to welcome her. Jane shook Edie's hand. The children cuddled their mother and clung to her like limpets, but Edie took no time in summoning Old Pelican and some of the young men to her front gate. She shifted in a white plastic chair with a rifle laid across her lap. This was a very angry English woman. She stared at the men, and then motioned to Old Pelican to sit down on the ground. The others sat near him and Jane stood at a distance straining to hear the conversation.

'So Boss fella, he's in the hospital, broken head, broken knuckles, fractured collar bone, broken arm, smashed teeth. Who killem him?' said Edie, as she fingered the rifle. Burnie stared at the ground and moved a stick in circles. Edie looked at each of them, or at the top of their heads, because they would not look up. Only Old Pelican stared at her with a smile. Jane drew breath, the red heeler walked by and growled.

'How about you, Sammy? You look up to David, don't you? Did David do this? Where is he? You believe in God, Sammy, you study to be missionary, you fella won't tell a lie? Wouldn't want to go to hell? Dat place where you burnem?' said Edie.

Sammy cringed and Burnie looked at the headman. Old Pelican nodded.

'Big fight, no fella mean hurtem him', said Old Pelican.

'I saw it Edie, no one was to blame. It was a fight. Hubert was drunk too', said Jane.

'If I want a school teacher's opinion, I'll find one with some sense, one who is not prejudiced in favour of certain people', Edie said.

'I was only saying …'

'Nothing. I don't care what you think you saw!'

'Okay.'

'That right? Burnie, you are the big edumacated man now, aren't you? You think we don't know about those letters to the gubberment? Land rights be damned. Too smart, that's what the Boss says, he doesn't like flash blackfellas'.

'It was drunk fight, sorry', said Burnie.

'Policemans coming, you know dat? You better watch out', she threatened as the men walked off.

Hubert came back to Harrison carrying his plaster casts with pride. His children decorated them with flowers. He settled down on his veranda to survey his kingdom, but kept his rifle by his wicker chair. Jane saw the rifle sticking out near his feet and remembered Harry and his terrible behaviour. Could Hubert shoot someone? Maybe he was a murderer of Aboriginal people like his grandfather. She skirted around the house, avoiding him and Edie.

David had left Jane and the school in the lurch. There was no other teaching assistant with any training at Harrison. Jane had to appoint one of the mothers to help at the school, but it was Margie and she was illiterate. Jane sighed at the thought that this lovely young man, his brown lustrous eyes and velvet lashes, his sweet smile was no longer in her daily presence. It was all too bad. She carried on; she was strong, and the school was great.

Some weeks later, no police officer had arrived. Jane walked to Edie's gate. She gave Jane a message from the School of the Air radio. It was from Brian in Katherine. He said that David was in the town lock-up. Jane's mouth twitched. Edie stared at it with fascination. She was smiling. It gave some kind of relief to Jane's anxiety; at least she knew where he was, but he was in gaol, where the isolation killed so many young Aboriginal men.

Reverend Wiltshire heard about David's incarceration and insisted that he drive with Jane into town. She left Aaron with Edie.

'It's school business; we can't manage without a trained teaching assistant.'

'We asked them to charge him for assault. He'll get a year in prison, see how he likes that', said Edie. She stood on the road and watched Reverend Wiltshire get into Jane's vehicle, she spat as they passed.

At two in the morning, after a gruelling silent drive, they stood on the step outside the police station. The grey paddy wagon with its steel mesh door stood alongside. *I will do this useful thing,* she thought. *I will not be scared or cowered in front of these men.*

It was a square red-brick and aluminium building with an old stone and concrete cell block out the back, a remnant of 'pioneer days' where it held Chinamen, Afghans and Aboriginals. Black iron bars, etched graffiti, it looked like something out of a Gestapo interrogation centre. Jane peeped into the cells. There were no glass windows for possible breaking. Nothing to cut your way out, or cut your throat. No rusted metal ring high up in the wall, suitable to tie a piece of ripped blanket attached to a neck.

'We should wait until morning.' Jane shook her head and knocked on the metal door of the station. Through the window, a thin blue light shone. The door opened. She looked inside. Pairs of football socks were pinned in a line to a wall.

'Yes, what can we do for you?' A hammering in her chest. The officer was so young, so gormless. So suspicious. But he was trained for this job. He would listen and she would be very polite.

'You have an Aboriginal prisoner.'

'We have several, Madam. Who do you want?'

'I want to see David Yaniwuy. Please, if it's no trouble. I am the head teacher where he works.'

'Not possible. He's been charged with assault. He has to face the magistrate.'

Reverend Wiltshire moved out of the darkness and his hand rested on the door.

'I am a minister of the church. May I see the prisoner?'

'Not tonight.'

They saw it all: the terror, rage, hatred, love – it flickered around her. The image of this young policeman possibly kicking David's head in – no, not possible. But it might be if David resisted incarceration.

'Come back tomorrow. Look he's alright, don't worry. I gave him a hot feed of stew. Home cooked.' The door shut slowly. They looked down the ghostly street. Jane indicated silently to Wiltshire to stay. What was she doing? She moved towards the road and a voice cried out.

'Jane, here. It me, David. Over here.'

At first, she could not see David; he was behind the cell bars. She smelt vomit on the floor. He stood shivering in a thin grey army blanket. The same blanket that her great granny wore in the orphanage. A red line ran down one side; it was frayed it smelt of wasted lives. Her smarter self had cautioned her to not go to the police station: 'Trouble'. Her fingers reached his as they clung to the bars. She stroked his cold grey skin.

'Go home – too much humbug here.'

'No, I will talk to the police in the morning.' She gripped his fingers in a goodbye. She stopped and stepped back against the cold stone. An Alsatian dog barked on its chain.

'What?' he whispered.

'Don't do anything stupid; you will be alright.'

Wiltshire appeared by her side, put out his hand and touched David's.

'It's just a building; they won't hurt you. You are a dissident, a political prisoner. I will pray for you. Jesus will protect you. They have no right to hold you, I will put in a complaint to our church head; he will instigate action on your behalf. We have a policy to fight the racist imprisonment of young people like yourself. Have faith in the good will of all men. We will overcome.'

She heard David sob. She hoped what the Reverend had said was true. For Aboriginal people there was so much fear in a cell: the ghosts of dead inmates, claustrophobia and the damp and cloying hell, fear dribbling from the concrete. The terror of being alone could kill. Jane saw the grey conglomerate walls, the cell held pain in its essence. She knew that for David the experience of a locked cell alone was the worst punishment he could endure. David would rather be flogged or speared. But she believed in his sense of survival, he was courageous.

The next morning something strange happened. Wiltshire and Jane were sitting in the police station when the sergeant answered the phone. The Reverend was bent over his clasped hands praying. The police officer looked at Jane.

'Mrs Reynolds, seeing as you have the minister with you, I can release the prisoner in your care.'

'Do I need to get bail money? How much?' she said.

'Nope. Mr Barkley has dropped the charge. He doesn't want to proceed.'

'Thanks be to God.' The Reverend laughed.

Jane slumped on the wooden seat.

'Thank you so much.'

'Don't thank me. I don't care. I'm being transferred back to Nightcliff in a few months.'

They collected David and he asked them to drop him at the Lanniwah town camp. He was quiet, thinking, and he didn't communicate. Jane was relieved that he was free; he needed to stay away from his country until people forgot about the incident. He didn't realise Jane was deeply afraid of police and all authority figures, a fear that was ingrained.

Her father had despised the police for their corruption. He watched mates dragged off to prison for being radical unionists or for just being Aboriginal.

Jane wondered how she as a single mother could be a threat to Australian society. She had shown her courage in just keeping her illegitimate baby. She had not allowed the Royal Sydney Hospital authorities to take him. The matron with her starched headdress had grabbed her hand and tried to force her to sign the adoption papers – 'How do you think you will feed the baby? You have no husband, no one to support you, how will you work? Give him up. Don't be so selfish.' But, Jane had stood up to the matron's ferocity and contempt. She had had the baby alone, a long labour, and then he was gone for a whole day. At last, when she held Aaron, she knew she would never surrender him. She signed herself out of the hospital. They lived on brown rice and Weetbix as she struggled to finish her honours degree. She was determined to become a teacher.

Now in the Territory, she received strange unsigned threatening letters, with words like 'black bitch' or 'southern do-gooder' or 'nigger lover'. Maybe people suspected she was a drug taker and not suitable to teach children. She was accused of putting them in 'moral danger'. Jane felt that there were people watching; her sexual freedom meant she was tainted. She could be sacked at any time. She had experienced the shame of having to collect store vouchers from the police station, with the burly copper leaning over the counter to look down her dress. 'You sleeping with anyone?' She had felt the shame that all the Aboriginal girls lined up behind her had felt. Jane had smiled and said, 'No, are you?' He muttered, 'He who eats of the fruit must water the tree'.

In the past her store vouchers were stamped under the regulation for *Food Famine and Flood Relief*, at least it was alliteration. Jane could only buy food from certain big supermarkets. The checkout chick would stare at her in contempt. She would barely touch the voucher with her fingertips. She said; 'You can't have sanitary products on this, only food. Can't you read?' Jane had felt a burning shame as she replaced the Modess sanitary pads.

'What's wrong, Mummy? Why can't you have your lady things?' Aaron said. Country women sporting broad bosoms had looked on with amusement or pity. Jane had picked up Aaron and her bag of groceries and slunk out of the store.

In her current position, Jane was not going to be pushed around. She would fight for her survival.

As they passed through town, she saw Daniel in a building construction four-wheel drive. He waved and pulled up. He was tanned, his bright blue eyes dazzled.

'I'm comin' out your way soon; want me to bring you anything? Fresh vegies? I can bring a slab', he said.

'No, I've got all I need.'

'What happened to you and Orlando? He looks like shit.'

'Nothing, all good. He was called back to town', she smiled.

'Come on Janey, lighten up – he loves you. Hey, I respect what you're doing out there, Jesus saves!'

Wiltshire waved. 'Yes, he does!'

'Okay, gotta go', they drove off.

It was exhaustion more than anything else that surrounded her on the drive home. Thomas Wiltshire chatted amiably most of the way. He was delighted that David was free, delighted to have been of use. Jane drove the long road back to Harrison. She needed to refuel when she got home. She knocked on Hubert's door. He grunted and she went inside the house to find Harry, the stockman who had terrorised her and the kids, sitting at the table eating peanut butter toast. Her face froze. She backed away. What kind of trouble would he be up to? Harry stood up and pulled out a chair for Jane. She was surprised. He seemed like a gentleman. He poured her a cold tea, but he looked nervous and embarrassed. Gertie was washing up; she raised her eyebrows at Jane.

'Get Missus Reynolds a hot cuppa, Gertie', said Hubert.

Hot tea from the tap was poured and plonked in front of Jane.

'I brought some mangoes for the school kiddies. It's a big sack from my tree at the homestead – they'll love em', said Harry.

'He's not all bad. Tell her about your plan for a tree house', said Hubert.

'We're gunna put it on the big coolabah tree. Your boy can play in it too.'

Jane wandered if Harry had sobered up or maybe he was trying to show a better side of himself. Harry walked down the steps to show Jane where the tree house would be. He stopped at the big white tree.

'I'm sorry for that business when your Toyota broke down. I drink too much; this country is tough. I get pissed and lose it. Sorry. I mean, I'm really sorry. It was shameful', he said.

'Okay, let's forget about it, Fourex can be lethal.'

'It's the Bundaberg rum that does it. You won't believe me, I joined A A in Katherine, yeah me. Twelve steps and all that. Dad made me do it.'

Jane felt prickly around her neck. He was actually trembling. He had his hat in his hands, strangling it.

'By the way, we saw your friend Daniel a few days ago. He's been up at the blacks' camp.'

'No!' she said.

'Saw him on his bike. He'd better watch it.'

Harry smiled and stared at her.

'They'll get him. It's dangerous stuff. I sleep with a rifle. It's a war', he said.

'Yeah, yeah'. She turned to leave.

'And another thing, yer teacher assistant'.

'What about him?'

'He was seen handing out land rights pamphlets in town. He's hangin out with radicals from Darwin – what an idiot. You see, this country is everything to me; my father worked himself to death lookin after this place. I love this land: it's in my blood'.

Jane walked away; she felt exhausted, and she needed to pick up Aaron.

CHAPTER 5

Policemans And Mardi Gras

Jane went to Katherine for the annual Mardi Gras parade, she stayed with Rosie and Brian. Early in the morning she was awake first. There was a knock on the door. Jane was surprised: it was not the light tap of the children; it was a loud assertive pounding. She was quiet; she remembered hiding behind the couch as a child, when the debt collectors or a woman from the Department of Child Services was knocking, voices telling her to be quiet. Maybe the visitor would come to check on the family, to inspect, and they would see the dirt and poverty and charge her mother with being an unfit mother, they might *remove the children*. What was this knock? Maybe it would bring the repercussions for her political work on land rights. Maybe a big thug who wanted to warn her off, to accuse her of provoking the locals into standing up for their rights.

Jane opened the door; a police officer stood there. Oh no, worst fears. Had he followed her after she arrived in town? The police officer was young, she recognised him from the lock-up in town. He asked respectfully if he could come in. Jane's heart beat wildly. He sat on the divan and wrote notes.

'Miss Reynolds, while you're in town for Mardi Gras, I have to ask you some questions. You're staying with known poilitical agitators ... Back in Harrison, have you been stirring up trouble in the Aboriginal camp? We believe that your teaching assistant is a cheeky bloke and the Boss doesn't like his sort.'

'I thought you were being transferred. No? My teaching assistant, David, has left. Look, I'm a teacher. I have too much to do to bother with politics', she said.

He nodded, unconvinced. Rosie had got out of bed and was standing beside him.

'Okay then, I have to ask these questions. Have you talked about land rights in the school room?' She winced.

'They can't even read – what possible way they would know about land rights?' Rosie spoke up.

'Miss Reynolds, you have been reported for signing up Aboriginal people to vote. Did you know that it is an offence to coerce Aborigines to sign up to vote?'

Jane smiled and put on her most innocent coquettish look. 'No, officer, I didn't. But even if I had, I would have signed them up anyway.'

'Mr Barkley, would be in his rights to stop you taking Aboriginal people to town to vote', he said. She got up and mixed coffee and milk powder in a jug.

'Iced coffee?' He nodded and sighed and an embarrassing silence enveloped them.

'To tell you the truth, the local conservative party doesn't like your activities. They have made a formal complaint to the Department of Education and to us. One of their people saw David Yaniwuy handing out pamphlets against mining. You would be advised to avoid getting involved with his sort. But you are already, aren't you?'

She drew in breath.

'Sorry, but this is your first and last warning. I don't want to go out to Harrison to find you.' He had a look of condemnation, as though he thought, *Whose side are you on?*

'I have some biscuits somewhere.' She stood up holding a dusty packet of Custard Creams. 'Want one?' said Rosie.

He laughed, and accepted a biscuit.

'Nice. I like Tim Tams best.' They ate in the quiet whirring of the fan.

'Hot, isn't it?' he laughed.

'Sure is.'

He closed his notebook and stood. 'I'll be on my way. If you see Yaniwuy, well, you better stay away from him, for your own good.'

Rosie stood on the step watching him drive away.

'The Northern Territory, a place of homicidal white men free of the morality that civilised cities can bring. Here they have the freedom to be lords over the blacks. Back down south they might have been bank clerks but here, kings. Starving Aborigines pushed into camps, squalid with no running water and no future, for God's sake. And the coppers, just lackeys, yes men.'

In Katherine, there was a Mardi Gras carnival, not a gay one, but a white community event with returned soldiers in old army tanks from the airfield. Jane scanned the crowd with Aaron; she hoped to see David or Orlando. There was a marching band with girls in silver mini-skirts badly throwing batons in the air. Boys dressed in woollen Scottish kilts banged drums and blew ghastly noises from bagpipes. It was an Australian town on the Queen's Birthday weekend. It was Edinburgh and the military tattoo mixed in with American marching. Then the new Northern Territory flag arrived. It looked like pair of white false teeth on a background of baby pooh – hideous.

In town, there were scratchings on toilet walls about white supremacy and the Ku Klux Klan. Aboriginal readers ignored it. Most couldn't read or even speak English. What the Lanniwah at Harrison wanted was their land back and access to Pink Lily Lagoon to harvest water lily seedpods and perform renewal ceremonies. In the meantime, they asked politely if they could have the gates unlocked. They wanted to sing the songs on country so the ancestral beings would wake up. It was in direct conflict to the white land usage.

On the corner, stood a lone Aboriginal man with another new flag – the Aboriginal one. It was David and he did not wave it, but stood still and silent. Jane watched him. He had a pride and dignity. He was vastly outnumbered by white people but he stood his ground. The flag had black for the people's skin, red for the blood spilt and a yellow sun for the land. It was beautiful. Everyone on the street ignored him but he stood there proud. Jane approached; he saw her and smiled.

'Like my new flag? A Koori fella from down south make it'.

'It's wonderful. Are you coming back home?'

'Not yet. I gotta see some Northern Land Council fella, there's a meeting with the traditional owners from here.'

'Some people here in town won't like you waving this flag.'

'They reckon some outsider fellas told Gurindji to walk off Wave Hill. But we are bosses ourselves.'

'Be really careful.'

'Don't worry, I got brothers in town, big fellas, they even talk to dat Shire Council. Not your worry no more, okay?'

Jane went to the meeting in a hall at the museum. Old Lucy, Burnie and David sat on a platform with the representative of the Northern Land Council. Photographs of Territory pioneers hung from the wall, old coloured streamers hung limply on windows. There were a few people in the audience, mostly Lanniwah local and Jane spotted Rosie and Brian at the back. The overhead fan turned, the Land Council man stood up to speak.

At that moment, there was movement outside the door, a loud voice. 'Let me in! I demand to be heard.' Rainer Shire Council Chairman, Renway walked in. With him was Harry, he pushed past the Lanniwah audience and waved at Jane.

'Look who's here', he said. Jane ducked her head; she felt fear and revulsion.

A local police officer cleared a path for the Shire Council chairman. Renway moved with power, his blue lapel shirt stretched across his huge girth. The whole room stared. He moved heavily like an ox to the stage.

'I'm Chairman Renway and I've got something to say to all of you.' He faced the people on the stage, his back to the audience. Jane thought he needed drama lessons. Some of the Lanniwah audience got up to leave but Harry blocked the door, his arms folded. Renway seethed and tore a land rights poster from the table and screwed it up.

'Look here, you fuckin' black cunts ....'

He turned to look at Jane. He pointed at Brian and Rosie.

'And you fuckin' do-gooders from down south! '

'This is a private meeting!' said Jane.

Renway leaned over David and Old Lucy; he pointed his finger at their heads.

'You're not getting fuckin' land rights! Not now, not in ten years' time, not ever!'

'We see about dat!' said Old Lucy.

His fist clenched and he slammed it against his other palm.

'We'll burn your house down first', yelled Harry.

'They don't have any houses', said Jane.

Renway pointed at Jane.

'You, we've got your name, lady. We know about your agitating. We'll fix you, all right. You'll wish you stayed in Sydney with your student radicals.'

'We wantem National Park for dat Rainer River; gib back tribe land for us mob; we look after dat sacred place', said Old Lucy.

Renway ignored the old woman.

'Sacred, my arse. It's our river, our place, our tourism money, my tour boats, the town's life blood. You're not goin to steal it or destroy it. You got that?'

He punched his fist against the wall next to David's head. The room trembled. David tried to stand. Harry walked forward and pushed him down.

'Stay there and shut up!'

'You fellas can't do this. We will fight you with white man's law', said the Northern Land Council rep.

Renway walked back and forth in front of the stage. He leaned towards David again; spit flew from his mouth. His huge body was full of beef; full of faeces; he was high-status nastiness.

'I'll send a group of my blokes round to your station to beat the living shit out of ya. How do you like that? No one will stop us!'

Burnie and Old Lucy moved out of their chairs and with great dignity walked from the stage. They moved to the door and the police officer nodded at Renway and let them pass. Jane was stunned; the room was now quiet. What could they possibly say?

Jane felt a rising terror as she imagined the worst, the men coming in the night, maybe killing her and her child.

Renway whistled to Harry like a cattle dog and they walked out of the room. Jane sat quietly with the historians. No one spoke … The Northern Land Council rep stood.

'Now where were we? Yep, land rights for Lanniwah.'

After the meeting, Jane walked over to David and hugged him.

He greeted Rosie and Brian.

'Thanks for coming.'

'Happy to support your mob', said Brian.

'We don't need you fellas to fight. We okay.' Jane was not certain if that meant she was too involved. She didn't want to feel offended, but she cringed.

'I'm happy that you don't need me.'

'That right; too hard for you' said the Northern Land Council rep.

'I come back to Harrison some time. That my true country'.

'I'll be glad to see you back; I need your help at school'. Jane stroked David's hand and he flinched. She was scared that she was drawing too much attention to him; she took Brian by the arm and left the room. Her chest pounded. She picked up Aaron from the child-minding centre.

Out of a pub staggered two Lanniwah men, drunk and laughing. Aaron called out:

'Mummy, here come funny men.' Down the street came floats: they were trucks decorated in crepe paper and balloons. A sign read 'Harrison's Butchery, Purveyor of Fine Meats'. The butchers were dressed in drag with red lipstick and frilly white dresses; they had on big bras with tennis balls in the cups. They lifted them lasciviously to the cheering crowd and threw lollies to the children. Aaron scrambled for Minties.

The celebrations culminated in a barbecue at the showground. Sides of beef were turned on spits, the beer tent was full and drunken cattlemen lurched in and out; they swore and spat and talked about beef. Aaron wanted a go on the 'shoot 'em down' stand, where boys honed skills with rifles. Jane held the rifle for her son; he shot down ducks and won a stuffed synthetic toy lion.

There was a plastic *thong throwing competition* with thongs emblazoned with bright red, white and blue union jack designs. Jane watched and thought how white and self-congratulatory it was, a commemoration of British invasion. Aboriginal families looked on in distaste from distant trees; they weren't included; they were *conquered and despised*. Jane bought a beer and drank in a tent with Rosie and Brian. They got mildly drunk like everyone else.

'Who controls the past, controls the future.' Brian said as he reached for a dry martini from his Esky.

Beatrice appeared with David and her grandchildren; they all held showbags full of rubbish and licked fairy floss *God knows where the money came from!* Some cattlemen lurched drunkenly across the road from the beer tent. Jane and Rosie greeted the Lanniwah with hugs.

'What dis for? Alla time Wunungah drunk?', said David.

'This one special ceremony', said Jane.

Beatrice looked. 'Where dat ceremony?'

'It's all about Captain Cook and then Captain Phillip coming to put English flag in Sydney', said Rosie.

'We hear 'bout dat Captain Cook, he wantem make little mission. Walk about here, dere, everywhere. He walkabout all across our country.' They all laughed and Jane touched David's arm and he nodded. She dropped her hand down: that was all she needed, to be reassured that he cared about her. She took the children to buy ice creams.

CHAPTER 6

David Returns

Lanniwah people gathered outside the dusty store. It had chain wire windows and peeling paint. Rubbish blew along the road. David was back. Jane was stuck dumb by his return. *I must be cool, not show anyone my feelings.* She saw him walk out of the store and she wandered why Hubert had let David in. He stopped and lent against a jacaranda tree, women watching him, curious. Coke cans tumbled in the hot wind, the sound of black cockatoos and distant ceremonies. Elvis music slammed from a portable ghetto blaster on a young man's shoulder.

Struggling to breathe, Jane watched David move in his tight blue jeans. How could she consider restarting the affair? The thought of loving him was so dangerous. *Oh yes, bring it on.* He was so black, his teeth so white, his smile so soft. She asked herself about her plan for redemption and her responsibilities as a mother. No, a forbidden affair would be unthinkable. She argued with herself as she drove her groceries back to her caravan. As she unpacked tins of corned beef and baked beans she decided to ignore her feelings and just be polite. She would ignore her burning in his presence. Yep, no problem.

She took Aaron to the little white church tent and prayed to someone or something. She prayed to a bark painting with wavy lines in red and black of Jesus on a cross. She prayed to the painted ochre crocodiles and stingrays with glitter borders. The fusion of Aboriginal and Christian beliefs resulted in a confusion of the spirit. Yes, even she was confused, not to mention sexually frustrated. She could believe in animism that respected living and inanimate things or she could worship a man from Jerusalem who hung in pain on a tree. Dark guilty feelings simmered in her stomach. Aaron pulled on her arm.

'Can we go now? Jesus isn't here.'

Aaron ran up and down the aisle with a tin truck. The lay-preacher's wife, Dixie, wearing a patterned sundress and a tennis eyeshade, came towards Jane.

'Welcome at last. We were praying that you would come along to Bible class. You have our pity because you are not yet saved. We will bring you into the fold to be reborn',

'Thank you. That's very nice of you, but school … does keep me busy.' Jane hurried away. The woman looked insane.

A Land Rover pulled up outside. She saw that David was with some boys wearing dark blue Boys Brigade uniforms. They marched in to the church and stood in formation. Jane took Aaron by the hand and moved to the back while the boys arranged wattle in vases. She sneezed; the Christian light could infect you. She wondered why David was keeping his distance. He had arrived back at Harrison quietly and was not working at the school. She felt ignored. However, Harrison was too small a place to ignore someone.

Jane was at the big house collecting medical supplies from Edie. As Jane stood near the door, David knocked. She averted her gaze; it was not the time or place for a reunion. He stayed on the veranda, smoothing his hat. Hubert walked out and swung his boot up on the railing. He indicated that David should stand further down on the step, so he could look down on him.

'Yer got something to say?'

David nodded and stepped backwards.

'I want to hear you say it.'

'What?'

'That yer bleedin' sorry you nearly bleedin' killed me. Yer flaming black prick. Next time we have a fist fight I'll be ready for ya.'

'Yep.'

'Yep, what?'

David looked at his foot.

'Boss.'

'Okay mate, shake on it, and no more cheeky fella business or I'll run you out for good! Too right. I don't like dobbers, so I made that call to the coppers. You should be bloody grateful. Grateful! I want to see it on your face. You could have gone away to Fannie Bay Gaol.'

Jane watched David's face twitch, but he was silent. They shook hands and David strolled away waving at Jane.

'Leave it, Jane. You don't know what you're playin' with. He needs you like a hole in the head', Hubert said.

'Hubert, I got a letter back from the police about the girl who was raped.'

'I said I would handle that', he said. Jane stood her ground.

'Really? By covering it up?'

'Grow up, teacher. You got nothin'.'

'They will keep investigating. You will get their attention.'

'And pigs might fly.' He walked away.

She watched Hubert hide behind his Hammond organ and she walked down the stairs.

PART FOUR

NORTH WEST WIND, DRY SEASON, YAMS HAVE GREEN LEAVES – 1977

A year passes and Jane feels at home in Lanniwah country, she is enjoying the cool nights. It is mungo season and everyone gorges on the fruit. The Whistling Hawk dives for insects and crocodiles are searching for food.

EIGHT MONTHS LATER

CHAPTER 1

Shirley's Baby

Eight long months passed, Jane's relationships had shifted and developed. The land was now swept with cool dry winds and the sound of distant ceremonies. The Lanniwah children had begun to read well; some were moving onto young adult books and their faces lit up with pleasure when they first read a whole page without faltering. Jane smiled and pinched their chins with affection. She was loved and grew in strength from the children's trust. Jane had trained Ricky as an assistant because David was absent, somewhere. The love affair with him was an on and off thing. Jane was not concerned: she knew it was his way and that he travelled around the country with little thought of her. Shirley's pregnancy was full term and every one waited for the birth. Jane's relationship with Hubert and Edie was almost non-existent. They pretended she was not there.

Aaron was a big seven year old and still king of the camp kids. Jane watched him rush along the road with a group of boys, their tin trucks belting out plumes of dust. In school, he was working on his reading but was not as quick to learn as the Lanniwah girls his age.

It was a beautiful Dry time, with clear blue skies and cool nights. Jane even wore a cardigan. Then Elvis Presley died; they heard about it from Raymond. All the community were mourning for the King of Rock and Roll. There was a ceremony and his songs were played accompanied by many tears and wailing. The cadence of the music swept through the camp and the girls cried in class and no one spoke his name. It was real grief.

One night, there was a hush over the community, Jane heard the unmistakeable sound of a woman in labour; the panting drifted down from Raymond's shack. She gathered up Aaron, put him in her vehicle to sleep, and drove through the dark to where Shirley crouched on her bed having her baby. Old Lucy and Gertie were attending and their steady cooing penetrated the room. Old Raymond stood outside, smoked cigarettes, and stamped them out half way through. The tension snaked around the dark tin walls. It was a long labour, too long. Gertie considered Jane for some time and Jane was afraid that she might accuse her of being somehow complicit in the whole event. That maybe Jane had been neglectful of her students and had allowed Shirley to be out late and get pregnant. That perhaps Jane was a person who put on a respectful face to the Boss and that she had not stood up to him. She walked out of the shack to stand near Raymond.

For want of something more useful to do, Raymond took an axe and swung at the red gum logs piled beside the shack. He had a big fire burning, two billies were full of boiling water, one tipped over, and he quickly pushed it up right. The smoke rose in tall pale blue shadows and quivered around the landscape. The crack of the axe burst through the sound of his daughter moaning. Raymond leant against the wall and ran his thumb over the blade as Jane sat beside him. 'In the old days, the station bosses fathered a lot of kids; some had ten or more and they were treated no better than slaves on the properties. I saw a bloke force his white son to tie up his half-caste brother and flog him on his naked back. Tears poured down his face as the young lad pleaded for mercy. God cursed Ham – is this why there is so much hate against black people? What life will my grandchild have? I'm too bloody old to be of use.' Raymond sighed.

Jane watched Raymond throw down the implement and sit on the woodpile, his head in his old hands. A desperate cry from Shirley broke the moment. Raymond tapped on the corrugated iron and Old Lucy called out.

'Might be baby too big, better gettim Missus Edie. Gettim help.'

Raymond struggled to his feet and lumbered into the dark towards the Boss's house.

The fear poured into the gloom and Jane huddled beside Gertie and held

Shirley's hand. Sweat poured down the girl's face, her body contorted in pain as Jane mopped at her face with a wet napkin. She stroked the dark hair away from Shirley's arched brow and a tendril was looped around Jane's finger, she unlooped it and placed it gently amongst the beautiful ringlets. Golden Shirley. It was suddenly quiet, just the breathing of the women; no one spoke, and terror filled their faces. What if the baby died while trying to be born? What if Shirley was too young and too tiny to deliver what was obviously a very big baby? Jane's anxiety pulsed, she watched Shirley sit up in fright, her face contorted with a contraction, and then Edie was beside her. She pushed Jane aside and motioned for the women to move out of her way. She had some forceps and she would want elbow room.

'Get out all of you, except Gertie. Give the girl some air!'

'Missus. She bad.' Gertie cried.

'Stop frightening her! We're alright as far as I can see. Just take a few minutes more. Hold on, my darling girl.'

Jane sat in the corner and watched in awe as Edie delivered the baby. Her thin pale arms were elevated as she pushed her foot against the old bedstead. The baby popped out, and it was a girl and she was fair skinned and slightly blue. Everyone sighed, the newborn howled and they all looked at Hubert's child. Edie tied and cut the cord with a professional flourish and tucked the baby into a bunny rug. Edie shrugged and handed the bundle to Shirley for a moment before helping to deal with the after birth. After a while, Shirley smiled and Gertie knelt beside her to look at her grandchild. Clenched tiny fists pressed against her mother's face.

'My granny used to say that babies bring their love with them.' Jane smiled at Shirley and patted Gertie on her back. Jane thought how weak she must sound – as if this child had been born with no cloud over her. So many Aboriginal babies born to white fathers had been murdered in the past, but this one was going to be loved at least by her mother and grandparents. The room filled with other family members and Jane stepped outside to see Raymond in tears by his fire.

'She is okay, Raymond. You can see her if you want.'

Edie walked out and washed as Jane tipped a jerry can over her bloody hands, the sound of the water was like a song, it splashed and Edie let it run over her legs and shoes. She looked like a woman exhausted by the truth of the baby's paternity. Jane wanted to say something that would comfort, something that sounded wise and that recognised Edie's pain but there was nothing to say. It was useless, and Jane watched the water run pink and trickle down Edie's legs then into rivulets that created snake lines across the yellow dust. As if there were words that could make it better, make it not like thousands of other stories of Australia's black and white history. Jane wanted this moment to be full of love and for the new baby to be accepted and not seen as a problem to be solved or a mistake or the evidence of betrayal and abuse of power. Edie just stared at the dirt and sniffed.

'Another yellafella, what a shame.'

'She is gorgeous! You saved Shirley.'

'Just doing my job. Couldn't let them die; wouldn't be right.'

Edie walked into the night and Jane watched her disappear; she looked defeated. There was a piercing cry in the stillness, like a howl of a wounded animal and Jane didn't know if it was from a broken woman or a man in distress or what. Then, she heard a name yelled:

'Damn you, Hubert!'

Jane felt tested and that she had somehow failed to be of use to anyone. She had been useless in the end, not able to offer support to a lonely Edie or advice to Raymond, in the way and of little consequence. A bystander who had not protected the young woman. She could not face Hubert, tell the police, make a difference, or protect any other young girl from abuse, or anything at all. She looked down at her dress: it was splattered with blood; she would be marked by this event, but a feeling of joy consumed her and she raised her face to the grey cloud that moved over a rising gold moon. The baby was so beautiful and alive and its huge black eyes had stared into the new world.

A night bird swished past and Jane imagined Edie walking into her house and telling her husband that Shirley's baby was here. Maybe a madwoman would come storming up those steps and maybe there would be screaming and rage. Jane pictured herself unclenching Edie's hand from a rifle. The evidence of his duplicity was now certain, or would they all ignore the child, the half-sister of Elisha and the others. Yes, that was how it had always been: no one would say anything; the lies and secrets would float and fall like so much confetti.

A few days later, Lanniwah women crowded around Shirley, admiring her newborn baby girl. Edie had visited and worried about the child. She was not drinking properly and Edie offered to take Shirley and baby Elizabeth to Katherine hospital for checking. Jane stood outside the school and watched them drive off; it seemed like a witch was kidnapping the pair of them.

In Katherine, the hospital kept the baby because she was sickly and sent Shirley home with Edie. They could not accommodate a young Aboriginal woman when the wards were crammed with spectacular evidence of a violent outback. The bull gorings, rodeo accidents, beatings and beer bottle wounds kept the nurses running. Jane was appalled that the hospital would not admit Shirley alongside her baby.

On their return, Jane watched in shock as Edie sat Shirley down outside Raymond's shack and bound her breasts with tight nappies to stop the milk. Tears ran down Shirley's face.

A few weeks later, the Lanniwah women waited for the return of the baby from Katherine hospital. The white nurse got out of the four-wheel drive with the child. Lanniwah mothers began to cry as Shirley took back her baby and she took the bottles and formula from the nurse's hands. Jane watched critically – why separate mother and child? With no way to wash bottles, the baby might not survive. Jane ached to look after this new baby and feared for her health.

Jane nursed baby Elizabeth and asked Old Lucy about David.

'They scared him bilka because dey not know his foot print. He might be making witchcraft. If he walk through a wangarr place, might be losem strength in bones, dey break. He might go crazy, *bamu'mitti*.'

'Lucy, do you know where David is?' said Jane.

'He in might be Arnhem Land; you not worry bout him.'

A few weeks later, Jane was suffering. Hubert and Edie totally ignored her because of her affair with David: she imagined them calling up on the radio to the education office and speaking to Mr White. She saw herself being run off the property with a bullwhip. The missionaries were leaving; they packed up their tents. There were omens everywhere: something bad was about to happen; Jane could feel it.

It was near dawn when Jane woke up; there was some strange sound close to her window. She sat up and looked out into the dim light. A huge owl sat on a gum tree branch overhanging the caravan. The bird was grey and had piercing light bulb eyes. His massive yellow talons gripped the wood.

A shiver of fear, a memory. Jane's dad had told her about owls and their dangerous power of foretelling, yes, death. If they arrived over your door, you had to be ready for the bad news. When her dad had drowned, she remembered the snowy owl, the same visiting presence, eerie and unfathomable, perched right over their suburban back door. Jane got out of bed and quietly went to the door. Aaron was sound asleep on his fold-out bed in the kitchen, unaware that an unwanted visitor was searching for them with gold, torchlight eyes. She opened the door and the owl stared at her. Still, he didn't move those eyes. Then the bird flew off with a flutter of powerful wings. Jane stood in pink light as the dawn broke.

That morning, the Toyota filled up with the cranky old women; all of them wanted good fishing and a ride to the outstation of Third River. It was a four-hour drive into Arnhem Land. Old Lucy and Gertie took the best spot next to Jane in the front. Aaron rode on the back with a crowd of children. He was one small blond head amongst the black haired ones. They travelled for hours bumping over a corrugated road.

The Dry season was full of dusty winds in the pandanus palms. Jane wrote letters to Batchelor College in case David was there. She missed him. She drove Shirley and Old Lucy to the coast to swim, and hunt turtles and dugong. They would eat wild food: fish, waterlily, sugarbag honey, wild yams, kangaroo, goanna, blue-tongue lizard, blanket lizard, fresh water turtle, plus flour, Uncle Toby's Oats, Corn Flakes, rice, sugar tea, syrup, jam, tobacco, molluscs, crustaceans, dugongs, duck, tern, jungle fowl, croc, kangaroo, wallaby, possum, bandicoot, echidna, reptiles. They drove with no one talking for an hour. Finally, Jane pulled up alongside paperbark bough shades and blue tarpaulin sheds. Spears stood in neat rows outside the dwellings. A generator thrummed, barrels of fuel were covered with branches. There were a couple of destroyed four-wheel drives and a new white Toyota belonging to the clan headman. There was a new bough shade for a mobile clinic and Shirley sat inside with her baby.

'You seeum dat ring of black stones, dey for big pot, trepang. Makassan cookem up, sellem. I dive for trepang when I young womans. Now alla ghosts. Yeeai, dat trepang sea slug pack in salt. Over dere, ghost men sail prahu ship to Makassar', said Old Lucy.

'You dived?'

'Yeeai'.

Cooing, laughing, barefoot children were everywhere. A palm bough shade became the clinic building. Hanging in the air was the smell of the old people, pungent and fishy. Jane's emotions were raw and extreme. She looked at Shirley's pale daughter and wondered if Hubert would ever come to look at his child. Jane sat on a blanket under a tree with Old Lucy; they minded baby Elizabeth while everyone hunted.

Dreams of other lives criss-crossed Jane's brain. Maybe she should have gone to Africa to work with Albert Schweitzer's team or joined the Hare Krishnas. They seemed light-hearted. She felt she was obsessed with caring for others.

Gertie tapped Jane on the shoulder.

'You white women think you know everything. You like little baby, like Elizabeth asleep alla time. Not see big trouble you make. You not take that man,' said Gertie.

'What man?'

'You know 'im. He promised. You break law; dey might kill you. Wake up! Not sleep no more. You take David, his woman from Gove might beatem you.'

Jane felt like running away, running into the bush to disappear. Old Lucy hugged her and laid her head on Jane's shoulder.

'I suppose you never made a mistake? You're too busy taking orders from Missus Boss. You like being treated like dirt?'

'I work for money, dat all. You break law, 'cause you thinkem you better than us', said Gertie.

'You've got no self-respect.'

'No fella respect you – look at yourself', said Gertie.

An azure kingfisher darted over the car bonnet; it shimmered with blue light. The air smelt of grevillea nectar.

Jane offered to look after baby Elizabeth while Shirley caught some fish.

The infant seemed feverish and she whimpered. She was a sweet pale delicate child, pink brown lips with bubbles of milk on her tongue. She had chocolate eyes that smiled into Jane's eyes. Jane carried the baby over her head as she crossed the flooded creek at low tide. Everyone else had gone out fishing from Raymond's tinny boat; but Jane misjudged the tide. It seemed as though it was going out but it was coming in, rushing, and she misjudged the crossing. As she waded into the water, she realised that it was very hard to keep going against the current of water. The strong rip pushed against her, getting deeper and deeper. Jane tried to turn back, her heart pounding, but she had gone too far. Panic filled her mouth and chest. The water got deeper and began to pull her in towards the crocodiles' mangrove home, *malu*. She struggled against the rush of water, up to her chin. The baby cried as Jane held her higher and higher and pushed on towards the beckoning sand on the other side.

At last Jane sat down, alone on the riverbank, she felt terrible – so close to killing the baby. The beach stretched out in emptiness. Not another human in sight. She felt lost. She knew it was madness to have had David as a lover; she would end it for good. In addition, she was a neglectful mother: she let Aaron run wild. She couldn't even be responsible for a sick baby. Jane lay Elizabeth on a towel in the shade and fanned her. The baby was hot. Jane washed her down with cool fresh water. Tears came; Jane fell on the sand and howled. All seemed lost, death hovered. It was not the end of the world but she could see it from here. When Jane told the family about the tide, everyone laughed at her.

Next morning near dawn, Jane felt Shirley touching her face.

'What's wrong?' Jane softly enquired,

'Baby sick, got fever.'

Jane knew that the old women had made a mistake. They were ignorant of medicine. She was angry.

Shirley was no more than a girl herself. Jane tried to look away, feeling rising panic, but aware of calm under the bough shade clinic. The Lanniwah health workers steadily processed every patient. Everyone clustered on plastic benches, quietly waiting, children held on knees. An old man with streaming nose held his ancient head in his hands. His granddaughter with saucer eyes touched his shoulder as it heaved.

With desperation in her eyes, Shirley shook the sick baby gently. The health worker had endless patience. She whispered in Lanniwah language a rhythmic purr with occasional mnymik, good. Everything was good – no one dying today. The women dispensed medicine in plastic cups. They offered drinks of water. The health worker was smiling, soothing the sick baby. She walked into the treatment room. Through the canvas and leaves, Jane could see her worried interaction with the mothers, heads shaking at the tiny form.

'You have to take her to town. This baby will die! What are you doing?' Jane said.

'You no tellem us Lanniwah what to do – you not queen here!' said the health worker.

Shirley pushed into the clinic, snatched back her baby and sat under a tree in tears. She wrapped the baby blanket around the tiny baby, and with her trembling younger sister walked away from the tin building.

'Will she be okay?' said Jane.

The health worker sadly shook her head. 'Maybe die.'

Jane felt a shock of indignation. She couldn't accept the situation. Her impotence burnt.

Sweat poured down her back, thirty-eight degrees and humid. She asked where the qualified missionary nurses were today.

'Day off, at bible study, no duty for them today. Dey not come.' Jane left the rough building. She walked past tamarind trees planted by the Makassans. Fragrant sticky pods clung to her shoes. Water glistened beyond flowering jacarandas.

Jane thought about how Shirley lived in the shack with Gertie and Raymond. There was no two-storey house like the one the council chairman at the outstation had – no new Toyota or light plane for her. She had to feed her baby from a dirt-encrusted bottle. Some misplaced reasoning by nurses had allowed for the weaning of the baby while they had her in the hospital. Shirley went home on a truck without Elizabeth ... Jane had taken note – was it a deal with Nestle to sell more baby formula?

At Third River, there was genteel eating with fingertips from the shared leaf-plates. The old women waited for Jane to take her share of crayfish. Old Lucy tipped seawater from a pannikin over cooked white fish; it was barramundi, with its crackling skin pulled back. The sun set in orange and purple. Tiny Elizabeth was hot, too hot. Jane and Gertie bathed her and administered miniscule drops of baby Panadol in boiled water.

'I can take you back to Harrison. We need to see Edie. She'll know what to do', Jane said. Shirley shook her head; it was too far, too many ghosts on the road, the danger of losing the Toyota in deep bulldust, and too many buffalo on the road. No, she would be okay: Old Lucy had given her some bush medicine.

Beatrice woke Jane from her swag. Jane thought a crocodile might be coming along the quiet black beach. The night was navy velvet, a cool breeze swept the white sand, and the waves were small and perfectly formed. Beatrice's face was close to Jane's.

'You come Jane, quick', said Beatrice. Jane followed to a group of women under a casuarina tree. Shirley sat with her head in her hands. Jane looked at the tiny bundle on her knees. Shirley's baby was still. Jane took possession of her, and held her close. The baby could barely breathe, she was burning up, and shaking breaths like puffing came out of pale blue lips. Jane handed her to Shirley; she shook gently, and the little breath came. Then her breathing stopped. Shirley shook again, and looked wildly at Jane.

'What wrong with Elizabeth? Help her', she cried.

Jane leant over Shirley and laid the baby on the blanket. She was dead.

The baby was warm but began to cool like a billy of tea. Jane cleared the tiny mouth with her finger; she gently rolled her on her back and knelt over the infant. Jane tilted back her head.

'Elizabeth, come on sweetie, come back, breathe, please', whispered Jane. She tasted the little lips and nose as she blew – one-two, one-two. Mouth tiny and pale. Around her in the dark, Jane could see only whites of eyes and gleaming Lanniwah teeth. She was desperate; the urgency beat in her throat; her heart raced. And it was too awful. Shirley shook the child again, willing to shake her life back. Jane's head throbbed, a knife in her brain, glass in her temple. She felt stupid and useless; she knew nothing about how to bring back life. She looked up at Shirley; her face was a wall of grief and tears bubbled out.

'You fixem, Miss Jane. You fixem Elizabeth – she not dead, she sleep. She sleep ...' Gertie took her daughter in her arms and rocked her back and forth. The tiny baby pressed between them in her rug. Grandmother, mother and daughter all one.

'My daught, your little one gone now; she fly away in the stars. You lookem, see her going.' Gertie pointed upwards to the night.

The wailing began; women fell in crumpled heaps on the cool sand. Gertie took a rock and beat her head; blood dripped down. Too much death, too much crying. When would it all stop? Shirley wrapped the little body in the cotton Peter Rabbit and Jemima Puddleduck rug that Jane had bought in Katherine. The baby's tiny hands were pressed in prayer under her chin. Shirley lay next to her all night, her small breast near her mouth, waiting out the terrible haunting night as her mothers and aunts sang, waiting for sunrise.

Back at Harrison, Shirley, Gertie and sisters, grandmothers and aunts, danced a desultory ceremony with their foreheads caked in white ochre. It was a day of dancing, a mortuary ceremony for the little wrapped body, as small as a package of rice. The men played didgeridoo for the child, but there was not much ceremony for such a little, yellafella life. Old Burnie sat with clap sticks in his old hands, spindly arms raised, his eyes cloudy with glaucoma. Robert played the didgeridoo; he stopped and stared at Shirley. Raymond sat on his plastic chair just outside his shack, tears running down his face. Jane wondered if she had the right to attend, as it was only her adopted clan.

'Come sit', they said.

'Come dance wid us for this baby. She gone to Jesus now', said Lizzy.

Aaron came up to the little bundle, wrapped in yellow flannelette and gum leaves, and stared down at the little corpse.

'Why is Elizabeth dead? Can't you give her medicine and bring her back? Jesus did that; he brought back Lazarus', he said.

Raymond blew his nose and called Aaron over to him.

'She's gone now, mate. Her soul is gone, just an empty little body now. It's okay to cry, we all cry in this life.'

Aaron sat on Raymond's lap and laid his blond head against the white beard.

Jane knew that this baby would join the hundreds of babies whose names were crossed off the lists in the health clinic book, little deaths due to gastro or bronchial infection – so senseless. So many dead at two weeks, one month, ten months, three years – all gone to Jesus.

Hubert rode by the ceremony on his motor bike, then stopped and parked in the dust. He walked towards the ceremony, his hat crumpled in his hands. No one looked at him openly. It was a Greek tragedy. Jane watched with fascination. What would he do? What did he dare do? Old Lucy grabbed her hand and leant her old eyes towards the ground, averted from the Boss. Hubert walked, a man on a mission. He squatted next to Raymond's chair and offered him a cigarette, lit it for him; they smoked in silence. Hubert's head bent forward, his shape like Rodin's 'Thinker'. Was he crying? Jane ached to see, but could only see his balding skull rocking above his bent knees.

Shirley was with the women dancing. She proudly looked away, intent on her best dancing for the baby's spirit. After ten minutes, Hubert stood up, touched Raymond on the shoulder, then he gave the old man the cigarettes – *a half packet of Benson and Hedges for a life?* Hubert moved towards Gertie, but she walked away. He followed and put something in her hand. Then he kicked over the engine and rode away. The motorbike roared. So was that it, the atonement? Jane walked over to Raymond.

'Thought you were going to kill him?' she said.

'He's a good Boss; didn't mean any harm', he said. Gertie took a crumpled fifty-dollar note from her bra. She held it out to Jane on her palm.

Jane looked at it. 'Okay, that's it then?' Jane said.

Gertie tossed the money onto the dirt in front of Raymond, brushed her dress down, and with great dignity walked away.

'The Boss is going to give me his old nag. She's a good horse; we can get around a bit, you know', said Raymond.

Jane's throat filled with green bile of rage. That night she wrote a letter to the Member of Parliament for Arnhem Land, Henry Cotton. He was a friend who dropped in on Lanniwah and Wunungah alike, a good honourable man, funny too, married to a Tiwi wife who was majestic and smart.

A month later, Henry wrote back from Darwin – 'A great letter, Jane; made me cry, etcetera'. He told her that he would look into baby Elizabeth's death. Jane's letter claimed that the missionary nurses had been negligent. They had allowed unqualified Lanniwah health workers to run the clinics at the outstation and babies were dying. She asked him why the nurses just prayed when faced with impending Lanniwah deaths. Why wasn't there an airlift to Gove? Why was there no air evacuation for Aboriginal communities? Hadn't this baby been very ill? Was she the only person who could see that? No flying doctors here: they were for the white cattle station people. Injustice burnt. Henry would hand the case to the coroner. A few weeks later, the missionary nurses called on Jane and solemnly tapped on the screen door.

'You have accused us of negligence!' The air crisp with anger and Christian repression.

'It's the devil's work', they said. Jane shamefully backed down, apologising, snivelling, and praising the church's missionary work. After all, she had to survive amongst majority missionaries and cattlemen both. She hated herself as she poured the tea.

'Powdered milk?' Smiling nurses accepted her apology..

Shirley was found *guilty of neglect* by the Darwin coroner. Charged with *not being a fit mother*, leading to the death of an infant. There had been no place to clean a bottle in a windswept shed; it was a scandal, a shame, and the mother's fault of course. Perhaps she would face criminal charges. Jane's letter was evidence, a piece of Judas kiss? She tore her hair in disbelief. Poor Shirley, poor golden Shirley. But nothing came of it. The weeks passed.

Aaron and some little boys played with Shirley outside the caravan. She pretended she was a teacher and they were students. They had a little piece of masonite as a desk, and she walked back and forth with a ruler in her hand.

'Shirley, where is your baby gone?' Aaron asked.

A look of great misery passed over her face.

'She maybe in the clouds; she not cry no more; we not cry no more.'

'I cry, Shirley. She was so little, we shouldn't have put her in the ground – she might wake up.'

'She no more wake up.' Shirley stopped and stared at the ground. Jane put her arms around her.

Jane sank into despair. Being in love with someone was hell; it tore out your stomach. So she withdrew and wondered what being dead would feel like. She thought about her body swinging from a rope. It looked simple. She knew from Girl Guides how to tie a hangman's noose.

Returning to the Harrison clinic, Jane watched to see if the missionary nurses attended, asking loudly when they would arrive. Having a social cause was a help; it made her forget about David. The Aboriginal health worker bustled around distributing medicine, laughing and filling the makeshift room with hope.

'Why no doctor come and stay here, Jane? We only got Missus Boss. We need a doctor so bad', said the health worker. There was no answer.

CHAPTER 2

Margie And Edie Cook Stew

It was a morning of wind, full of dust and leaves. Jane sat by Margie at recess. The stockman's breakfast sat cooling in the makeshift kitchen. There was a big fire and griddle on bricks under a roof of gum branches and tin. No walls, stinking hot at midday. Margie had swept the dirt floor with a broom of twigs; her sister's small child was hanging from her shoulders. A grey dog licked the meat fat from stones at her bare feet. She threw some beef livers on the hotplate and sprinkled it with salt; the smell was pungent, something between urine and hamburger. An eaglehawk perched on a mulga tree; she threw it some fat. Margie winked at Jane.

'My meat, totem, that bird; can't hurt him', Margie said.

Every day, Margie cooked stews and damper at the bush kitchen near the school where a huge piece of salted green bullock hung in a meat safe. The damper of flour, water and salt was huge and cooked in a big iron camp oven on the fire. Flies buzzed. Jane sat in the shade. Edie walked in and emptied packets of dried vegetables into the iron pot on the fire. She was avoiding Jane, punishing her. Edie chatted amiably to Margie as she stirred the stew.

'Don't put a whole box of curry powder in – you'll ruin it', said Edie.

'My stew, Missus, my way. You know nothing. I cook for twenty years for big mob men, and you only cook for a few kids', said Margie.

'Okay, Margie, next time you're in labour you can do it yourself.'

'My mamma had six kid all by herself at Pink Lily Lagoon. One tree there my Dreaming place. True', said Margie.

'My Dreaming place must be under the bridge in Manchester, then', Edie said.

Jane laughed, and Edie gave her a withering look. 'What do you want?' said Edie.

'Company', said Jane. Margie looked at the Missus and kept stirring the stew.

'You wantem some stew, Miss Jane?' said Margie.

Jane nodded. Edie shook her head.

'She doesn't eat here', said Edie.

Margie dished out some stew for Jane. Edie looked at the plate and pushed it out of Jane's reach.

'I hear bout dat teacher fella at Kelly Downs. He was too lonely, so he jump off that cliff, true', said Margie.

'Reverend Wiltshire said he had been drinking metho', said Jane.

'Why would an atheist like you be talking to the Reverend?' said Edie.

'I have to talk to some adults. Aaron mostly talks about Lego, and the Reverend has a duty to talk to lonely women, doesn't he Edie? He has compassion, and if you want me to define that, it is "with proper grace, informing a correct compassion".' Edie slammed the meat cleaver into the block and walked out. Margie whistled.

'Nice one.' Margie said. Jane cut herself a piece of damper and piled on golden syrup. It was the end of recess.

Edie turned and stepped back under the bough shade.

'Just because you helped me when I was under the weather, doesn't mean I want you in my face. I have other friends, good Christians. Why don't you move up to David's camp?'

'Sure, whatever you want, I can be the devil incarnate, I eat babies, I teach Satan worship, I am corrupt … I have sex with all the Lanniwah men. I am not perfect and you are so … judgemental', said Jane.

'You have to be a respectable person: you're the teacher. The missionaries are upset, you abused Dixie; you swear and commit adultery; you have immoral habits; and you had an affair with David. Sex with an Aborigine – how could you? We think you're having a nervous breakdown. You might have to leave. We are going to write a letter to the Department; we are going to make a complaint! How do you like that?' The rage poured out of Edie's face.

Jane edged away. She ate her damper and said nothing, but Edie had her in her sights.

'And don't you ever spread rumours about my husband! He is a saint, you hear that? A wonderful, kind and generous man and he was not the father of that pick bastard child! ' Edie sat down and blew her nose. It was over.

Margie whistled and kept stirring. Jane stood stock still. She examined her foot, no shoes; it seemed to be part of someone else's body. Maybe she was losing her mind. She had an idea that she might throw the stew pot at Edie, but it looked too heavy, too hot; she would need a potholder, no two; it would scald her, third degree burns, it would hurt. Jane observed Edie's face up close: she needed a facial, and she had blackheads.

'My job is very hard. How would you manage?'

'I already teach my children. Would you like me to take on your picks as well?' said Edie.

'They are not picks; they are children, valuable human beings and a lot smarter than your drongos.'

Margie leaned forward and removed a carving knife out of Edie's reach.

'That so? Well a gin would say that. Go on, get away from my kitchen. My boys built this. Don't come near my drongos or me! And keep your illegitimate brat away too, you witch. I hope the loneliness kills you!'

'And Hubert is a rapist, and you let him abuse those young girls', Jane shouted.

'He was never charged! You got that through yer thick head?' Edie lunged at Jane and her punch missed as Margie grabbed her from behind and held her until the rage subsided. Edie spat at Jane, shoved her in the chest, and walked out. Jane caught her breath; she was panting. Margie watched Edie go.

'You don't worry 'bout Missus. She gone thick in the head since dat Reverend he bin go America. You like Lanniwah now. You not leave us.' She hugged Jane and the two women stood before the boiling pot.

CHAPTER 3

Wrong For You

During the terrible pre-Wet build up, some young men climbed trees covered in green ants and refused to come down. The heat drove everyone mental ... Jane had kept up her letter writing for land rights. One day, she came back from school and saw the door open: something was wrong. All her things were torn up and thrown around the caravan. She reached down and picked up the photograph of her family; it was torn in half. She sat in the mess and wondered who had done it. She looked into her bedroom and over on the mirror was a scribbled sign. "Stop the land rights shit or die!" She traced the Texta words with her finger. She shook with fear, rocked back and forth with her arms pressed around her chest.

Jane was going mental by wanting David as a lover, boyfriend, assistant – or what? They were all waiting for the rain, the black clouds built up and crashed together, lightning pierced the sky, tongues flickered and white light lit up scenes from Fellini movies. A flash, revealing a girl in a white dress running with a bunch of bananas on her head, shattered blackness. Another flash and Raymond was seen with no trousers, holding up a bible – or was it Dante's *Inferno*? – pissing on the front door of Reverend Wiltshire's tent. Again, the light revealed Dixie, the missionary, tearing her blouse while her husband beat her with a switch of bamboo. Jane cowered in her caravan; she was alone again with a child and a missing husband. She told herself to be strong, run away, or jump off a cliff.

Jane watched the sky, black clouds, the end of the Dry. And the monsoon was late. David said that the young men went crazy, they made love with wild girls at Third River in the mangroves, crocodiles watching – if they could find a girl, that is. The teenage boys at school reckoned they needed a whole packet of Black Cat condoms for every weekend.

The missionaries seemed oblivious that the school classrooms were the scene of wild love making every day after school. The youngsters simply removed louvres and took over the juniors' beanbags with libidinous abandon. These same innocent teenagers dressed in boys or girls brigade uniforms and assembled outside the church on Sundays. They had bibles in hands, scrubbed clean for God.

On weekends, Beatrice sometimes knocked on the classroom walls with her stick and yelled at the children to get out. She was a lawmaker. All the Lanniwah respected her. They scattered at the sound of the old lady's voice. She was a force to be reckoned with. Jane watched her throw a stick at Hubert's truck as he drove by, she cursed him in Lanniwah language. She saw Jane walking home from the store, and called her over.

"Gotta watch out for whitefella: dey go mad in dis season. Dat Boss, he gotta chasem young girl cause he got little fella in pants, real tiny one. Poor fella, eh?' Beatrice fell about laughing. Jane wandered how she might know something like this.

'You now forget David. It might be killem you. You no go to him. Too hard mixem marriage. He got promise', Old Beatrice said.

'You're right, it's no good. Bad business. I forget about him', Jane lied.

'Yeeai, I likem young fella too. I lookem alla time, yummy.'

'But you are fifty', said Jane.

The old lady touched her head. 'Might be fifty up here, but I fifteen down dere!' She roared with laughter.

'You bad womans', said Jane.

'Yeeai, young fella feel real good – drive 'im hard.' She wiggled with laughter

Jane was in turmoil: she couldn't get David out of her head. She became obsessed, hands thrust in panties, caressing her clitoris, madness, lust, touching, wanting, and daydreaming of him. Was she some sort of sex maniac? She asked permission from Old Lucy to drive the long road to the coast with some older girls. They drove through trees laden with sticky grevillea flowers, the nectar glued to the windscreen. Lizzy and Shirley tore off branches and licked the gold flowers. Jane joined them and the nectar ran down her chin. When they arrived at the azure sea, they broke off rocks, smashed open huge oysters, and slurped them down. Jane drew David's name in sand and erased it.

Old Lucy was getting very weak: her multiple sclerosis, or whatever it was, had made her crippled, and she could barely walk. Jane helped Old Lucy back to her camp; laid the old woman down and covered her with a blanket.

David had kept quiet about Jane, but why bother? Everyone knew about the affair; they might as well have announced it on the community loudspeaker at the church. The Lanniwah women whispered and laughed at Jane but she just walked past, head held high.

Back at school, time moved slowly. Oh God, every day the bloody same. Jane thought, 'I sit here at this teacher's desk, writing plans that nobody will read or care about.' She waited for small disasters: a snake in the school, nit infestations, a wild bull, a baby born blind, Edie to report her, the missionaries to set her on fire or stone her to death. In her world of duty and books marked, each day she waited for, what? Someone to come, a move to a bigger school?

She thought about David while she worked. David put his head in the door, girls squealed, and some hid behind desks. He laughed and looked at Jane. David held Jane's eyes for a second too long and the girls noticed it immediately.

'Missus, he still lub you, oh Missus Jane'.

She blushed and ducked behind a desk, pretending to search for a book. David whistled and strolled down the track as the girls rushed to the window to admire his backside.

Sixteen-year-old girls fluttered their eyelashes at David while they were rehearsing a Hawaiian hula dance. The girls were sensual, dark or golden skin in coloured grass skirts. ' Miss gunna dance too?'

Mayda began wearing hibiscus flowers around her beautiful face to school. One afternoon, after school was finished, Jane saw David talking to her. He was leaning across Mayda as she pressed her back against a school wall. Jane felt a flash of violent jealousy. She pushed it aside. It was embarrassing. He could do whatever he wanted: he was not promised to her, and he could have any relationship as long as the woman was in the right subsection for him.

Jane began to monitor where he was in the school. She would find excuses to drop into his class. She asked him for extra assistance with the boys. He could treat scabies and take them to the showers. Jane was entering an inner world of obsession with a man she couldn't love.

One night, Jane woke up because she could hear a distant car. It pulled up near her home and someone got out. She looked through the slightly open door and suddenly it opened. A large man in a brown floppy hat stood there. She was frightened. Time slowed down and everything became unreal. She could smell his cigarette breath, his sweat and unwashed clothes.

'You Jane Reynolds?' he said.

'Yes.'

'I've been sent to give you a message.'

'What? From who?'

'You keep out of land rights agitation or we will kill you and your son! You got that. We'll all root you, then shoot you, and bury you where no one will find you, ever! Just a pile of bones in an ants nest. I was in Vietnam – I know how to kill gooks', he said.

Jane tried to push the thin door shut but his foot was jammed in it. He pushed his arm through the crack and grabbed her by the face. His fingers squeezed her cheeks, the grip steel. Her skin white and sweating. She shook and tensed in terror. Her teeth chattered. The hand was cold and it penetrated her skin ... Time slowed down and her tongue gagged; she felt like she was rushing towards a brick wall, about to have her face smashed; she was frozen and no sound came from her strangled throat. Minutes seemed to pass, he didn't speak. Then she heard Aaron wake up, she struggled out of the ice grip and felt like she had a sudden strength and would turn into a she dingo and tear the man's arm off ... She snatched his wrist and gave a vicious judo twist; the man yelped.

'Who is it, Mummy?' said Aaron. The man dropped to the dirt. His face had a red bulbous nose with a carcinoma on it. He wore an army camouflage jacket.

'See you', he hissed, and then he laughed. She felt a rigid terror as walked away and slammed his car door. He drove back along the track towards town. Jane moved to the bedroom and held Aaron in her arms. He cuddled her and asked for a drink. Jane went to the fridge and found she couldn't open the milk tin because her hands were trembling ... She sat on the floor and held her hand over her mouth; she choked with tears. She hated the Territory; she hated the power of all the old men who ran the place. The black and the white.

CHAPTER 4

Pity

One afternoon, thunder cracked and big drops of water fell from the grey sky. The sublime relief. Jane felt certain everything would turn out fine. She would ask Hubert to talk to Renway. She would surrender and stop writing letters: men like Renway could win, and she didn't care anymore because her son's safety was paramount and the Lanniwah could fight their own land rights battles. They had told her to stop. David would carry on without her. She felt a kind of release.

It began to sprinkle and everyone rushed out of the school to drink the rain. Children ran in the rain and it began to pour. Everyone was jubilant, face upturned to the teeming rain, even Reverend Wiltshire, back from America, danced outside in the rain in his 'y-front' underpants. It was ecstatic; pink tongues lapped the liquid catching the droplets with joy. It was the renewal of the soil – rebirth. For the Lanniwah it was literal, it was spiritual.

It was *Dangurreng*, knockem down season with violent storms. Jane was getting desperate for a break. She looked across the plain and prayed (actually prayed) for someone to take pity on her. Storms flattened the spear grass; plants bore small sour fruits and it was time to harvest yams and light fires to clear grasses.

Reverend Wiltshire had returned with new skills: he was able to speak in tongues and exorcise the devil and the Edvard Munch Ministry of Silly Walks had replaced the caring mission. Wiltshire was seen standing in the middle of the road outside the church laying his hands on unsuspecting Lanniwah men. Jane walked by with a pile of books.

'I am now a member of the International Organisation of Exorcists. Out!

Out!'

The Reverend grabbed Ricky by the shoulders, trembled and shook, rolled his eyes and panted, and looked upward and cried out to God for the salvation of the Lanniwah. Ricky squirmed and his eyes asked Jane to help him. She stood nearby and reached out an arm for Ricky to hold. Her arm shook with his, a chain reaction. She carefully took hold of the Reverend's hand and unpeeled the gripping fingers; each one reattached like an octopus and Jane again unpeeled them. Ricky slid out from the grasp and ran off. The Reverend's warm eyes fell on Jane. He sniffed the air; he seemed to be trying to detect brimstone or the smell of sex. He moved up close, still sniffing. She held his arm and squeezed it and they both stared at blood beginning to ooze beneath her nails. He cringed.

'Wilt, do not even think about exorcising me. I like my resident devils!' Jane let him go and walked away.

'I am doing God's work!'

'You are just another white interfering shithead. Leave Aboriginal people alone, my people alone!'

'You? Look at you! You're not black, you're a fake!'

'Not as fake as you. I saw you!'

Jane had heard that the Reverend had held Sammy in a room for two days for exorcism. The Reverend forced Satan out of Sammy's thin body by preaching to him. However, Sammy had agreed to train as a Lanniwah pastor: miracles could happen.

Edie and Hubert attended a meeting where the Lord spoke to them through the Reverend and they were happy to wait in love for the last judgement. They waved with insane smiles at Jane; it was the first kind thing Edie had done for her in months. She ran over to Jane and gave her a bottle of lemonade. It was warm.

Jane wondered if perhaps she was missing something, and above all, whether Edie had reported her. Maybe they were grinning in triumph. Maybe they knew about Renway and his connections. Maybe they had stood behind their window and laughed while that terrifying man threatened her. She put a big latch on her door. A plank of hard wood across the inside. Still, she found it hard to sleep.

'You can sleep in our bed if you're scared – it's a Sleepmaker king size', laughed Hubert.

She worried about unemployment. A terrible meeting with the authorities in Darwin. Dismissal. She was skin and bone, a mess of fear and anxiety. She was ill and Aaron was very weak with gastroenteritis.

Wiltshire saw Jane as she came out of her caravan, a haggard skinny mess. She hung out washing with shaking arms and he rushed over and grabbed her by the shoulder as curious Lanniwah watched. She wriggled, but his grip was iron. His other hand waved up and down; he moaned like a maniac.

'Out, out, Satan! I say, out!' Jane grimaced and leant forward.

'Fuck off!' she said.

The Lanniwah women wept with laughter.

'The devil speaks in filth. It is the devil, not you. Beware, Jane, of Satan's grip. I can help you. You trusted me when David was in gaol. Let me help you, please!' he whispered. She wrenched her arm away and ran off down the road. Lanniwah women slapped their thighs and fell about – it was better than Charlie Chaplin.

Jane became thinner and the gastroenteritis took away her strength. She sat for days on the toilet, shitting yellow water, and she feared that she might just die and no one but Aaron would notice or for that matter, care. All day she didn't eat; she drifted with her mind clinging to an idea of redemption. Her child must get better; he was a messenger for Jane. His life was more important than hers was; he was a lesson in love ... Jane recovered by starving herself but Aaron was thin and weak and she went to see Edie. Her feet were heavy on the big house steps.

'Please Edie, my little boy is sick. Do you have any medicine?' said Jane.

'Get off my steps!'

'He has bad gastro, I'm really scared, and I have run out of Gastrolyte. Please!'

'If you let him drink out of the picks' cups of course he will get sick – use your head, woman.' Edie handed a bottle of liquid and sachets through the gate rails and walked away. She showed a little compassion.

After a few days, Aaron was well, and ran back up to the Lanniwah camp. Jane struggled to school and ran into Hubert in his truck.

'You feelin' better?' he said.

'Yeah. But I'm frightened that I will get another visit from Mr Renway's thug. I'm scared.'

'Don't worry, I can protect you. Just give a yell if anyone comes near and I'll come over and punch their lights out. No one hurts a teacher on my property. I can give you a rifle if you want … Look, I care about your safety. Edie and I are responsible for everything that happens out here. It's not your fault. Some townies are too political – why can't we just leave this land rights stuff alone?'

David arrived back in the community but did not work at school. He sent a note with Shirley. Jane read it and walked straight over to his house. He sat quietly by a fire reading a cowboy book.

'Are you coming back to the school?' she said.

'Narr, no good for you.'

'I want you to keep your job: the kids need you.'

'You might be train up Ricky, or Shirley?'

'I want you to do it.'

'I go over Rainer River soon; might be work at dat school', he said.

She looked at his face; it told her of compassion and a hidden history.

'My mother and father, they die when me little fella. Uncle raise me up. Teach me cattle work. I look out for my little sister and aunty, she blind. I can't be with you.' he said.

His face was lightly lined and he had deep brown eyes that smiled but never held their gaze too long. His warmth oozed; he was open and awkward. She watched the top of his curly head as he used his bare foot to trace circles in the dirt. The air rippled with heat … She still felt alive in his presence.

'I understand. Do you still want to finish your certificate then maybe go on to become a teacher?' she said.

'Might be, study in university. I go back to Darwin, but it's big city, lotta bars and lotta white people. But make me feel like a stranger, and dis my own country. I gotta do some land rights work myself.'

'I could come with you?' she said.

He looked at her and smiled; he reached out his hand but withdrew it. He held it against his red-checked cowboy shirt. She looked at the mother of pearl buttons. She stared at the hand, his beautiful hand. Her words hung in the space between them. She wanted to take them back, and she was ashamed of her longing. She ran her hands through her long hair; he watched the tresses as she stroked them. He swallowed and turned to watch the horizon.

'No, no more. No more love, sorry.'

Jane's face crumpled. She knew this would happen – it was all impossible. They struggled to change the subject.

'I worry about bilka men; they watch all things from miles. Dey sneak in my house, might be payback. Takem hair and makem poison that poison body.'

'What's that poison?' said Jane.

'Made from dat ant bed and stuff and you know singem, make it real strong and you can't see him. Then I might be wake up dead, lookim down on my body like bird, from far away.'

'But you haven't committed any crimes? Why would they hunt you?'

'Might be for some crime. Might be for that Daniel.'

'You're frightened?' she said.

She was devastated. He was not going to love her any more. Her face showed all the hurt but she kept up a cheerful conversation. *Keep a happy face.*

'No, not for that. I wantem wife, Lanniwah. I not have promise wife long time yet', he said.

Jane was relieved to hear this; he wouldn't marry for many years. The old men took all the beautiful young women. It wasn't fair. Now she knew she was not a candidate for David. She never would be. The pity of it.

'I go Katherine soon; might be find new job with Northern Land Council. Sorry, I got to do this. Too much trouble here. Sorry 'bout that.' She felt devastated, he was going out of her life and she would have to live through the pain all over again.

CHAPTER 5

A Fight At The Hotel

Jane went to the next remote schools meeting at the conference centre at the rear of the Crocodile Hotel. It was hot and sticky, like life was being sucked from the atmosphere. Aboriginal people stood in the shade near the post office, they waved to her.

She knew that it was time to stop acting: she was going to be outspoken about her Aboriginality when necessary. She was sick of pretending to be something she wasn't. It would be a peaceful professional time. She had no time for men or traumatic relationships. She left Aaron with Rosie at their house.

She moved through the hotel lounge, velvet curtains stinking of smoke. Jane knew she couldn't avoid Orlando. She didn't want to avoid him. He must be there somewhere. She would be cool, sensible, kind but distant; they could be friends. Yes, she had a plan. She looked around. The people looked familiar. Horror of horrors, there was also a conference with bigwigs from Canberra and Darwin and teachers from local schools. They were all getting blotto, the women hugging glasses of moselle, the men vying for the opportunity to become the biggest imbiber of Cooper's beer. Some of them called out to her across the mayhem. She walked around with an averted face; a man kissed her cheek. Someone was vomiting in a corner.

Mr Pageworthy was back. The Education Department inspector pushed his face into hers. 'How is Orlando?'

Jane smiled weakly. 'I haven't seen him since last year. He'd be here somewhere, I guess. Same old Orlando, a real character', she muttered and kept moving, a smile plastered on her face.

'Fancy meeting you here! I was going to come out for a formal visit. How's it all going? I heard there was some problem at your school.' He looked concerned. It was a man from the Darwin office, Mr White. He wore a brown cardigan, with shorts and a red spotted tie. There was tomato sauce on it. He grinned at her. She squirmed, thinking, for a terrible moment, that he was going to tell her about receiving a letter from the station, that she was on probation and there was a review of her contract or something and she was about to be sacked.

'Marvellous, great pedagogical outcomes that meet my objectives, fabulous Aboriginal people', she said. He sipped his brandy and dry.

'No trouble then with the relief teacher?'

'All marvellous. The Lanniwah are wonderful people, despite being massacred and exploited. It's amazing, isn't it, how one survives? Must go. Lovely to see you again. Give my regards to Darwin office', she said.

'Come into the regional office on Monday, I have to talk about some serious issues.' Mr White watched her push through to the main bar, where it was wall-to-wall men. She felt that a pile of shit was towering over her, and she might just expire on the spot. Hadn't Mr White seen *Wake in Fright*?

This main bar, the Sports Bar (no blacks allowed) was loud with beer swilling and poker machines ringing out. The miners were drinking with the contract builders after work on Friday. The men's eyes flickered around her. Jane searched nervously ... She was uncomfortable, unwanted, in the male domain. She looked about for Orlando, she just couldn't keep away. She would utilise a talking cure, summon up Freud. Expel him forever from her consciousness. Perhaps she could go somewhere with him and talk: it seemed like they had unfinished business. A group of men were nudging each other; she was a cockroach about to be squashed. They were talking about her, it wasn't pleasant, and it seemed to be funny.

Jane pushed past and slipped into the hotel kitchen. She leant against the stinking industrial Simpson dishwasher, like the ones she had unloaded as a seventeen year old at Basser College. She breathed in the smell of unwashed dishes, fat from steak and chips and there he was, Orlando, the name a song. He stood in front of her and smiled and she fell into his arms.

'Thank God, I was about to run. It's like purgatory in there'

'You look beautiful. It's been far too long. I forgot how you make my heart leap. Hey, stop hiding in the kitchen! Come on; we won't eat you'.

'Hey Orlando, I'm sorry about all the…'

He took her hand and led her to the bar; his flesh was gentle and caring, and he gave her a lovesick look.

'No, darling, I'm in the wrong, not you … We need a drink. God, it's great to see you … Come and meet the boys, you know most of them. Johnno, Nobby, Bluey, Curley, Robbo, Dan.' The men all greeted her. They stood against the bar, boots on the trough with hands gripping overflowing schooners of ice-cold beer. They leered and licked their lips.

'Hey, I'd rather be on Lanniwah country fishing with Old Pelican, but here we are', said Orlando.

And, yes, Daniel was there. She looked at him: standing with arms crossed, legs apart, muscled. Staring at her. Right into her personal space. He now specialised in building houses on mining sites: fly in, fly out.

'Look who's here, the most beautiful teacher in the outback!' He took her hand and kissed it, she blushed and the group of men laughed.

'She's working in an Aboriginal school', said Daniel.

'Good on you! Here we work alongside Aboriginal blokes, that bulldozer driver; he's a blackfella isn't he? Or is he an Indian?' said Robbo.

'Sure, we're all really sensitive. We love our footie, our women in the kitchen or on the bed – narrr, just stirring you. And our fishing.' said Daniel holding up his glass. He could be reasonable when he was apart from the other builders, but some kind of group macho atmosphere overtook him at the pub. Jane could smell his cologne, Armani or something. She whispered to Orlando.

'Can we just go?' But Daniel was zeroing in.

'What you drinking, Jane? You look good enough to eat. They haven't got cabernet sauvignon blanc on tap here. No, sorry. You like whisky. I hear you've been adopted by the local Indigenous people. That's an honour. Seriously, I am part of that tribe too, so I've been told by a certain person. What does that make you in relation to me? I am a Jabiru man, and you'd be what if Orlando's my father in law? Hey, you'd be my mother-in-law.'

'That would be a taboo relationship', said Orlando.

'Can't even look at you. That right, eh Andoboy?' said Daniel.

'Sounds good to me', said Jane.

'Come on, be a good girl. There's not too many white guys left to talk to. Did ya hear about the bloke snorkelling off the point? Got eaten by a salty croc. His wife saw him lifted out of the water in its jaws. True. We going drinking or what?' said Daniel.

Jane pulled on Orlando's arm. 'Let's go Orlando. I thought you might want to talk.'

'I wouldn't be such a snob with your juicy reputation', said Daniel. Orlando simmered.

'Just leave it, he's drunk.'

'Sorry, sorry. I am a respectful admirer. And I'll have you know that I am not drunk, just slightly inebriated.'

Another man walked into the bar; it was Harry, but he had fallen off the wagon. He was also drunk. Kenny Rogers squealed "Lucille!" from the juke box. Harry staggered towards Jane and held out his hand.

'Oh gawd, it's the pretty hippy teacher. You remember me from last year don't you? That's me, the Boss's love child. I saved your life in the outback; you could have perished, and those kids. Gee, I love those little pickaninnies … that other stuff, you've forgiven me, I hope. You'll be pleased to know that I still go to Arseholes Anonymous; but tonight I'm drinkin'. I'm gettin' charged up so I better not run into those land rights uptowners. You see, if anyone tried to take my land, I'd neck myself.' He held up a schooner glass.

'Leave her alone, Harry', said Orlando.

Jane nodded and shook his hand. He gripped hers hard and smirked. She felt like vomiting; the scene was getting worse by the minute. It was creepy. There were whispers behind her back while someone stroked her hair. Orlando was laughing but he looked terrified. Why? Jane felt like she was witnessing a conspiracy. The men kept looking over at the Blacks' Bar outside.

Then she saw David. It was one of those terrible coincidences, an agonising gulf between them. She caught him watching her. He stood outside in the beer garden, with some Aboriginal men wearing white shirts and land rights badges. They looked like the Northern Land Council men. She wanted to walk over to David and greet him, but the long walk past white men with beers was too much. It was a walk between two worlds, and she would stand out like dog's balls.

Harry pulled an object from his back pocket and showed it to Orlando and Daniel. Jane strained to see it. My God, it was a knuckle-duster with a silver skull and green glass eyes. He put it on his hand and made a fist. He tucked it into his crocodile-skin belt. They all laughed, all of them, even Orlando. She wanted to scream. It was some sort of plan, for what? For who? Why?

Jane could see David drinking a bottle of Fanta orange outside, his white shirt unbuttoned to the waist, his dark chest visible. He was still a non-drinker. He helped a drunken uncle to his feet. She wanted to move outside and squat down under the palm trees next to the Lanniwah and let them know she was with them, but she was rooted to the spot, embarrassed, imagining herself leaning on David's shoulder.

Daniel was in her face; he ate up her discomfort. He could read the whole thing: he could see her duplicity, her cowardice, her submission, and how she sometimes ignored the prejudice and hate. Jane reached for a white wine and chugga-lugged.

Daniel and Harry picked David out from the rest outside the Crocodile Hotel. They had seen Jane watching him, admiring him. Orlando wanted them to stay out of it; he couldn't condone it. They wanted David badly. All the land rights bullshit. Other nights they cruised for Aboriginal girls to screw in the casuarinas, needles in the sand.

'We like to lay out a bloke. Or get laid out. I like a fight with anyone, really. You know me, keeps me fit, doesn't mean anything. I was a champion at boarding school. Lionel Rose, he's alright.' Orlando turned his head to laugh it off.

But Daniel was getting himself into the red zone. Half yelling as he moved into the car park.

'White, black, I'm not a racist.' His eyes locked on the Lanniwah men. Jane moved away from the advancing Daniel. All night, this had been going to happen, a drunken disaster. She was stunned, out to the side watching Daniel advance ... She had a few tears, it was pathetic; the past and the future stormed together at this moment.

'There he is. Hey you, fucken David!'

David had been onto it from the start. He stood free, at the paved edge of the drinking area. Jane saw Orlando dropping away from the blaze of Daniel. Now David moved, she saw him going to avoid trouble, moving through the shadowy patch of eucalypt trees by the hotel exit. Moving fast across the sand, leaving the area of lit street behind.

Daniel slid into the car park, turning to his audience of mates, jangling the keys to his Land Rover. Jane became aware of Orlando's arm next to her. She clung to it, watching the boarding party, Harry co-pilot. Daniel's energy was revving through the engine, wailing in the night. He beckoned them, jerking his arm through the window. Jane knew she couldn't prevent anything or raise a protest. She got in the car.

The car's suspension was wrecked; they thumped along the corrugations, on the hunt.

The engine roared, gears crunched, low gear over white sand. A cassette came on, loud. The Bee Gees. 'Saturday Night Fever'. Music to disguise the hatred.

'Having fun, Janey?'

Orlando leant towards Harry in the front seat.

'Come on, I don't want this. He's on foot.'

'Put your foot down. We'll teach him to go sniffin yer missus.'

Jane laughed.

'We broke up a year ago! I'm not with him. It ended.'

They were on fire, the boys, the posse with a hanging rope. A black wallaby beat across in the headlights.

'Get that wallaby! Hello dinner.' The Land Rover swerved and missed.

Still she couldn't speak up. Taken over by the crushing weight of it all. The terrible significance. The violence and lashing out. The idea of a white woman with an Aboriginal man, the sex and smell of the act, the luscious black skin, pumping big man, the squealing pink flesh – it frightened them, it enraged them: it was all linked. Ancient hate, envy of the dark man. No, envy it was of the freedom they had, and the Aboriginal belonging to the landscape. Owning nothing in white law, but they had it all.

'That's him!'

'We'll get him with the spotlight.' They gunned onto the bush track, David, clearly alone, walking in the dark, pulling the trouble away from the others.

Orlando dropped his head. Daniel screamed, frenzied, as Harry's spotlight trapped David.

'Hey Davo, I want to bust you like a roo on the bull bar.'

Jane tried to open the car door. 'Stop this! I will get the police onto you!'

Orlando was stirred.

'I can't stand this. Let me out. I'm a pacifist.'

'Hey Orlando. He's rootin' your missus. You're an idiot, mate, to take it. Stand up for yourself!' Daniel laughed. Jane pulled at his arm as he reached beneath the seat.

'I don't care!' said Orlando. Daniel slid a rifle out from under the seat.

'Want a lend of my gun? Watch it – he's hiding in the pandanus.' The headlights now held David, standing, shading his eyes. He held up his fists, a boxer's stance. Jane hid her head in panic as Daniel smiled, then he jumped out with the other men.

'Look at him. Stunned like a wallaby. Got ya! Off with Orlando's woman. We oughta cut it off, eh! How about it, fellas? How'd Davo go without it? Come on Ando, where's your manhood?' The other builders, one drawing a plank of wood from the tray, were forming behind Daniel. Then Orlando turned and jumped backwards, fist raised beside David.

'I don't have to beat up people to be a fuckin' man. You'll have to take me too!'

David and Orlando, nodding in unison, moving, warming up with raised forearms.

'My brother here', exhaled David.

Daniel had the plank, starting a low rotation then faster and rising up, eye level. Jane couldn't scream, the sounds wouldn't come. She held up her hand, to what? Was she going to run in and stop it? Her hand was pathetic. The plank curved through the air and found its mark with a crack.

David's skull bubbled in blood. His head sagged sideways. Blood spurted in the dark air, crimson. The plank dropped. He'd been belted with a four by two. David staggered, his feet separating trying to stay upright, while he lurched backwards. Jane slumped to her haunches, fist in mouth. David looked at her and fell to the sand. Blood around his mouth.

His eyes closed and he lay still. Harry kicked the form of David.

'That'll teach yer to want land bloody rights! How about white rights? You fucker.'

Orlando moved to kneel down between Harry and the body. The howls coming with a repellent frequency. Harry wavered, uncertain. He kicked at the dirt, spent and drifting backwards.

Jane, slumped at the tree, saw all the blood, saw it glimmer as he twitched. Blood covered one side of his face, then she screamed at the Land Rover, at its cargo of cowards, dumb with hate. She wanted to touch him, feel his body limp and fallen. The blood tasting of salt or sweet, could she remember? Yes, from being punched in the mouth, an explosion of broken skin against her teeth. She wanted to lift him in her arms, tear bandages from her dress.

Daniel moved into her vision, bringing her back. Daniel, hot and sweaty against her side, holding the builders' wood caked in cement, now blood. Orlando on his knees, sobbing. His shirt was off, bunched up to press against the head wound. Thunder rumbled out there, the pandanus trees bent in the sudden wind. Rain began pelting, bullets of rain to turn the track into sliding grey mud.

'Oh God what have you done? You might've killed him. David, can you hear me?'

Jane was up, tending the crumpled figure. Harry moved in; she stared him off. But not Daniel.

'We'd better get going. Come on, Jane!' He pulled her up as she thrashed at him, frog marching her into an opened door of the Rover. Harry and the others were in. It smelt like wet dogs. Daniel leant out of the car window.

'Orly, come on, mate, he'll be fine; he's got a head like concrete.'

Orlando sat in the wet sand, David's head cradled in his lap. Unconscious David. Orlando was facing up, rain flying on him.

'Go on, fuck off, cowards!'

Harry wheelied off, honking the horn. Jane watched Orlando diminish through the window. He looked destroyed. The Land Rover skidded against casuarinas, shunting Jane into Daniel, her tormentor, mad Daniel. All of them, faces silent, stunned at what they'd done. The only sound the unrelenting swish of the window wipers.

'I have to help him. We've got to go back, Harry.'

'You came along to save him? Yeah, right!'

'For Christ's sake, I have to go back!'

'You played them off against each other.'

'We have to get help. He might die – he could have a fractured skull', she said.

Daniel pushed his face into hers, pressed his leg against hers.

'You were there Jane, limp-wristed; you didn't even try to stop us! Did you get a thrill from being the woman that men fight over? Get you hot? It's your fault, ever think of that? What does Freud say about that? Make you feel good about yourself? Your righteous goody-goody act?'

She didn't answer; she felt sick. Daniel, he might as well just stick his hand in her chest and poke her in the heart.

Harry drove up onto the hotel room pavement under the neon light. 'Pokies, Keno'.

Jane got out and they drove off, honking the horn. Jane sat on her bed sobbing, then she picked up the phone. She called the Aboriginal Legal Service in Sydney, left a message on the machine and then dialled the local ambulance.

Breathe deep, then go forth and act. She splashed water on her face, then took the keys to her car. She drove out to the spot where she had last seen David and Orlando, but there was nothing there. Just a pool of blood amongst the casuarina seeds in the white sand. She touched the blood and it stuck to her fingers. The white sand looked different now; it was a post-apocalyptic paddock, with cracked black bones, beer cans, mussel shells and leaning pandanus palms blown by the howling wind.

That night, she heard the psychotic alcohol-driven frenzy of Aboriginal men and white men shouting – degrading, strange and terrible. She huddled in her room and tried to block out the fear. She had heard horrible things said about Aboriginal communities, the whites' pathological dislike, Aboriginal people described as animals in filth and squalor. That was why she had chosen the Lanniwahs: no alcohol. She sat until she lost a sense of time.

Later, outside Jane's motel room, Orlando leaned against the wall, soaked and in mental pain.

'David's in the hospital. I'm sorry. But he will be okay. I can't say no to the mates and their expectations of loyalty, the brotherhood, never let a mate down. It got out of control. It should have stopped before the violence. He'll recover. We all will, I hope.'

She looked at him and said nothing, shut the door to her room and heard him walk away. She wanted to call him back, but it was too late. The whole thing was over; she was glad, it was all horrible and she wanted to be alone to face herself. Where the hell was her moral judgement? What kind of so-called compassion did she exhibit? In the end, Orlando had stood by his Lanniwah mate. Not her. It could only be fear; she had been in shock, utterly frozen and unable to move to stop her complicity. Jane willed herself to face her weakness: she wasn't brave.

An urgent tap on the door – would this night ever be over? Orlando again maybe? No, he would be back at the hospital; he had taken over her role as concerned friend.

Knocking gain, urgent. She pulled back the polyester sheet. She ached all over. She looked through the peephole. A blur.

'Who is it?' said Jane.

'It's Rosie, are you alright?'

Jane was not surprised. The invisible gossip-line in town, better than a phone. Rosie sat on the only chair in front of the vanity table. Whose vanity? Jane was a wreck.

'The whole town knows about it'

'They love a scandal.'

'Orlando came to us; he was desperate.'

'Let him be a hero.'

'He tried.'

'I will go to the police. Make them write a report.'

'Don't do anything. The police will only go for David again; he'll get a record.'

'I have to do something right!'

In the morning, Rosie held Jane's arm tight as they approached the police station. She sat on the bench as Jane wrote out her version of events.

'They'll most probably throw this paper away when I leave – they won't care.'

'In Katherine, there are fights and beatings every night. It's just another weekend rampage. But just do it, Jane.'

After the police, the women went to a café and had a coffee. Jane rested her head on her hands and Rosie patted her head. Surely, the worst was over. Jane could just get on with her work, but first she wanted to talk to the town Lanniwah elders – she owed them an explanation.

CHAPTER 6

Lanniwah Revenge

Jane walked through the tall elephant grass behind the riverbank between cardboard humpies, empty port flagons and dogs to the Lanniwah town camp. It was a humid stifling day. Black clouds tumbled overhead. She entered the camp with trepidation: she didn't belong to this Lanniwah town world. She walked over to a fire and stood at a distance. No one looked at her but she had to find some self-respect and stand by what was right. She stood a way off and waited for someone to acknowledge her, to invite her in. One elder nodded, she crept in.

'Can someone please tell me where David Yaniwuy is?' She stood alongside the old people until a smiling man offered her a spot on his blanket.

'Sit here, girlie.' She was grateful, sat on a corner of the blanket, and put down some canned drinks, bread and fruit. The old man nodded and opened the cold lemonade.

'What you want?' he said.

Jane heard that David's cousins had found him caked in black blood and a pool of broken teeth, but he was alive. They had helped him into the ambulance and Orlando had gone with him to the Katherine Hospital.

The word had gone out on the grape vine, faster than lightning. Lanniwah brothers and cousins gathered at Yellow Grass Camp. She had brought a medical kit for David, but he was in hospital. The older men muttered about revenge; others argued that they should just take it to the police: it was a clear case.

Finally, three young men stood up and left the camp with David's cousin, George, who had trained in boxing at the YMCA in Darwin. He was tough and agile; he would be David's back up. Grim faced, Jane sat in the back of the battered Land Rover with an old woman. They drove to the hospital and signed David out. Head down, shrouded in bandages, he hobbled into the front seat.

It was hot; the sun was high. David's brothers pointed the way out to George and they turned off onto the mining road. Black crows flew overhead. David still didn't speak to Jane; he spoke in language to his brothers. They drove for ten kilometres to the builders' camp and stopped behind some spindly trees. It was the hottest part of the day and they knew the builders would knock off at three o'clock and head for the pub. Jane sat silently and watched. It had to be this way.

Jane was melting with anxiety; she saw herself running through the bush, covered in prickles, tripping on ant beds, pathetic. The men whispered and used sign language to indicate where to hide. A low whistle let them know that one of the builders was walking towards the back of the aluminium shed. David looked out and recognised Daniel as the one who had used the wooden plank on him. He was a good target – alone just as David had been. David moved to sit near Jane, leaning against her. She was frightened but comforted David by stroking his curls. The bandage around his head seeped blood. Jane watched with a grim fascination as the Lanniwah men grabbed Daniel from behind, covered his mouth and dragged him struggling into the bush. For a moment, she wanted to cry out a warning but she held David's head on her lap and couldn't move. Daniel's eyes bulged with terror. David leapt from the car, hit Daniel in the jaw and shook his broken hand with the pain of it. His cousins took over with a punch each. The builder staggered and pleaded for his life as tears sprayed from his face and he went down on his knees.

'Don't hit me! I'm sorry. I didn't even know your brother. I just like to fight', said Daniel.

'You racist! You hate us. You lucky we don't spear you, that's all.' George leapt forward to land another punch in the builder's face but David stopped him.

'That enough now. Let 'im go', said David. George reluctantly pushed the white man onto the ground and the Lanniwah men walked away. Daniel crawled into some prickle bush. His nose looked broken. Jane saw his eyes on her, a look of shock on his face. His eyes met hers in accusation; she suddenly felt part of the revenge. It was a kind of justice, but she still pitied him.

Jane and the Lanniwah men heard the knockoff whistle and saw the builders put their tools in the shed and hang a chain around the door. Jane and the men waited round a corner to see what would happen.

'Where's Dan?' yelled the foreman.

'The bludger's left his gear all over the place', said his mate. One of the men saw him stumbling towards the gate, blood pouring from his eye.

'What the hell happened to you?'

'Black fellas, got me. Where were you when I needed help?' said Daniel. The other men stood shocked with disbelief. It was rare that they felt the revenge of the blacks. They were used to always being the men who bashed, not the other way round. They spotted the Land Rover, but Jane took off with the Lanniwah men. She looked out the back window at the builders shouting and shaking their fists.

Jane took David back to hospital where they nursed his broken cheekbone and fractured arm. Jane knew he wasn't a violent man, but he hated people pushing him around, hated putting up with the white arrogance. It was his people's land, after all. She felt enormous regret at her actions: her love affair that had exposed David to the attack. She admired him: he was heroic; he had taken the beating because of her – and because he dared to speak up for his people, for their land.

Sometime later, Jane heard that David was seen driving with his cousins towards Oenpelli. The women told Jane they thought it was best for him to go. Arnhem Land would swallow them up with no trace. David was one of the young educated people who would go a long way. He was also a learned man with deep responsibilities to his people. He would inherit custodianship of sacred sites, have further initiation, be carrier of tradition – and he would fight to get their land back. Old Pelican had chosen him to go further with his education so he could one day be a leader. Jane was not part of this picture.

Jane knew that she wouldn't see him again, and that, right now, alone, she would have to face any consequences of the whole mess.

CHAPTER 7

Stones of Blood

At Harrison, Jane hid her guilt and sadness. She was the happy head teacher, full of confidence, then at night a sobbing wreck. Loud thunder broke the night, lightning spirits crashed above. The terrible sight of David on the ground, bleeding and pale. Her memory of the scene made her ill. It had been wrong to run away from the scene, and she'd showed no courage. Forgiveness was what she needed. She had let him down. She may never have the chance to tell him how remorseful she felt.

Jane went to Old Lucy to tell her everything. The ancient face watched and listened.

'No one help you – we not dere', Old Lucy said.

'How could anyone help me? It was all my doing. He was beaten because of me.'

'You not hittem. Mens do it. Bad mens.'

No one meant to be bad. She thought that it was all reactive, some kind of genetic imperative for violence. It made them feel good. Black or white, some men needed to hurt each other, needed to draw blood.

Old Lucy was sick. Her face close up was a skull, frail thin skin stretched across it like a painting, her cheekbones prominent. Jane saw that the old woman was not quite ready to go – she had more to do in her life, one last reconciliation. Jane went with her to the stone place. She wanted to ask forgiveness for all the treachery and pain.

They took the Toyota a short distance across brittle spinifex grass, then there was no road. They got out, and the two women walked to the secret solemn place, Jane holding the old woman's shaking arm. A sheer stone wall against a red hill. Many Lanniwah had warned Jane to stay away, but on this day Old Lucy wanted her to come. It was a moment of prescience. Jane realised that all times were living, all pasts were the present. The ground brought up hundreds of insects. The land was full of signs, singing out, clickety-clack.

'Land speaking now.'

Old Lucy sang softly with a quavering voice, high notes ringing against cliffs. She gripped Jane's hand. Old Lucy pointed to a tall pile of smooth reddish stones against a hill, like huge marbles.

'See dark colour?' asked Lucy.

Jane squinted in the sun. 'I can; what is it?'

'Blood splash der when white man smashem babies.' Jane looked at the dark arc like a boomerang; these were the rocks where the children who had run from the massacre were murdered, their heads shattered like melons against the granite stones. It was unbearably poignant.

'Lookem here', said Old Lucy. The old lady parted her thin white hair to show Jane a raised scar. Jane touched it and tears came from her eyes. She listened to Old Lucy's story and touched her face.

'Sit quiet now, no talkem.'

Jane sat in silence and Old Lucy sang a soft song.

'Eyes shut, you go dere. I come too, in mind not real, slow now', she said.

Jane was in a trance; her mind went to the place amongst those rocks.

'What you see?'

'Nothing, just sand.'

'Lookem.'

'I can see a hill, I'm walking past it. Now, there on the dirt ... something. It's no good, Lucy, I can't do this.' Jane opened her eyes.

'Closem, I come too. I dere wid you, likem dream, you see me.'

'It's cold, dark, down a tunnel or something.'

'Yeeai, dat thing is dere.'

'What?'

'Babies dere. My face cold now; dis side real cold.'

Jane opened her eyes. Old Lucy nodded.

'Were you here in 1929, Lucy? Did they try to kill you?'

'Yeeai, little girl. One mans throwem me, but I lie still, not movem; dey think me finish up.' She sobbed and embraced Jane, their arms encircled, great cries echoed against the red stone wall. Jane wiped her old friend's face. Lucy's grace and trust in Jane restored her faith in humankind.

Dark tumbling clouds rolled in from the west. From the hot plain, Jane felt someone was watching them. There was a tension. Who was it? One of the enemies? Some horrible person wanting something? A shadow crossed the women and they froze. They couldn't see in the glare of midday sun. He stood up high on the cliff against the sky, his outline, tall and lean, was unmistakable. Jane shaded her eyes from the glare. It was David, barefooted, Akubra hat shading his face. He bounded down the rocks and touched Old Lucy's face.

'Granny, I'm looking for you.'

The old lady looked up, her face alive. She hugged him and her delicate bent frame leant against his chest. His eyes met Jane's.

'Okay, Aunty; all okay.'

Jane waited for the old lady to let him go, and he came to Jane. He put his hand out and took hers, and held it for a long while. He had forgiven her.

'Eh, that Orly, he tryin' to be a boxer, but he no Lionel Rose! True, eh?'

Yes, Orlando had stood his ground. He had been strong, had stood up to be counted, not like her. She did not trust her own voice. Her hand shook; there was a lump in her chest, making her incapable of speech. He waited, looking worried but not angry.

'Not your fault.'

'Yes, it was.'

'No worries', he said.

'What will you do?' she said.

He looked back towards Arnhem Land and swept his arm in an arc in that direction, his lips pursed.

'You will finish your course?'

He nodded, turned and walked away, disappearing into the grey green mulga trees. Jane watched him go, and felt that she would never feel a love like this again with a man who was capable of such tenderness.

Jane drove Old Lucy home to her dogs. There, Old Lucy pointed at a tree full of white flowers. 'Dat tree my daddy, he clever man, can light fire wid stick, find water in desert, not needem white fella.'

Jane looked at the paintings Old Lucy had created, and saw they contained history and metaphor. The peaked black hats on some figures, which looked like interesting decoration, were police hats. The large round shapes were majestic hills, markers for a hundred deaths. The pathways that led them away from the killing were strokes and footprints in a line. They were a touchable ochred insight into the essential frailty of humans, a mythic screen indelibly printed. The images were incredibly sad.

It was dark when Jane arrived to pick up Aaron; she carried him across to the caravan. She felt suddenly strong in her belonging in the Aboriginal world, powerful. She was growing in knowledge, had opened her awareness into a mystical place.

CHAPTER 8

Jane's Revenge

Jane knew she had compassion, that underneath she was a virago. She travelled towards the mining camp across the unchanging landscape with its dirty grey and green spinifex, pale orange rocks and pebbles and mulga. Dead buffaloes, black and bloated, with legs up, and piles of Fourex beer cans marked the way. 'I've counted fifteen dead kangaroos.' Aaron said. The names and geography of the great sandy continent were its history – Slaughterhouse Creek, Poison Swamp Creek, Treachery Point, Gins Leap, Diggers Rest, Humpty Doo, Chinaman's Patch, and Leichhardt's Stand. A sign – 'You are entering Aboriginal Land. Permit required' – had been peppered with shotgun pellets.

She was moving towards a confrontation, with no idea what to say, or what to do, but she suspected it would be awful, and redemption of sorts. She would confront the stupidity of these men; tell them that she was Aboriginal too – as if they gave a shit. She blamed her cowardice, her failure to have moral courage, for letting it all get out of control. She had passively let men piss all over her. She had failed to look after those who really needed her.

Jane arrived at Jalilinka mine. Dirt blew off piles of yellow rubble across the dirty landscape; it looked like the moon. She parked under a tree, put the windows down and got out of the car. She closed her eyes; a sob sprang up from her throat. She was doing it, facing up to herself, and them. She smiled as she asked the guard on the gate where to go.

Jane woke Aaron and took him to the canteen. A tired cleaning woman agreed to look after him for ten minutes; that's all it would take. The woman gave Aaron an ice cream.

'Where is Daniel's lunch room?' she said, all sweetness. The woman waved her over to an aluminium demountable building next to a line of yellow bulldozers.

Everything that had happened seemed to lead to this moment when she would turn the aluminium door handle. A creak of flyscreen. All the struggles of the last few years rose up in front of her. The humiliations, the poverty, the craven desperation and mad longing for stability. Now was the moment to be strong, to have clarity and stand up for something she believed in. It was time to confront the hatred. The handle turned; she was in...

Inside the lunch room, workmen sat around a table eating their corned beef and pickle sandwiches. That looked tasty, she was hungry. A man was pouring boiling water into a large teapot on the table. Daniel had a bandage over his eye. He saw her and stopped mid-sandwich. She held a piece of paper out to him, her hand shook.

'What's that?' he asked.

'It's a police statement sheet from Lanniwah men about a criminal assault. Read it!' she said.

He looked down. The other men watched.

'Oh, I forgot; you can't read. Will I read it for you?' she said.

'Piss off', he said.

'Why did you assault David Yaniwuy?' she asked.

The men all laughed,

'Nice to see you too, Janey', said Daniel.

'He didn't do anything to deserve that', she said.

'How's Orlando? I thought he was your boyfriend.'

Patsy Cline music poured out of a cassette player. It was the climactic moment in a scene from a bad play.

She was fury incarnate; her chest pounded. 'You smashed his face in with a four by two, you broke his arm, and you bloody near killed him!'

Daniel pushed back his plastic chair.

'Take a look at my face. Your damn black boyfriend's mates did that to me', he said.

'I wish they'd killed the lot of you, you lousy racists, self-satisfied colonising white pricks. You can't even recognise that the mining company is exploiting you – look at your living conditions; you live like pigs! And you're paid shit. Not even an Australian company that's ripping you off – it's bloody British, even Queen Elizabeth has shares in it!' she said.

'Come on, Janey, calm down; we're all friends here.' said Daniel.

'No, we're not. I have a witness to the assault who will testify in court about your attack.'

'Who?' he said.

'Orlando Kerekov. The Aboriginal Legal Service is sending a lawyer up from Sydney. They see it as a test case for the Territory. He has the backing of a top Sydney barrister. You won't get away with it. And I've called the newspapers.'

'Well, fuck me dead', said Daniel. The men laughed.

'You'll be charged', she said.

'I didn't hit him, he fell. I'm the victim here. Hey, you were there, Janey – limp wristed. You didn't try to stop us. Did you get a thrill from men fighting over you? It's all your fault, ever think of that. Make you feel good about yourself?'

'I wanted to stop you.'

'You came in the car with us to … what? Save him?' said Daniel.

'I don't know.'

'You played them off against each other.'

At that, moment Jane's eyes fell on the edge of the table.

'Okay, I'm sorry… calm down!' Daniel said, but it was too late. She lifted the table. It was time slowing, scalding tea flew over the men, they jumped, sandwiches falling to the floor. They stood up yelping and brushed the hot water from their thighs.

'You stupid bitch! You burnt me!' yelled Daniel. He mopped at his shorts as Jane picked up crockery plates and began throwing them at their heads. The men ducked in shock and some laughed. Shattering crockery slid down the plastic walls.

'Take that, you pathetic arseholes. I hope you all get VD from your town whores and your dicks drop off, and your wives find out and leave you, and take all your bloody money!' She grabbed Daniel's collar, pushed him against the plastic wall and twisted his collar into his throat, her knuckles white.

'Don't you ever go near David again!' she said.

Daniel smiled. 'Or what, Janey?'

The whole room laughed, someone shouted: 'Show us your tits.'

The atmosphere was ugly, like a rape pack. She let go of Daniel's shirt and hissed into his face: 'Or his countrymen will track you down and kill you with a Kadaitcha man! And I will help them find you, because I have Aboriginal blood too and I will go to gaol and enjoy every minute because it'd be worth it!'

'So you're a mad black bitch ... but I kind of admire that', said Daniel.

A voice yelled: 'We've called the cops!'

'Go ahead. And you know what? I am an Aboriginal woman, and I am proud of it!'

She straightened her blouse and summoning up her dignity, walked out of the building. Her face was rigid with anger, steam from her ears. Fury made her powerful and totally fearless. A wind blew yellow dust into her face. Pools of brown poisoned water dribbled into the wild river.

Jane collected Aaron, got into the hire car, and drove away. It was fantastic. After twenty minutes, she began to sob. What if the police came after her? What if she was charged with being an accessory to the assaults? What if she went to prison? What would happen to Aaron? He looked up from his book.

'Mummy, don't cry', he said. She drove with her chin on the steering wheel and blobs of hot tears fell.

'I don't need a present if we can't afford it. I've got lots of Matchbox cars. We can go to Aunty Rosie's house, she will make you better.'

She held out her hand and stroked his blond head. 'Let's go to town and get a chocolate thick shake and then presents!' she said.

At that moment, she knew that she would never go back down south to live. The power of the Territory was too great. She had swum in the Rainbow Serpent sacred billabong. She was destined to stay. She drove back along the dirt road. At last, she'd been able to find some strength. She'd taken on the misogynist, racist, white men and she felt triumphant. They stood for wiping out all Aboriginal rights, all Aboriginal people for that matter, and keeping women subservient. They wouldn't win in the end. It felt fantastic.

CHAPTER 9
More Gossip

Black eyes followed Jane and people still talked about her. Life back at Harrison was as difficult as ever, but she was nearing the end of the teaching year; she felt confident in her skills at managing the school ... After all that had happened, it was inevitable that she would leave. The visiting missionaries crossed the road when she passed; she didn't care.

Reverend Wiltshire brought her into his office to talk.

'We need to talk about the situation. We feel for you; God cares. People want you off the community: you're too uninhibited, too bohemian, and not suitable. It's about holding up community standards, and demonstrating morality. I struggle also to reconcile my human needs with spiritual values.'

She nodded and smiled.

'I am sorry if my behaviour has not been acceptable.' His hadn't been either.

'All right, Jane; look, we are all sinners. You will come through this. People just like to observe others and they're jealous. You are very brave. I have respect for you.'

'Yep. Look, I won't come to your services because I am an atheist. I do like the teachings of Jesus but not the church stuff. I appreciate the work you are doing for the clinic; the supplies are very useful. Thankyou ... Look, you have tried to help. I recognise that.'

The Reverend attempted to place his hands on her head. He was giggling – was he all right?

'I just want to say goodbye. I might have to...' he stopped mid-sentence as though he no longer knew where he was; he looked around to see Hubert walking towards him, carrying his whip.

Jane nodded and was about to walk out, but stopped and turned towards the Reverend: 'Does it ever bother you that you are preaching on land where there was a terrible massacre?'

'We are not responsible for evil carried out before we were born', he said.

'I think maybe we are.'

'By the way, Mrs Reynolds, I have been visited by the Boss. I am ... I have ... I want ... I have decided that I am wanted elsewhere', he mumbled.

'You're leaving?'

'Have you ever thought what if it is all a fairy story? The Father, Son and the Holy Ghost? What have I based my life upon? Am I a fraud? Will Hubert forgive me?'

'Yes, you probably are.'

'What?'

'A fraud.'

'The rainbow billabong will wash away sin. I must make a flight into the wilderness.'

'There's a road house at the rainbow billabong, and a caravan park. Time to take stock. Love fades, believe me.'

He hurried over to his tent and began packing, his ute filled up with his belongings.

In the afternoon, Jane walked to Hubert's veranda. He sat with his foot up on a squatter's chair, and beckoned to her. Edie sat shelling a bowl of peas. He stared and sat forward; he seemed very serious. He was scaring Jane.

'We've had to tell the Department of Education about what's happened, Jane. About your behaviour'.

'You could have told me', said Jane.

'What do you think this is?' said Edie.

'We talked on the radio. The inspector was interested', said Hubert.

'Okay.'

'You'll be getting a letter', he said.

'About what?'

'We just want to help you', said Edie.

'Sure. Thank you. Anything else?'

'Why would there be?' Hubert smirked.

'Don't get us wrong. We appreciate your work here, eh Hugh? But it's so stressful; they might want to send out a doctor to you, for a psychiatric assessment', said Edie.

'What for?'

'Your health. We had to tell them.'

'About?'

'Your improper behaviour with a ... ahem ... a co-worker', said Edie.

'You made up some good words, didn't you, Ede?' said Hubert.

'Moral laxity. I had to use a dictionary. Putting the children at risk.'

'That's good coming from a rapist!' Jane spat.

'Hey, watch yer language! Did you know that my dad's old mate Joh Bjelke Peterson is the new premier of Queensland. Don't underestimate me.'

Jane smiled and walked away.

They were hypocrites. They would have liked her head on a plate. They had taken to religion but still wanted something ... what ... from her? She would be a sacrificial teacher. It would be so easy to wreck a lone woman out here. Now she wouldn't sleep a wink again, waiting for the damn mailbag. What would it feel like, shooting them both? Where did Hubert keep his rifle? Alternatively, chopping them up into little pieces and putting them on an anthill?

The next day, Jane sat under a tree teaching Aaron to read; she looked up and saw Reverend Wiltshire in his ute hurtling down the road towards the gate. Hubert was close behind him on his motorbike. He pulled up and walked around the front of the ute. The Reverend was crouching down in his seat. Hubert unlocked the gate and stepped aside and the ute drove through it. The dust billowed around and Hubert stood still in the middle of the road with his hands on his hips, staring at the disappearing car. A pile of hymn books flew off the back and blew away amongst the trees.

CHAPTER 10

Daniel And Mayda

The air was cooler somehow, late in the day. Jane was folding washing on her lounge. Daniel stood at her door, his Bob Dylan shirt looking back at her. He looked ashamed and hung his head. Jane couldn't believe he was there.

'I've come to apologise to you and your friend Davo', he said.

'Please just get on your motorbike and go back to town. I can't have you here.'

'I came to explain what happened. I was a shithead.'

'Alright, don't worry about it. Now will you leave, please?' she said.

'It's a bit late. I might hit a bullock in the dusk. I'll just make a camp here for the night.'

'Don't bother me again. Go somewhere else.' She slammed her door.

In the middle of the night, Jane heard loud shouts from some men outside. She went to the door in her nightie and there was Daniel standing in the light of a torch. Mayda was with him, quivering with fear, her dress undone at the front, her breasts exposed. She held Daniel's hand. Burnie and Old Pelican stood in front of them. Jane walked towards the scene in slow motion. She looked at Daniel and shook her head. She was finding it hard to fight the anxiety. This was not good. This was a problem with huge consequences.

'Can I help you, old grandfather?' said Jane.

'Nothin', you do nothin'. This fella bin jig jig my promise wife, jig jig in bush', said Old Pelican.

'I didn't know', Jane said.

'I love him', said Mayda.

'Don't say anything, honey. I want to take you away', said Daniel.

Dogs barked furiously and Beatrice arrived with some women from the camp. Before Jane could move, Beatrice hit Mayda on the back with a waddy. Beatrice laid into her.

Jane cried out. 'Please don't hit her. It's not right. Leave her, I beg you.'

'She bad girl. She wife now. Not come to school no more.'

Mayda fell to the ground. Beatrice dragged her up to her feet and walked her away into the dark. The men looked at the ground in front of Daniel. Awkward. Then Beatrice returned and pushed the young woman in front of Jane. Beatrice pulled Mayda's head up by her hair. Her face arched in pain. Daniel said nothing.

'This girl she lay down wid dat teacher', Beatrice said.

'Which teacher?' Jane whispered.

'Dat Orlando fella.'

Mayda began to cry. It was a low pitiful moaning. Jane nodded; she felt sick. Beatrice pushed Mayda into the dark.

Daniel didn't move. Old Pelican put his spear thrower under his arm and followed. Old Burnie stood in the dark, looking at Jane. He put his hand over his eyes and sighed deeply.

'This fella no good. He your friend?' asked Burnie.

'No, I hate him', said Jane.

'Yeeai, tellem to get. You my daughter. I watch out for you alla time now.' Burnie disappeared.

Daniel lit a cigarette and stood awkwardly in front of Jane. She didn't know what to do. She wanted the ground to swallow him up.

'Well, that went well', he said.

'Do you realise who you are insulting? How important a man Old Pelican is?'

'Look, be cool. I really like Mayda. I think I'm in love. She's sensitive and funny. She's eighteen; she knows what she wants. They do have some human rights, you know. What about your feminist stuff? One day, I'd like to take her away from all this … We can go to Sydney; we could have a life. My family might act up a bit, but hell, they'd grow to love her too … Okay, I'll be gone by morning.'

He rolled out his swag and climbed in, relaxed and oblivious.

Some hours later, just before dawn, Jane heard strange noises. Daniel was singing and mumbling as though he was very stoned. She watched out her window as he staggered to his feet and rode off towards the river through thick bush. His motorbike roared and wobbled, he fell off then remounted. The last she saw of him was his back fading into shadows of acacia trees.

Three days later, Hubert drove with a slow pace to Jane's place. He pulled up in his truck. He looked worried, and very serious; his face a mask, white and staring. He rolled a cigarette with violently shaking hands. What on earth had happened? Perhaps he had been charged for his crime. Had Edie done something? Suicided? Run off?

Jane stood fixed to the step of the caravan, unable to move. Against the white earth, there was a silhouette of Hubert's body, earth, his shadow large, towering. He beckoned to her. Why? If only he had spoken, given her some hint, a warning. Her eyes stopped on the green canvas in the back of the truck. It covered … what? A fresh killed bullock? There were no stockmen, no guns, no gum leaves to keep off flies.

'You got a minute, Jane?' he said.

'What's up? If Flash has been after your chickens, I'm sorry', she said.

'Nope, we found something up the river, a long way up in the mangroves. The boys tracked it.'

He had his hand on the canvas. She saw kapok fluff balls gathered in the creases, lifting and whirling in graceful arcs. A bluebottle fly landed on Hubert's hand; he brushed it away.

There seemed to be some accusation floating in the air, the smell of rotting garbage, mangrove worms and mud, a putrid dead animal, a stench that made bile rise up, gagging green fluid. A riding boot stuck out of the mess. Hubert leant his head on his arm, exhausted, on the metal gate of the truck. The red cattle dog jumped on the back of the truck and stole something, then moved off the truck and began to eat it. Hubert kicked the dog, took a handkerchief from his pocket and carefully picked up the flesh to replace it under the canvas. His eyes led hers to the large shape. She walked towards it. Black mud oozed on the wooden floor of the truck tray. Was he going to show her a crocodile? Why was he showing her? Didn't he hate her? She certainly hated him. Was it a sick joke? Or was it Aaron? Fear choked her. Where was he? No, he was up at the camp. It was so quiet. Hubert wouldn't look at her. She approached the greasy canvas and Hubert pulled it back.

Jane peered at the greenish mess of a half-eaten human body. A terrible stink. A croc had been eating it, the face blackish and gouged, only one leg remaining. She gagged and blocked the smell with her shirt.

Then she saw it … the ragged remains of the Bob Dylan tee-shirt, 'Don't Look Back'. She cried great gasping sobs, her body convulsed with the grief and horror; she dry retched and Hubert put his arm around her.

'Oh hell, it can't be! It's not Daniel?' she said.

Hubert replaced the canvas and wiped his face with a handkerchief.

'Sorry, it's a bloody awful shock. A croc will do that; drag a feed up the mangroves to eat later. I'll get Edie to make you a cuppa. He's Orlando's mate.'

'I don't understand it – why would Daniel swim a crocodile infested river?'

'Must have gone troppo. Are you okay?'

'I feel terrible, it's devastating.'

Hubert let his head roll forward, he scratched his scabs. He sniffed. No tough bloke now. Jane thought about how fragile life could be. The terrible uncertainty. The extremity of the violent death was horrific; everyone would reel at the devastating impact of his last hours. Who would tell his family? He must have had one – who would talk to his crying mother? So painful and ghastly. The crack of huge jaws, the gleaming yellow eyes, the reptilian massacre. All for what?

Aaron ran back down the road and over to the truck. Jane stopped him. Hubert covered the corpse. He turned to face Aaron and patted the child's head. All casual. Jane almost loved Hubert then.

'No, Aaron, let's go up to the school. The Boss has some business to do.'

'Why are you crying, Mum?'

'Nothing, darling; it's just I feel a bit sad today.'

She choked back tears and walked away. Hubert drove to the back of his house and called to Edie to help him pull out their old freezer. He had something to put in it.

CHAPTER 11

Letter From Head Office

A few months passed and brought a new period for Jane. She was light, had a sense of freedom from the stress of relationships with men; she was single and strong with a rush of energy. She had applied for a transfer to a new school. She gleamed. People had basic goodness; no one was all evil.

Then one morning, a letter arrived for Jane from Head Office. Edie pulled it out from the mailbag and held it in her hand. Jane reached for it. Edie pulled it away. Jane felt like punching her. Then Edie reluctantly handed it over. The letter said that Jane had to travel to Darwin for an interview. It wasn't clear about what. Jane wasn't worried about her job. So what? If she were fired, it would be all right; she could get a job anywhere now. She didn't give a damn anymore. She was a good teacher who could take on any remote position and be very successful. Why, she could work for the Catholic schools or even become an overseas volunteer.

The Darwin night was humid; Jane strolled past pandanus trees and riotous pubs. A sailor fell at her feet. She saw lonely men looking in shop windows and she had a flash of single motherhood, a child's tears for absent fathers, no money, and pathetic nights in front of television. She might have become one of those women who always got dumped, but she was not going to be a failure. She grabbed a taxi to go to the YWCA. The taxi driver slid his arm along the back of his seat and adjusted his crutch.

'You look like a nice chick; want to come for a drink?' She declined and looked out the window, watching the tropical red hibiscus shrubs and palm trees as the taxi swerved down the street. As he dropped her off, he cocked his head out the window.

'You're gorgeous', he said.

'Sorry', she said. Then she walked the dark street without her usual fear of attack and crawled into bed.

The next day she had the interview with a handsome young Department of Education man in brown shorts with a grey tie. He wore white long socks with sandals, of course. She waited for him to read the report on his desk.

'A large Lanniwah Aboriginal community of students in one demountable class room, an occasional teaching assistant and for a few of those months just one relief teacher. Is that about it?' he asked.

Jane sat twisting her scarf in her hands, her mouth dry. The report would say more.

'Yes, that's right. We taught all of them some basics of reading and writing in English and maths. It's been a big two years.'

'Your Aboriginal teaching assistant went away? Is that right?' he said.

'Some important ceremonial business, I think.'

'There always is', he said.

'David is an excellent teaching assistant, a teacher really. I can give him a great reference.'

'I'm sure you can … It says here that there were, how shall we say, some personal difficulties, Mrs Reynolds. Is that correct? I have a rather peculiar letter from a Reverend Wiltshire.' He looked sharply at her and she shrank in front of him, then raised her face and looked directly into his eyes. He winked.

'No, absolutely nothing wrong. It was wonderful all the time. Two professionally rewarding and challenging years. Academically excellent, and we had great sporting results at the annual carnivals. Can I go now? I have to pick up my son from the child-care drop-in centre', she said.

He smiled and smoothed the paper; he took off his glasses and slowly wiped them. He sighed.

'You know, I really admire you. Anything you want to say, um, the need for a doctor's assessment?'

'Do I look mad?'

'I didn't say …' he said.

'I have waded to school in chest-deep crocodile infested water, while carrying my seven-year-old son on my back and balancing my books and lesson plans on my head, during the three-month flood. I have taught fifty-two children to read and I have planted a garden of Chinese cabbages, bandaged scabies infected legs, cleaned nits from hair, dealt with a racist cattle station manager, kept my caravan nice and clean and written the school's semester reports. My little son and I survived gastro, king browns and wild buffaloes and being broken down in a Toyota some hundred kilometres from help. I was nearly raped; a Lanniwah man punched me in the mouth. I undertook to enquire about Aboriginal land rights on behalf of the head man and learnt a considerable amount about Lanniwah culture, language and history. I was adopted into the clan and a number of very important elders hold me in respect. A baby died. A crocodile ate a man. I managed.'

He sat forward and stared at her with his beatific smile. He closed the folder on his desk. Frangipani trees blew outside in the breeze.

'Okay, that seems to be all we need. Thank you for coming in.'

'Is that it?'

'Yes.'

He stood up and walked her to the door; his hand was on her elbow. She stepped out into the hallway. He called out.

'Any comments about the Reverend Wiltshire?'

'No.'

'Go on, just a hint.'

'Well, alright, you might be interested to know …'

He leaned forward and looked alert.

'… that the Reverend Wiltshire ran away from his mission post.'

'I guessed that.'

'And was found naked in the Rainbow pool at Churinga Springs, shouting in tongues and preaching to the flying foxes; that is, after he was caught having sexual relations with Mrs Barkley, and her husband threatened to shoot them both. However, Mr and Mrs Barkley forgave each other. Oh, and he trained a new Lanniwah pastor and was supportive to me in obtaining release from prison of a young Lanniwah man. All good work.'

'Priceless', said the officer, and gave a loud raucous laugh. He held his hand over his mouth to gain control.

'You know, you are very funny. We will let you know about your request for a transfer and the outcome of these other matters', he said.

She stepped out the door, then turned around and looked straight into his eyes.

'One other thing – please put it on my records that I identify as being of Aboriginal descent, Darug from the Hawkesbury River. Make sure it says that – it's very important.'

'You don't look Aboriginal.'

'And you don't look racist', she said.

He smiled and ushered her out of the building.

Jane walked into the bright sunlight of the city and felt that a huge weight had lifted. It would be difficult to leave the Lanniwah but it felt like she had experienced with them a true homecoming. The old women had enlightened her, she was awake to her Aboriginality, and it would never leave her. She had entered a new realm; it felt like the revelation of strength. Nothing, no government department, or fear of authority or white or Aboriginal man would ever oppress her again.

She walked past young soldiers out on the town, drinking themselves into oblivion in the outdoor bars. They sang while she danced up the street.

CHAPTER 12

Death Of Old Lucy

Old Lucy's family were in the dark, under the canopy of the bough shade. They sat near the deathbed. It was very quiet with no movement, just faint snuffles from babies. Jane knelt by the bed. Old Burnie played didgeridoo nearby. She felt a great pulsing of emotion as she looked at the tiny hand laid on the sheet, twitching. The frail hand waved upwards and took Jane's heart with it. Jane moved forward and laid her head next to Old Lucy, unable to pull her eyes from the wizened face, the white hair soft as it crowned her head, transparent tendrils lying on the pillow. She hoped to hear some last words. The family leaned as one into the old woman's approaching death; sounds of crying began to waft around the figures. They were waiting to be with her spirit, to see it through to another world.

Didgeridoos played and the singing of the old men was loud, and heart breaking, and never ending. Edie sat on a plastic chair and held the old woman's other hand. At her feet was a bunch of pink tea roses from Edie's garden. Old Lucy lifted her head, pain etched on her face.

'I go now, grand-daughter. You tell em about dat place', said Old Lucy.

'What place?' said Edie.

'Where her family was killed', whispered Jane.

'I've heard about that place, alright', said Edie.

David stepped into the space, his presence magnetic. He washed the old woman's face with a towel and held her head up tenderly to drink some water. He seemed taller, stronger, as though there was a shift in his aura; he wore a land rights tee-shirt.

'I can give her a shot of morphine for the pain', said Edie.

Lucy looked at Edie and shook her head. David sat on the ground and laid his head against the sheet. Jane looked up at the sheaves of fresh wattle and gum leaves hanging from the branches above. It was beautiful and full of peace. Edie moved from beside the bed and sat down with Jane amongst the wailing women. Old Beatrice cried and hit her head with a stone. Blood ran from the sorry cut. Every member of the family walked past, all leaning forward to say goodbye, little children clasping the old woman's hands. Shirley wept and rocked back and forth, the end was coming. Edie put out her hand to the girl.

Old Lucy looked up again. 'Take Missus to that place', whispered Old Lucy.

The old woman sighed and stopped breathing. She was gone. A great wail of crying burst out from the family.

Later, no one was allowed to mention the old lady's name; the ceremony went on for a week. The women painted Aaron and the Lanniwah boys in white ochre. The girls – Shirley, Lizzy and Mayda – danced alongside Gertie, Margie and Old Beatrice. Flags of batik and plain bright colours flew in the breeze and Jane joined a procession to pay her respects to the coffin. The coffin was painted with ochres of orange, yellow, cream, black, and inscribed with the old lady's Dreamings. The wailing kept up hour after hour and women beat their heads with sorry stones, blood mingling with tears on their cheeks. Babies cried and people danced each ceremonial moment of the dead woman's Dreaming cycle. For Jane and Aaron, it was sad, ancient, and overwhelming.

Jane went to the mortuary ceremony after school. Hubert stood nearby with his hat in his hands; he hung his head. The coffin was first mounted on a four-wheel drive truck and slowly, with dancers alongside, the procession moved through the land. People were dressed in full ceremonial costume, with men in feathered headdresses with sacred dilly bags in their mouths or hanging from their shoulders. Their ochre-painted bodies glistened with their Dreamings – animals, fish, birds, goannas, and turtles all attended the mortuary ceremony. Jane, covered in white ochre, danced with the women. They arrived at the gravesite in the small cemetery and men carried the coffin to the edge. Jane looked at the mounds of shells and small white stones; she touched the lucky stone in her pocket. Wailing rose to a crescendo. The dancers leapt in and out of the open grave. Men carried spears and the drone of the didgeridoo roared out. At last, the men put the wooden coffin in the grave and Sammy read the short service and closed the bible.

CHAPTER 13

New Job

The letter was on her caravan steps, an unmistakable envelope with a little window. The Department of Education wrote of her 'outstanding two years work in a remote school'. Jane received her promotion and she would be the new head teacher at Kiperinja School, six hundred kilometres away. She was not going to be sacked. She was admired. She was professional. All her fears washed away. This was her redemption, her spiritual rising. Jane picked up Aaron and danced around the yard. Flash barked and ran in circles.

Jabirus flew overhead where Edie was planting new geraniums. She waved. Jane felt like a woman who could do anything, teach anyone. An incredible feeling of happiness welled up. Aaron sang and they hugged each other. Flash was up front in the Toyota and barked as Jane packed up their belongings.

Shirley sat inside the caravan and helped her sort out things to give away as Aaron played on the floor and counted Lego pieces.

'One hundred and two, one hundred and three … I've got more than when I started. Yeeai.'

'Who get dis present?' said Shirley. She held up a royal blue cowboy shirt.

'Old Pelican', said Jane.

On the day they left, Jane tied the painted boomerangs and bark paintings carefully on the back of the vehicle. All the schoolchildren stood outside the school and sobbed. Jane sobbed. Raymond cried. Jane handed him a new copy of *The Complete Works of William Shakespeare*; she hugged him and everyone. The Lanniwah mob walked over to sit in the shade of a gum tree.

Old Pelican strolled over to say goodbye.

'You know that one builder he bin finish up?' he said.

'I know. Poor bugger. Crocodile got him.'

'Might be Kurria spirit take him. He might got footprints stab with hot wire, might be his shirt got em poison, he go mad in bush. What you reckon?' He laughed and walked away but turned to look at her. She felt sick. It was too horrible – the greenish skin, the vile mangrove mud smell, the memory of the body.

'Old man, please, it all has to stop', she said.

'You got present for me?' he said.

Jane looked back; she felt cold, a shiver of illness and pain. She was afraid of him. He was so dangerous, but she went into her room, took out the new cowboy shirt, and laid it on the bed; she stroked the royal blue cotton and white tassels, the pearl shell buttons. She put it back in her suitcase and closed the lid. She walked out to the old man.

'No, sorry. I got nothing for you. All gone.'

'You got tobacco?' he said.

She looked at his outstretched palm, pale with black lines. He looked innocent and needy but his eyes were of steel. Jane looked into them and held the gaze. Not respectful.

'No tobacco either.'

'Yeeai.' He turned and shuffled back to his camp. She thought: poor stupid Daniel, he didn't stand a chance against this man. And what about Mayda? A life of sleeping alongside Old Pelican and his four other wives. She would be their drudge and be beaten if she strayed.

Shirley cried as she hugged Jane, and Lizzy lifted Aaron onto her shoulders and ran towards the billabong. 'You not go wid her. You stay wid me', she said as she swung him around. Aaron giggled and they ran back to the packed Toyota. Shirley had a present for Aaron; it was *Arabian Nights*, a treasure.

'Let's go, Mummy', Aaron said. Then Edie whistled for Jane to come to the fence. Jane walked over and Edie kissed her.

'I don't think the next teacher will be so interesting, Mrs Reynolds', she said.

'I'll miss you, Edie, and Hubert.'

'I doubt that.'

'I'll come back one day for a visit.'

'No, you won't. And with any luck we'll be in Brisbane', Edie said.

Jane drove out of her gate. Hubert rode up on his motor bike. He waved at her to stop.

'See you around like a rissole. Here's a little gift for ya.' He handed her a small soft tanned crocodile skin. It was gold and smooth. She took it from his meaty hand and thanked him. It was a strange gift, she didn't really appreciate dead crocodile skins and no doubt, it came from Harry.

They left Harrison Station and Lanniwah country. Lanniwah people stood along the road and waved. Jane felt devastated to leave them. Leroy and the other little boys ran up to the car. Aaron waved and shouted: 'I'm going to big school! See you when we come back!'

Jane thought, *"We will never come back"*. Leroy, Ricky, Shirley, Lizzy, Robert and Mayda all ran along beside the car, and then they stopped to wave one more time, their outlines against blue sky. Jane saw the last line of mulga trees disappear as the Brahman bullocks chewed on.

Some weeks later, at the new remote Aboriginal school, Jane slept in her lovely new fibro house; it smelt of fresh paint and cleanliness. A sound woke her. She sat up in bed and there before her, the old woman's ghost. Her presence filled the room. She stood dressed in feathered string and a long white feathered headdress, with her Dreaming painted in yellow ochre across her breasts. She danced her Dreaming Ceremony and sang with high clear notes. Jane sat up in bed, stunned. Old Lucy spoke swiftly in language to her, but Jane could not make out the words. Jane was alert; the moist sheet clung to her shoulders and she was about to ask her granny something, when the old woman faded into the venetian blinds like dust.

Jane was part of the supernatural world that Aboriginal people treated with a sense of common acceptance. It was not strange; it just was. Jane's experiences with the Lanniwah linked Jane to who she was – her history, her genetic heritage – and she knew she wouldn't go back to the uncertainty.

Jane phoned her Darug aunt, who advised her to take a crystal, hold onto it in the night, and ask the ghost what she wanted. Aunty Emily suggested it was like getting the phone on – once you saw one ghost, you would always see them. Jane did not welcome this information. She smoked the house with peppermint gum leaves that she burnt in a wooden coolamon. She cried out, 'Have peace; go away, ghost'.

ACKNOWLEDGEMENTS

WARNING: Some deceased Aboriginal persons are named below.

I am indebted to many people who have assisted me in the creation of *The Crocodile Hotel*, both as a novel and a stage play. Firstly I acknowledge my father Neville (Jedda) Janson for his teaching about the bush and hidden Aboriginal story. My mother, Jovanna Janson for her artistic encouragement and my aunt Rose Pickard for her reading of the novel. I especially thank my husband Michael Fay who has given unswerving support to my writing. Thankyou to my children: Morgan, Zoey and Byron who are an inspiration. Thanks also to the Darug mob and the Buruburongal clan of whom I am a member. This mob has encouraged and facilitated my search for family history from the Hawkesbury River country. I especially thank Shane Smithers and the Darug Tribal Aboriginal Corporation.

I also wish to acknowledge the many individuals from the Aboriginal Education Assistants Program, University of Sydney, who nurtured my writing through theatre improvisation in the 1980s and '90s. Without them, my stage plays *Gunjies* and *Black Mary* would not have been possible. In particular, I am grateful for the talented assistance of; Veronica Saunders, Emily Walker, Wirrunga Dunggirr, Delma Davidson and Robyn Williams. I acknowledge the support and input of Aboriginal actors: Justine Saunders, Kevin Smith, Lillian Crombie, Pamela Young, Margaret Harvey and Billy McPherson. I also acknowledge the teachings of Yolngu friends and adopted family past and present: My old mother Dupawal, old father Gulpa Gulpa and elder Burramurra.

I thank historian, Peter Read for his guidance and support in the research for our project www.historyofaboriginalsydney.edu.au.

I acknowledge the recognition given to my plays *The Crocodile Hotel* and *The Eyes of Marege* through the shortlistings by The Patrick White Playwrights' Award and the Griffin Award.

This novel is vastly different to my play *The Crocodile Hotel*. It has new characters and incidents as it portrays the world of an imagined Northern Territory Aboriginal community and the non-Indigenous people who surround it.

The novel *The Crocodile Hotel* would not have been written without the support of the Australia Council's B R Whiting Studio residence in Rome 2013.

I also wish to thank those who assisted in completing this novel: Jannawi Dance Clan; editor Brigitte Staples; editor of 2 chapters Wayne Grogan; designer Michelle Ball; proof reader Nigel Parbury; mentor Bem Le Hunte; readers Polly Ryrie and Lesley Giovanelli; John Ogden of Cyclops Press; Tony Gordon of tonygordonprintcounsel.com; and the NSW Writer's Centre.

*The author acknowledges the invaluable support given
by the Literature Board, Australia Council for the Arts.
The writing residency at the BR Whiting Studio,
Rome, contributed significantly towards the
completion of this novel.*

Australia Council
for the Arts